BIOTOXIN

A NOVEL (?) OF ENVIRONMENTAL TERROR

By

William Gartner

This book is a work of fiction. Places, events, and situations in this story are purely fictional. Any resemblance to actual persons, living or dead, is coincidental.

ISBN: 1-4107-6501-6 (e-book)
ISBN: 1-4107-6500-8 (Paperback)

Library of Congress Control Number: 2003094406

This book is printed on acid free paper.

Printed in the United States of America
Bloomington, IN

1stBooks - rev. 6/13/03

THANKS

This book would not have come to be if it hadn't been for the long-time friendship with my first editor, John Jiambalvo of Downers Grove Illinois.

My gratitude would not be complete without thanking Irene Plagge, who corrected my endless mistakes in the proper use of quotations and references.

DEDICATION

This book is dedicated to my lovely and loving wife Jennifer and my 5 beautiful children Kathryn, Kimberly, Andrea, Ben and Greer, along with my four precious grandchildren Gunnar, Dakota, Kelsey and Carmen.

SECTION ONE

IT BEGINS

As the huge, nearly luminescent Coho salmon rose from the depths of Lake Michigan, she felt the same inner stirring she had come to know every spring for her eleven years. She began the strong rhythmic strokes that would take her to the nesting area; the same well protected spot that had been used every year for her eggs. The Coho had gradually begun to bloat with the thousands of roe that hung heavily in her belly. The steady, fluid movement of her powerful dorsal and tail fins had brought her toward the surface where she began to notice the light-density shift. As she rose nearer to the light, the penetrating rays of the sun had begun to play off her spring "coat", used to attract a virulent male to fertilize her eggs. When she approached a depth of about twenty feet, she began to move northward, directly against the strong southwesterly flow in the lake. She reveled in the light and clarity of the water at this depth. With the temperature of the water nearing forty-five degrees Fahrenheit, her skin rippled with the warmth that came every spring. After nearly five months at temperatures around thirty-four degrees, in the ninety-foot depths of the lake, she felt more vigorous than ever before.

FRIDAY 9:00 p.m.

CHAPTER 1

The keyboard felt cool to the fingertips as his hands moved methodically from function keys to alpha keys. Smiling at the computer screen, Jon realized that his near symbiotic relationship with the high-powered Hewlett-Packard was truly addictive.

He had been at the screen for nearly five straight hours without a break and he'd about had it. Jon noted that his stiffening neck reconfirmed his thought that he was more of a computer jockey than an environmental chemist these days. He pushed the gunmetal gray chair tick ticking away from the glowing terminal and began to slowly rotate his head with melodious creaking to relieve the tension.

With a final quick thrust of dual victory-fists, he rearranged himself in front of the video display, momentarily pausing with thoughts of food. Brushing those aside, he listened for any unfamiliar sounds, besides those of the clanking pipes and sighing thermostats.

Trying to get his mind back on track so he could wrap up here, he was startled by the tinny little voice that could only belong to Laura Thomas, his lab assistant.

"Dr. Kepler," she chastised, "I can't believe you're still here. Do you have any idea of what time it is", sweeping her eyes from green wall to green wall finding only a ring of dust where the clock was until yesterday.

Jon came around slowly in his swivel chair with his best Cheshire Cat grin firmly fixed to his strong, slender face.

"No, Miss Thomas. However, I do have an idea about how delighted I am to see you."

As Laura felt her face glow crimson, she attempted to counter with a clever remark, "Sure. It's just Beauty and the leering Beast."

She had been working with Dr. Jon Kepler since the beginning of January, having opted for a special lab intern program at Northwestern University. The National Science Foundation sponsored this new approach to tedious lab classes for senior students at the university. It allowed them to work in certain jobs for a full semester earning money for school and receiving credit in their major field of study. As a guest speaker at the Northwestern campus just north of Chicago, Jon was impressed by the depth of Laura's questioning relative to the chromatography of environmental organic compounds. In their repartee he sensed a strong set of Watsonian abilities and pegged her as a deductive analyst. His effervescent email to the head of the department automatically uplifted her application for an internship from One-Among-Many to Head-of-the-Class.

Jon had spent this past week analyzing a plethora of water and sludge samples from a project near Waukegan, Illinois. He was unhappily working at the request of a contractor for the U. S. Army Corps of Engineers. Jon had decided to stay late today and finish analyzing the samples to avoid working the weekend.

"Laura, I'm really glad you came by. How do you feel about helping me clean up the lab and we'll both get out of here?" With a sweep of his hand he said, "See, there really isn't much that needs doing."

Laura looked around at the myriad of flasks, vials, Pasteur pipettes and Kudner-Danish extractors that covered the counters in windswept disarray. "Doctor, this place is a disaster. It'll take hours to clean up and I came here to work on my research paper, not to play janitor.

Jon grinned at her with his best innocent boy look, "Laura, if you help, you can name the price; anything at all.

Laura stared into those gray-green eyes and moaned, "Oh God, Doctor Kepler, who will be your slave when I'm gone? And besides, I'm supposed to be learning how to operate the Mass Spectrometer, not working like some lab grunt.

Laura had barely strangled her racing heart when she had found him still at work. She was convinced that he had no hint of her feelings for him. She adored him with an almost overwhelming lust at the well-fortified center of her feelings. As she glanced back at him, she noted that he was still wearing that really beautiful smile that made the nearly invisible, soft brown hair tingle on its descent from the soft curve of her neck to the cleave of her butt.

At barely six feet Jon literally towered over Laura, but that only made it more convenient for her to stare at his body. 'Thank god he isn't skinny,' thought Laura. His 190 pounds were well proportioned over a large frame, just showing a hint of the move toward softness and middle age.

"One of these days," she thought out loud, "One day soon!"

"What did you say, Laura?"

She blushed and bumbled nearly spurting, "Nothing, Doctor. I was only muttering about the shitty life of a dedicated student. Friday night with no date and here I am stuck at the EPA lab with the Chief Organic Chemist—who is far too old for me."

Jon stood, smiling down at Laura. His Pierre Cardin navy slacks, stripped blue shirt and wild tie didn't portray the usual picture many had of a scientist for the Environmental Protection Agency. Jon Kepler was a brilliant analyst and a dedicated environmentalist, but didn't feel compelled to stick with the usual tan slacks or jeans and sloppy-shirt-styles of his fellow chemists.

"Laura, I really appreciate your helping. You've saved me the inner struggle that would make me want to leave the place like this."

As they began clearing the traditional black slate bench tops anchored to mottled gray metal cabinets, Laura asked, "Doctor, why did you decide to even run these samples tonight? They're nothing super-special, are they?"

"Not really," he confirmed with a soft voice and strong shrug, "But you know that on Monday, some schmuck from Haltec will be on the phone for the test results and I wanted my weekend clear for some fun. I have tickets for the Cubs double-header on Sunday against the Mets. Anyway, our benevolent boss should never have agreed to analyze these samples for an outside contractor. The Corps of Engineers gave the job to that contract-engineering firm, Haltec, who should have been responsible for the entire project.

As Section Leader for the Organics group, Jon was totally responsible for not only the quantity and quality of work done by his people, but also for the budgeting within his lab. The U.S. Environmental Protection Agency operated its system of laboratories with substantial budgets for equipment, but always seemed to skimp on manpower. As usual, there were always too many Superfund sites, waste drums, and contaminated soil samples for them to analyze and categorize.

Projects like this one in Waukegan always screwed up Jon's budget and being a little preoccupied with the interesting parts of his job, he kept forgetting to keep track of the reasons for his budgetary infractions. Time sheets and supply requisitions just drove him nuts.

Sure as hell, his Department Manager, Wayne Ely, would begin the sermon in his usual fashion 'Chrissakes, Jon, you over-spent again. How can I continue to approve your budget, if you never follow it? Engler and the rest of those bean counters will be on my back, like white on rice.'

Well this time, Jon thought, 'I'll plaster a big yellow Post It Note on my monthly report and remind Ely that it was his fault for accepting the Corps project that caused me to blow the budget.'

Jon broke from his thoughts to find that he and Laura had managed to return the lab to a semblance of organization, while she had continued to toss her head amid comments on the life of a lab grunt. The government green paint in the brightly lit room was in contrast to the clutter of charts, posters and chromatograms that littered the walls. Jon's lab in the EPA office building was a little unique with the glassed cubicle for the instruments looking like a communicable disease isolation room. A special air conditioning system ran even in the deep Chicago winter to soak up the heat generated by the equipment in this windowless glass cage.

Jon walked through the positive airflow toward the softly humming Mass Spectrometer intending to reduce its operational mode for the night. With the automatic movements of oft-repeated actions, Jon glanced at the multi-colored screen to make sure the last sample was finished. The graphics had played across the terminal face and everything was ready for the computer equivalent of a nap, when Jon's peripheral vision clicked on something.

Noticing Laura looking around for her one submission to fashion, Jon flipped his hand into an exaggerated pointer at the small desk she usually occupied. Her blue and gray Gucci purse with the well-worn corners sat on top of the neatly stacked chemical journals.

Jon used their mutually developed sign language to say, 'If you wait a minute, I'll walk out with you as soon as the computer gives me a printout on this last sample.'

Jon was still amazed by the speed and precision of this newest generation of instruments. At nearly $230,000, the stylish, beige metal sat like a miniature cityscape on the $89 folding table he kept meaning to replace. This unit was a testament to the successful marriage of chemistry and microelectronics with its knobless instrument face. Jon had learned his basics for the analysis of complex organic samples at Purdue University before these electronic miracles had been developed.

With a nearly poetic reflection, his memory's camera ran the film of his old Mass Spec in the darkened chemistry lab on the southwestern corner of the Purdue campus. The instrument face was splattered with more than 35 individual control knobs. Micro-bore stainless steel columns, some encased in fabric-wrapped heating tape, ran from one valve to another. There was no fully automated sample injector with its robotics and self-cleaning syringes.

As his memory-film flickered to an end, Jon's eyes roamed across the front of the soft beige instrument to the one control knob. He almost reminded himself out loud that this electronic miracle just needed to be told to RUN or STANDBY.

Jon's lips bent into a smile as he thought of Professor Breitmeyer lecturing him about the ultra-low vacuum in the bombardment chamber and how the instrument was only turned OFF when it needed servicing.

"Listen to me Jon Kepler," the sharp-eyed East German refugee continued unabated, "when samples aren't being run or when data isn't being processed, the machine is put in the STANDBY mode, which is like idle—like your mind, you Dumkbkopf".

A shot of pride came to Jon's mind as he refocused on the tracing on the screen, that he still averaged about 20% of the compound identifications before the ultra, hi-speed HP-4000 Chemstation could search the library and come up with the compound that matched the spectra. The color graphics displayed several forms of the emerging data, as the computer finished its data analysis and provided a huge wealth of information, in both table and graph forms.

Jon's well practiced eyes flicked across the screen to see that his added surrogate compounds were showing up and that this sample had run just as smoothly as the other 8 he had done that day. He followed the tracing on the monitor as it snaked its way up and down the screen in the typical "fingerprint" pattern of a particularly nasty pollutant, Arochlor 1352.

Jon automatically flexed his memory without speaking, cataloging complex sets of peaks for the Arochlors, the trade name for most PCBs.

The chromatograms of all of the Polychlorinated biphenyls or PCBs were so well known, and Jon had run so many, that the 9 major peak points on the screen perfectly matched the file in Jon's mind. Then the memory upload hit a snag. He noted that this sample-run typified the previous ones and he was about to turn away, when his eyes saw the chromatogram curve begin to move upward again from the baseline.

'What in the hell is that,' he wondered. 'I have never seen a signal of any significance in that area of a PCB chromatogram before. He kept reviewing his mind's filing system of previous tests, trying to figure it out before the Mass Spec finished the run and the computer began its spectral library search. Jon gave up and waited with a respect for the machine's capability to look at 135,000 spectra in less than 10 seconds. It would take two Ph.D.'s like himself, with 10 years experience, at least 20 days to complete a manual search of that magnitude.

Laura was just picking up her purse and jacket to leave, when she saw the strange look on Jon's face. "Doctor Kepler, you look like you've messed in your pants".

Jon simply continued to stare at the computer screen with a twinge of dismay about this run. Recalling that all of today's samples were samples of fish tissues, Jon pondered the potential problems that an anomaly would cause. Jon asked Laura to come and look at the strange peak being displayed on the monitor.

Shrugging, she walked over to him, having to squeeze in front of his height to get a look at the screen.

Jon simply leaned back to let her in and offered the peak on the screen with a strong hand.

Finally he asked, “Have you ever seen this kind of a peak in this position? Whatever caused this had to be present in considerable quantity or it would have been a much sharper slope and smaller area under the curve.”

Laura reminded him, “Doctor, I’m just a lowly plebe in the EPA intern program and can’t see what you’re concerned about.”

“Look here,” he began to explain with his finger tracing the curve on the screen. “In all of the previous samples, there were no compound peaks anywhere in this area.”

“Now I see it, Doctor, I’ve run a lot of PCB samples by regular Chromatography and I’ve never seen a peak like that either. Can’t it be just a screwed up standard solution or something simple like that? Maybe it’s something as simple as the sodium sulfate crystals you used for cleaning the concentrate.”

The run was just ending as the hard drive on the main computer signaled that it had completed its library search for a matching spectrum. Its low whine and clicking indicated that it might be finding some things to compare this mess to, when suddenly the monitor flashed with the data.

“Shit!” he blurted, “the damn computer identified the primary PCB compounds with a 97.9% confidence but says ‘no match’ on that last peak.”

Straightening up, Laura said, “I’ll tell you, Doctor, that peak is just some small error and we can resolve it Monday. It’s after 11 o’clock and I’m heading home. Oh, Doctor Kepler, if you’re really that interested in this sample I’ll be glad to come in tomorrow, extract it again and have it ready for you to run again first thing Monday.”

Jon looked up at her saying, “I would really like to rerun the sample tonight, but I’m fadin’ fast. If you will prepare the sample from scratch tomorrow morning, I’ll come just before noon and shoot it again. Thanks for bearing with my Sherlock Holmes complex, Laura. And thanks for stopping by tonight and helping."

Moving away from the instrument, he turned to take one last look at the laser printer. The strange tracing was just being spit out at 12 pages per minute. He was again momentarily tempted to try the rerun tonight, but shook his head and turned to leave the lab with Laura.

'Laura's probably right,' he thought, 'it's just some little detail I missed that brought up that peak. We'll find it tomorrow and still be finished in time for me to have part of the weekend to work on my car and go see my Cubbies Sunday afternoon.'

Exiting from the stainless steel elevator, Jon and Laura parted in the austere government-building lobby, Laura was about to make a production out of the goodbye, but saw that Jon was deep in thought.

Jon was still thinking about the errant data while he walked toward his car parked in the lot next to the building, curiously shared with the regional office of the FBI. Jon had always liked the strange mixture of government employees in this office building. The EPA people were always in their open-necked shirts and beards with a League-of-all-Nations personnel roster while the Feds looked like a little gray army in their suits and ties.

This laboratory was part of the main office of Region V of the U.S. Environmental Protection Agency. The building housed the labs, the library, offices and support services for all of the EPA functions. Jon had never quite understood why the EPA put the lab in a multi-story downtown building, but he liked living and working near Lake Michigan.

Scanning the bright orange illumination of the Iodine lights in the parking lot, Jon spotted his car sitting like a panther on a black patch of sand. He smiled lovingly at the car. Most of his co-workers drove Japanese look-alikes mandated by heavy city traffic and the price of gasoline.

A few drove old "beaters" rather than buy a good car for the commute into downtown Chicago. Several even had one of the new breed of sexy sports cars like the BMW Z-3, but Jon did not like the sameness and the lack of romance in any those cars.

To Jon, the Pontiac had class. It came in the color everyone scampered to buy in 1965. Heads did turn when his metallic blue-black giant hunkered up to a traffic light, its sycophant dual exhausts making that seldom heard muscle car rumble. Jon strode briskly to the sleek-lined Grand Prix.

He unlocked the chrome-laden door on the hardtop and climbed behind the huge steering wheel. The Pontiac had the original upholstery and a total of 21,200 miles on the odometer. The instruments glittered in an array of gauges and knobs. No CD player here. Just Hi Fidelity, push button AM-FM. With multi-colored leather seats, this was Pontiac's famed muscle car of the 60's, capable of nearly 100 miles per hour as a stock car running the quarter mile drag strip.

Jon rarely failed to remember the day his great Aunt Vera had called him from Neenah, Wisconsin, just north of Green Bay, to say that she had a special gift for Jon.

Jon had gone up to see Aunt Vera by bus just in case the car she talked about was worth driving home. Sitting with her in the neat little living room, with its soft, filtered light looking through photos, Jon felt a familiar closeness returning. The same closeness he had felt when he had spent that long-ago summer in Neenah with Aunt Vera and Uncle Andrew. Jon was only twelve that summer of 1972, but he reveled in the outdoor freedom of the woods of Wisconsin. He always remembered that Andrew was the oldest of his father's brothers with just over twenty years separating them. Jon always thought it fun when his Dad called Andrew "Pops" and teased him about being old. His Aunt and Uncle were quiet, loving and wonderful people. He was not sure why he had never gone back there, especially since he often remembered that free summer in the north woods.

After all the photos had been seen and laughed about, Vera's eyes flickered up and welled with sadness, looking toward the graying skies. Jon was told to go to the little barn in back of the dairy building. Vera had given him the key, and said she didn't like to go near that barn.

"Andrew got it ready for you this past week. When you're ready, Jon, just get in it and drive away. Please don't let me see it. I'll say goodbye now. Remember that Andrew wanted you to have this car because you made us feel very good the summer you were here. You were like a son to us".

With Aunt Vera watching from inside the screen door, Jon twisted the key in the padlock of windowless, graying shed and opened the sagging double doors. Sitting there was perhaps the only never-driven 1965 Pontiac Grand Prix in the entire world.

Like a tidal wave flattening a village on the beach, Jon's memories crashed in on him. He remembered the stories of his aunt and uncle's grief when their only son John was killed at the start of the conflict in Vietnam. The only explanation for the car was the family rumor that Uncle Andrew had ordered a car for his son in anticipation of John's college graduation in June of '65. Andrew was not rich by any expansion of the facts, but his dairy farm had done well. It was told that Andrew ordered the car on May 6th, not knowing John had signed on with the Marines the day before. On the day after graduation, the graceful blue machine rumbled into the farmyard during John's going away party, proudly delivered by the local dealer. Andrew held his son's wide shoulders in his large weathered hands and with tears welling told him that he would care for the car until John returned. John was killed in a special marine "wet mission" into Haiphong that "had not taken place" according to all of the war records. A few months later John's commanding officer visited the farm to tell of their son's bravery and belief in his country's mission.

It took several minutes for Jon to wander around the Pontiac inspecting its sleek, high fenders, dual taillights and rows of chrome on the high-backed trunk. The white walls were barely an inch wide, making a target of the oversized 16-inch tires. Complete with fender skirts and a massive 492 cubic inch engine, sporting 3 deuces, the two-ton "road cruiser" was one of the last really fast cars off the Detroit assembly line before the U.S. began its slide into automobile mediocrity. Jon got in, slowly slid his fingers around the cold steering wheel, turned the key and drove away. He had glanced up just at the right time to see Uncle Andrew come straight in his tracks and throw his strongest salute since seeing Omar Bradley on the Bridge at Remagen.

Until the day they died, Jon would send flowers to Aunt Vera and a book to Uncle Andrew on their birthdays. He would call them on special occasions and at Christmas. They never discussed the car or those not with them, but talked mostly of Jon's career. He recognized the substitution but it didn't depress or anger him. Aunt Vera, Uncle Andrew and the cousin he hardly knew always came to mind when he got in the car.

Just as Jon started the Pontiac and slipped it into gear, he saw the security guard standing in the harsh light of the side entrance, waving frantically in his direction.

FRIDAY 9:00 p.m.

CHAPTER 2

About two hours before Jon got into his car in the EPA parking lot on Dearborn Street to head north to his apartment, a brilliant white 38-foot Chris-Craft had cruised into the deep blackness of Monroe Street Harbor.

A somewhat disheveled and windblown figure prepared to jump to the dock and tie up the boat. Cindy Farrell was totally exhausted having spent nearly 11 tossing hours in the boat. She was fed up with this project. Tossing the wind snarled hair to one side, she jumped lazily for the edge of the pier and damn near fell short, stumbling slightly and stutter-stepping toward the tie-down.

Methodically securing the front and aft lines, Cindy continued her career evaluation that had been in process nearly all day. As a field biologist for the Haltec Corporation, Cindy had changed her college ideals of a glorious mission to save the environment. She had accepted the job offer from Haltec just before receiving her Masters in Aquatic Biology. The company's employment information waxed philosophically about research into the grand scheme of the ecology and the company's great contributions to the science of "environmental rebuilding." Cindy had found, after nearly six years on the job, that Haltec's business was centered on the environment, but primarily concerned with very profitable government contracts. While the work itself was right up her alley and she was applying what she had learned at Vanderbilt, Cindy was convinced that her real contribution to the saving of Mother Earth was insignificant.

Haltec's lone female vice-president, Joan Blacker, who made it sound like she was giving Cindy the biggest break of her career, assigned this current project to her. Blacker emphasized that if the job was screwed up, she would drag Cindy bare-assed across a football field of hot coals. Cindy had found the project to be almost a repeat of a 1999 study of the entire Waukegan Ditch ecosystem. The big discovery of PCB's in the harbor was initially made in the mid 70's, but no method of cleanup was ever conceived that satisfied all of the interested parties. The current testing was yet another attempt to find some way to deal with the polluted bottom sediments that were slowly ebbing out of the river basin into the harbor. Cindy and her team took the project in stride and did their best to see it through to a professional conclusion.

Cindy really enjoyed the two people she worked with for the last few years, having come to find them mentally stimulating and fun to be with. She liked them both, but for totally different reasons. Jerry Wittner was a somewhat bulky, curly haired, straight shooter from Ohio. Rubin Anderson was a small thin black from a southern Chicago suburb working his way through college.

Within several days of joining each other on their first project, the three had developed a mutual respect for each other's talents. Jerry was a chemistry major from a small college in Dayton, Ohio; he had a minor in biology but had declared his distrust for the "science that relied on Latin names to keep the rest of the world impressed."

Jerry Wittner continually demonstrated his competence in the field with a strong background in sampling methods and a great knack for equipment repair. They had seen each other socially for several months, but after only three or four dates, they rapidly found that they were really just great friends. Their relationship had become a mutually delightful one of movies, plays and canoe trips.

Cindy pulled lightly on the aft line until Jerry hollered, "Hey, that's not a piece of linguine; you can pull a little harder, you know."

Cindy laughed, dropping the rope and scampering to catch it before it fell in the still chilly waters of Lake Michigan. Jerry, realizing that she had been down lately, had worked to keep her spirits up during this project. They had averaged ten to twelve hours a day out on the choppy lake—sometimes getting caught in cold showers that blew in suddenly. It had not been one of the better jobs for Jerry either. He had begun to notice some kind of unexplainable brooding from their third team member. Jerry was certain that it wasn't a dislike of Rubin's color or work ethic, but his deepening silence.

As Cindy walked back toward the boat to begin unloading equipment, Jerry couldn't help but wonder why he had come to treat her like a sister, rather than like the bedmate he had first hoped for. Jerry loved the tight jeans and tee shirts she wore when out sampling. She claimed that jeans kept her warmer than the special jumpsuits issued by Haltec. Jerry still thought she had the best curve to her behind that he had ever seen.

Cindy called back, "Hey, Chubs, are you gonna stand there and play with yourself or help with this equipment?"

Just then, the deep blue-black face of their field technician, Rubin Anderson, appeared in the opening of the small cabin on the Chris-Craft.

"All battened down in here. Do you need help with the equipment or shall I haul out the sample coolers," Rubin said, still in the gangway?"

Rubin had always been an enigma to Jerry and Cindy. He had been easily trained in his new job and was a genuine assistance to them. He seemed to enjoy the work but rarely laughed or bantered with them. Rubin kept a disconcerting solitude about himself and Cindy had seen Jerry's quizzical expression surface more and more lately. Still, with the usual unpredictable Illinois spring weather and the rather boring project, the three of them had managed to function as an effective field sampling team.

Unlike most other powerboats on the Lake, the HALTEC NINE carried 6 large, red plastic coolers and no beer. The special 48 quart, insulated boxes were used to store the water, fish and bottom sediment samples they collected. Jerry sometimes kidded Rubin about his quickness with a knife when gutting the fish to take liver or fatty-tissue samples. Rubin's answer never varied, "In my neighborhood you either have a fast knife or fast feet."

Having gotten things organized quickly and the boat cleaned up, the three moved all the gear into the white Chevy Astro Van with the Haltec logo. Just before Jerry kicked over the engine, he reminded Cindy that she had promised to take the samples to the EPA lab tonight.

"Chrissakes, Jerry, it's damn near ten o'clock and I'm beat!" growled Cindy. "Plus, there won't be anyone at that lab on Friday night," she whimpered hoping to get out of making the trip downtown.

Jerry said with what little sympathy he could muster, "Remember, Cindy, that Miz Joan Blacker herself told us to get this last set of samples to that lab tonight in order to avoid any statements in the data about samples being received after allowable holding times.

And besides," Jerry continued, "You promised me that you would make the last trip and then weaseled out of it."

Cindy turned in the cramped seat and with feigned anger flaring from her tumescent green eyes, she hissed, "Shit, Jerry! How do I know there will be someone at the EPA lab to take the samples and log them in?"

"Cindy, you've got the number for the chief chemist right on the project sheet. Blacker got the idiot's direct dial number for emergencies. Use it," Jerry chastised.

Rubin just sat by the window and enjoyed his inward smile, while the two playfully hassled each other.

"All right! All right! You really owe me for this one, you bag of fish guts," Cindy taunted. "I'll call the schmuck and run the samples down there, but only if you guys will load the sample coolers into my Jeep back at the office."

With that settled, Cindy, Rubin and Jerry headed back to Haltec's office.

It always amazed Jerry that it could be so difficult to travel the short distance from the Monroe St. Harbor to their prestigious Michigan Ave. location. In sum, Lake Shore Drive's curving black ribbon along the gray-green waters of Lake Michigan is beautiful for the tourists but not too practical. As soon as they arrived at the loading area for the building, the trio quickly transferred the coolers into the back of Cindy's beat up CJ-7. Jerry and Rubin dispersed with exhausted good nights.

Cindy decided to call the EPA guy from the pay phone in the parking garage, rather than her undependable cellular. She looked on her battered clipboard and found "Dr. Jon Kepler, 278-2522."

Cindy quickly judged the name and said to herself, "With that Ph.D., this guy is probably so old he farts dust."

Dropping in her only quarter, she quickly dialed the number only to wait while the phone rang at least eight times. Cindy was about to stuff it back onto the cradle when a raspy, panting voice said, “Yeah, EPA night desk. This is Security. Hold on! My goddamn keys are still in the door.” Cindy looked at the phone in the dim white light of the garage and mouthed an obscenity to the security man.

“Yeah, whatcha want,” the guard said with his usual I’m-put-out attitude.

With the long day’s muted anger evident in her voice, Cindy replied, “This is Cindy Farrell, from Haltec Corporation and I am looking for Dr. Jon Kepler at the EPA laboratory.”

“Scuse me, Miss Farrell,” he said straitening up, “but Dr. Kepler just walked out into the parking lot.”

“Please. It is very important that you catch him. I have samples to deliver to him and I must bring them tonight. Please try to catch him for me.”

“Hold on!” came the response that was evidenced by the twanging hollow noise made by the guard’s having laid the phone on a metal desk.

After an interminable wait, a slightly out of breath person responded, “Miss Fowler, you’ll forgive me but I don’t know why you insisted that the guard drag me back in here. I don’t know anything about any samples and it’s nearly midnight.”

Cindy retorted with, “Doctor Kepler, if you’ll let me explain. First, my name is Farrell, not Fowler. Second, perhaps you need to be enlightened as to your responsibilities regarding my project. Now! Your name is listed as the emergency contact for the Haltec sampling of the Waukegan Ditch for the Corps of Engineers project and I am declaring this an emergency”.

Mustering his best vitriolic tone, Jon countered with “Well, Farrell I am well aware that the Haltec project is my responsibility, but why are you calling me? Do you need directions to the Lake?”

“Look, Buster, I practically froze out on that lake today and now I get a friggin’ Ph.D. who thinks he’s a comedian. Let’s just finish up this little job and part ways.”

Jon had immediately formed an impression, no, a complete picture of Cindy Farrell. Her use of "buster" told him that this little lady was a tough one and probably a hideous Medusa whose primary purpose in life was to turn all men into eunuchs.

Cindy was fuming! She had begun to sweat. She wanted to scream. Wait! Why was she letting this lab jockey get to her? She was a field professional and knew her job and her position. She decided to pull rank.

"Dr. Kepler, according to the arrangement between Haltec, the Corps of Engineers and the EPA, all field samples must arrive at the laboratory within the time limits stipulated by your own Quality Control Section. Your name has been provided as the emergency contact and your superior has authorized this contact. Therefore, will you please wait for me at the laboratory to take these samples for disposition?"

"Ms. Farrell, that was well recited. You are within your right to call me as the emergency contact. However, I am still uncertain as to why you must bring in the samples tonight."

"My dear, good Doctor", Cindy spat out with her best, I'm-Now-In-Control-Voice, "Today is Friday. Previous late arrivals of samples have taken place on Monday through Thursday, when it was allowable to hold the samples overnight in refrigerated storage at Haltec. However the 24 hour maximum time limit would be exceeded, if I waited until Monday to deliver the samples."

Cindy and Jon both seemed to hear the high pitched squealing of radial rubber on urethane-coated concrete as the Dodge Viper came skidding around the pillar, exiting from the lower level. As Cindy screamed and Jon sucked air with that typical unsighted awareness, the Viper braked hard, whirled to the right and missed Cindy by three feet. The driver shot a glance at the girl on the phone, but elected to rev up for a fast exit from the parking garage.

Jon had not heard the phone bang against anything, so he figured that she couldn't have dropped the thing. Then with a resounding bellow, he heard, "Holy Shit!

"Cindy!" He called urgently.

She wanted to scream at him as if it was his fault, but she mustered her cool. "Yes, Doctor, I'm here".

Before she could go on, Jon interrupted with "What was that? Are you OK?" he demanded.

"Please forgive the interruption, Doctor. I'm in the first level of the parking garage at the Haltec building on Michigan and Oak, and some adrenalin addict damn near hit me. Now could we finish our business?"

Detecting a softness he had not heard before and almost feeling the fright-induced pounding in her chest, Jon said, in a much softened, almost demure tone, "My apologies, Miss Farrell. Perhaps we could start this conversation over if you are up for it?"

Cindy slowly wondered what the hell was going on, but recovered to say, "That is a good idea. I apologize for my gruffness. It has been a long day and I just want to get these samples to the EPA lab within the allowed holding time", she said with a wide-fingered stroke to her hair. "Could you help me with that?"

Jon was about to give her directions, when Cindy interrupted, "Should I just meet you at the side entrance to the EPA lab by the Security Guard station?"

Her face changed once again when she actually paid attention to the deep resonance of his voice. She said incredulously to herself, "You can't possibly be old enough to fart dust."

Jon was impressed by her change in attitude and smiled to himself while glancing in the direction of the guard, who seemed to hang on every one of Jon's words. Jon gave him a smile and agreed to wait at the side door for Cindy's arrival.

After setting down his briefcase, Jon was just getting to his response to the guard's third question about the weird smells that came from the lab, when they both heard the muted beep of a small car through the insulated steel door. They both reached the push bar at the same time and were greeted by the beguiling behind of Cindy Farrell protruding from the back end of her Jeep, where the rest of her was dutifully searching for the paperwork amongst the sample coolers.

Jon caught the sharp elbow from the security guard and tried not to smile as Cindy unfolded from the inside of the vehicle.

Standing in the unearthly glow of the Iodine lights, Jon and Cindy simultaneously performed that physical inventory that runs head to toe. Catching each other in the act, they both tried to appear nonchalant, knowing that they had been caught.

Jon spoke first. “Cindy Farrell?”

Her face changed when she recognized the voice. All of the earlier animosity melted away as they each stared at the other in disbelief. Cindy’s beautiful, wind-blown, sandy hair partially covered her face but could not hide her total surprise at Jon’s appearance. Was it the fright from the auto’s near miss or the magic of the moment that caused a rising of her libido? She just stared up from her 5 foot 7 inches into steely eyes set in a chiseled pale face. Jon stared back until the guard noticed.

FRIDAY MIDNIGHT

CHAPTER 3

"OK, Doctor Kepler, I'll be willing to log the samples…"

"Cindy, its Jon, not Doctor. If you say it again, I'll have to prescribe something horrible."

"Jon it is then," Cindy mumbled demurely. "As I was explaining on the phone, I had to call to get these samples signed in tonight", pointing toward her Jeep CJ-7. They are the last samples from this project. The coolers are in the back. Where shall we take them?"

Jon was studying her features. He carefully noted the sandy blond hair loosely tumbling down to shoulder length in apparent disarray from the day out on the lake. He paid a moment's too much special attention to the fullness of the lumberman's plaid shirt. Her tight jeans gave plenty of apparent support to the rest of her body though. As his appraisal moved up to green sparkling eyes, he felt swallowed by an overwhelming lust.

Cindy blushed again with a familiar stirring that was rarely elicited by a male's glance. She stuttered, "J-J-Jon, what do we do with the samples?"

His assessment interrupted, Jon suggested, "How about if we load the samples onto a cart and take them up to the EPA lab and log them into refrigerated storage. That will take care of the holding-time issue and get us out of here." With a throw of his hand, Jon indicated their parking lot surroundings.

Cindy nodded her head in acknowledgment and suggested that he bring the sample cart over to her Jeep.

Jon lifted the first cooler onto the cart and quickly followed it with the second. Judging by the weight, he figured the samples were heavily iced. It was then that he suggested, “Cindy, why don’t we combine the samples into one cooler and dump the ice out here in the storm drain to avoid the mess in the lab.

Cindy smiled her agreement and opened all of the coolers.

They had transferred all of the bottles of water samples and the jars of fish samples to one cooler. Then they took care of the plastic Whirl-Pak bags with the muddy-black sediment samples. Quickly dumping the ice water from the coolers, they watched it swirling down the parking lot storm drain like a giant flat black bathtub, leaving the remaining empty coolers in Cindy’s trunk.

As they pulled the cart up the loading ramp into the building, the security guard glanced sideways from his stand-up green metal desk without meeting their eyes. He looked at a very familiar Jon Kepler and shot a look at Cindy letting them in while giving Jon a poke in the ribs followed by a lewd wink.

Moving into the elevator, Cindy muttered a comment about the guard and the inability of all men to think with their big heads.

Jon almost spurted an answer, but decided to focus on the numbers silently clicking away above the slot that would open to reveal the laboratory floor. The doors opened and they moved the samples into the main lab for numbering and storage.

Jon noticed Cindy looking around at the rather dismal laboratory storage area. “Even bright blue paint wouldn’t help this place,” Cindy said nearly exclaiming. “I couldn’t work in this damn place. It feels like a hospital but looks more like a shiny metal dungeon.”

Jon pushed the cart to the sample log-in desk and began removing them while Cindy continued her appraisal of the main chemistry area. It only took Jon a few minutes to remove the samples and begin organizing them by group. Cindy moved next to Jon and realized she had stepped just slightly too close. She found herself reluctant to step away. She assumed the sample organization from Jon who automatically stepped around the corner of the low counter to take a spot at the computer terminal. Jon quickly placed his fingers on the dirty keys and oriented himself to the Master Sample Log-in Prompt. He began to flash through the screens pulling up previous information on the Haltec project, when something made him raise his eyes within a steady head to see Cindy Farrell staring at him. She couldn't look away fast enough to prevent the red tinge that crept up from the collar of her warm shirt.

Cindy wondered while they worked in silence.

Things moved quickly through the process. They placed the samples on a hospital type cart, having stuck barcode labels on each as they had spat out of the miniature printer. They wheeled them into a large white-doored walk-in refrigerator.

At that moment they both seemed to realize their reason for being together had evaporated with their efficiency. Jon quickly asked if Cindy would like to see the rest of the facility.

Finding a clock in the room, Cindy declined with a glance at the large battery operated timepiece, curiously displaying an electrical cord hand-drawn on the wall below the otherwise cordless device.

"Someone's rather odd sense of humor, Jon?" Cindy asked with a pointing nod of her head.

No answer from Jon was an admission of guilt, as far as Cindy was concerned.

With a shake of the head, Cindy declined his invitation for a tour citing the late hour. Jon garnered his courage and turned to Cindy. Too late he saw that she was about to speak to him. They blurted simultaneously, "How about coffee?" Smiling at the occurrence, they answered "yes" to one another at the same instant, imitating some old TV comedy routine. Both chuckled with some embarrassment while they strolled to the elevator.

SATURDAY 9:15 a.m.

CHAPTER 4

Jon awoke from his nocturnal reverie with a heart-pounding start and a throbbing erection. Lying in bed waiting for both problems to subside, John recalled the fascinating late evening, or rather, early morning, spent with Cindy Farrell.

'Christ, it's Saturday,' he thought, 'Why am I up so early?' Glancing at the clock, Jon found that his body had said early, but the clock said 9:15 a.m. Then he remembered why he was tired. He and Cindy had sat in the Golden Cup coffee shop by his near-north side apartment until nearly three in the morning. Escorting her from the restaurant back to her Jeep, with nary a peck on the cheek, he arrived home to collapse wide-eyed in bed.

Then the message came to him that was registered in his mind's memo pad. He was supposed to meet Laura back at the lab to rerun that one strange sample. He'd better get his butt in gear or lose her respect and possibly the extra efforts she made on the job, like working this Saturday. He hustled around the large studio apartment, taking little notice of its disarray.

Less than 20 minutes later, Jon strolled into the lab to see Laura's back. She was laboring over the last crucial stage of the sample extraction and he hesitated to speak or move forward, lest he startle her into dropping something.

As she set the glassware down, Jon spoke with a rising lilt, "Laura!"

Before he could continue, Laura turned and the frown of concentration flipped into some Gargoylesque full-faced grin that seemed to disfigure her normally conversational face.

“Dr. Kepler, how good of you to come. I hope you did manage to get some sleep,” Laura chided.

It took Jon more than a moment to pick up on the taunt. “Whatever the guard told you was greatly exaggerated and she was just a biologist delivering more samples from the Haltec project,” he said so fast as to lend no credence to the statement.

“Oh, Doctor,” Laura continued, “You do not owe me any explanations. Whatever you do in the lab at midnight on Friday with a beautiful woman, is completely your affair. Oops! Was that a poor choice of words?”

“Come on, Laura, lay off”, Jon grumbled with a faked scowl. “I’ll buy you lunch as soon as we rerun that sample from last night. Now, where do you stand in the prep?”

Laura blinked rapidly in her best, if poorly done, imitation of a vamp and said, “Doctor, I’ve completed the entire sample preparation and you now have your required one milliliter of solvent extracted fish tissue, along with all of the Q.C. standards. Oh, by the way, I also finished setting up the samples you logged in last night. By the way, you almost did the whole thing right, but I fixed the two entry errors in the log-in data.”

Comedically grimacing at Laura’s very bad vamp imitation, Jon took the tray of nine miniature vials with a sweeping hand and a stiff smirk. He reviewed in his mind the quality control procedures that mandated the need for standards, sample duplicates and spikes that magically turned a single sample into nine computer runs. He proceeded to load the vials into a few of the 99 places in the round rack of the instrument’s robotic autosampler.

Hitting the start button while simultaneously giving mental “start” instructions to the GC Mass Spec, Jon stood and anxiously awaited the first appearance of the tracing from the computer. As always he was unsatisfied with the time element. Even though these samples would have taken one chemist three months of solid work just twenty years ago, Jon still wanted it to be faster.

While Jon had been tempted to run the sample first, he had followed proven analytical protocol and was running a series of five standards or “knowns”. These samples were dilutions of pure PCB that were prepared in advance to calibrate the instrument. Each of these took only 8 minutes with the amazing new Hewlett-Packard. Just 2 years ago, each of the sample analysis runs were over one hour. Quickly following the standards, came several more qualifying runs with duplicates of the first two standards and a blank using just ultra-pure hexane.

As the first compound peaks began to appear from the sample being rerun, he attacked the keyboard, commanding the computer to retrieve yesterday’s chromatogram for the same sample. The computer obeyed with stoic machine information:

YOU HAVE REQUESTED
A PREVIOUS ANALYTICAL SAMPLE RUN

DO YOU WISH IT DISPLAYED OR PRINTED?

Patiently Jon instructed the computer to put the run on the video display for comparison to the currently running sample. As the third peak was appearing, the run from yesterday flashed into place occupying the lower half of the screen, while the new data was being traced onto the upper portion.

“So far so good,” he mumbled to his screen. Laura walked up wanting to make a comment about his talking to the monitor again, but passed the opportunity when she noted his concentration.

With their eyes so strongly focused, the two scientists almost melded into the glow of the screen. As peak after peak matched on the horizontally split screen, Jon seemed to tense as the cursor approached the atomic mass unit window where the previously unidentified compound had shown it self.

“I’ll be dipped in shit!” Jon shouted. “There it is again Laura”, he exclaimed making a rat’s nest out of his normally neat hair. “Now, before we go any further, was there anything different about your prep technique?”

“Doctor, I even got the Procedure Manual out and checked everything before I started” Trying to lighten the electrified atmosphere, Laura panned, “Following my standard excellent lab techniques, I also checked the reagents to make sure none were outdated.”

"That could be it, Laura," he started, nearly cutting off her last words. "The reagents might not be old, but could be contaminated! Let the Q.C. samples finish at the end of the run, and then check the results. If there is no contamination, we'll run five extraction solvents and another complete set of standards through the instrument and a set of duplicate method blanks. Then we'll shoot two standards."

It was a good thing that Laura had been there a few months already or Jon would have lost her with that batch of instructions. She easily recognized the USEPA Method for GC/MS verification of sample runs. Pleased with her expanding capabilities, she immediately began organizing her thoughts around the task. Then it hit her.

"Dr. Kepler, you are talking about 4 or 5 more hours of work and it is Saturday. I might consider doing it for time and a half," she whined, kiddingly.

Jon had already turned to the H-P Chemstation and was engrossed in the final minutes of the chromatogram run. He hadn't waited for Laura's answer since he naturally assumed that anyone would be fascinated by this strange analytical phenomenon. Laura shrugged her shoulders, shook her closely cropped, soft brown hair and began the long grind of checking the sample run from top to bottom.

At 3:30 that afternoon, while Jon mused with his electronic mistress, Laura interrupted with a resplendent rare curse. "Shit, Dr. Kepler, don't the slaves here even get fed lunch. Anyway, you promised me the whole story on the late night sample delivery."

Jon looked up from the notes he was making, which included an even longer run of standards and check samples for Laura. "Laura, my dear, the conscripts in the service of science don't require food. The quest for knowledge is sustenance enough and don't try to make me think I promised you any talk of last night." He grinned at her.

She only stood there with one hip akimbo and a tight fist poised on the opposite side.

Jon turned back to the instrument and just as quickly spun back around with a loud screech from the worn chair.

"Laura, I'll buy you a fabulous early dinner while we let the automatic sample injector finish up for us. Then we'll come back from dinner and see what we've got on the computer."

SATURDAY 4:00 p.m.

CHAPTER 5

Jon and Laura weren't the only ones working this Saturday. Joan Blacker sat in her nearly sterile office reviewing the status report sheets from the field crews under her direction.

She was the first woman ever promoted to this level within Haltec's corporate structure, and she was determined that she would also be their first female Division vice-president. After getting her Engineering degree at the University of Illinois and her MBA at the University of Chicago, Joan had worked for the world's largest gasoline retailer. Headquartered in Chicago, Joan worked very hard in the old stone tower only to find that her career goals would never be fulfilled. She had discovered that her primary function was simply to be part of the oil giant's "female quota" for management personnel. She moved on to Mid- American Oil where they at least promised to utilize her combined engineering and business talents. In her four years at Mid-American, Joan found that professional skills were defined both by the skills of one's intellect and the skills of one's body. She had honed her capabilities in both areas.

Haltec hired Joan Blacker because the Division President, Stewart Phillips, found the trait in her that signaled profit. Joan was a climber. She had something to prove. Phillips knew that Joan would produce the kind of results that his office needed in his own scheme to push his Division in unprecedented growth. She would stop at nothing to get what she wanted, he said to himself, after interviewing her. She will walk over anyone that gets in her way. Phillips hired Joan Blacker and immediately put her in charge of five major environmental contracts currently being operated by Haltec. They would get done, done well and done on time. That meant profits and attention for Phillips.

Joan finished her project review and summed it up for herself. All ahead of schedule, except for the Lake Michigan study here in our own backyard. She gave herself an A-. She opened her leather bound appointment book and made a note to get Cindy Farrell in here on the carpet to give justification for the delay in her project completion. The contract with the Corps of Engineers did not have a stringent performance clause, but Joan knew that timely performance would look good—both to the client and to Phillips.

In her reflections on how the dressing down for the project delay was to be handled, Joan recalled her total dislike for Cindy Farrell. Joan knew, however, that Cindy wouldn't be a problem, but simply a distraction. Whenever Cindy had to come onto Joan's floor in the Haltec building, the men were gaping and jabbing each other. The attention Cindy got infuriated Joan and goaded her to heap some special criticism on Cindy. Joan had been on the negotiating team that had handled the Lake Michigan project with the Corps, and she felt that Haltec had received a golden job. The project had not been put up for bid due to the time constraints and the Corps had simply called in Haltec to negotiate a price. Because of the extensive and continuous publicity about the PCB problems related to the Waukegan Ditch and the nearby areas of Lake Michigan, the Corps of Engineers had finally made the decision to proceed with the dredging project to remove some 20 million pounds of bottom sediments.

This sludge was destined for barge shipment to the central southern part of the state where it would be used as top dressing on the "naked hills" that were left by strip mining operations.

The U. S. Army Corps of Engineers would not make any friends over this project. Everyone had a different theory and opinion on how to handle the problem. The Corps decided to select what they thought was the best approach and take whatever flak came with the decision.

This allowed Joan and her team to come out with a contract for the final Environmental Impact Study that was worth at least a thirty-one percent profit on a total of $687,000. Phillips had congratulated the team, all of whom agreed that they had simply followed Joan's lead and convinced the Corps of the need for an extensive re-study of the Waukegan Ditch area to cover everyone's ass.

Joan had assigned the project to Cindy because she knew that Farrell and Wittner were probably the only people dedicated enough to go out on the Lake in the spring to collect samples. The wind, waves and cold rains would normally make a project like this go on interminably, but those two would get it done. Joan had carefully constructed a scenario of how important this project was, first in terms of its impact on the area ecology and with respect to its importance to Haltec.

Remembering her summation in the oak paneled warmth of the project meeting room, she repeated to herself. 'Cindy! Jerry! This can be the best project ever awarded from the Region V Hazardous Waste Superfund. If we can do a great job, we will not only save the Lake from continued spread of PCB's but we will most certainly establish a solid reputation with the Corps for service and quality.'

Joan had been disappointed to find out that the Corps had contracted the sample testing and analysis directly with the USEPA lab, because as the general contractor, Haltec was usually able to pick up a 15% management fee just by subcontracting the analytical work to a commercial laboratory. That would have looked even better on her record.

Joan was just about to leave her office when she remembered the promised call to her grandfather. She punched #71 on her custom mauve autodialing telephone and waited for someone to stop the incessant buzzing by answering the phone. When a woman answered she was taken aback momentarily.

"Is Isaac Blackman there, please?"

Not being certain she had gotten the correct number, Joan quickly checked her personal directory to confirm the AutoDial number. Just then, the familiar gravel voice of her grandfather came on. "Hello Liebchen! I knew it was you. No one asks for Isaac Blackman except you. Everybody just asks for old Isaac. I just love it when you do that."

Joan despised her grandfather's acceptance of his role in life. A tailor for 58 years, he said he loved his work and would consider none other. His obvious Jewishness was embarrassing to her. Since her parents died in a private plane crash nearly 10 years ago, Joan only visited her grandfather when propriety demanded it. She usually invented excuses to skip one occasion after another.

"Isaac, I cannot make the reception tonight for Mrs. Braun. It is really important that I complete some work here today, but I'll see you Tuesday," she lied.

Isaac Blackman loved his granddaughter and was proud of her accomplishments. But he was concerned over her apparent disdain for their heritage.

"Ya, Liebchen. I'll explain to Mrs. Braun. You take care and God will do the rest.

'That dear old man is so unbelievably sweet, but sometimes his god-crap can get to me,' she thought.

Joan Blacker started her separation from her family when she changed her name as a junior in college explaining that a Jewish name kept a girl from getting ahead in business.

Joan shoveled her material into the briefcase for some work at home tomorrow, after she worked on Phillips tonight.

SATURDAY 4:20 p.m.

CHAPTER 6

Jon and Laura came back from a quick dinner at the not so quaint Italian restaurant on Dearborn just up from the EPA building. They were both smiling. He and Laura had spent the forty-five minutes telling stories about college professors. Each one had gotten funnier and had thus produced an ebullient mood.

That all changed when they returned to the lab and Jon unfurled the computer printout, studied the data summary, and announced, "Well, Laura, we cannot solve the mystery by calling it a mistake. We have found some kind of heavy molecular weight organic compound in that fish tissue sample that has no match in our computer. We don't know what it is."

"Doctor," Laura said seriously reflecting Jon's mood change, "There are still a number of possibilities that we have not checked out—possibilities for obscure errors that we may have missed."

"Certainly there are a lot of items to be checked, but I'd bet my diploma on the fact that we have some really weird compound here."

Jon began reciting a list of things that had to be done as if Laura was to automatically record his words. She quickly grabbed a pad beginning to pick up on his list.

Wandering in small circles in front of the instrument with a cupped hand on his pensive chin, he threw out his growing list, "First, we have to rerun the sample in triplicate and spike it with some known compounds to check recovery. Then we will rerun all new blanks and check samples followed by a complete set of new sample extractions. While you get started on that, Laura, I'll back up the hard drive onto tape and take it over to FDA lab and see if their computer library can find a chemical that matches our spectra."

Laura smiled then frowned. "Doctor Kepler, it is five p.m. on Saturday. Do you really think anyone will be at the FDA lab now?" She had smiled at his forgetfulness, but that changed to a grimace when she realized that Jon's list meant a greatly increased workload for her.

"You're right, Laura. We've already been here too long today and are probably not at our sharpest. Let's come in early Monday and get at it."

Laura's mouth was still hanging open when Jon smiled at her and picked up his jacket. "Well, Laura, let's blow this joint."

Laura still couldn't believe it even as they left the building together. Normally, he would have asked me to start tonight or come in tomorrow, Sunday or not.

As Jon and Laura left the nearly lifeless building, they went their separate directions in front of the building, Jon's mind was racing with conflicting thoughts of an unidentified compound found in the tissue of a Coho salmon and his teen-age infatuation with Cindy. He had not intended to be at the lab this late and had wanted to call Cindy for dinner. Climbing into his Pontiac and pointing it toward his apartment, he vacillated between thoughts of strange compounds and Cindy Farrell.

Suddenly he realized the Pontiac was not even running. He concentrated on the scene in front of the windshield. The pitted gray face of a concrete wall stared back. "Shit! I did it again," he chastised out loud. "I'm parked in the garage stall at my apartment and I don't remember even one stoplight or turn. There must be a God!"

Once inside the apartment, Jon immediately felt a strange emptiness that had not been there before. He went to the phone and called information for Cindy's number, not having thought to ask for it last night. Thank God, he thought to himself, she doesn't have an unlisted number.

After several rings, Jon began to sense his falling mood. Just as he was about to replace the receiver, "If this isn't Mel Gibson or Tom Cruise, I'm hanging up to get back in the shower."

Jon could only wonder if Cindy was always so saucy and abrupt on the phone.

"Cindy, its Jon, from the EPA lab."

"No shit, Jon. You really work for EPA?"

"Cindy, I just finished up some things at the lab and wondered if you would like to go for coffee and hear about the really strange compound I've stumbled across." Jon held his breath waiting the answer.

"Coffee!" Cindy spat into the phone with a false wrath. "Are you addicted to that stuff or just cheap? You could at least buy a girl a drink. Wait! I have a better idea. Instead of your waiting while I get dressed, I can be presentable by the time you get to my place and the drinks will be on me."

Jon thought to ask the address and even wrote it down in case he had a memory lapse. "I'll be there shortly, but I didn't bring the data home with me. So you'll have to settle for a verbal report."

Jon brushed his hair, tapped the cologne bottle twice for luck and ran out the front door. Using the stairs, instead of waiting for the elevator, he hopped in the Pontiac and pulled out of the garage. Hitting the brakes, he slapped the steering wheel with both hands in mock anger. It just dawned on him that the address was less than three blocks away. Returning the rumbling muscle car to its slot, Jon hustled out through the large driveway door and broke into an easy jog toward Cindy's building.

Knocking on the door in less than six minutes after their phone call, Jon heard a soft "Shit!" from the other side of the recently refinished mahogany door. Through the peephole he heard "If you're selling I don't want any; if you're Gibson or Cruise, I'll buy from you."

Through a sputtering of chuckles he answered, "Cindy, its Jon." This was quickly followed by another expletive from the wooden barrier.

Whipping open the door, Cindy smiled at Jon with her best charming school manners allaying the fact that she stood there wrapped in a towel with her wet hair hanging over her face.

Brushing it aside in a careless manner, she said, "C'mon in, Jon, I'll just slip into something a little less comfortable and be out in a minute. There's wine and whiskey in the kitchen; just look around for the supplies."

Watching her swish down the short hall with only the magenta terry cloth towel, left Jon somewhat dumbfounded. He smiled to himself, 'That girl has panache.'

Strolling into the combined kitchen and dinette, Jon got a sense of organized chaos. Undoubtedly, Cindy knew where everything was, but there was no logic to it. Glasses in the cabinet with baking dishes, pans in with the cereal and plates sitting with the spices. He would go crazy. Opening the refrigerator to check for wine, he literally yelped.

Cindy immediately called from the bedroom, "Don't worry Jon, it's dead. The wine's in the vegetable bin. I'll have some of the Pinot Grigio."

Jon stood there staring at the biggest rat he had ever seen. It just laid there smiling from inside a Ziploc bag on the second shelf.

"Holy shit! That is really disgusting," Jon exclaimed. "All biologists are weird and this one may be the weirdest," he mumbled too loudly.

Cindy tapped him on the shoulder causing him to jump away from her and simultaneously yelp again. Cowering in the corner of the countertop, he took longer to recover than he should have.

"Goddamn it, Cindy! You've got to warn us normal folk who really don't expect to find a stiff rat in a fridge. Why that damn thing has his eyes open and a grin on his face."

"Jon, in the first place it's a girl and in the second place I picked it up near the tie-down at Monroe harbor one night last week. Look at it. There is not a mark on it and there is very little decay or dehydration. It also seems to be limp like it has no skeleton. I wanted to take it to the lab at Haltec to check it for some viral infestation. It has to be something a little strange to cause a rat to drop dead, like she did."

“Jeez Cindy, shut the door. It’s staring at me with the crazed look that Bela Lugosi had in those old movies.

“Protect me,” he feigned with his best whimper.

She pulled him into her arms with a playful swing to continue the frightened boy routine. As their bodies touched, both felt the static electricity flow. They quickly parted knowing that they dare not chance a continued physical encounter. They both knew the other wanted nothing more than for it to go on.

SATURDAY 9:00 p.m.

CHAPTER 7

After a glorious, mind bursting kiss, "I could tell by the taste," Jon smiled. Cindy smacked him on the shoulder playfully but with some force.

"Really, Jon. I smoked for nearly six years, quit two years ago and this is the only time I smoke now. As a matter of fact I have a pack in the kitchen drawer that I bought a week ago and there may be one left." With that, she leapt from the rumpled double bed with Jon grabbing for her.

"Christ, Cindy, if there are 20 cigs in a pack, you've been a busy little girl," he said with detectable sadness in his voice.

Rolling her head around and glancing over softly sloping shoulders, Cindy smiled to the side, "Boy, Jon, you are too easy."

Only mumbles were audible from the bedroom as she made her way into the kitchen and back…"pack is so old I'm really afraid to light one." Jon grabbed the pack and checked, finding it full.

"Had you goin' there, didn't I, big guy?" Cindy grinned at his boyish, scolded puppy look.

"Cindy, you're beautiful! You're sexy! You have an incredible body, but it's really your mind I'm after. Let's talk about you."

Drawing deeply on the cigarette, Cindy coughed and immediately stubbed out the dry, foul tobacco. She turned to face him and said, "Jon, let's go shower, get dressed and go for coffee and burgers. Now I'm starved. We never even brought the wine in here." You are some kind of sex freak but WOW, the motion of that ocean was great."

Grabbing Jon's hand, Cindy ran naked into a shower stall that was definitely not made for two. In order to soap each other, they had to reach around and then switch. That kind of action didn't take many turns before the stall became plenty big enough—Cindy and Jon were up against one wall with cries for everything that could be given. With near screams of pleasure, they almost collapsed right in the shower.

Cindy held Jon inside her by pressing her thighs together, looked into his eyes with a total absence of shame or embarrassment and said, "I have to tell you that never in my life have I taken a man into my shower."

Cindy pushed him away and purposely scanned his body from top to toes. "You make me feel good, Jon. Please don't tell me you love me or any other bullshit. Let's relish the moment, the day and see what happens."

Jon pulled her toward him, but Cindy bolted from the shower into the bedroom and quickly began pulling on nearly sheer white panties. As Jon strolled into the room toweling his hair, she was already pulling on her white jeans and T-shirt. Jon moved the towel down to dry his chest and looked at her expecting to get an unnoticed moment to smile and reflect at this extremely unusual and striking girl. Instead he could not avoid focusing on those perfect nipples still erect and outlined by the damp cotton of her shirt. Then he refocused to read the shirt BIOLOGISTS ARE BUGGERS.

"Umm, Cindy, are you wearing that to the coffee shop?"

Cindy looked down at her shirt, while pulling it out at the bottom, as if she couldn't remember what it said. "Oh shit! I forgot about that. I'll change."

Pulling the T-shirt over her head with both arms exposed her breasts with a sensuality that struck Jon like a jolt. With a rush, his erection grew to full bloom and Cindy just stood there with shirt in hand shaking her head. "Will you look at that. I feel like I've been gang-banged and he's ready again."

Jon blushed and attempted to cover himself with the towel. This only started Cindy laughing again. With a final shake of her head, she collapsed face down onto the bed in a fit of jocularity that created a need for revenge in Jon. He walked over to the bed and removed the towel from his waist and was rolling it for a "towel whip". Cindy finally noticed the quiet. Rolling over quickly, she quickly continued rolling to the end of the bed.

Catching the playful mood, Jon grinned while not yet understanding his incredible desires for this woman. Then he began to sing, "I deserve a break today…"

* *

Just seven blocks east and 5 blocks south from where Jon and Cindy were now walking along the dampened street toward the coffee shop, Joan Blacker was stepping from an otherwise empty shower. She had spent a long time scrubbing herself after her sweaty romp with Stewart Phillips. She prayed that he would be sleeping and not want to go again. While not unhandsome, her boss was both the least considerate and quickest jump she'd ever had. Joan always liked that expression—'jump'—because that's what it was used for. If she jumped Phillips, it was possible that she could 'jump' up the corporate ladder even quicker. Her short-term goal was to be head of the Chicago office and be rid of this idiot.

Joan wrapped a towel around her head and a large one under her arms, carefully tucked in. She strolled into the living room as always taking pride in the accouterments she had acquired. The brightly slashed paintings, multi-colored metal sculptures and spectacular wall hangings were perfectly toned to set off the furniture in the room. She prided herself in making the apartment look like it was $3,000 a month, when in reality it was slightly over $1,800. It was just close enough to Michigan Avenue to be an "in" place for a classy, single executive. Opening the wine cabinet, Joan selected a half-bottle of a hearty Beaujolais and removed the cork with precision. Pouring a glass, she curled up on the sofa and listened to the flow of sounds in Revel's Bolero.

Reflecting on her status at present, she saw all her activities in order—with only a couple of possible hurdles. Her present concern was the timely completion of the Lake Michigan study for the Corps of Engineers. A mental review brought forth her usual projection of rapid progress up through the company. With everything on an even keel, her promotion to Chicago Division VP was in the bag.

The growl from the bedroom startled her, “Joan, where are my shoes?” Phillips called with a panicky edge to his voice.

Like the professional actress she was, Joan replied with as much syrupy whine as possible, “Oh, Stewart, must you leave so early?”

Walking into the room looking like he was about to enter a Board of Directors meeting, her boss said with his usual post-coital stammer, “Joan, you knew that my wife was expecting me home about midnight; why didn’t you tell me it was so late.” With a supposedly sexy grin, he turned to adjust his tie and check himself for any possible telltale signs of extra-marital female contact. “Well, better run, babe. You were really dynamite tonight. You can’t get enough of me, can you?”

Wanting to retch, Joan managed, “No, Stewart, you ARE the best. Will you be in Monday morning?”

“Of course. Don’t you remember that the fiscal year review is due before the 25th? If it’s not on Bonner’s desk that morning, that bitch will throw a fit.

“Stewart, you know how to handle her. Don’t worry; everything will look great with the profit numbers we’ve turned in this past fiscal year. Ole Loretta will probably lick her lips all the way to the bottom line.

“Joan, I’ll want your memo of support for the next board meeting for expansion of the Chicago region to include the new branch in St. Louis.”

“Don’t worry, Darling, I’ll be backing you up all the way.” Joan followed with her inner thoughts, ‘Just more for me to take over when you’re out of there, Turkey.’

“See ya’ Monday. Oh! Would you be able to give me a final completion date for the Lake Michigan study before the meeting?”

Joan thought for a moment and said, “The answer is yes, but only after I get a hold of the field team lead. You know her, Cindy Farrell, the blonde. She has complained a lot about this project. I suspect that is a cover for her loss of interest in the job.”

“Now, Joan,” Phillips drawled imitating Loretta Bonner, “Don’t be catty”. Let’s just get the job done for my report to Mrs. Bonner. You are well aware of our little leader's wrath. With the door closing behind him, he repeated his standard exit line, "Remember now, Joan, these little get-togethers are our secret."

Locking the door with a violent clang of the dead bolt, Joan resumed her position on the couch, wondering if she could have gotten this far, this quickly, without screwing nearly every boss she'd ever had.

* *

After a smiling, quiet 2:00 a.m. breakfast, Jon and Cindy walked slowly back to Jon's apartment. Like two students fresh with the bloom of love, time was at a standstill. They strolled hand in hand along the dusky north-side streets of Chicago. This area of rebuilding and rejuvenation was quizzically referred to as "Old Town." Nobody asked why. It was a great place to be in love. The buds of spring could nearly be felt waiting to burst forth with the inclining sun. When Jon and Cindy stood in front of Jon's building huddled against the cool early morning air, they watched as the spring mist began to form, signaling the deepest part of the night. Both felt that this would last forever as they rode the elevator to Jon's floor. They slowly undressed each other to get back into bed, full knowing that the outside world would cease to exist, at least for the next few hours.

MONDAY 7:10 a.m.

CHAPTER 8

Sitting at his desk, coffee in hand, feet up, head back, eyes closed and a smile on his face, Jon doodled in thought while he waited for his computer to give him a complete printout of the Waukegan Ditch data.

Slipping in the lab door to get a head start on what she knew would be a grueling week, Laura turned to find Jon, head hanging back, with an uncharacteristic mellowness about his posture. Look at him! She thought. There is no doubt in all the world that this is a man without wanting. Laura walked slowly up to Jon almost sliding her feet across the tile. As she neared his back, Laura wanted to reach down to lightly caress his hair.

"Good morning, Laura. Are you ready for a long day in the pursuit of truth and knowledge?" he asked as he leaned his head further back to look up into her eyes.

"Oh God! Doctor, you have the most disgusting grin on your face. I wish you could see yourself. Why not hang a sign on the back of your lab coat. It could say something like

NO DANGER—SATISFIED."

"Well, I admit that I did have a wonderful weekend, for having started it so late, but ever since this morning about five, my mind has come riveting back to our project."

John turned to her and said, "We must move to a decision point here by noon. Is this or is it not an identifiable compound? If it isn't, I intend to stay here until I am totally positive we are dealing with some bastardized molecule."

"Doctor, I'm with you. Believe it or not, I have been thinking about this since Saturday. I'll tell you what; if we really crank out the data today, you have to give me some of the details of your weekend," Laura grinned.

"That's a deal. You start all of the new sample and standard preps while I get the data and the computer disk over to the FDA and check it against all of their spectral libraries. I should be done by noon, and then we'll get lunch. That gives you just about four hours, so get humpin'."

Meanwhile, back at Jon's apartment, Cindy awoke with a retina-burning awareness of the sun pushing its ultraviolet photons directly into her brain. She immediately noticed that she was bare-assed naked with all the covers down past her feet.

With the sun in her eyes like that, She thought that Jon must need some shades under his curtains. She looked to the window with slitted eyelids and became horrified when she saw that not only was there no shade, there were no curtains. Rolling over, she was disgusted that some pervert might be out there salivating on his undershirt hoping she'd start to play with herself.

"Shit!" She rolled across the bed and crawled toward the bathroom door grabbing what clothes she could find. Cindy was getting madder by the second. She pulled on panties and her T- shirt. Keeping to the walls, she angled toward the window to try to catch some weirdo with binoculars. She jumped square-faced into the window area and blurted laughter. She looked left and right with teary eyes and saw only blue sky. The only reason to have curtains here is if one of your neighbors flies a helicopter, she thought.

Flipping on the TV as she went toward the kitchen, Cindy noticed that her drawers were not fitting right. She looked down only to see Jon's bright blue Jockey shorts. With a smile, she thought of being inside his pants—better yet she thought of him being in her pants, right now. "Christ, I'm as bad as he is," she said aloud. But even while attending to distractions like sausage, potatoes, toast and coffee, she got hornier and hornier. Finally, after cleaning up the impeccably arranged kitchen, she languished in the shower with herself and Jon's beautiful body in her mind's eye.

Finding all of her clothes, Cindy finally felt ready to face the world. She glanced around for a clock and seeing none, turned to the TV to see if she could recognize the newscaster.

"A.M. Chicago is being brought to you by the folks at General Mills, giving you such fine foods as Corn Flakes and Rice Krispies. Now here are the local headlines at noon. Mayor John A. Daley will probably announce today that his older brother and former Mayor Richard M. Daley, is to head the Lakefront Festival Committee. Negotiations at the School Board have finally progressed to an agreement on teacher's rights under tenure. Chicago Police have arrested a man who was found swimming in Buckingham Fountain around six this morning; he claimed that the lake water temperature was still too low and he felt like a swim. Finally this. Three men were rushed to St. John's Hospital in Waukegan this morning after a jogger saw all three writhing on the ground near the lakefront. Hospital officials would only say that the men had been fishing since late Saturday night and may have eaten something not kept properly refrigerated."

Cindy flipped off the TV figuring she would stop home, change and head into Haltec to work on her project report on the Lake job. Then maybe dinner with Jon. She remembered that he had awakened her near six this morning and said he wanted some early quiet time at the lab to review his data and prepare for a computer run at FDA. He promised to call her before he left the lab so they could have dinner at her apartment.

Cindy reflected quickly about the incredible weekend. First the hilarity in the EPA parking lot, then Jon coming to her apartment Saturday night, then back to his place Sunday night. It had been quite a weekend.

Her smile weakened and Cindy felt some tug in the back of her mind - some quick glance of gloom. Shaking her head, she left Jon's apartment already framing her report in her thoughts, but some minor dread nipped at her subconscious.

* *

Jon's knee crashed into the open drawer as he spun into the lab. The computer disc slammed onto the bench top, scattering glassware from its path. In a limping hop, Jon came to rest in his chair in front of the GC/MS. 'Keerist!' he thought. 'What asshole would leave a drawer open in that spot?' As if on cue, Laura rounded the corner from the hall leading to the bathroom.

"Well, Doctor. Don't just sit there playing with yourself, I mean your knee. What did you find? What is it? We sure as hell musta missed something. Did you get a match? What was the percent confidence?

"Whoa! Hold the questions and check my knee. I have shattered my knee cap and you go on and on about the friggin' samples."

Laura stood there with the rack of prepared samples and slowly let a spanked-toddler look creep onto her face. As six or seven responses spun through her mind in rapid succession, Laura simply continued to stand in her place and stare at Jon rubbing his knee.

Suddenly Laura began to cry silently. Several emotions had run through her mind following Jon's outburst. She actually felt cheated. After nearly 22 hours in the lab since Friday night, she really felt that more consideration was due than the nasty way Jon had reacted.

Limping over to her in response to the tears "C'mon, Laura, I didn't mean anything by that. It was simply a reaction to a nasty crack on the knee. I apologize for that. Now, let's sit down and look at the printout I got at FDA. You'll be blown away by the data from their mainframe library. It confirms what we thought from the beginning."

Jon began to rattle on and explain how he had set up the search of the FDA's spectral library. His total rapture with this project only made Laura seethe inside. He was apparently ignoring all of the extra effort she had put in. Then she tuned in to his words in the middle of a sentence…" which proves that your sample preparation and standard dilution techniques were impeccable, Laura. That should make you feel damn good after all of your extra work."

All was forgiven, as Laura began her examination of the 'fingerprint' chromatograms. The tracings and data were 100% in agreement with their initial runs and confirmatories on Saturday. After looking through some thirty laser printed sheets, both Jon and Laura fell silent momentarily as they simultaneously read the computer's conclusion

NO MATCH

Jon thought, '135,000 compounds in the spectral library and not a damn one came close.'

"Laura, this can only mean one of two things. Either that fish has consumed some radically new organic chemical or some reaction took place within the fish tissue itself to be manifested in the analysis."

Laura sat there and thought about the permutations of Jon's statement. The ringing phone caused her to jump from the chair and literally run to answer it.

"Doctor, it's for you." With what seemed like a little less vitriolic manner, Laura added, "And she really sounds sexy."

Jon smiled at her, walked to the well-worn spot in the gray-green floor near the phone, and kissed Laura lightly on the forehead. "You are very special. I'll take this and then we'll get on with the additional runs on the instrument to see if this mysterious compound is in any of the other samples."

He turned to the phone, "Kepler here."

"Kepler is a bastard!" Cindy said with a hiss that seemed to spray from the phone. "Laura, you're special! What gives, Buster? The bed's barely cooled down and you're trying to get into some other chick's knickers? Not only have you not called, but you're onto some Bimbo at work."

"Whoa! Hold it!" Jon interrupted. Number one, that is my lab assistant who has worked her buns off on your fish samples, and that makes her special. And number two, you are out of line with the rest of that crap, Cindy." Jon had managed to talk even faster than Cindy in answer to her tirade.

"Oh, and by the way, we have verified that there is a totally unidentifiable compound in one of your fish tissue samples, Jon added.

Cindy mumbled an apology sounding something like I'm sorry. "But shit, Jon, when you didn't call I couldn't help myself. You should have heard your conversation from this end especially with the evidential smacking of lips.

"Cindy, I love you," Jon said softly, "And didn't you hear what I said about your fish sample?"

Stunned by Jon's statement, she felt compelled to slide past it with an invitation to lunch to look at his data in the Haltec cafeteria.

After hearing Jon's quick acceptance of the invitation, Cindy hung up her Mickey Mouse office phone by putting the hand set in Mickey's upraised glove. She sat with her elbows on the fake wood top and succumbed to the high schooler's malady.

MONDAY 10:30 a.m.

CHAPTER 9

Cindy was simply doodling with her report when the intercom line buzzed. She assumed it would be the receptionist out in Haltec's simplistically stunning two-story lobby to tell her that Dr. Kepler was here to see her. Instead, a steely female voice ripped the humming silence before she even said her name, "Farrell, this is Blacker. What is the status of the draft report on the Lake project?"

Cindy immediately recognized the voice as belonging to Joan Blacker. Whenever she talked to Blacker, the picture of her Patrician beauty jumped into Cindy's mind. The business-like hairstyle failed to disguise the raven nature of her hair. Joan Blacker was 100 percent woman but had to be tougher than any of the men at Haltec. Cindy never understood her work ethic of "beat the men at their own game in their own world and you'll get to the top." Cindy always felt that enjoying your job and doing it to the best of your ability would take you far enough; but apparently Joan Blacker would never be satisfied with "far enough."

"Yes, Ms. Blacker, the first draft is under way now and I am meeting Dr. Kepler from EPA for lunch to pick up additional data. With that I'll be able to have the draft on your desk by this afternoon. Of course, the final report won't be ready for at least 10 days after we have the verified data from EPA," Cindy replied in her usual staccato fashion.

"OK, Farrell, just make sure that this government lab-jockey doesn't slow us down. It is imperative that we produce the final report in advance of the due date."

Joan Blacker always resented Cindy Farrell's outlook on things because of her spirited cheerfulness. Joan thought that Cindy was a typical biologist with slanted views about the environment and an inane love of all creatures great and small. In some ways Joan envied Cindy's approach to business but knew that Cindy would always be a field technician. Joan respected Cindy's abilities in the field as the only non-male team leader, but never seemed to be able to establish any person-to-person communication with her.

Thus it seemed that both of them greatly disliked each other, but were never openly critical of one another to other Haltec employees. Joan occupied her somewhat plush office with the southwestern wall covering, beige carpet, couch and great V-shaped whitewashed desk, while Cindy's office, shared with Jerry, was a model of austerity. The 15-foot square was piled high with sample containers filled with foul smelling Formaldehyde and holding critters ranging from nearly microscopic Daphnia to a 22-pound prehistoric appearing salamander.

Jerry and Cindy had an agreement—an office was simply a brightly lit cubicle out of the rain—a place to sit while you think. It definitely was not very important to them. This was in direct contrast to Joan's approach with psychological color coordination directed towards calming the visitor. Jerry had even added posters from his collection of "fantastic photos with a microscope" that somewhat disgusted his and Cindy's rare callers. The 1000 times enlargement of a tapeworm's mouth, with its thirty outward oriented teeth and pointed raspy tongue was the worst.

Cindy commented quickly before Joan hung up, "The EPA chemist, Kepler, did say that he had found some variant compound in one of the fish tissue samples that he wanted to discuss".

Joan responded quickly and harshly, "Farrell, it's your job to keep this guy on track toward completion or we'll blow the finish date. Don't let him try to convert this into a research project when it's simply a confirming study prior to dredging. The Corps of Engineers wants to get under way; the damn thing has been in court for fourteen years. Don't let some asshole scientist screw up the schedule now.

The incessant buzzing in Cindy's ear signaled that Joan Blacker didn't feel a salutation was necessary. "That chick really pisses me off sometimes," Cindy hissed while replacing the receiver.

Jerry looked up from his logbook where he had been reviewing the sample cataloging data to say, "That can only mean that the Wicked Witch of the 12th floor has honored our cubicle with a call."

Jerry was always amazed at the obvious friction between Cindy and the infamous Joan Blacker. Those two were both striking females, for very different reasons, but they always seemed as if they were shacking with the same guy on alternate nights.

"Joan Blacker is a climber, Cindy. When are you going to realize that she isn't out to shit in your nest, but just to keep her nest as high up the tree as possible?"

Cindy turned to scowl at Jerry for defending Blacker but immediately forgot when she noticed Jerry's famous grin.

"Damn it, Jerry, I don't understand her. She seems to carry some kind of grudge against the world. All I did was mention that Jon Kepler from EPA had found some anomaly in one fish tissue sample and she lets fly with this crap about keeping on schedule. Sure, it's probably nothing, but why not at least discuss it and see if there is something that's gone unnoticed in previous studies."

"Cindy, I agree," replied Jerry with his affixed professional grin, "but you must remember that Blacker isn't a scientist and is not the least bit interested in what we see or find in the field work. To her the report isn't an informational piece about a particular ecosystem, it's simply a typed and bound backup to an invoice signifying a completed project—another gold star in Joan Blacker's 'attaboy' scorebook. So relax! Go meet your new love for lunch and find out about this variant data point."

Cindy was turning back to her desk when it struck her, "What the hell does that comment mean, Mr. Wittner?"

"Pray tell madam. Of what do you speak?" replied Jerry with his always-changing characterizations.

Cindy glared her answer, "The 'new love' crack, buster".

"Pardon me, madam, but ye must recall that ye were off to the laboratory for sample delivery on the evetide and did not return 'til past two bells Saturday morn."

Jerry, cut the Sherlock Holmes routine and explain how you knew that I was out with Jon Kepler until after two in the morning," Cindy sputtered in her demand.

Jerry loved knowing when Cindy didn't know how he knew. "Well, Cindy, it is the basic deduction process made popular by Detective Holmes that allowed me to determine the nature and timing of your meeting. Follow along. You leave myself and my black Watson with the samples in your car about 11 o'clock Friday. Allowing about an hour and a half to get the good doctor to the lab and unload the samples, you should have been home about 12:45 with the 15 minute ride home."

"Jerry, that doesn't tell me how you knew what time I did get home."

"Ah yes, that is true," he turned while he began to blush with his little joke turning on him. "Actually Cindy, I was a little worried and since I was in the gin mill near your place, I drove by about 12:30. When I didn't see your lights on, I waited around for a few minutes…'til a little after 2 am."

With a flip of her swear finger to Jerry, Cindy smiled and didn't press his embarrassment. Jerry laughingly recognized their familiar signal and turned back to his desk to work. The intercom line buzzed again and Jerry felt a quickening of his pulse signal the telltale signs of jealousy. He knew though that this was a father's jealousy of his daughter's boyfriend. That age-old protective instinct. He shook his head trying to get back to work while Cindy answered the phone, and then hustled out to the elevators.

While Cindy waited, toe tapping, for the elevator, Joan Blacker was making a note to find out who this Dr. Kepler was at the EPA lab. She liked to be prepared in case it became necessary to apply some pressure. Without looking, Joan's hands unscrewed the top of her granite-smooth Mont Blanc fountain pen. The gift from her father at high school graduation had been from his heart. It was the only "soothing stone" she needed. It reminded Joan of him. Joan began to write. "Check out Kepler at EPA. Standard package of info."

Jon smiled at Cindy from the back of the sterile elevator. He lewdly motioned her in, but she cocked a hip, put a disgusted look on her face and waggled her finger at him to disembark, Getting in line in the already bustling, chrome-and-rented-plants cafeteria, any casual observer could easily see that this was not the typical business lunch meeting. The touching of arms, the smiles, and the nods signified the courting routine of the human species.

Cindy paid and Jon got flustered. They moved from the end of the line out onto the ninth floor sundeck where they selected a secluded table.

"Okay, Jon, what do you have for me," Cindy began.

He smiled with a full mouth and pointing to his loaded cheeks gestured for a little time. Cindy reveled in his newness, thinking of their time together and reflecting that this was a man she could love.

Jon pushed their trays to the side of the table before Cindy even started her lunch. Then he could remove three stacks of computer sheets from his file folder.

"Cindy, how much chemistry did you have in school? I need to know where to begin."

"Jon, when you mention chemistry to me, I break out in hives. I almost switched majors because I had such trouble with it" Cindy had posted her only B's at Vanderbilt in Chemistry; they had kept her from having perfect scores throughout her four years. She exaggerated her difficulties for Jon.

"Well, these are chromatograms and Mass Spectra from the GC/MS at the lab. As you possibly know these are like fingerprints. No two organic compounds regardless of their complexity or molecular weight have the same spectrum." Cindy remembered all of that so far from Advanced Qualitative Analysis.

Jon continued with his explanations. "This first chromatogram is of a common PCB material specifically that of Arochlor 1352. Notice the pattern of peaks in the 12 to 14 minute retention time frame. Now look at this one; it's exactly the same except for the shoulder on the peak at 15 minutes. That tracing is of Arochlor 1260, another of the PCB's."

Cindy interrupted, "Jon, is that Polychlorinated biphenols?"

No, but you're very close. The last syllable is b-i-p-h-e-n-y-l-s. They are all chlorinated derivatives of phenol compounds but are pronounced with the 'el' sound instead of the 'ol'; and it's written as a single word. They are nearly indestructible in the environment unlike DDT, which does break down after 25 or 30 years. The PCB's as a group of chemicals are about the most stable organic compounds ever developed by science. You know that they were invented for high temperature transformers, lubricants and fire-retardants. Plus they found hundreds of uses in the 60's, 70's and 80's for other applications until EPA's testing showed them to be carcinogenic and mutagenic."

Cindy remembered some of what she had read about PCB's, but defended herself with, "Yeah, I remember most of that but when I look at a fish sample, Jon, I'm more concerned about its appearance and the possible worms or lesions signifying some biological problem. I rarely think of the chemical contamination aspect."

"Well, Cindy, even a chemist like me is aware of areas other than his primary field. I've been working on PCB's ever since the problem was first brought to full light in '82. The long term impact of these materials on the environment and the food chain isn't totally understood yet, but let me continue."

Flipping to another printout, Jon rolled on. "Pay particular attention to this one. Notice that it is exactly the same as the Arochlor 1352 except for the significant peak at 19 minutes. In all the analyses I've ever done, I have never seen one like this. There is no organic compound I know that gives this pattern. At the end of this run, the GC/MS computer ran a check against its spectral library and came up empty handed. That's not even the biggie. I took my data disk over to FDA's mainframe system and ran it against their library—hell they have three times as many spectral patterns in theirs. Not a damn match anywhere," Jon said with an emphatic blow to the table with his right palm.

Ignoring the stares from inside the partially opened glass doors that separated them from the main group inside the cafeteria, Cindy asked, "Well, Jon, this material certainly wasn't sent from outer space. If it was in the fish tissue itself, it had to be from something the fish actually ate."

Jon smiled sardonically and emphasized with a finger in the air, "Or it was created by reaction within the fish itself."

“Jon, that is impossible. Even a chemist should know that organic matter is reduced within a fish’s body just like a human’s and the resulting compounds are very predictable. There are not any weird or unknown materials ‘created’ in a fish from the food it consumes.”

“Please consider, Cindy,” Jon said softly, as if afraid someone might laugh at his idea, “That the compound inside the fish’s body was a PCB that was just approaching some minor degradation conversion when the reaction was interrupted by another organic compound. That would create quite a flurry among the molecules. BAM! The molecule shifts to take on the new atoms forming a heavy molecular weight material we do not even have a name for.”

The frown on Cindy’s face was noted by Joan Blacker who watched the conversation from inside the cafeteria while not even noticing the lunch she toyed with.

‘If that’s who I think it is, I do believe I had best move Dr. Kepler to the top of my priority list,’ she thought.

SECTION TWO

SHE HUNGERS

The Coho was old, but not yet one of the slow lumbering giants that she had passed on her way up from the deep blackness of the lake. At thirty-four pounds she was a trophy fish but had never experienced the life threatening, mouth-ripping sting of the fisherman's barbed hook. Her thirty-one inches of sinewy muscle imparted incredible power to the primary swimming fins on her upper and lower body. The large fantail she carried was somewhat unusual for a female of her species but she had seen several others with the strange triple pointed tail fin. As she glided through the water she began to search for food. The smaller fish in the lake at this time of year gave a wide berth to the prowling Coho. They knew that even with their darting quickness they were no match for the hungry female's need to build her reserves.

MONDAY 12:20 p.m.

CHAPTER 10

Jon and Cindy were completely unaware of Joan Blacker's observation of them while they went on with their discussion of the lab data.

Cindy sat staring out over the railing separating them from 140 feet of non-stop fall to the sidewalk below with a look that was a cross between non-belief and puzzlement. Jon looked at her, waiting.

"Really, Jon. It's bad enough that we can absorb PCB's, Chlordane, Lead, and other pollutants by eating the fish from the Lake. Now, you're telling me that the PCB's are reacting with living fish tissue in some freaky chemical metabolism."

"How can that be?" Cindy said with a rather frightened quiver in her voice. "I mean, the thought of that happening really scares me. That really screws up this biologist's thinking about the sanctity of biochemical balance in nature."

"It is the only logical conclusion based on the data. Neither my computer library, nor the one at FDA could identify this compound. But, I need to do more work with the sample."

"Perhaps this does bear some additional work, Jon, but I have two problems. The first is that there are no funds or time allotments in the project for that kind of work, and, secondly, my boss would cut off my hands if my report wasn't in on time."

"Why not let me talk to your boss and see if she'll give us an extension and maybe cut loose with some money."

Cindy didn't know whether to laugh or cry. Jon just had no idea about the way a company like Haltec ran. Bidding on government contracts was tricky business, contrary to popular belief. It took very careful planning and follow-through to make money on a project that came to the lowest bidder. While everything was run at razor edge efficiency at Haltec, there was no room for goofing off or personal research projects. Add to that the fact that Cindy didn't want Jon near Joan Blacker.

"Jon, you really have no idea how impossible that would be. Haltec has no interest in environmental research. We are a consulting engineering firm specializing in environmental impact studies. We contract bodies and brains to our clients for projects they want done. Hey! Could you get something out of your people?"

Jon grinned, "Well, we're kinda in the same boat there, kiddo. Nobody has the money to track down some potentially fascinating concept making it possible that we could miss a completely new piece of biochemical information. Where do we go from here?"

Cindy jumped in, "Let's announce that we've found that there is a carcinogenic substance in the fish from Lake Michigan—we would surely get some attention that way."

"Right. That is exactly what we need—some notoriety about an unidentified compound, which is most probably harmless and which we know is present in only one out of 54 fish tissues we tested. I do hope that your little joke is not a premonition though."

"Jon, I just realized something. That is the first time that you have mentioned that it occurred in only one sample. Why would that be? How is it possible for only one fish to have this weird substance when all of the fish were taken from the same area? To boot, you guys have analyzed hundreds of fish from the Waukegan Ditch ever since it was earmarked as having the highest sediment PCB concentration in the world. Why haven't you seen this before?"

"Whoa, one question at a time, my dear. First of all, it is possible that only one fish was experiencing this strange metamorphosis at the right moment and secondly, this may have been the very first time this happened."

"Oh, Christ, Jon. Do you expect me to believe that we caught the first and only fish in all of Lake Michigan that contained this compound? That would be a ten billion to one shot. There must be others."

"That's it. Let's see if we can't get some more samples that contain the substance. That would lend credence to our need for time and money. Could you get a boat to use and the equipment we need?"

Cindy was somewhat taken aback by Jon's rush to pick up on her thought about additional fish that might have the mysterious substance. But once she thought about it, she figured that it was the logical way to go.

"You're probably right, Jon. I'll see if I can get Jerry and Rubin to help us make a special run back to the site and pick up a few more of those Coho, and then you could analyze them. It would have to be before Thursday. That is when my first draft of the report is due and I'd better not be late. Blacker would have my ass. She would shit a brick if she knew I'd take out a company boat without a valid project to charge the costs to."

"Who, may I ask, are Jerry and Rubin," Jon said with a slightly cold question.

"Don't get on your chauvinistic horse with me, buster," Cindy said with a slap to his shoulder that had some sting to it.

Jon grabbed his shoulder with the other hand feigning injury, while Cindy's surprised and embarrassed look made him grin inside.

"Oh, Jon, I'm sorry. I didn't mean to do that quite so hard. It's a technique I learned from Jerry—the hard way. Jerry is Wittner and Rubin is Anderson. We work together on several projects and now on the Waukegan Ditch project. Speaking of Jerry, let's get him down here to discuss the midnight boating raid."

Cindy jumped up with her tray and walked unnoticing past Joan Blacker to call Jerry. Joan moved to take her place at the table with Jon. She intended to start her check on Dr. Kepler with some first hand information as long as the opportunity had presented itself. Joan picked up her tray and started out onto the sundeck as if looking for a spot to enjoy lunch.

"Excuse me, but if you're eating alone, I'd be happy to chat about the weather, the environment, business management, or at least thirty other topics in which I'm completely versed," Joan purred to Jon.

Jon looked up to see five feet nine inches of a cross between Cindy Crawford and Raquel Welch. While pushing back his chair to stand up, he hit his knee on the table in the process, and became totally tongue-tied. She sat down with her tray conspicuously not between them.

"Hello. My name is Joan Blacker. Do you work here at Haltec or are you a visitor? If you are a salesman, please tell me so I can sit elsewhere."

She had totally stunned him. He still had not spoken because his mind was whirling. This must be Cindy's boss, he thought. I remember her saying Blacker. Holy Shit! I've never seen eyes like that—empty black pools.

Still not realizing that he hadn't spoken a word, Joan continued, "If you would prefer, I can sit over there where I won't bother you."

His brain finally engaged. Jon replied, "Please stay. My name is Jon Kepler and I'm from EPA so I can't be a salesman.

He gambled that his guess was right and continued. "You must be the Joan Blacker that is in charge of the Waukegan Ditch project. I have just been discussing the initial data with Cindy Farrell. We have come up with an interesting deviation from the usual PCB results."

Joan couldn't believe her good fortune and hoped that Farrell would be a while. All she needed was a few minutes with this scientist to extract all the required information. Her mind quickly noted that she hadn't used her usual "geek" adjective in front of scientist.

Joan began, "Yes, Jon. I would be fascinated. I only have about few minutes before my staff meeting, though. Can you give me a quick synopsis in that time?"

Joan Blacker knew this guy was easy. She had him with that lead-in and played it all the way.

“Before you begin, Jon, should I address you as Doctor Kepler, or what? I really believe that anyone who has earned their Ph.D. deserves to use it,” she smiled.

“Really, Joan, I’d rather not stand on formality. Just plain Jon is fine. The Doctor coat goes on just when I really need it.”

Jon slipped into his scientific mode. “To give you a quick summary, I would say that the project was rather mundane, analytically, except for one item that I’ll come to in a moment. All of the water samples along with the sediments and fish tissues were pretty much along the lines of the previous results from the Ditch. That is until we got to this one particular fish sample.”

Jon proceeded to review the chromatograms with Joan in a similar fashion to his discussion with Cindy. Joan Blacker just smiled, nodded her head and asked quick probing questions. Interrupting Jon just as he was about to launch into an in-depth explanation of the analytical procedures backing up his strange discovery, Joan reminded him of her meeting and quickly picked up her untouched tray.

“Jon, I am really captivated by what you have found, but I must get to my meeting. I would be honored if you would consider having dinner with me tomorrow night to review the information in more detail. Say around seven at my place. My secretary will call you later this afternoon with directions. I’m looking forward to it. Thank You.”

As Joan Blacker walked away, Jon realized that he hadn’t even said yes. ‘Miss Blacker is not used to getting a negative answer,’ he reflected.

While Jon was contemplating his meeting with this captivating woman, Cindy approached from the hall with a bulky friend in tow. Joan had left by the other exit, turning in time to see Cindy go out onto the sundeck. Joan smiled at her timing.

“Dr. Jon Kepler, I’d like to introduce you to Jerry Wittner, my fellow technician on the Waukegan Ditch Project.”

“Jerry, it’s a pleasure to meet you. Has Cindy told you about our plan?”

“Well, Doctor, she gave me a quick run-down on the way here and I for one am rarin’ to go. This is conceptually intriguing,” Jerry smiled in response.

“That’s great, Jerry. Drop the Doctor stuff and let’s talk about our plans,” Jon replied.

“Before we get engrossed in the project, Jon, a quick question for you. How will we proceed politically with the information once we are completely confident of its basis? Who gets to unravel the tangled web we will weave?”

Cindy interrupted, “Jerry, we haven’t talked about that yet and I’m not sure that this is the place for that. Why don’t we get together at my place tonight for pizza and cheap wine for a technical planning session?”

Jerry and Jon replied in unison, “Sounds great. What time?”

“I’ll bring the wine,” Jon added, not sure if Cindy was serious about the “cheap” part.

“OK, guys! Let’s say six o’clock and see where we can take this thing,” Cindy directed as she rose with her usual abruptness.

As they were walking out toward the elevator, Jon remembered that he hadn’t mentioned meeting Joan Blacker. ‘Maybe it’s better if I just let that go for now,’ he thought. ‘I’ll meet with Joan tomorrow night to see what she really wants,’ he thought with a harbinger of guilt.

With that, the three of them parted at the elevators. Cindy and Jerry were already in a spirited discussion about the equipment list for their little sojourn.

As Jon was riding down in the elevator to return to the EPA office, Joan Blacker was punching the intercom number for Stewart Phillips. She could handle this on her own, but felt that he should be completely aware of the possible snag in the Waukegan Ditch project, just in case it wasn’t completed on time. With him being in the know at this point, there would always be Farrell or that simpleton Wittner to blame for the delay, she reflected as Phillips picked up the line.

“This is Phillips,” he started.

“Stewart, this is Joan. We may have a small problem on that Waukegan Ditch Project we’re doing for the Corps of Engineers. Would you have a minute to discuss it with me and perhaps advise me how to proceed?”

Stewart Phillips knew that Joan Blacker didn't really want his advice, nor did she likely need it. However, he knew that as long as he was in his position, she would snuggle up to him to get what she wanted. Deep down he realized that his relationship with Joan was a mistake, but, Christ, that body and sexuality were hard to turn down.

He replied, "Yes, certainly, Joan. Please come to my office in say, thirty minutes and we'll review the situation."

Joan murmured an affirmation and hung up the handset with a grimace. She almost despised Stewart Phillips. He didn't have half of her management capabilities. She hoped it wouldn't be too much longer before the president of the company realized her potential and gave her Phillip's office.

On her way up to the fourteenth floor just after two, Joan remembered that she had promised to see her father tomorrow night and had also invited Kepler to dinner. She would have her secretary call her grandfather and offer some excuse along with a promise to make it up to him the following week. Joan arrived at Stewart Phillip's office having decided to call grandfather herself. She found the office guarded by the piece-of-fluff Phillips called a secretary.

"Ah, Miss Blacker, please go right in. Mr. Phillips is expecting you," the girl said as she continued typing.

Joan didn't even answer as she swept through the walnut door into Phillip's corner office. His desk was strategically placed in the corner so that the light was always in his visitors' eyes.

There must be fifty feet of glass in this office, Joan remarked to herself and just as much carpet to cross. She always made directly for the small, softly lit conference area in the opposite corner, not waiting for Stewart to direct her there. She noticed that Phillips didn't even think about objecting, but picked up his legal pad to join her on the fawn-colored leather couches.

"OK, Joan," he began. "What is such a big deal that you need my thoughts? I was under the positive impression that the project was just about completed."

Unwillingly, Joan appraised Stewart Phillips as he walked to the couch. She saw the fiftyish paunch detract from the solid features of English ancestry.

The waddle of the non-sportsman always made Joan think of a penguin. The Brooks Brothers tailored suit and expensive shirt and tie helped with the image, but left the man underneath unchanged. Even with their sexual relationship going on three months now, Joan still thought of Stewart Phillips as a cardboard figure. His thinning brown hair and dulling eyes were contrary to her management image, but Phillips was moving his way up through the company by driving his people and turning in the profit scores that pleased the Board of Directors.

Joan caught his eye and established a position with her expression. "Stewart, I just sat with the EPA scientist that has been doing the sample analysis for this project. He has stated that they are nearly done, but he has found a fish tissue sample that contains some, as yet unidentifiable compound. It appears that this Dr. Kepler is sufficiently concerned, perhaps, to go to the Corps of Engineers or upwards at EPA with the information. He still hasn't checked out his data completely, but feels certain that there is something there that bears additional work. If he keeps pressing, he may be able to convince someone that he has found something. That could cause all kinds of problems for us, Stewart. Not only would it delay the close of the project and the billing, but it may reflect on our performance and possibly on future contracts."

"Do you think this Kepler has found something that could be a problem out there in the Ditch, or is the guy just fishing for some glory? Did you check him out, by the way? Is he on our list of environmental crazies?"

Joan smiled at Phillips' questions and answered, "I'm having a file started on him now. I'll have something by tomorrow morning. This guy seems sincere though. And I really don't think he is pursuing this for one of those meaningless journal articles. He expressed concern both for our lack of information about this unknown substance and for the potential ecological implications."

Stewart Phillips replied quickly, "After you get a file together on him, send it up here and I'll see if we can put some pressure on him to back off. I've bought the regional administrator enough dinners to get me something in return. I'll tell him that this Kepler is screwing up the works and may start something that could delay the project. Engler doesn't want this thing put off any more than we do. EPA has been in court so long over the dredging of Waukegan harbor that they probably wish they had never found it. I'll let you know what comes down from that end. You just get me some background on Kepler."

Joan nodded her reply and uncrossed her legs to leave, being certain to give Phillips a look up her fashionably slit skirt. His look confirmed her move. She smiled as she reached the door making a mental note to get rid of the awful tweed carpeting when she took over this corner suite.

MONDAY 3:00 p.m.

CHAPTER 11

Stewart Phillips sat back down on the couch to think about Joan's report on the Corps project. He really wasn't quite sure how much of a problem this Kepler could cause. He would definitely call Engler, the regional administrator for EPA, and apply a little pressure. He also knew that he had better make another call first. Moving toward his desk, he reviewed the strange conversation of three months ago, that presaged the call he was about to make. Stewart Phillips hated any deal that might hurt his career, but couldn't pass up the insinuated promise of a position jump that would finally move him into corporate management. 'Wouldn't Joan be delighted to know that my job will be opening up shortly,' he thought while punching #62 on his auto dialing phone.

"Mrs. Bonner's office. Derek speaking," was the answer.

He replied, "This is Stewart Phillips at Haltec in Chicago. I would like to speak to Mrs. Bonner, please."

Stewart could picture the "fruit" that answered Loretta Bonner's private line. Of course, he had no way of knowing that the "fruit" was indeed a homosexual, nor could Stewart know that the 27 year old MBA was one of the highest paid employees in the corporation because of Yale class rank and his astounding genius in business planning.

"Mrs. Bonner is tied up in a meeting right now. May I have her call you when she is free?"

Shit!" Stewart thought. The first time I use this special number to call Loretta Bonner and she's not available.

"Yes. Please have Mrs. Bonner call me as soon as possible. It is important. My direct dial private number is 312-155-9944. She'll know who it is."

'And don't forget to give her the message you faggot,' he muttered silently, as he hung up not waiting for a reply.

While Stewart Phillips was looking up the phone number of Dr. Russell Engler at EPA, Joan Blacker was already in her office calling Haltec's "Information Specialists" at the sumptuous Outer Drive East office complex. She wanted to stress to the anomalous agency that her request was urgent and most confidential. She knew from a few previous experiences that she would have a fairly thorough file on Jon Kepler within twenty-four hours. She wasn't sure how or where they got their information, but knew that it would be accurate. This so-called executive information company was an expensive group of computer-oriented private detectives that Joan jokingly thought must be populated by some former CIA agents.

When the agency answered, Joan told them what she knew about Jon Kepler and the person confirmed that Joan would have a standard information packet on her desk via messenger before 11:00 am the next day, Joan was impressed with their skills, but was somewhat wary about the firm's techniques. They were almost too good, she reflected as she hung up. But then they are certainly well paid for their services.

While reviewing the progress of events so far, Joan returned to her mental picture of Jon Kepler, trying to look at him from several different viewpoints. She thought of her invitation to Jon and his ready acceptance. Perhaps, it will be necessary to squeeze some information out of him, she contemplated languidly. Joan shook herself back to other tasks at hand getting back to her review of a request for proposal on another large Government contract in northern Wisconsin.

* *

While Joan began skimming the RFP for particulars, Jon was back in the lab seeing what additional progress had been made by Laura.

"Dr. Kepler," Laura said, calling his attention to her presence back near the lab supply storage area. "I have finished a review of all the data generated in previous runs of the fish, sediments and water samples from the Ditch and have come up empty. There is no indication whatsoever that our mysterious compound was present. I hope that doesn't mean that we may still be faced with some error that has gone undiscovered."

"Laura, I am convinced that all of the techniques were sound and that the substance we have found in that Coho tissue sample is something that has never been seen before. I have arranged to get some new fish samples for analysis, but they will have to be analyzed first thing Wednesday morning. We've got a deadline to beat," Jon announced.

"Really, Doctor. If you insist on creating new and more demanding deadlines, you may have a full revolt on your hands by the peons in this lab—most notably me," Laura proclaimed.

"Well, no promises this time for lunch or dinner," Jon said smiling, "but it really is important that we somehow verify the presence of this compound in more than one tissue sample from the Ditch. I have made arrangements to go out with the sampling crew to get more fish by electroshocker and see if we can come up with more contaminated samples. We are probably going out Tuesday night."

MONDAY 6:30 p.m.

CHAPTER 12

Jon, Cindy and Jerry sat around her glass-on-wrought-iron dinette eating pizza that could only have come from the master maker of Chicago style thick crust pizza. Pizzeria Uno at the corner of Ohio and State had made their works of art for over 40 years in that location and the richness cum gusto seemed to get better every year. Letting business slide for a bit, the three "conspirators" scoffed down the cheese-laden crust followed with gulps of fruity red Chianti.

Jerry broke the reverie with the comment, "You two had better realize that Haltec could report the boat stolen and have us thrown in the slammer."

Cindy thanked him for the pleasant dinner thought and countered with, "It's a one in a million shot that they would ever find out, Jerry. We are the only ones who use that expensive puddle runner in the lake and who would be down there to check if we had it out or not?"

"I believe that you two should consider getting out of this because of your Jobs at Haltec. Perhaps there is somewhere else that I can get a boat," Jon responded.

Together Jerry and Cindy responded with a neck snapping sharpness, "Bullshit! Kepler."

Cindy then continued, "We want this too, Jon. If there is something out there, we want to know. Besides, where would you get a direct current electroshocker and all the equipment needed to go with it? Just the special rubberized gloves and boots cost over $600. Hell, without those you might as well stay home and put your finger in the air conditioner outlet. The voltage from an electroshocker can easily be a killer. The fish are only stunned because of the diffusion of current through the water."

"OK! OK! I only wanted to give you two an out if you were hoping for one. Besides, I don't have many skills in the fish-netting business. To be honest, the only Coho salmon I ever see are the little tissue samples we analyze. I'd probably go out there and come back with a bunch of carp."

Laughing at Jon's assessment of his biological talents, they moved the conversation into Cindy's small living room.

Jon remarked, "Cindy, you've made this apartment look twice its size by the way it's decorated. My place is half again as big and looks smaller than your living room."

Looking around, Cindy smiled at Jon's compliment. She was pleased with the effects achieved with her limited funds. The apartment was really a studio with a partially separated bedroom. The use of grouped colors or patterns provided a semblance of separate areas. The blue cabinets in the kitchen were complimented by the blue and white-checkered curtains, tablecloth and towels. The iron dinette served as Cindy's office at home with the floor to ceiling bookshelves on the wall where a server would usually be parked. Interspersed with the reference texts, Danielle Steele novels and spy stories were little statues, baskets and plaques. The "living room" was separated only by the contrast in Country English comfort. A pretty, but small couch, a rocker, a cedar chest/coffee table, TV and an ottoman were simple but pleasant.

Jon kept glancing at the bookshelves, studying the various titles to get some insight. He was convinced that there was two of her. The magazines piled in the old rope-handled Anheuser- Busch crate helped some. Business Week, Working Woman, Sports Illustrated, Field Ecology, and Cosmopolitan made Jon wonder if there was a message in that combination.

Jerry brought Jon's mind back to the task at hand. "Ok, Jon, how many fish do we want and from what locations. Normally a suspected area is sampled and then fish from an uncontaminated area are collected for comparison. You've already analyzed fish that do not contain your mystery chemical, so we can eliminate the comparative samples. How many do we want from the

Ditch area? And are we sticking to just the one species or will we collect multiple varieties?"

"My God, Jerry," Cindy interrupted. "This is not a federally funded project. We have limited time, both with respect to sampling and for Jon's analysis. We must have the information we need by Thursday, or the initial draft of my report will be filed with EPA and our first volley will have far less impact."

"All right, I just got a little carried away is all. I'm too used to doing things right—and in the daylight I might add."

After discussing and listing everything they would need, which took almost an hour and a half, Jerry thought for a minute and added, "Cindy, I think we should ask Rubin to help. Even with Jon along, we still need two people shocking and netting, plus someone to log and tag samples, and a driver, of course."

After a brief discussion on Rubin's interest and trustworthiness, all agreed. Cindy would find Rubin tomorrow and ask him.

About 11:30 Jerry could see that things were dragging out and Jon was not about to be the first to leave. Jerry stood and stretched his squat, solid frame followed by the announcement that he was ready to 'hit the rack'. After his offer to help pick up was refused, he headed for the door escorted by Jon, while Cindy went to clean up the kitchen.

Jerry hesitated at the door, turned slightly toward Jon, looked into his eyes and said, "Treat her well, Jon. She is a special person. Besides, if you ever hurt her, I'd personally make your body a candidate for organ donorship."

With that, Jerry turned out the door and down the hall to the stairs. Jon stood there staring at the empty corridor. With a moment's realization, Jon knew that Jerry loved Cindy with an easily apparent big-brother mixture of feelings.

As Jon moved into the kitchen to help Cindy, he looked at her with deepening respect and feeling. This girl is something special, Jon Kepler, and if you aren't careful you might fall in love, he thought musingly. Slipping up behind her, Jon gently slid his hands up under her typically untucked man's shirt and caressingly cupped her breasts. Cindy didn't even hesitate with the pizza box. It fell to the counter splattering a few drops of the remaining sauce onto the tile wall. Cindy moaned and turned into Jon's arms, eyes closed, mouth open and hungry. Jon's fingers traced her waist around to the belt on her shorts. Cindy's hands, fingers splayed, roamed through Jon's hair seeming to have a mind of their own. She quickly diverted them to Jon's trousers to find him ready for her.

Cindy's only words on the way to the bedroom were, "A few times tonight I could barely talk, I wanted you so bad, Jon. Please make love to me; I want to wake up with you in my arms."

* *

Earlier that evening, at the Haltec offices, the Michigan Avenue traffic was emerging from its daily commuter load, to the gold coast's nightlife blare of horns and rushing hotel conventioneers. While Cindy, Jon and Jerry were just beginning their pizza fest, Stewart Phillips was sitting impatiently in his now-silent office awaiting a return call from Loretta Bonner.

In a review of his first conversation with her, he recalled his initial belief that she had absolutely no involvement in the management of the company. He was to find out that she was far more than just "involved."

After Mrs. Bonner had introduced herself as the majority shareholder, she made it clear that Stewart's assistance would not go unnoticed at the next Board of Directors meeting. He learned that this old war-horse owned the holding company, which had a controlling interest in Haltec. In essence, she ran one of the largest privately owned conglomerates in the United States. She controlled them all through various trusts and desktop corporations that were rarely known to the public. While Bechtel was the world's largest engineering company and Haltec was about one-twentieth their size, the Bechtel family as a whole was worth less than half of what Loretta Bonner's holdings now totaled. She was president and chief executive officer of ATI. That conglomerate had controlling interest in some large manufacturing concerns and several of the biggest leisure time industries in the country.

A powerful woman, Stewart reflected. Having her in my corner will make the climb easier. His recollections were broken by the shrill buzz of his private line. Far too quickly he answered, "Phillips here."

"Mr. Phillips. This is Loretta Bonner. If I understand Derek's message, you have some urgent need to talk to me. I apologize for the lateness of my call, but other business needed my attention. Hopefully, my tardiness has not kept you at your post too long past your normal departure."

Stewart realized that her standard claptrap was just part of the game to let him know that she knew he would sit there dutifully by the phone until she returned his call.

"Of course not, Mrs. Bonner. I had some details to clean up myself and was glad to have some time without interruptions. I hope the weather in Knoxville is agreeable."

"Knoxville is delightful as always this time of year, Mr. Phillips. Please tell me the nature of your urgent call," she said cutting short the amenities.

Stewart began, "If you recall our conversation of several months back, you wanted to be kept abreast of any unusual developments in our project for the Corps of Engineers at the Waukegan Ditch. While I had assured you that it was simply a check of sediment contamination prior to dredging, you instructed me of your desire to know of extraordinary findings prior to their availability to the Environmental Protection Agency and the Army Corps of Engineers."

Loretta Bonner sat in her 900 square feet of nearly palatial office fuming at this Dantesque dance. Stewart Phillips was an effective manager. Haltec had functioned well under his direction and he had maintained his allegiance to the company. He was typical of the ruthless executive who used everyone in his influence to become even more powerful. She despised treating him like a fellow executive. In her calendar of events, he was necessary and effective. She played along with the Casablanca intrigue.

"Yes, Stewart, that is correct and I must reconfirm my confidence in you that will certainly be born out in future corporate movements. Now, what do you have for me?"

"Mrs. Bonner, a development has occurred on that project that may need your guidance for resolution. The EPA chemist, a Dr. Jon Kepler, who was assigned the job of conducting the analytical work, has come up with an unidentifiable organic compound in a fish sample taken in the area of the Waukegan Ditch. He has already interested our biologist on the project and has hinted of the need to be granted some additional time to research the findings. While this may be of no consequence, I thought you should know of some possible delays in the project and even some additional governmental interest."

With a quick assessment of the information, Loretta gave Stewart Phillips an unmistakable direct order, "Stewart, you are to intercept Dr. Kepler's information, curtail his ability to continue with the project, and bring such probing to a complete halt by any method necessary."

Taken aback by her stringent command, Phillips stumbled over his reply, "I'm not precisely sure what you mean, Mrs. Bonner. Do you want me to clear Kepler off the project? If so how can I accomplish that when he works for EPA? How could I bring sufficient pressure to bear on the guy to get him to give up what is obviously of great interest to him?"

Loretta Bonner spoke slowly as if trying to get a child to understand her meaning, "Stewart, I am only saying that any disruption of the final cleanup schedule for the Ditch could cause me great difficulty. It is up to you to see that this Dr. Kepler does not add tinder to a fire that has taken nearly ten years to douse. Please do whatever is necessary to divert his attention from a pursuit of some 'cockamamie' search into an area that is more complex than you could ever know. Now I trust that you can handle some unimaginative scientist with your contacts amongst the powers that be in Chicago. If that is all, I must get to yet another meeting."

Realizing that Loretta Bonner had ended their conversation without even a perfunctory salutation, Stewart Phillips gently replaced the handset into the walnut box that was the earmark of higher floor executives at Haltec. He continued to stare at the instrument as if afraid that she might not be done and he had hung up on her. His mind reeled with the implications of her orders. Did she really mean for me to use ANY method I deem necessary or was that just an expression of confidence in my judgment to use normal business tactics to control Dr. Kepler's safari into the unknown?

Shaking his head at her orders, he smiled at the thought of Loretta Bonner's southern manner and refined drawl. Removing his briefcase from its daily precision placement on his walnut credenza, he began loading papers into it without really noticing their relevance to the evening's needs. 'If I can meet her expectations with this job, I believe that it will speed my drive to the top.'

On his way to the elevator, he forced his mind to occlude thoughts of professional danger with this assignment. ‘After all,’ he thought, ‘What the hell could Kepler’s compound be?’ It’s probably just some fuckup in his lab and can’t possibly be anything of significance.’ Boarding the late evening train for the ride to Kenilworth, Stewart didn’t even stop at the page two headline on his way to the stock market report to check his investments.

He didn’t see the bold words:

THREE DIE FROM MYSTERY AILMENT

TUESDAY 10:30 a.m.

CHAPTER 13

Cindy suddenly jerked up and took a few moments to realize that she was sitting at her desk staring at Mickey Mouse. She hadn't been able to concentrate all day. Pushing the report aside, she began reviewing the list of equipment that she, Jon and Jerry would need that night for their sampling job. As she worked her way down the list, she would occasionally tap the pencil on her teeth. Jerry called that her 'snarl' look. Then she remembered that she was to call Rubin and ask for his help. Popping the receiver out of Mickey's hand, Cindy dialed Rubin's extension down in the technician's bullpen. Cindy simply asked Rubin to come up to her office.

Within minutes, they were sitting nearly nose to nose, while Cindy quickly explained tonight's planned secret mission and asked for Rubin's help.

Rubin listened intently to Cindy's summary of the PCB's and the strange compound in the single fish sample. At the same time, Rubin's mind was reviewing his personal situation and the threat this brought to bear. Rubin's father and mother lived in a simple, small two-bedroom house in suburban Robbins, Illinois. This south Chicago suburb certainly wasn't the inner-city ghetto, but it sure wasn't the lily white west either. Rubin had been born while his father was in Vietnam. Between his dad's service pay and his mother's job as a keypunch operator, his Mom had managed to buy their house with a low-money-down VA loan.

When Rubin's father had returned minus his arms, he cried. He knelt in front of his two-year-old son, Rubin, and wept, unable to hug him for the first time. Rubin's Mom worked full time and they got by with his Dad's army benefits.

While he never got great grades, Rubin worked hard in high school. He failed to win any scholastic achievements but hoped to get grants or at least financial aid to one of the Illinois universities. Rubin quickly learned that his parents' hard work and pride had come back to bite him. Rubin's parents owned a house. A prerequisite for full financial aid or grants was that the assets of the family could not include real estate equity over Ten Thousand Dollars. The quirk in the law forced Rubin to study the Biological Sciences at the local Community College called Governor's State.

"Cindy, you know how much this job means to me. If you feel that this whole thing is that important, I'll pitch in."

Cindy took his hand and said, "Rubin, this thing has me scared. For some reason, I have a growing feeling of dread about what we'll find in these new fish samples. You haven't met Jon Kepler yet, but I really feel that you'll like him and come to trust in his view of the potential problem here. Do you remember when they first found that the Waukegan Ditch had the highest concentration of PCB's anywhere in the country? Well, Kepler is worried that this unidentified compound he found in the fish may be related to that. Even underlying that is the possibility that some reaction has taken place in the fish itself due to the high concentration of PCB. No one really knows about Kepler's results yet. He isn't about to release information based on one sample. Our people at Haltec don't want the project delayed, so we've got to get some additional samples on the sly. If you go along, you'll be a big help. Jerry really felt that you'd make things go smoother and it would also be a lot safer."

Rubin couldn't believe that Jerry wanted him to come for any reason other than gofer duties, but Rubin wanted to help Cindy in anyway he could.

"Well Cindy, you've always been white with me," he said with a grin. "I'll go tonight and we'll see if we can do our part to save mankind from themselves."

"Oh, Rubin, that's great. I feel much better with you going. I was a little worried about the two of us and Dr. Kepler trying to do the job and getting it done right. Let's meet down in the parking garage at 5:30. We're meeting Jon at the harbor."

As Rubin was leaving her office, Cindy was already grabbing for Mickey to let Jon know that everything was all set. When she found that he wasn't in, she had to leave a somewhat cryptic message in case he didn't have a chance to call her back.

Cindy told the soft, little voice at the EPA Analytical Lab, "Please tell Dr. Kepler that Cindy Farrell called and would he return the call. He has the number. If he can't call, please tell him that he should rendezvous at 6:30 for the catch of the day."

Laura hung up the phone with more than a little vigor, repeating with curled, catty lips, "Tell Dr. Kepler that *Ms. La Dee Da* called. Up yours honey," she said to the empty room.

Walking back into the prep lab, she felt a pang of guilt and picked up her little pad of sticky memos to quickly pencil the note to Jon. She stuck it in the middle of the screen on his GC/MS terminal.

While Cindy was hanging up the phone, Joan Blacker was just cutting open the heavy messenger envelope from the executive information agency. She began to read the data with great intent hoping that the material would give her a lead toward understanding one Dr. Jon Kepler.

As she scanned the computer printouts, she began to get a picture of a serious student who was low key and had more on his mind at Purdue than the social activities. His curriculum and grade point showed that he was top notch in his major field of analytical chemistry. His doctoral thesis was entitled "Identification of Long Chain Polymers Using High Pressure Liquid Chromatography".

Joan knew from some old Haltec reports that HPLC had to be in its infancy during Kepler's final years at Purdue. She knew then that the guy was probably a genius in his specialty.

Reading on, she noted that he carried a tough course load with a lot of it geared specially toward intensifying his chemistry education. Joan made special note of the fact that Jon Kepler had been nominated as a Rhodes Scholar. Likewise, he had so impressed the Chemistry department at Purdue that they awarded him special grants to pay for his Ph.D. studies.

Joan finished reading about Jon's college days stopping at a handwritten note at the bottom of the printout. She didn't know whether to laugh at Jon or feel sorry for him after reading the note. It read, "Registered as Jon Kepler. Rhodes Fellowship nomination for same in the full name of Johann Copernicus Kepler."

"Holy shit," Joan said aloud, "I'd go by Jon too, if someone stuck me with Johann Copernicus."

The best part about these reports was not the confirmation of your guesses or suspicions. The fun stuff was reading the items that always made you say "I don't believe it."

First his name and now the fact that Jon Kepler went through undergraduate school at Purdue with a fifty percent scholarship for football. Having grown up in Indiana, the report continued, Jon apparently played throughout high school and was good enough to get a partial ride.

He just doesn't seem big enough, Joan thought. Of course she was unconsciously comparing Jon, a 1970 backup tight end, to the giants that currently played for the Chicago's Bears.

Another "I don't believe it." Joan sat up and held the printout with both hands while she read Jon's service record. He had gotten several U.S. Army deferments while he finished his Ph.D., hereby avoiding the service. The record showed that Jon went to work for the EPA immediately after graduating from Purdue. He then volunteered for a special project in Kuwait following the success of Desert Storm.

Curiously, Joan noted an italicized segment denoting unconfirmed information. It stated that while with the Corps of Engineers in Kuwait, Jon's special assignment was working with the emerging complaints about the drugs used to fend off Saddam Hussein's chemicals he had stashed.

Just twenty-four weeks after Jon arrived in Kuwait, he returned following the ragtag surrender of the Iraqis.

Reinforcing her concentration to continue, Joan came to the section about Jon's career. She found less in that section than she thought. Apparently, he had spent his years since Vietnam in the service of his country's environment because he had been with EPA the whole time. She did find his record was marred by a number of reprimands from his superiors regarding Jon's management abilities relating to budgets and monetary controls.

Joan remembered that nowhere in Jon's college credits, did she notice any business courses. Boy, that's a mistake these days, she thought. In what business could even the greatest scientist survive without basic fundamentals to deal with businessmen and bureaucrats?

Then Joan came to her favorite part of these reports. The private lives of the previous four people that she'd had requested reports on, had their spicy moments, to say the least. While Jon's social life did not appear to be the background for a good trashy novel, he wasn't a slouch either. She quickly reviewed the credit records showing a few expensive gift items that required 90-day terms. She noted several credit card purchases for short trips skiing up in Michigan…the fact that the trips were always for two did not slip past Joan. The report continued about his parents and known family, his income at EPA and finally the personality profile as interpreted by the Psychiatrist at Executive Search. Surprisingly, the only interesting thing in that section of Jon's dossier was that he drove a relatively rare 1941 Pontiac.

Closing the file, Joan reflected that tonight's dinner with Jon could be stimulating and productive. She smiled the smile of the Sirens, as she turned to her inter-office mail to finish the day. She knew that she would have to leave a little early to get ready for her dinner with this somewhat intriguing and complex specimen.

* *

Just then Rubin was five floors below, leaving a note on the duty desk for the guy he had ridden to work with that day. "Going on special sampling tonight—see you tomorrow."

Sandra White sat at her desk on the executive floor at Haltec whispering furtively to her best friend of the week.

"That asshole has sat in there all morning just calling me every 30 minutes or so to get him some more coffee. I really think he has gone off the deep end or is suffering an incredible hangover. You know how I've told you that he almost slobbers when I wear this low cut dress. Well, today I might as well have been Herpes Hanna for all the looks I got. He was a little strange yesterday, but you know that a lot of us are weird on Mondays. Well…Oh shit, there he is again with the damn buzzer. I'll see you in the cafeteria at lunch and fill you in on the rest of my morning."

Sandra was right. Even when she gave Stewart Phillips her best bend-over shot, he didn't bat an eye. He just asked for more coffee not even offering a thank you.

Stewart was very deep in thought following a nearly sleepless night. His conversation with Loretta Bonner last evening had left him somewhat adrift. Deep down he knew what she meant by "curtail his ability to continue and bring such probing to a halt."

Never before had Stewart been involved in such an affair. Certainly there were the well-known fancy presents for clients, big dinners and nights on the town, etc. etc. etc. But this was the big time. Stewart didn't even know where to begin. Where one finds a shin-buster, he asked himself. Do I wander around at 35th and Halsted until I see a likely hit man, he wondered.

When Sandra returned with his umpteenth cup of coffee, he asked her recklessly, "Sandra, I'm in a bind and need a favor. There are always plenty of rumors going around this place," Stewart stated with flitting eyes. "Have you heard anything about Cindy Farrell's project or her carryings-on with some guy from EPA?"

Almost before Stewart could assure her that the information would go no further, Sandra was in his side chair launching into a plethora of scuttlebutt.

Stewart sieved the data as she went interminably on about that whole section at Haltec. "…She's already slept with the guy…Jerry Wittner might have been banging her—oh, excuse me, Mr. Phillips, I meant having sex with her—six weeks after they started working together…Joan Blacker is really jealous of Cindy…There is a special sampling project tonight…Jerry Wittner has weird things in bottles in his office…"

"Sandra! What was that about a sampling project tonight? Where did you get that?" Stewart asked nearly coming across the desk.

Sandra was proud that she always remembered her sources, but she had to work for this one. "Let's see now. Yes! It was Jamie, the pool secretary down in the technician's area. She said that she saw a note on the duty desk that Rubin had a late night sampling job and couldn't ride home with Jeffrey. Jamie figured that Rubin really was trying to line up a hot one with that girl in data processing and…

"Wait a minute, Sandra, who is Rubin?"

"I'm sorry, sir. I just assumed that you knew that he is the technician assigned to Cindy Farrell and Jerry Wittner for the Waukegan Ditch Project. He is the cute black one…"

"Sandra, that may be exactly what I'm looking for. Can you check around and find out anything more about this little sampling job?"

"I'll be happy to, Mr. Phillips, if you promise that any information I pass on won't be tagged back to me. I don't want everyone around here to think I'm a gossip," she grinned sheepishly, as she rose to leave.

Finally, a break!" Stewart said aloud as the door closed. "If dimwit can turn up some details on Rubin's involvement in this Farrell-EPA thing, that may get me started." He continued to think about the possible ways to curtail Dr. Kepler, when Sandra burst back into his office.

"Mr. Phillips! A good friend of mine in the supply room just told me that she heard from her boyfriend that Rubin and Cindy are taking a Haltec boat out tonight to get some samples from the Waukegan Ditch site. Apparently, Rubin had called to check on the special insulated gloves Rubin had lent him. Will that info help by the way?"

Stewart Phillips was already around his desk moving for the door when he told Sandra that he had to go out and probably wouldn't be in until tomorrow morning. Sandra lifted her eyes and gnawed on a pen as she thought that this would be the perfect job—Company detective.

TUESDAY 1:30 p.m.

CHAPTER 14

Meanwhile, Jon Kepler was still sitting in the research library at EPA's office center hoping to find some reference to an elusive compound appearing during the analysis for PCB's. So far, he had come up with zip…nada…nicht.

Jon looked up to see 'ole thunder thighs' the chief librarian glaring at him. He checked to see if his fly was open or if he had some lunch on his shirt, but came up empty. What the hell is she glaring at, he wondered. As she strolled over toward him, Jon almost started laughing while he watched the rather massive thighs undulate with the miniature steps she took. Watching her approach, he finally noticed that he was looking over the top of his shoes at her. Oh Christ, he thought, I've got my feet on the table again. Red-faced he dropped his feet to the floor and causing the library matron to halt in her tracks. With a shake of her finger, another stern warning had been issued. As she wheeled around to head back to her desk, Jon gave her the finger and felt much better.

As the afternoon wore on, he kept running into blind alleys while searching for any real documentation on a heavy compound like the one he had found in the fish tissue. It could be several years of work coupled with a sizable grant to determine precisely what the material was, Jon reflected. Here he was with a day or two and NO budget.

"That's it," he said aloud, getting a SHUSH from the fat broad. "I'll lay the whole thing on Ely," mumbling.

He jumped up and was out the door before he could get another lecture. He headed down the hall to Dr. Wayne Ely's office. Ely and Jon didn't necessarily always hit if off. Ely's Ph.D. was in Economics and he rarely understood the complex analytical problems brought to him and why projects needed a little extra budget allocation. However, one thing Ely did understand and was good at—numbers. Jon always thought the guy got off on a balanced budget.

Opening the door to Ely's office, Jon felt it smack into something. Peering around the edge of the door, Jon saw Ely with a grimace and rubbing the hand that had been about to turn the knob to open the door.

"Lord in heaven, its broken!" Ely exclaimed, looking up at Jon from dull brown eyes under bushy brows, Ely frowned.

"Doctor Ely, if you have a moment, there is something that I must really discuss with you," Jon said too demurely.

"Christ, Jon! If you promise not to hurt me again, I can spare about 3 minutes. I was just on my way to a meeting concerning the new budget. As you know Jon, the new USEPA budget director is a woman and I've always thought that few women understand numbers."

Before he could ramble on, Jon interrupted with, "There is some data from one of the fish samples taken in the Waukegan Ditch that demonstrates the possibility that a totally new compound now exists in the fish subjected to the high levels of PCB's in the food chain in that area."

Ely stared at Jon for a moment as if Jon had recited the first 12 verses of The Koran.

Jon repeated, "There may be some entirely new compound…"

"No need to repeat, Dr. Kepler. I heard what you said and was simply guessing how much this little tangent will cost your group's budget. Not only is your group over budget, but you haven't even turned in your capital requests for the next fiscal year," Ely continued.

"Doctor Ely, please! This may be extremely important. We must delay the data release to Haltec and let the Corps of Engineers know there may be a problem at the Ditch. You know that they might start dredging within 10 days of receiving our report. Please take a minute and listen to what I've found." Jon heard the plea in his voice.

No need to be so desperate, Dr. Kepler. I'll just give you a ring as soon as I get back from my budget meeting and we can discuss the entire matter; especially your capital request budget forms."

With that, Ely accelerated past Jon and down the gray over green hallway.

Jon just muttered something about the lower orifice of the human body and began walking back to his office to call Cindy about the sampling tonight. Returning to the laboratory from Ely's office, Jon sat in front of the terminal at the GC/MS. He was fuming. It seemed that no one was interested in his discovery and even less willing to listen to the possible implications. Booting up the computer for one more look at the spectral display of the elusive material, Jon saw the note left in Laura's flowing script. He reached for the phone and rapidly punched in Cindy's number as he envisioned her grabbing the receiver from Mickey's upheld hand.

"This is Jerry Wittner", came the unexpected male response.

"Jerry, it's Jon. Are we set for tonight? Am I meeting you at Monroe St. harbor? Where is Cindy?" His questions flew like shots from a Gattling Gun.

"Whoa there, Jon-boy. If you talk that fast all the time, you are bound to hurt yourself," Jerry replied in an attempt to lighten the tension. "We're all set for tonight. Rubin is coming to help. Cindy is downstairs getting some coolers for the samples. See how calmly I answered all those questions," he said with some forced antipathy.

"OK, Jerry, I'll calm down a bit. It's just that Cindy's message was rather cryptic and I thought things might be tightening up for some reason," Jon said with deliberate slowness.

"OK! We'll meet you there at about 6:30, Jon. And, Doc, slow down, you'll live longer," Jerry mocked.

As Jerry hung up, Stewart Phillips was stealthily following Cindy into the equipment storage area in the sub-basement of the Haltec Building. Cindy was so intent on the task at hand that she didn't noticed Phillips. He watched as Cindy went to the marine equipment cage and began filling out a requisition to pass to the equipment manager. The coolers were the large red ones typically used for water, soil or tissues. Stewart saw the manager throw a box of Whirl-Pak sampling bags on top of the coolers. With a remembering glance at the plastic bags, Cindy turned to take the two coolers onto the elevator toward the garage.

As soon as Cindy walked away, Stewart calmly strolled over to the equipment manager and asked, "Have you seen Cindy Farrell? I have some data sheets for her."

"Mr. Phillips, if you hurry, you can probably catch her in the parking garage. She picked up a few coolers and supplies for a re-sampling at the Waukegan Ditch. Seemed like she was in a hurry though."

"Thank you, but I'll catch her tomorrow," Stewart lied in case anyone checked on him.

Phillips then took the elevator back to the executive floors to see what else he could learn. Arriving back in his office somewhat breathless, he dialed the dispatcher to find out where the boat assigned to the Waukegan Ditch project had been berthed. After being told the slip number at Monroe harbor, Phillips' plan began to take shape. So far he knew that Cindy and Rubin were taking a Haltec boat on an unauthorized sampling mission sometime today. He still had to find out if Kepler would be there. Gambling on the fact that about half of the people one calls in business are out, unavailable or on another call, Phillips dialed the main Centrex number for the EPA in Chicago. He asked the operator for Dr. Jon Kepler and after a great deal of clicking and humming, a vaguely female voice answered, "Organics lab, Laura Thomas."

"Miss Thomas, this is the project coordinator at Haltec. I am calling for Dr. Kepler in the hopes of leaving a message for our Cindy Farrell who may be meeting Dr. Kepler later."

"Well sir," Laura replied with an acerbic tinge, "Your Ms. Farrell called earlier and left a message for Dr. Kepler about meeting him at the harbor or something. I see that the note I left is gone, so it can be assumed that the message was received. Dr. Kepler is gone now and I don't know if he will return. Is there anything else I can do? Can I take a message?" Laura responded a little more properly.

"No thank you, Miss, I'll catch Cindy tomorrow. Thank you very much," Stewart replied not quite believing in his luck.

Leaning back, Stewart's plan fell into a final version. He opened the lower drawer of the solid oak credenza and extracted his L. L. Bean Swiss Army Tool kit. He kept one in his office and one in his shave kit when traveling. A somewhat expanded version of the Swiss Army Knife, the tool kit seemed like it was able to fix anything from TV's in hotel rooms to report binders on his desk. Sticking it inside his suit coat, Stewart told Sandra he was done for the day.

After arriving at the Michigan Ave. door, Stewart hailed a cab for the ride to slip 37, Monroe Street Harbor. Just before telling the driver his destination, Phillips froze momentarily and finally blurted "Lincoln Park Zoo, please."

* *

As Stewart Phillips was heading north toward the zoo, which is within easy walking distance of Monroe Street harbor, Jon was trying to decide how to handle one Ms. Joan Blacker. In all the confusion, he had forgotten his date with her. He really wanted to meet with her; she intrigued him. He certainly couldn't be late for the sampling. Checking his watch, he decided to try for a double play. After calling Information and then dialing her number, he inwardly hoped she wasn't home and thus could avoid his conflict of interest. Two rings and his hope began to rise. On the third ring, she answered.

"Hello, Joan? This is Jon Kepler. Do you remember our conversation at lunch yesterday?"

"Well of course, Jon. I really expected to see you before I talked to you on the phone. The dinner preparations are just about to get underway. Will you be here on time for the antipasto?" she asked with the smile of a panther.

"Well, Joan, that's why I called. I wanted so much to talk with you, but something has come up and I am really pressed for time. But I'll tell you what. To make up for canceling out on dinner, let's go to Irish Eyes for a quick drink and we can at least chat and get to know one another."

"Jon, I'm sorry about dinner, but are you certain you wouldn't rather just stop here. It's quieter and we can talk. We'll save Irish Eyes for drinking and singing some other night," Joan countered in her sultriest voice that drew a picture of breasts exposed beneath chiffon and wet lips slightly parted.

"OK, Joan, I'll stop by at 5:00 but I'll have to leave by 5:30 to make my meeting. At least we'll have a chance to be civil over a cocktail."

* *

Jerry, Rubin and Cindy decided to grab a bite at the great little deli around the corner from the office. While savoring 3 hot corned beef sandwiches with the biggest, juiciest Kosher dill pickles in the world, they reviewed the equipment needed one more time and came up prepared. Figuring 40 minutes to the Ditch in the boat and 40 back, they totaled a maximum of four to four and a half-hours for the whole job. That should put them back in the garage between 10 and 11. That wasn't late enough to require any special check in or out. Finishing up, they walked around to the street level entrance to the Haltec garage and went down the driving ramp to Cindy's jeep that had the coolers and other supplies.

* *

Stewart Phillips had already walked from the zoo area to Monroe harbor and was on board the Haltec boat. He stripped the insulation from a piece of heavy electrical wire he had found in the boat's spare parts locker. He attached the wire to the electroshock generator and then to the steel railing used for support when netting the fish. Normally the special insulated bushings would prevent any electrical flow to the railing, however, the short wire would make the railing "live" when touched by anyone. The clever thing was that the railing wasn't live until the generator for the electroshocker was activated. Stewart guessed that Rubin would run the boat while Kepler operated the shocker and Cindy bagged the fish.

Stewart was about to "curtail Kepler's activities" just like Mrs. Bonner said. Stewart Phillips was not a scientist. He suspected that an electroshocker that stunned fish would simply stun a man. He didn't know that without the dissipation of the water, a fish shocker was the equivalent of an electric chair.

'A good shock from this thing should help Dr. Kepler come to his senses or it will eliminate his senses,' Stewart thought.

However, Stewart had never kept up on project team assignments and had no way of knowing that Jerry Wittner would also be along to help Rubin, Cindy and Jon Kepler as they sought additional proof of their genuine concern for the Lake Michigan ecosystem.

SECTION THREE

MOVING NORTH

As the now ravenous Coho moved in closer to the western shoreline of Lake Michigan, she was nearing a bedding area of crustaceans. The sprawling community of lake crabs signaled not only an abundant source of protein, but a full meal that would not forestall her continuing movement northward. As the crabs scattered in front of her, she noticed several other Cohoes in the colony eating their fill in a random, rolling fashion that advertised their maleness. She quickly sliced her way through a corner of the crab colony, releasing any accumulated sand from her gills with a rapid fluttering of the outer flaps. She had no intention of letting herself be seen by the male Cohoes. Their size and friskiness had told her they were yearlings and would not yet be sufficiently virulent to produce strong fry from the eggs she carried. Moving outward from the sandbar, she resumed her relentless push toward the north.

TUESDAY 4:30 p.m.

CHAPTER 15

Jon was just preparing to leave for his rendezvous with Joan Blacker when Laura walked into the lab.

"When did you reappear? Did you get the message from Ms. Farrell? Laura asked with an abundance of snottiness.

"Laura! Just the person I need," Jon said smiling at her. "What would it take for you to come in very early tomorrow to start on some new samples that might contain our mystery compound?"

"Doctor Kepler, you and the entire EPA don't have enough money or perks to get me in here for another 20 hour day. I may be approaching executive burnout stage IV and I'm not even an executive."

"Laura, this is so important to the entire project that I will personally arrange it so your time-due gives you a four day weekend starting on Thursday," Jon blinked his best starving dog look at the weakening technician.

"One thing and one thing only, in addition to the long weekend, could get me in here before nine tomorrow morning. You must promise to take me to see that new play at the Shubert sometime this weekend. But, it must be a real promise and not one of your usual varieties."

Jon smiled at her with sparkling eyes and smiled, "It's yours and you're beautiful." As he jumped up to kiss her cheek, the phone rang.

Jon grabbed it to hear Ely's mousy voice, "Dr. Kepler, I'm free now for that discussion you wanted on some chemical that turned up on your project."

"Oh shit," Jon muttered. "Excuse me Dr. Ely, but I have to get to another meeting. I'll catch you tomorrow."

Not really realizing he had hung up on his boss, Jon turned back to find Laura already arranging the glassware and supplies for the early start tomorrow.

"By the way, Doctor," she started, not looking up from her work. "You must look at the pile of papers on your desk. There have been five or six people from the Hazardous Waste Group looking for you. And, you were scheduled to give a talk to that consumer group tomorrow."

Jon muttered his 'oh shit' a little louder and headed into his small gray office to quickly fly through the papers beginning to pile up on his desk.

Jon's office was somewhat atypical even though it had the standard gray desk, black armchair, side chair and a two-shelf bookcase. Instead of the usual Chart of the Elements, calendars and yellowing travel posters, Jon had nine advertising posters. Each of them had cost more than a few bucks, but his visitors were always fascinated. People in their twenties marveled at the fins, huge hoods and giant steering wheels, but squealed at the prices. Other visitors in their fifties or above reminisced. Jon had collected sales materials used by auto dealers to announce the "new cars" for the year. The collection included a 1955 Packard convertible, a 1951 Studebaker Champion and even a 1949 Hudson Hornet.

Hardly noticing his collection this time, Jon was out of the office within ten minutes firing a list of things for Laura to do.

"Whoa! Whoa! Whoa!" Laura said finally screaming the last one. "I'm an analytical technician, not a secretary and definitely not a magician. Let me write a few things down and see if I can save your ass again. Oops, I'm sorry, Doctor, That kinda slipped out."

With a rewarding smile, Jon went down the list slowly as Laura made notes on extricating Jon from the consumer talk, putting off a meeting with the

Quality Assurance Coordinator and trying in general to free up Jon's day tomorrow for the analysis of the fish. As Jon rambled on, Laura interrupted.

"Doctor Kepler, if you are meeting your Ms. Farrell at 6:30, you'd better hustle; it's 5:45 now.

"Oh Christ," Jon exclaimed grabbing his jacket. Whirling from the door, he told the ever-faithful Laura, "Call a Miss Joan Blacker; the number's on the pad somewhere on my desk and give her the first bullshit that comes to mind that will apologize to her for my not meeting her."

Watching him blow out through the door while standing with her mouth agape, Laura walked into Jon's cubicle wondering what was worse—the five a.m. crap or falling in line behind yet another wench craving for the attention of one Dr. Jon Kepler.

* *

Barreling to a screeching, dust-blowing halt, Jon bolted from the Pontiac at a gallop to reach the dock with glares from the other team members. Glancing at his watch, he saw that he was nearly 15 minutes late and the others were not appreciative of the added strain imposed on them by a fellow conspirator's tardiness. When Jon started to explain, none of the three wanted to hear.

Somber introductions of Jon to Rubin followed while the lines were cast off and the glistening white Chris-Craft rumbled to life.

Jon was glad that both Jerry and Cindy had made the run up to the Waukegan Ditch a number of times in the daylight, because the western shoreline of Lake Michigan looked very mysterious and foreboding in the failing spring evening light. While there were occasional patches of lights, there were long stretches of total blackness. Or perhaps it all seemed so sinister only because of the task at hand—illegally collecting fish samples in a stolen boat. All of this worked its way through Jon's mind as Jerry wheeled the sturdy white cruiser toward the harbor made famous in the newspapers as the Waukegan Ditch—largest deposit of PCB contaminated bottom mud in the entire world.

Jerry broke the silence, speaking over the rumble of the engines. "The geography and geology of the southwestern shore of Lake Michigan, especially right in this area, is incredibly diverse, Jon. The Lake is the result of the withdrawal of the Ice-age glaciers that left this area of North America with the second largest surface water supply of non-salt water in the entire world. Something like 80% of all the fresh water in the U.S. is in the Great Lakes."

Jon confirmed the knowledge with several listening noises. He couldn't help but think about the trip they were taking. As Jerry continued to steer north, Lake Shore Drive receded away from the water and left black cliffs that began to rise dramatically, with private residences perched atop them. Then, suddenly, the cars reappeared, the cliffs were gone and the huge Waukegan Harbor appeared with masts swaying like so many reeds in the wind.

As the boat turned behind the seawall and into Waukegan harbor, it slowed to a crawl. Zigzagging up into the industrial area along the shores of the Ditch, the Haltec people began to ready the boat for the Job at hand. Jerry idled the engine just downstream of the huge Nautical Marine Corporation plant that had created this environmental disaster. The blame had been fixed and they weren't in a boat at this time of night to reflect on the guilt of the parties involved. They knew their jobs. All of them began a bewildering set of tasks totally foreign to Jon. Finally he bellowed, "Goddamnit, what can I do!"

The three specialists turned to look at him as if this was the first time anyone had noticed him. Jerry grinned and said, "OK, Doc, sit at the wheel blow air through your lips and make a sound like a motorboat, then nobody will notice that we're almost standing still." Three people laughed, one scowled.

"Oh, shit, Jon, relax and just stay out of the way for a few minutes. Cindy winked at him.

"Say, Jerry, how about if Jon drives while you and Rubin net the fish. I'll run the instruments and log in the samples. That should speed things up."

"Cindy, I really wanted to try electroshocking," Jon said trying to pout.

"No, Jon, that takes some experience. Jerry and Rubin can handle it."

“Rubin, start up the generator and I’ll get ready at the bow with the netting equipment,” Jerry directed with his normal take-charge efficiency.

The bow of the cruiser had been specially outfitted to do electroshocking with the heavy metal railing to support the weight of 2 or 3 people leaning over the side. The netting of the shocked fish was laborious. Hauling up 10, 20 and 30 pound salmon could be very taxing.

“OK Jerry, here she goes. Instant start tonight. None of the problems we’ve had the last few trips,” Rubin announced, trying to keep it light.

One touch of the electric start button and the 8.0 KVA generator coughed into life. Cindy was showing Jon how to maneuver the big Chris-Craft as 15-foot tendrils of steel cable were unreeled from the bow to deliver the non-lethal shock to any fish within 25 feet of the boat. Rubin flipped the switch, thus delivering power to the cables and nearly instantly small fish began to appear at the surface. Jon watched with total fascination as those fish floated about for 30 to 40 seconds on their sides, then suddenly righted themselves and casually swam away.

Rubin increased the power flow to the steel cables to bring up the larger fish like the Coho salmon, steelhead and lake trout. As the first ruddy steelhead appeared, Jerry took his place, picking up his long handled landing net. Normally Jerry and Rubin both leaned against the safety rail. It seemed to help a sore back when the crew was out there all day.

Rubin reached over to pick up his dip net when he noticed a wire running from the generator to the safety railing. He had never seen that before. Realization hit Rubin like a hockey slapshot. He scrabbled for footing on the Fiberglass decking, not yet able to release his stricken vocal cords to shout a warning to Jerry. As Rubin saw Jerry begin to lean over to net the first “sample” of the night, he knew there was no way to stop him from being fried.

Rubin suddenly knew there was only one thing to do. He calmly took hold of the wire at the generator and laid his right leg over the gunwale into the water.

When the perfect grounding of 4,000 volts ripped through his body, Rubin wanted to ask Jerry if he had ever thanked a nigger for anything before. That would have been impossible as the electrical energy sought release from this "organic resistor" and began blowing holes where Rubin's fingertips, toes, nose and genitals used to be.

Nobody screamed. The incredulous, muffled sound of Rubin dying only caused each of them to turn toward the crackling and then away from it in total revulsion. As Jon's stomach knotted, he thought, "Anyone who says most people stare at gore could never have seen anything like this."

Jon pulled back on the throttle and stopped the boat. Staring straight ahead, he caught Cindy's face as she began to come apart. He reached for her and smothered her with his chest. She grabbed on and was immediately torn by a timpani-shattering scream. Jerry dropped the net and leaped for the generator to switch it off in the hopes that Rubin could be saved. The generator was already off. The direct discharge through Rubin's body to the water had placed such a tremendous load on the system, that the circuit breaker had cut the power.

Just as Rubin's body began to slip away from the hand that had grabbed the wire, Jon reached for Rubin's belt and pulled him back into the boat. The stench of burnt human flesh began to creep into the suddenly still lake air. Jerry quickly moved to pull a crumpled tarp over him. Cindy began to wail.

Jon watched as Jerry began cursing and kicking the generator trying to destroy the instrument that had blown Rubin apart. All of this caused the wire leading to the safety railing to go unnoticed.

After a number of solid kicks, Jerry looked for something else to blame for Rubin's death. He snatched up the long handled dip net and began pulling up nets full of the fish stunned by Rubin's electrical transfer to the water. As they flopped about on the deck he started screaming at Jon.

"Here, you sonofabitch. Here's the fucking fish you wanted. Rubin's dead so you could toot your fuckin' horn about some goddamn chemical. Maybe I'll shove these up your ass until you die like he did." Jerry's ranting was short-lived as Cindy moved from Jon's grasp to take Jerry into her arms. It looked like a transfer of strength from Jon to Cindy and then to Jerry. In a moment, Jerry stopped screeching at Jon and stuttered an "I'm sorry" through the start of coughs and tears. His body sagged.

The three of them sat there for quite a while before Jon stood and began kicking the fish into the live well at the center of the boat. Cindy began gathering others and putting them into the coolers. Jerry sat there for a minute or so and then began to pull in the cables. It was as if no one needed to talk. Some strange unspoken agreement had been reached.

Even as the Haltec boat returned to Monroe harbor, not one of the three surviving crew members had noticed the wire still attached to the generator terminals, nor did they even consider that Rubin had literally sacrificed his life to save Jerry Wittner. Their story to the police, who arrived shortly after Jon's call, was that Rubin must have slipped when rising from his position at the generator. He may have been reaching for his net when his foot slipped out from under him and into the water. While he grappled for a handhold, Rubin must have grabbed the generator terminal.

The police officer was taking down all of the pertinent information, accepting without question that the group was on a sampling run for a Haltec project.

The policeman finally said, "You folks will have to wait a bit longer until the Medical Examiner gets here. He'll want to see the body before it's moved and before the scene is disturbed further. Please just wait on that bench there."

As the three shuffled to the concrete bench, a black station wagon pulled up to the chainlink fence surrounding the dock. It was then waved in by a night guard who had been posted to the gate by the police. A small crowd was gathering, but it wasn't a problem because of the fence.

A gum-chomping, bluejeaned mountain unraveled itself from the car and wandered over to the policeman standing near the boat. Climbing onto the deck of the Chris-Craft, he lifted the corner of the covering. The coroner studied the lifeless body of Rubin Anderson for quite a while. He then turned and said something to the policeman. The officer moved quickly to Jon and told him that the Medical Examiner wanted to talk to him.

Being singled out hardly registered with Jon, until he looked up in to the smiling, consolate eyes of Fred Donnolly. Jon began to smile and cry as the Chief Medical Examiner of Cook County and former Purdue roommate of Jon Kepler, simply braced him up by the shoulders and walked Jon toward his friends.

TUESDAY 11:30 p.m.

CHAPTER 16

After introductions and comments on the grizzly business of the Medical Examiner's official duties, Dr. Fred Donnolly told the police to check the boat carefully and to get in touch with him if any thing turned up.

"I'll be at Dr. Kepler's apartment."

Handing the policeman a small sheet of notepaper, Dr. Donnolly continued with the total authority of a man that knows his job and the depth of the responsibilities that go with it.

"I'll be taking a full report from these folks, Officer Grayson. If there are any developments be sure to let me know. Kepler's phone number is right below the address."

Everyone piled into Donnolly's black wagon without batting an eye. Even if they had noticed, the color was certainly right for the occasion. They rode in total silence until they got to Jon's place. With Jon's key still in the lock, the four of them walked in the door to the ringing of the phone.

Jon picked up the receiver and answered in a complete monotone, "Yeah, this is Kepler."

An officious voice replied, "Dr. Kepler, this is the officer at the Monroe Harbor. May I please speak to Dr. Donnolly?"

With no surprise at all, Donnolly answered, “That was quick Grayson. What do you have?”

“Well, Doc, you may want to get back down here. We were going over the boat and found a wire connecting the safety railing and the generator. No way was this an accident. The Anderson kid was murdered.”

Dr. Fred Donnolly displayed the emotionless face of a Medical Examiner and simply told the officer to contact District 2 Homicide and get a complete evidence crew to the scene. Fred turned to Jon, Jerry and Cindy as he put the phone down.

Carefully moving his eyes to make contact with each of them, Fred carefully and stoically phrased his announcement to them. “Well, folks, it looks like your friend’s death was no accident. There was a wire connecting the safety railing to the generator. It appears that somebody was after him or one of you.”

The three looked at each other with pained, quizzical faces. Who? Why? When? Were just a few of the questions flashing through their collective minds?

“Fred. Very few people even knew we were going out in that boat tonight,” Jon offered.

They were each beginning to think that something must be done. The perpetrator had to be found.

Donnolly watched the metamorphosis of shock. They were coming out of it just like 99% of them do. It always that same pattern of shock, sadness, rage, revenge and finally reason. You could usually tell the ones that wouldn’t make it all the way through. ‘The hollow eyes never really fill in on the ones that won’t pull out,’ he thought to himself.

“Jon, maybe you should explain our relationship before I start questioning these nice folks,” Fred said with a directing gesture to Jon.

Jon related his four years of life with Fred Donnolly at Purdue University.

“Fred was in pre-med and I was in Analytical Chemistry. We both had to work our asses off because of the added sports load. Of course, Fred was the big first stringer on a full ride, while I was just a lowly backup receiver. We roomed together for about half of our semesters there. I was really impressed with the amount of Chemistry they made the pill-pushers take.

Fred interrupted with an observation on Jon's skills as a wide receiver. "When ole' J. C. here went into the game, the fans knew we were desperate and usually started to leave to beat the traffic." He grinned at Jon.

Jon turned with a smile to see wondering looks from Cindy and Jerry.

As Jon was not about to tell them his full name, the phone rang again postponing the explanation.

Picking up the phone, Fred said to them, "It's always for me when I'm at someone's house on business."

Turning toward the table where the phone sat, Fred took out his always-necessary notepad and began to repeat segments of the conversation to give himself time to make the notes. Fred still hadn't caved in to get a Palm Pilot. He always figured these pads from Target at a $1.98 were less painful to lose.

"Yes, yes, it's ok that Grayson gave you this number. What's up now? How many have come in? How many of them have the symptoms? Oh No! All of them? Have the results started coming back on those blood toxins yet? Are all the bodies in the same condition? Are there any trends showing in the computer data tracking."

Jon couldn't help but bend an analytical ear toward Fred's conversation. They had always gotten involved in each other's work in college and had continued that in their renewed friendship here in Chicago. It was really an accident that they found each other again after graduating from Purdue and losing each other for 7 years. The Medical Examiner had contacted the EPA for possible utilization of the EPA's Mass Spec because theirs was down for repairs. The call had gone to Jon and instant recognition renewed a strong friendship starting with lunch that day.

Jon was always impressed with the delicacy with which Fred manipulated even a fork at lunch. Fred had played left guard for Purdue and had never looked like a pre-med student. At six feet seven inches and 265 pounds he seemed to tower over everyone else around him.

Looking at him now and listening, it appeared that Fred was involved in something big. Jon tuned in a little more carefully, while Cindy and Jerry verbalized their continuing disbelief to each other about Rubin's murder.

Hanging up the phone, Fred began, "I'll be dipped in shit." He muttered, while staring at the notes on the miniature spiral pad.

"This one's a beauty, J.C.," he said, slipping into their familiar routine of bouncing problems off one another.

"Look at this," Fred said pointing to his notes. "We've got something going on and it looks like it could get bigger. The number correlation is just right for an epidemic, but these people are not being dropped by any ordinary bacteria or virus. It appears to be some toxic substance in their system, but we haven't identified it yet.

Jon interjected, "Whoa, Fred. What the hell are you talking about…these people…number correlation…epidemic?

Forgetting their fond reminiscing of only moments ago, Fred nearly hollered, "Christ, J.C., haven't you been listening to the news or reading the papers in the last couple of days? Nine people have died an agonizing, screaming death. Nobody knows what's causing it. Granted, nine is not a big number for a city like this to lose in 3 days, but this is the most horrible thing I've ever seen. Try to imagine being electrocuted like Rubin but it goes on for a day and a quarter.

Turning to see Cindy and Jerry staring at him, Fred apologized for his comparison to Rubin's death. It was easy to forget personal feelings when the sky was falling.

"The detectives from District 2 will take over Rubin's investigation. My office will verify his cause of death and there will be a statement for the District Attorney," Fred continued while moving toward the door.

"Rubin is dead. No one knows if Rubin was the right person. In other words, should someone else be dead or what? I'll contact the dicks from District 2 and tell them to come over here for some background. I have to get back to County Hospital and see if we can't make some progress on our mystery disease."

Opening the door, Fred was startled by the three scientists nearly hurtling themselves at the knob to stop him.

Fred smiled weakly and said, "Got your interest, did I?"

As the four piled into Donnolly's county car, they were excitedly asking questions about some possible mysterious toxin. Dr. Donnolly assumed their interest to be normal scientific curiosity.

"J.C., there are several newspapers under the seat on your side, if you want to catch up on the news. The Tribune probably has the least sensationalized version of what has been happening."

Rummaging under the seat, Jon came up with the papers and flipped on the overhead light. Scanning the pages, he began to read segments of the story leaving out the non-essential details.

"Police brought three men to St. John's Hospital in Waukegan today…the three appeared to be suffering Delirium Tremens when first examined at the hospital by emergency room physicians…screaming in agony for hours…drugs of no assistance in reducing the pain…no evidence of injuries, internal bleeding or organ damage."

"What the hell is this Fred?" Jon asked, searching the paper for more details.

"Go to Monday evening's paper on page four, J.C. and look at the right hand column," Fred instructed.

Jon searched through a now mounting disarray of newspapers and finally found page four of yesterday's paper. Forgetting to read aloud for everyone's information, he was quickly censured by Cindy.

"Hey, J.C., don't forget the rest of us here," she said getting no reaction from Jon. She was dying to find out why Fred called him that.

Jon read on. "Today six more victims of the 'North Side Malady' were brought into Presbyterian-St. Luke's hospital, each screaming and tearing at their bodies like they wanted to get out of them. Doctors have no answers yet and have had surprisingly little to say. It has just recently been determined that these six are totally unrelated to the three victims in Waukegan and have had absolutely no contact with them. Doctors have said that it does not appear to be a bacterial agent and ruled out the spread of the disease."

Fred said, "Monday's late night edition had a neat headline on page two—THREE DIE OF STRANGE DISEASE. There were so many calls to the hospital you wouldn't believe it. The place has been mobbed. When my team and I began to conduct the autopsies on these three guys, J.C., I made sure we all reviewed the case files first. They were gruesome reading. The doctors had tried everything on those three. Nothing stopped the pain. They tried Demerol, morphine and even resurrected an old time favorite called Dilaudin, a ketone derivative of morphine. Those people died screaming. One special note was that as time wore on, their mobility decreased to the point where they had muscular movement but no structural strength.

Cindy's question was on everyone's lips—"What does no structural strength mean, Doctor?"

Fred began to answer just as they were pulling into the six-story parking lot at Cook County Hospital at l6th and California. The complex was indescribable in size and layout. Even though it has had a past rich in politics and doctors' strikes, The County was still one of the top teaching hospitals in the world. It was famous for its burn unit and discoveries in the art of skin regeneration.

Stopping the car in an assigned spot, Fred turned to face the passengers.

"The easiest way to explain that statement is to tell you what I found when we conducted the first of the three autopsies. A male Caucasian, age 28, 6 feet even, 195 pounds, no apparent wounds or contusions, bones turned to rubber."

The three sat staring at Dr. Fred Donnolly with no change in their expression. Not disbelieving, but simply not grasping the concept.

Fred Donnolly showed the strain of the last 19 hours and screamed at Jon, "They had no fucking Calcium left in their bones, Jon! You hear me! They were human SLUGS! Their bones had turned to a cartilage-like material. Their screams were due to some kind of metamorphosis; some kind of chemical leaching of the Calcium. The pain was probably the most intense ever experienced by any human being."

He was almost whispering now. Jon reached out to hold his shoulders. As Fred's head began to sink onto his chest, his eyes closed. The jaw muscle tensed to its limit. Slowly it passed and Fred raised his head, in control again.

"No one has any idea how it happened or why. The place where they had been fishing was checked more thoroughly than if the mayor had been mugged there. The coolers of food they had with them were checked for bacteria, viruses and we were just getting into looking for toxins when the call came in from the police about you guys at the harbor. Normally one of the other ME's would have taken the call, but I heard your name mentioned. I thought that maybe you could help me if I helped you."

Fred looked at Jon and felt that deep consolation that only total friendship can bring. He looked at the quiet faces of Cindy and Jerry.

Jon said, "Fred, tell us how we can help and we will."

"Well, J.C.," returning to his more familiar address, "it's actually your Mass Spec I need. You have a more complete toxic compound library than we do here at County, Could I get you to run some tissues, bone, and blood samples and see what you can come up with?"

"Consider it done, Fred." Get me a lift back to my lab and I'll get things ready. Have the samples delivered and I'll run them myself ASAP—No.1 priority."

Together, the two biologists complained about being left out. "Can we help somehow?"

Jon took over. The sound of his voice was commanding. He told Cindy and Jerry how the rest of the night would go. "Both of you have some chemistry background. We went out to get fish samples today for our own important reason. Now the Medical Examiner of Cook County has asked our help. Let's get everything done at once and not try to assign priorities. We'll get over to the EPA building and get going on the fish samples and Fred's tissues, etc."

Turning to Fred, he said, "Get us a cab or a ride back to Monroe Street Harbor to pick up our cars. Get me copies of anything that your lab has run so far."

As they all got out of the car, their minds apparently were so consumed with the work that had to be done that the mood had shifted from morose to intense.

The four of them walked across the skyway into the third floor of the hospital. Fred headed for a hall phone to call a taxi for them. Jon was already explaining to Jerry and Cindy what was in store for them as lab technicians.

Fred Donnolly walked back to the group in small anteroom off the hall to find Jon giving a lecture on organic chemistry sample preparation.

"OK, J.C., I'll call the detectives up at the harbor to authorize the release of your fish samples and have them sent down to your lab. A cab is on the way. My people will bring out samples for you in just a few minutes. By the way, did I tell you that I know tomorrow's headlines?

Donnolly looked from one to the other. They didn't move. Each was more afraid to ask than the next.

Finally Fred spoke. "Eleven more dead of mystery ailment."

"When did it happen, Fred? Was it like the first three?"

"Jon, the call I got at your apartment was to tell me that the bodies were on the way here. I tried to keep a solid front for you and your friends when we left your place but I guess I lost it out in the car, I'm sorry for that."

"Christ, Fred. Facing this kind of thing with absolutely nothing to go on could put anybody in the booby hatch. Let's get on with the analyses and see if we can't turn something up to get us rolling on a big batch of answers."

Jon looked at Fred and then turned to his new lab assistants standing in the middle of the soft blue hallway with those colored tiles telling which way to go to something. "All right people. It is now 2:00 am Wednesday morning. If we want answers, we gotta get busy."

WEDNESDAY 8:30 a.m.

CHAPTER 17

Wednesday morning broke blue-skied and unseasonably warm for this time of year, especially in the Windy City. Stewart Phillips was particularly pleased with himself as he strolled down the hallway gleaming with azure blue marble wall tile and matching floor to arrive at his office, ordering coffee while strolling past his secretary.

'The first thing I'd better get out of the way is to call Loretta Bonner with a report on our Dr. Kepler,' he thought.

Settling in while waiting for his coffee, he wondered if Joan Blacker had come up with anything on her end. Finally appearing with the coffee, Sandra asked if there was anything else she could do for him. Phillips loved that straight line, but didn't have time this morning for banter.

"No, Sandra, not now. I'll be making some important phone calls, so please, no interruptions until I give the word."

Turning to leave, Sandra responded to the ringing phone and walked back to Stewart's desk. She leaned over to get the phone and gave the boss a hell of a cleavage shot for so early in the morning.

"No, I'm sorry Miss Blacker, but Mr. Phillips is tied up right now and...

With frantic hand movements Stewart signaled that he would talk to Joan Blacker, just to brag a little before the news came in about Kepler.

"Joan! Yes, this is Phillips. I just walked up to my desk. What can I do for you?" he watched Sandra's ass swing across the room and out the polished mahogany door.

"Well, Stewart, I just had to tell you that I was to meet with Dr. Jon Kepler last night. I got a call from some stumbling little technician at his lab with an excuse that made no sense.

Stewart was already gloating about his successful investigative work and Joan Blacker's failure. He was startled to see Sandra come rushing back in. Without even waiting for Phillips to hang up or a signal to speak, she blurted her news.

"Sir, Rubin Anderson was killed last night in a boating accident while sampling with Cindy Farrell and Jerry Wittner. Isn't that horrible?"

Stewart Phillips simply dropped the phone onto his desk, ignoring the questioning calls of his name from the receiver. His hands went to his perfectly brushed hair and ran from front to back. Sandra assumed it was shock or something. Stewart Phillips only wondered what Loretta Bonner would say when she heard that he had killed an innocent employee of Haltec. He had done it in the service of the company, but he had killed the wrong man. All he could say was, "OH FUCK!"

Joan Blacker couldn't figure out what had happened in Phillips' office, and no one was answering her calling of Stewart's name. She was trying to decide whether to run to his office or try the phone again. Just then her other line rang and she automatically answered.

It was Joan's secretary with the morning's list of call-ins. Joan wanted the list every day. She kept extremely tight control on the sick day usage in her group. The short list was routine until the girl came to Cindy Farrell and Jerry Wittner.

Hanging up the phone Joan's mind was jumping back and forth between two questions. What had upset Stewart so and why were both Farrell and Wittner absent on the same day? She spun to her computer and pulled up the Chicago Division schedule that had every project listed. She wanted to make certain that they weren't out on some job site. She knew the answer but needed to be certain. The blue, green and yellow scheduling software quickly loaded and she simply typed in Cindy Farrell's name. It was blank for the remainder of the month. Checking again, she found the same yellow blank lines for Wittner.

Having checked that, she called Phillips back to ask what had happened.

Phillips' secretary answered with, "I'm sorry but Mr. Phillips is not in; may I take a message?"

"Look, Toots, this is Joan Blacker. I was talking to Phillips when we were interrupted. Now get him back on the line.

"Well, Miss Blacker, I don't know if he can talk right now. He is really shook up after I told him that Rubin Anderson was dead. He seems…" The line was dead.

Sandra White would have a heyday gossiping about all the executives being so bothered over one black kid getting killed in an accident. She punched another line on the button set to tell one of her fellow grapevine specialists that Haltec must have a real problem with Rubin's death because, all the executives were really in a tizzy about it.

'Phillips almost had a coronary and Joan Blacker hung up on me' was the lead-in for her gossip line this morning as the receptionist on the third floor picked up the intercom line to answer Sandra's call.

Joan Blacker was certain that something was up.

'Rubin Anderson is reported killed in an accident and both Wittner and Farrell call in sick,' Joan reviewed.

She had to get some information and quickly. She moved her chair back and bolted across the room determined to see Phillips. With determined, long strides Joan made it to the elevator in record time smashing the up arrow with an angry fist. She bolted out of the elevator and nearly knocked over one of the staffers, who glared after her mumbling an expletive.

Stewart Phillips simply sat at his desk wondering how things had gotten screwed up. 'One of our own people dead,' he thought. 'What the hell is going on? Where was Kepler when Anderson was killed?'

All of these thoughts simply generated more unanswered questions in Phillips' mind.

‘I’d better call Loretta Bonner and let her know that there was a small problem and ask her for further instructions,’ Stewart directed himself.

Lifting the receiver to dial the special number, he tried to come up with a plausible discussion of the many possibilities for an apparent screw-up. As the phone rang, he was still undecided and hoped that no one would pick up the line at the other end.

WEDNESDAY 8:40 a.m.

CHAPTER 18

Cindy, Jon and Jerry sat in the lab slouching in the gray, uncomfortable, government-issue desk chairs. They had been at it for nearly 7 hours and up for at least 25. The weariness of that first full day with no sleep was just setting in. After the adrenaline rush of beginning the analysis and the newness of the techniques had worn off, the work became drudgery. Yet it required total concentration due to the sensitivity of the equipment. Even the slightest contamination would ruin an entire run. Jon had watched over them carefully. They had decided to prepare all of the samples before they got too weary and then begin the analyses. The three of them had prepared all of the fish tissue, blood, human tissue and bone samples. Getting that many samples ready for GC/MS analysis was no simple task, even with all the equipment in the EPA lab. There were dirty pipettes, beakers, flasks, columns and glassware of every sort littering the counters. They had voted on a break before starting the instrument runs.

"Hey J.C.," Cindy glittered, "How about some real breakfast instead of this machine coffee. Don't you have a petty cash fund here for all night employees to rob?"

Jon finally caught the J.C. "OK, Miss smart-ass, where did you pick up the J.C. business?"

Cindy and Jerry both grinned and nodded at each other knowingly. "Progress at last," they said to each other giving away their plot to get Jon.

Jerry told Jon that Fred Donnolly had called him J.C. all last night. Jon admitted he hadn't noticed because he was so used to Fred saying that.

"OK, everybody! Let's get back to work," Jon said jumping up from his chair with feigned vigor.

"Hold it, buster," Cindy commanded. "Fess up right now on the J.C. business. We let you get away with it long enough. Let's hear it right now or no more work from the biologists."

With a groan Jon sat back down.

"On your words of honor. No one else is to know."

With nodded affirmation, Jon continued, "J.C. are my initials. I've always gone by the name Jon because I didn't like my full name. It would have been a well kept secret except that the Rhodes Scholarship committee at Purdue insisted that my complete name be on the record. Well, Donnolly worked part-time in the Records Office one semester and stumbled onto my file—so he said. I really think that the bastard pulled my file to see if there was any dirt. Well, he came running into the dorm howling and shouting my name. From that point on the whole campus knew that my real name was Johann Copernicus Kepler."

"The first biologist to snicker dies!" Jon glowered.

Restraint was already impossible. Jon tried to intensify his stern look but began to laugh along with them.

As the laughter subsided, Cindy only had to say, "I'm sure every line possible has been used so just allow me to say that I love it. Personally, I love good looking Pollacks with a name like Copernicus."

For everyone's benefit, Jerry lectured that Copernicus was the l5th century Polish astronomer who preached the sun-centered solar system concept, and that Johannes Kepler was a mathematician from the l6th century that a lot of people thought to be Polish but was actually German.

Continuing, Jerry said, "Johan's major contribution to mathematics was his 'Music of the Universe Theory…"

"All right! Enough already! You've had enough fun was, now let's get back to it," Jon ordered somewhat timidly.

They stood and began collecting the results of their efforts. Cindy was bringing all the samples over to Jon with the sweetest smile she could muster. He pretended not to notice.

"If we ever get back to bed, Copernicus, I'll show you how much I love cute Pollacks with sexy names."

Jon blushed. "Cindy, whatever the outcome of our work here and I might add that I'm more than a little frightened by what we will find, you should be the first to know that I love you deeply. I'm sorry for what happened to Rubin, and when this is over we'll make up for some lost time. Now, what say we find out where we're headed?"

Cindy set down the tray of samples and took Jon's face in her hands lightly kissing him on the lips. Jerry pretended not to notice.

"It will take me a few minutes to get the run started. Why don't you and Jerry call Rubin's family and see if they need anything. You should also decide about your jobs at Haltec. How are you going to handle things now that they will know about the boat and everything?"

"Oh, Christ, Jon, I hadn't even thought about it, but the first thing that comes to mind is that we'll dodge it for now," Cindy said. "We called in sick and we both have some time coming. We can handle Haltec. I'll give Rubin's family a call. Jon, you get the GC/MS runs started and Jerry, why don't you take a scouting run over to Haltec and bring back some eats."

Jon turned to arranging the sample vials in the GC/MS auto-sampler, while Cindy grabbed Jerry and headed out the door lecturing to him in her usual rapid-paced manner.

As Cindy returned through one door, Laura Thomas came in the other. Both stopped dead in their tracks.

Laura stood there like an owl with only her head slowly swiveling to take in the disaster. Jon turned to watch her and then looked at Cindy. No one spoke for an interminable period.

Finally Jon said, “Laura, I would like to take you on a tour of our new city dump.” Cindy smiled weakly. Laura simply continued to survey the lab. Just as she was about to speak, Jon sensed rather than heard the silent laser printer begin the first chromatogram output. As he turned to watch, Cindy came to look over his shoulder. Laura was still riveted to her original spot.

Time slipped slowly along as the computer traced out the chromatogram. The tension could be felt in the room like the lack of humidity in the winter. Cindy had never seen a computer plot like this but seemed to sense the approaching point. As the stylus was about to pass the point where the unknown compound peak had shown up before, there was a total absence of sound, even breathing. Laura had moved closer knowing that Dr. Kepler had gotten to an important point in his work on the mystery material.

As the curve continued past the previous compound time window, there was an audible expulsion of air from the people standing entranced by the monitor. Jon turned to look at Cindy expecting to see relief and puzzlement. Instead he saw fear. He turned back to the screen to see the peak just beginning to form. It was slightly delayed from the previous sample runs most likely because of some matrix interference.

Cindy could only say, “Well Jon, your mystery compound is in more than one fish in Lake Michigan.”

Jon didn’t even realize that he had sat down. He swiveled the chair, stood and walked to the lab bench. Leaning on the countertop, he said without raising his head, “I changed the sample order just to make sure we didn’t inadvertently add some forcing factor to the sample runs. Our mystery compound is definitely in Victim A’s blood.”

* *

While Jon was reaching for the phone to call Fred Donnolly with a preliminary result, Loretta Bonner was answering Stewart Phillips’ electronic demand for attention.

“This is Loretta Bonner,” she growled with her normal voice tone.

“Mrs. Bonner, this is Stewart Phillips at Haltec Corporation in Chicago,” he said so fast as to be nearly unintelligible.

“Yes, Mr. Phillips, I know where you work. Now what do you have for me? Have you put a stop to Dr. Kepler’s meddling?”

“Well, Mrs. Bonner, we have a little problem. I followed your directions and attempted a curtailment of Dr. Kepler’s activities, but in the attempt, one of Haltec’s technician’s was killed. Now, there is…”

Loretta Bonner was unable to contain herself and spoke with barely repressed anger. “First thing, Mr. Phillips is that WE do not have a problem; YOU have a problem. Second, you have two hours to hand write a complete summary of the incident, from start to finish, with names, dates and places. That report should not be dictated nor must any copies be made. Send it directly to the FAX machine in my office. That number is 1-615-555-4321. I will cover for you and attempt to repair the damages you may have wrought. Is there anything else?”

“Mrs. Bonner, don’t you understand? I killed an innocent boy for you. My attempt to distract Kepler was at your direction and now Rubin Anderson is dead. What shall I do?”

“Stewart! It is imperative that you regain control of yourself. There should be no fear of reprisal unless you left a trail of bread crumbs back to your office. Now get that report to me, so I can take care of things.”

Before Stewart Phillips could continue, the line went dead. He was near panic, but afraid that displeasing Loretta Bonner would make his protection vanish, he began a summary of the last 24 hours, taking care to use an ordinary ballpoint.

Meanwhile, Loretta sat at her expansive burled black walnut desk, absently pulling at her hair as if trying to straighten a wave. She thought that Phillips would follow through with his report and she would be covered. With a cynical smile she reflected on his miniature intellect. That idiot is sending me a written confession, but it will be very concise and to the point like any other intercompany memo. She had always been able to pick Phillips’ weak-willed types from among her middle level management for her dirty work. They were so anxious to get ahead in the company and knew, subconsciously, that they lacked the skills to do so. That made them perfect “cyborgs” for her tasks.

Snapping into action, Loretta picked up the receiver, not even needing to refer to her ATI corporate phone directory, and punched in the private number for Blake Thompson. She couldn't wait for Phillips report to get something done about Kepler, and, while Thompson wasn't one of her most loyal lackeys, he would do the job. She had to make certain that there were no information leaks from his direction.

The buried knowledge that Nautical Marine Corporation was the probable source of some hideous chemical killer could not be let out. Loretta Bonner's only concern at this time was for the possible damage to her company—there were no thoughts of the danger to the ecosystem.

Quickly reviewing her mental file of Blake Thompson, she remembered his good looks, quick mind and abilities in problem-solving. She had hired him to take over the badly troubled Nautical Marine Corporation in Waukegan, Illinois soon after the news about the PCB's broke in Chicago. The company's sales had plummeted and it looked like it would go down the toilet. Thompson came in and with the slash of a sword, ridded Nautical Marine of the liars and those wanting to hide. He took the full brunt of the media scorching on the irreparable ecological damage to the Waukegan Ditch and Lake Michigan. He answered every question from every reporter, environmentalist, senator, etc. Never did Thompson sway in his commitment to admitting the unintentional error made by the company. But, never did he once offer to take the blame. His position was simply that PCB's were not restricted until recently and the company knew of no limits on their use or dumping. He explained that the PCB's were additives to the transmission oils used in the outboard engines and until EPA announced the findings relating to their carcinogenic properties, Nautical Marine discharged only the PCB's spilled onto the assembly area floors and washed into the Ditch with routine floor hosings. He ordered the immediate cessation of all utilization of PCB containing products. He ordered the company to seek out every purchaser of a Nautical Marine Engine and offered to replace the engine's fluids at no charge.

Within 18 months of the biggest waterway pollution event in U. S. history, Nautical Marine's sales were back to normal. Thompson had won. He had convinced everybody of the company's innocence in the act and of their desire to be "good citizens". Even the final announcement from EPA that nearly a million pounds of PCB's rested on the bottom of the Waukegan Ditch, didn't make new waves. Blake Thompson simply said, "Not one ounce of PCB's have been discharged into the Ditch since EPA told of the compound's potential harm to our environment."

Loretta's smile grew when she remembered Blake's late night call that everything was over and he had managed to keep secret the theory that PCB's may be mutagenic. Loretta had praised his work with a very handsome bonus. Nothing of consequence had happened since the whole thing had broken loose in the press, but she wanted to be absolutely sure that the lid stayed on.

As she heard Thompson say hello, she wondered what had become of that one scientist at Nautical Marine who had wanted to publish his written report on the mutagenic potential of PCB's.

WEDNESDAY 6:30 a.m.

CHAPTER 19

A rather frazzled sounding female answered the phone in Fred Donnolly's office in response to Jon's call.

"Just a minute please. I'll see if he's out of the cutting room yet, she said.

An even more tired Dr. Donnolly mumbled into the phone, "Hullo."

"Fred, it's Jon. Do you film all of your work for posterity, now?"

Jon's feeble attempt at 'lightening the load' was missed by Fred, evidenced with his quizzical, "What the hell are you talking about, Jon?"

"Well, the girl said you were in the cutting room, so I figured you were editing films of your work."

"Jon, the cutting room is where we do autopsies, not a damn movie editing area." I probably would have laughed at that two days ago, though. I appreciate the effort. Now, what have you got?

Jon tried to empathize through the wires. He felt better about his try at some humor.

"Fred, I really hate to say this but that bad joke was the good news; now for the bad news. The first tissue sample, designated as Victim A by your group, definitely contains the exact same compound that we found in the fish tissue samples. The chromatogram has just run up and we have 25 more samples to go, but I thought you should know. We have set the autosampler to run with the remaining samples and will give you progress reports as we proceed. Any thoughts, yet Fred?"

"Too many, actually. I've played every scenario in my head as I proceed with the autopsies, but I keep coming back to one. Every victim that I have examined has precisely the same symptoms. Total Calcium depletion, no apparent bodily damage, no detectable bacteria or viruses, no clues anywhere. Each of the people has been brought into the emergency room at one of the area hospitals screaming and tearing at themselves. Even in death, this strange metamorphosis continued. This last batch of guys died 12 hours ago and their bones have continued to deteriorate to the point where they are like stiff gelatin…not even cartilage. From what I've been told, Jon, these guys were pumped full of pain killers and never stopped screaming."

"We'll continue here, Fred and let you know if the substance continues showing up in your samples and whether or not we find it in our fish. I still haven't been able to get a match out of the computer, but with our new ENVIROQUANT program, we can simultaneously acquire data from the samples while trying to come up with an ID out of the data banks. By the way, did I tell you that I tried running the data against the FDA computer spectra and didn't find a match? Where else can we get some reference libraries besides EPA? Should I try the National Science Foundation and the American Chemical Society?

"Shit, J.C., that about covers the gamut. Some manufacturers may have their own data but it probably wouldn't have been run under the same chromatographic conditions. You might give Dow Chemical and DuPont a call. Hey, try Hooker Chemical; I understand that they did some good GC/MS work in their research labs after the Love's Canal thing.

"Ah, Fred, remember me, I work for EPA. Ha! Ha! We did a little work up there, too."

"Hey J.C, I'm just a little wacky about now. But, c'mon, be honest! Had you thought of that?" Fred asked teasingly.

"Honestly? No damnit! But I'll get right on it. Are you agreeing that it's some kind of toxic material and not some weird new virus or something"? Jon queried with thoughtful probing.

"I'm not sure of anything yet, but to cover that aspect we have sent additional samples down to the Center for Disease Control in Atlanta for review. And, by the way, J.C., I haven't told anyone about your mystery compound yet. My feeling is that we'd better have some hard facts and substantive data before dropping that bomb. That would really panic everybody. Christ, if we told everybody that we have discovered a mysterious substance that turns your bones to foam rubber, we would have bedlam. Keep me posted. Get some sleep, guy.

Jon replaced the receiver gingerly and turned to find Cindy and Jerry slouched in their chairs. Jerry was making a noise akin to the Pontiac with tune-up problems, while Cindy more or less purred. Jon lightly kissed her forehead. She awoke with a jump, hitting his chin with her forehead. Both swore.

"Jon, this is not the movies. I don't awake demurely and flutter my eyes while looking deeply into your baby-blues. Besides, I was having a bad dream. What the hell is going on?"

Jon was still rubbing his chin and tasting the iron flavor of blood in his mouth when he responded, "Cindy, I'm not sure, but I may have bitten off the end of my tongue."

Just then Laura strolled back into the lab and announced that all of the carrying's on were strictly forbidden by Dr. Kepler in this lab and anyone caught fooling around would be dismissed without vacation pay. Laura smiled and warmly read the return smile from Cindy. Jon and Jerry grinned.

"Seriously folks," Jon announced, "Let's go grab some breakfast. The autosampler will inject while we're out and we'll have something to look at when we return. C'mon Laura, you too. We'll clean up later. Anyway, I'll fill you in on my conversation with Fred.

"Wait a minute," Laura interrupted, "Who is Fred?"

"Laura, he's the Chief Medical Examiner for Cook County and I'll give you details over fresh coffee and whatever at the Sippery."

"Dr. Kepler, do we have to go to that shit-hole…OOPS, I'm sorry, I didn't mean…"

"Speak up, Laura," Cindy jumped in, "Let's make the cheap turd take us to a decent place."

Jon held up his hands for attention. "It's either there, or you pay for your own. Besides, they make the best sausage gravy on biscuits anywhere in the world—well at least anywhere in downtown Chicago."

Jerry looked at Jon with feigned nausea and said, "Dr. Kepler, sir, may I have the honor of treating you and the gang here to Huevos Rancheros at Cafe LaMargarita?"

Cindy responded with, "Oh Christ, Jerry. You guys from Ohio would eat buffalo chips if they had Mole' Sauce on 'em. How about some Eggs Benedict at Diamond Jim's?"

Laura put her hands on her hips, looked around at each person and said, "There will never be a consensus here, so I will choose since I have the most class. We will go to McDonald's for pancakes. It's only two blocks."

They all shook their heads to concur. Looking for jackets, purses, and so forth, they began peppering Jon with questions as they went out the rear exit toward the elevator.

Many times before, Jon had seen people function under pressure by relieving the stress with this kind of banter. He was glad that familiar relief spread through his friends.

Nodding, as he took another draw on his third cup of coffee, Jon affirmed Cindy's rhetorical question about Fred's theory.

"Fred is really leaning toward agreement that some kind of toxic substance is the cause of these deaths because there is absolutely no trace of bacteria or viruses in those bodies. They are clean."

"Yeah, well, what about Legionella when it was first discovered." Jerry looked around for agreeing nods. "It took them weeks to discover that a new microbe existed and was causing the illnesses and deaths."

"That's a good point, Jerry," Jon responded. "Fred is covering himself there by sending samples to CDC in Atlanta for a complete workup. The fact that our mystery compound was found in the fish tissue and in the human tissue indicates that some material has found its way into the ecosystem and it beginning to show itself just now. But try this on for size—a toxic, organic substance from say an industrial waste begins to react with living, organic substances to form an entirely new family of compounds."

Cindy and Jerry just stared at Jon with no understanding showing on their faces.

Laura practically came out of her chair with, "You mean that some company's waste product could react with the fish tissue to form a new compound and cause this horrible disease."

"Well, Laura, it can't really be a disease, because it's simply a chemical reaction. I doubt that the waste would react directly with the fish tissue either. It would have to be a completely new chemical concept to have a reaction that could cause these tremendous changes or damage to the human metabolism." Looking at nowhere, Jon softly said, "I would call it a "biotoxic chelator".

Jerry and Cindy just looked at each other and smirked.

Laura immediately began to explain, "A chelating agent, that's pronounced liked its spelled k-e-y, but it's really c-h-e, is a substance that surrounds another and removes it from reactive potential. Jon calls it a chelator because it removes or exchanges the Calcium out of the bones somehow. It is "biotoxic" because it reacts with living tissue with an unfavorable result."

Just as Jon was complimenting Laura for her explanation, Cindy jibbed, "and we were always kidded for biologist talk like 'hypolimnion'."

"Sheeeit, Jon, we've got nothin' on you smart dudes in chemistry," Jerry added.

"Ok, ok. Let's get back and see what we've got," Jon interrupted.

Jerry said, "Cindy, why don't you go back with Laura and Jon while I kinda stroll over to Haltec and see what's humming on the office wires. I'll get back with you folks later to get an update."

"Good idea, Jerry, Take my Pontiac; it's still in the lot from yesterday."

Jerry stopped in the doorway of the McDonald's with an exaggerated, stage right halt. "Take your Pontiac? I must be entering that period in my life where I have a face that can be trusted. Have no fear, Jon; your machine is in the hands of a true connoisseur. Lead me to the gorgeous beast."

The girls just shook their heads at grown up boys with toys and took the lead to walk back to the EPA lab.

SECTION FOUR

HER BEGINNING

This particular salmon was a descendant of one of the first yearlings hatched in the gigantic experiment to repopulate the Great Lakes with game fish in the 1970's. The program undertaken by the U.S. Fish & Wildlife Service was derived from research begun when it became apparent that the Lamprey eel had become a permanent resident in Lake Michigan. The Lamprey was originally a sea creature with sufficient natural enemies in the oceans to control its population and contain its voracious appetite. With the completion of the St. Lawrence Seaway in 1954, the Lamprey eel made its way up the completed waterway and within 10 years became the scourge of the Lakes. At this time, Lake Michigan was still a large commercial fishing ground based on the popularity of the yellow perch. The Lamprey feasted and spread like a disease in an unhealthy animal. As commercial fishing declined, various experiments were tried—all of them failed miserably. Then scientists of the marine research institute at Florida University discovered that the adult Coho salmon could be taken from its fresh water spawning streams and maintained in fresh water environment indefinitely. The Coho Salmon is the most aggressive, natural enemy of the Lamprey eel—it was the perfect answer. Possibly man's greatest success in solving a natural biological problem by using nature's own balancing power.

WEDNESDAY 9:00 a.m.

CHAPTER 20

Joan Blacker came into her office Wednesday morning to find it buzzing with the news of death. She had a nagging hangover; she always did when she drank alone. She used to think it was the wine or the bourbon but had finally come to the conclusion that it was loneliness. She just sat there last night after Kepler's message had come. She waited in her sexy silk dress with slits up the thighs and drank a bottle of Pouille Fuisse. Now she grabbed coffee, sat down and called her secretary for a full grapevine report. Sitting there sipping the strong, black coffee, she had the feeling that things were going wrong. Kepler's message to her last night, the news of the strange deaths on the TV and the death of that kid, Rubin, sat in her mind like lead weights. They wouldn't succumb to a reasoning process. They just created an uneasiness that bore on her like the humidity of a Brazilian rain forest.

Joan leaned forward to signify that she had enough gossip and, with that, disposed of the secretary. She punched the buttons on her phone with intent to do harm and waited for Stewart Phillips to answer.

"I'm sorry, Ms. Blacker," Sandra said, but Mr. Phillips refuses to talk to anyone. Says he has an important report to get out. Say, did you hear about…"

Joan hung up with frustrated intensity and caught her index finger in the cradle. "Goddamnit to hell!" she screeched. The phone rang immediately causing even more pain in her head and finger. She reached for the phone, practically ripping it from the cradle and answered, "Blacker here."

"Miss Joan Blackman?" came the returning question.

"Who's calling please?" Joan demanded.

"This is Beth Israel Hospital. Are you Joan Blackman?" requested the caller again.

"Yes, this is Joan Blackman. If this is about a donation or a fund raiser, would you please call Haltec's Public Relations office," she answered, picturing her father giving her name to another Jewish charity while telling someone that his daughter was a "bigvig" and can make a good donation for her company.

"Miss Blackman, this is the Dr. Anna Froehlich and your father is ill. He was brought to the hospital early this morning and then was admitted to the intensive care unit. You should come right away, if at all possible. This is quite serious. No questions now. Please come. Ask for me, Dr. Anna Froehlich at the front desk. I'll come and meet you. I've known him a long time, since the old country, and he needs you."

Joan started to make an excuse and then said, "I'll be right there."

Hustling past her secretary and grabbing her coat, Joan ran for the closing elevator doors. She whirled into the walnut lined box only to knock a package from the hand of a courier leaning against the wall.

"For Chrissakes, lady, watch it!" came the sharp report from the man.

Without thinking, Joan bent to pick up the envelop and noticed the names showing SPECIAL COURIER DELIVERY from Stewart Phillips to Loretta Bonner.

Joan looked up to find an attractive young man in a typical brown uniform wearing a beautiful smile. She shrugged and withdrew into her thoughts.

Now what is wrong with that old man? She wondered. He always picks the most inconvenient times to get sick. He doesn't take care of himself, works too hard and carries on like a 30 year old.

The courier didn't waste one of his "have a good day" specials on her. 'What a smug bitch,' he thought as he walked out of the elevator toward his red and white delivery van.

Joan Blacker arrived at the hospital not even remembering the cab ride over. The hospital entrance just seemed to appear, as if she had stepped out of the Haltec building right onto the steps of Beth Israel. Joan walked up to the desk and asked to see Dr. Froehlich. When asked who was calling she started to reply, caught herself, then said, "It's Joan Blackman."

Standing at the desk, fiddling with her tailored burgundy blazer, Joan heard her name. She looked to her left to see a somber, but smiling woman hustling toward her. Joan had still not spoken.

"Miss Blackman, I'm Dr. Froehlich. Isaac's friend. Please come with me."

Joan was surprised at the Doctor's age. She remembered her saying she knew her father in the old country, but Joan had not assumed that the lady would be Isaac's peer.

Following the doctor to a small conference room, Joan focused on her as she said, "Miss Blackman, I'm not sure where to begin. Your father's heart is even older than he is. His hard life has aged him beyond his years. We continue to do everything possible, but I am not sure if he will regain his strength with the condition of his heart. Did you know that he has had angina for twenty years, at least?"

Joan was trying to find the words. She seemed unable to answer the Doctor. Joan was just being to fumble out her questions, when the Doctor continued.

Tuning her mind to the doctor, she heard, "I don't think you should see him, just now. We are trying to control the pain and guard against further deterioration. I think you'll be able to talk to him in a few minutes. I'll go…"

"Dr. Froehlich…Dr. Froehlich," came the page with a crackle over the cheap wall speaker, "Code Blue ICU…Code Blue ICU."

With a perceptible concern, she turned with a snap and turned back, trying to conceal the fear on her face. Fear that showed the worst.

‘That might be Isaac’s heart giving out to the pain,’ Anna Froehlich thought. ‘I’ll go in there and go through the drill knowing that the old man’s paper thin cardiac walls have blown apart. But I’ll go anyway for his little girl’s sake.’

“I’ll be right back, Liebchen. Isn’t that what Isaac always called you? His Liebchen. Sit here and don’t go away.” She turned to respond to the demanding speaker.

Turning into the second hallway, Dr. Froehlich did not see Joan Blackman/Blacker rise to move toward the main entrance.

Joan walked out the front door, down the steps and up the block until she arrived at Michigan Avenue. She registered the speeding mid-morning traffic with glazed eyes and calmly looked over the crowd of shoppers of the Gold Coast of Chicago. She thought that everybody seemed so happy.

Then Joan realized that she was happy too. She began to smile, always bubbling when her father and mother took her to the Lincoln Park Zoo for their regular Sunday visit. Joan reached into the empty air for her father’s hand and then her mother’s. Feeling safe in their grasp, she stepped off the curb to cross the busy street on the short walk to the zoo.

A bored cabby, low on fares in the beautiful Michigan Avenue sunshine, scanned the walkers for any signal. Nobody ever wants a ride when it’s nice out, he muttered to the steering wheel. He looked ahead just in time to scream “LOOK OUT” to the black haired girl stepping off the curb into his path.

As the steel impacted her hip, crushing the pelvis and driving the fragments up into her abdominal cavity, Joan looked at her empty hands and wondered how Mommy and Daddy would let her get hurt so badly.

WEDNESDAY 10:00 am

CHAPTER 21

Jon sat in the chair staring at the computer screen with the data summary of the sixteen samples run so far. Cindy and Laura stood silently, knowing, that the mystery compound was present in every sample run thus far. The eight fish tissues, six human bloods and two bone samples all contained what Jon had called a "biotoxic chelator".

"Well Jon," Cindy said breaking the silence, "Shouldn't you call Fred Donnolly right away. Maybe you should even take these results down to him at County, so that he can review the data. Laura and I will sit out the remainder of the runs to make sure it goes OK."

Jon continued to stare momentarily and then rose slowly. "Yes, I suppose that reviewing them with Fred would be best. Tell you what. I'll take care of getting the results to County while you girls get this place cleaned up. I have the feeling that there is a lot more work to do."

Once the groans subsided, Jon continued, "My guess is that Fred will need a lot of additional samples run and no one else has our experience. Laura, get one or two of the other technicians in here to help you guys. Grab every available extraction rig and K-D concentrator. If necessary, use my name. Hell, use Ely's name. I'm now sure that we have at least found a link between the fish samples and the deaths. There are still a lot of unknowns, though. As soon as I get back from Fred's, we'll get Ely, and anyone else that will listen, in here for a briefing session. Be back soon."

Watching Jon practically run out the door, Cindy and Laura began their tasks with no discussion. A comradeship had developed that required little talk, especially considering the subject that lay on their minds.

Meanwhile, Jerry was just arriving at the Haltec building when near-pandemonium came at him like a surprise green wave on a still, blue ocean. Trying to make sense of the unintelligible squawking, he gave up and went to the elevator for the ride up to his office. As the doors closed, a slim, dark-haired goddess boarded. Before he could use his best line on her, she nearly screamed at him.

"Did you hear? Joan Blacker was nearly killed up on Michigan Avenue. They are even saying that she may have been trying to commit suicide by walking in front of a cab. She must be in a million pieces, with blood and guts all over the place. I always thought she was strange."

The doors opened on Jerry's floor and he almost didn't make it out before they closed. He just stood there, riveted by the girl's announcement. 'That must have been the verbal insanity that was flying in the lobby,' he thought. Christ, what else could happen around here? 'Why would she do that?' was the next thought that came to him. 'Shit, she had everything going for her here. And, yes, she was a little strange.'

As he walked toward his office, Jerry felt a pervading sense of increased, yet nonproductive activity in the office area. That feeling you get when you come into an office the day before Christmas. You know that not one damn thing will get done that day; everybody just flits around and chats. As Jerry surveyed the nearly all white surroundings of the general office area, for perhaps the first time, he noted the sterility of his work environs. White walls, white partitions, light oak desk tops and beige carpet. Maybe that was why he and Cindy kept to their shared office with its wild posters and colorful junk.

As he strolled toward that island of color in this sea of white, Jerry picked up snatches of conversation. "Yea, Blacker was depressed over her grandfather's death…Rubin Henderson was an OK guy…No, Joan Blacker was straight; she was screwing Phillips regularly."

The assault on his senses ceased when he closed the door to their cube, something he rarely did. He had to think for a few minutes. Maybe he should go to Phillips with the complete story and see what help he could get within the company. He had been concerned about the slow track that their discovery was taking. Jerry felt that the news should be made public so people could take precautions. Phillips could help there.

Jerry was about to pick up the phone to call upstairs, when it rang.

"Jerry? Cindy. If things are OK there, come back to the lab. We're going to meet with Donnolly to figure our next moves. All the samples so far show the "chelator".

"Cindy, Joan Blacker was almost killed by a cab. Her father just died this morning," Jerry interrupted with a whispered monotone.

"We've got to deci…" Cindy halted in mid-word.

"Cindy, this friggin' place is up for grabs. People are wandering around like the company folded, just talking about Blacker and Rubin like they were two people from Iowa—not fellow workers. What shall I do?"

"Jer, get back over here. We need you. Do it now," was Cindy's command. She had sensed Jerry's overload and hoped that an order would bring him back.

He simply said "OK," and hung up.

Jerry stared at Mickey's smile, rose and said to him, "What the fuck are you so happy about."

Entering the elevator to return to the EPA lab, Jerry fixed on the descending numbers to avoid talking to the other person riding down with him.

"Jerry. Jerry Wittner," were the words that broke through to him.

"Don't let this thing bother you too much, Jerry. Joan was a great gal, but the loss of her father was just too much."

Jerry turned to see Stewart Phillips move closer to place a consoling hand on his shoulder.

Like a rifle shot through a fish bowl, the words were released from Jerry's mouth with no seeming connection to his brain. He began spewing all he knew about the discovery of the mystery compound, Rubin's death, the nearly 30 hours without sleep and working in the EPA lab to run samples.

Stewart Phillips barely contained his shock at the outpouring. His worries were deepened by the news of Kepler's activities.

Exiting into the lobby, Jerry continued to ramble. Stewart was envisioning the saving of face in Loretta Bonner's view. 'If I can get to Kepler and stop him, Mrs. Bonner would be very pleased, he thought. He tried to calm Jerry with peaceful soft talk about stress and friendships. He advised Jerry to go home and rest before continuing his work. Stewart offered to take him home. Jerry declined, adding that he had to get back to the EPA lab to help.

The last statement caught Stewart's ears just a shade late. Before he could inquire about this meeting, Jerry Wittner was out the front door. Stewart knew that a meeting signified some kind of big development and that he had to get to Kepler before he could bring more people into his ring of guilt. Stewart stopped with a thought, and then turned back into the building, heading for the basement storage area.

"I know just the supplies I need," Stewart smiled to him self.

Fred Donnolly walked into the small conference room just outside the Medical Examiners Office and practically fell into one of the unpadded chairs next to Jon. Rubbing his eyes with both hands, he softly moaned. Jon just sat and waited for Fred to collect himself.

Looking up Fred quietly exclaimed, "You look like shit, Kepler. Fill me in and go get some rest before you're more worthless than usual."

Jon grinned at Fred. "Don't look in any mirrors, Frankenstein. You roughly resemble some of the fish samples that we analyzed today."

Fred smiled weakly and straightened in his chair. "Jon, the best thing about our friendship is that we are always so complimentary to each other. I don't want to pass from this lighter mood to ask why you came down here again, but I will."

"I'm really wondering if I should even lay this one on you, Fred, the way you look. How long since you've slept?"

"Goddamnit! Jon. Just give me the report," Fred screeched at Jon with a wrenched mouth and frightened eyes.

“Oh shit! I’m sorry, Jon. The last 24 hours have been a living nightmare. The place is crawling with bureaucrats. The hospital Board of Trustees is convening. The mayor’s office sent over a delegation from the Health Department. Add County Health to that list and you have the sum total of my day. There must be 150 reporters down the hall. I’m up to my ass in the dead and dying and now you come to see me. I’ll bet it’s not to invite me to your wedding.”

Jon’s lips compressed as he started with his report. “Fred, I am one hundred percent convinced that this plague is the result of an environmentally induced mutagen.”

“Whoa! Back up, Jon. First, why do you call it a plague and, second, what in the hell do you define as an environmental mutagen?”

“Fred, this thing scares me. Every fish, every tissue and every blood sample we analyzed contains this mystery compound we discovered before. I call it a plague, because we saw it in none of our samples before and now it’s in every one of them. It seems to be spreading like the plague. It is a mutagen because it appears to have never existed before now and couldn’t have come from some natural biological source. So, to retrace my process for this conclusion, the substance we have found appears to be the result of a mutagenic reaction brought about by some environmental contaminant.”

“Jon, are you extending your original theory saying that the PCB’s in the sediments were consumed through the food chain by the Coho salmon…?”

“And the Steelheads we collected, too,” Jon interrupted.

“The PCB’s in the fish,” Fred continued with a nod to confirm Jon’s addition of another species, “just happened to get to the right concentration to react with the fish tissue to create a whole new chemical.”

“That’s it precisely,” Jon confirmed. “We believe that when the contaminated fish is eaten by someone, the biotoxic chelator immediately goes about its business of removing Calcium from the system.”

“With what is happening here and with the information that you have Jon, we had better organize a meeting with the Public Health people and start getting the warnings out. I’ll go call the DPH right away.”

Fred Donnolly raised his huge frame up out of the chair looking paler than when he sat down. Just then, the paging system blurted loud and clear for Dr. Donnolly to report immediately to the ER Fred spun and started toward hallway leading to the Emergency Room. Jon followed.

As the two nearly flew into the ER, they were met with what sounded like screams from across the River Styx. Jon stopped and stood with mouth gaping, watching a woman flopping around on the floor of the room, banging into examining tables while bleeding profusely from self-inflicted scratch wounds scattered about her body.

Three doctors and orderlies were trying to grab the woman and restrain her to prevent any more injury to herself. They were finally successful, allowing Fred to grab a syringe and pull up some syrupy looking liquid. Fred plunged the needle into the Subclavian vein just below the collarbone to give her instantaneous pain relief.

Fred knew that the nearly lethal dosage of heroin would only last a few minutes, but it would be time enough to secure the patient. He glanced over to see Jon's look of fear. Just as the orderly tightened the final Posey belt, the woman's eyes burst open and the horrific screams came again.

Fred moved away to let two other doctors take over. He said softly to Jon, "This is the worst stage for the pain, but the final stages are the worst to see."

Fred led Jon into an isolation room where a man lay on a bed with his head lolling back and forth. Jon still had not spoken. He became even more withdrawn watching the man drool and sputter in an effort to speak. Just as they turned to leave the room, Jon noticed the man's arms hanging over the side of the bed in an unnatural curve.

As they walked back toward the ER exit, Jon finally spoke, Good God in Heaven! Fred, that is the worst thing I've ever seen in my life. The pain must be unbelievable. But, that pathetic final stage is more than I could bear."

"Jon, it has been like this for several days now. It is becoming obvious that the number of people contracting the disease is growing steadily."

Another doctor came up to Fred and told him that he had been paged because the ambulances had just brought in seven more dead patients from other hospitals. There were also many questions about quarantine procedures.

Fred turned to Don at the exit and simply said, "Find the answer, Jon.

He grabbed Jon's shoulders. Looking at him with exhausted eyes, Fred said, "Buddy, I think we are in deep shit. Maybe we need more than just the Public Health Department. Let's start getting everybody together. You get EPA, I'll get Public Health, the folks here and I'll call the Mayor's office. Let's suggest a meeting in the Mayor's office at 3:00. Jon, don't discuss this with anyone yet, but we have reports from around the city that now list a total of 4l dead so far and it will get a lot worse before we even begin to find the answers. Now get out of here and get your people and all of your information assembled for the meeting."

WEDNESDAY 11:45 a.m.

CHAPTER 22

Jon arrived back at the EPA lab to a loud clamoring for sleep. Cindy, Jerry and Laura had done yeoman's work in cleaning and organizing the GC/MS lab. They mockingly reminded Jon that his offer of help from the other technicians had not been too realistic when they had considered the need for secrecy.

Jon headed for the door to his office and made a note to call the EPA Regional Administrator and Ely right after a quick review. He then ushered everybody to the conference room for a needed break from the lab. Jon began to fill them in on his meeting with the Medical Examiner.

"Fred concedes the probable existence of a biotoxic compound that was a reaction product of the PCB and the fish. The more I work on the idea in my own mind, the more it seems to become concrete. In sum, the fish are the carriers, like aquatic Typhoid Mary's."

The other three sat in the vinyl-covered chairs of the dingy room, with coffee cups frozen in movement. The concept of live fish carrying some mutating disease agent was just a little overwhelming. Jon continued with his summary.

"Fred wants us to get all of our information together and prepare a summary of the findings to date. He and I are going to get on the horn to begin setting up a large meeting with Public Health, EPA, the Corps of Engineers, Haltec, etc. Everybody must be informed of what we've discovered here and its connection with the increasing number of deaths. Public warnings must be issued as soon as possible."

Cindy finally asked the question that everyone preferred be left unasked. "Jon," she said, "How many deaths are there now?"

"Well, Cindy," Jon replied, "There are some that are not at County Hospital yet, so Fred isn't positive about these numbers. There is no way to know how many are at other hospitals until an alert is issued. It appears that 41 people have died as a result of the strange chelation process. The deaths continue to be agonizing.

Laura asked, "Dr. Kepler, are you sure that we have real evidence? Actually, all we have proven is that some unidentified compound is present in both the fish and human tissue samples. The study really needs to be expanded to include healthy tissue and reruns on the previous tests. We must try to find how this is transmitted? Are we all carriers right now?"

Jerry squeezed Laura's shoulders when he noticed the slow building tears start to roll down her cheeks.

Jon took charge with a show of firmness. "OK. Everybody home for some rest. That will give me time to begin compiling all of the backup data and printouts for the big meeting. It would be better if all of that was started now. I'll need a complete printout and that takes time."

"Besides, Fred wanted me to call some of the people and get confirmation for attendance at the meeting," Jon continued.

"Hold it right there, buster," Cindy interjected. "It sounds to me like you're trying to be the martyr here, sending the three of us home for R and R while you sacrifice yourself. Fill me in on this meeting," she demanded.

Just as Jon was about to tell what he knew of Fred's plan, Laura interrupted before he started.

"Just a damn minute, Jon Kepler. Let me just tell you that after what I've been through, I'm in this to the finish." She dared his refusal with a thin mouth, hard eyes and a strong nod of the head.

Cindy took up the gauntlet, "Jon, I really believe that each of us has changed the priorities in our lives and we share the common goal of solving this mystery. It's a mystery of nature not born of natural things, but one that must be solved. I think that can best be accomplished as a team," Cindy finished looking to Jerry and Laura.

They looked at each other and nodded their concurrence while Laura said, "She's right, you know."

As the four of them made their way back toward the lab, their clutching hands nearly went white with the pressure. Deep in thought for the short walk, they didn't even look at each other until they got into the lab. Then, it was as if their batteries had been charged. They began to come alive.

Walking into his office to the ringing phone, Jon walked to his desk, peered out at the brightly lit lab, took a deep breath and answered.

As Cindy watched through the streaked glass, she noticed for the first time the real difference between her life at Haltec and Jon's at EPA. The years of hearing about government waste and dollars ill spent could not be proven in these rooms. Slowly turning she saw that every dime had been sunk into the analytical instruments and none in the usual items considered necessary to make a place livable. The entire lab depressed her to the point where she wanted to bolt and seek the safety of something that reeked of familiarity. Having completed her visual tour of the room, she caught Jon talking animatedly into the receiver gesturing to an unseeing recipient.

Then Jon hung his head briefly in resignation, replaced the phone in its cradle and walked out to Cindy.

"That was Fred. One of his assistants has been calling all the area hospitals to survey them about strange illnesses and any fatalities. Well, no one had put it together until now. The private hospitals have been getting one or two patients each with no knowledge that this thing was spreading. They haven't even finished calling all of the hospitals in Cook County yet and it looks like there are over one hundred people stricken."

Cindy looked at Jon and wanted to cry. The combination of no sleep and worsening news was almost enough to shatter her.

Instead, she looked at Jon and simply said, "I'll begin getting the data sheets copied on to transparencies so you can use an overhead projector in your presentation. How else can I help you get ready for the meeting?" An inner spirit that seemed to reside deep within was beginning to show in Cindy's resolve.

"Cindy, you make the copies. Jerry, you collect all of the printouts that are in the laser printer. That will be the backup to the graphics. It will be important to avoid burying the Mayor and other non-technical with information they don't understand. Laura, could you see what you can get out of the graphics program for the geography of this thing."

As Jon dialed the phone for Dr. Engler's office, Cindy began gathering up the data sheets.

She asked Jon "How do you intend to lead into the involvement of Haltec people in this picture and what will you say of Rubin's death?"

With his hand on the mouthpiece, Jon replied, "Personally, I would want to keep it simple and just go directly to the discussion of the probable cause of the deaths we are seeing. If I try to cover all of that background before I touch on the "chelator" concept, I may lose them." Rubin's death is a tragedy that someone created. When we have this thing under control, we'll do everything we can to help find Rubin's killer.

Cindy nodded an unseen agreement while Jon began leaving a message for Dr. Engler that was to the point, "Please find Dr. Engler and tell him that the Cook County Medical Examiner has ordered a meeting for 3:00 p.m. today at the Mayor's conference room regarding the Waukegan Ditch. Dr. Engler must attend. He should decide if Ely should be there also.

Jon was already listing the samples tested and the results on a large piece of white cardboard from his last continuing education lecture. Although bowed in the center, Jon thought the visual aid would help present the information. Cindy welcomed the grin spreading onto her face when she noticed that the only large felt marker Jon could find that wasn't dry, was a shocking pink.

WEDNESDAY 2:20 p.m.

CHAPTER 23

As Jon and Cindy were stuffing the final papers into file folders trying to keep some organization about them, Jerry and Laura were working with the sample-planning program in the Pentium III PC on Laura's crammed desk. This powerful desktop computer was networked into the mainframe data storage on the big Hewlett-Packard 1000.

This program was being utilized to list all of the human samples collected so far and to identify the source and type of sample and whether the sample was positive for the biotoxic chelator. This part of the program, while being very handy, was not unique. The real marvel of modern electronics was about to be unfolded.

Laura said to Jerry, "Now, Mr. Wittner, you are about to witness one of the genuine blessings brought about by machines like this in our field. Previously, some poor slob like me would have to set for days and days plotting data onto maps in order to get a pattern. Watch this!"

Jerry watched her fingers fly gracefully over the keys and then watched the screen scroll upward.

CRUN 2 MENUF PLOT

RUN GRID LOCATOR PROG

SEC: 51/0 39/15

SPREAD: 0.1

Jerry listened to the slight change in pitch from the CD-ROM drive of the computer system. The hiss from the drive was immediately assimilated into the myriad of other soft noises in the lab. The cursor disappeared and the screen pulsed momentarily.

“Holy shit!” Jerry exclaimed.

Laura smiled, leaned back with crossing her arms with authorship pride. She then began an explanation of what had appeared on the screen in vivid, full color.

“This is a really new concept, Jerry. In effect, the U.S. Geological Survey has digitized all of its maps. These are stored in the computer system and you call them up by segments or sections of any size you want. As you saw, I asked for an area at 51 degrees 0 minutes North and 89 degrees 15 minutes West. I just happen to know that is State and Madison in Chicago. Then I told the computer to give me a 0.1 degree spread on that. That means to go 10 kilometers in all four directions, because one degree of the earth’s circumference is about 100 kilometers. That has given me a map that I will use as a starter just because I know the coordinates.”

Picking up speed, Laura continued. “You will notice the red data points that correspond with the sample numbers of the sediment or fish samples that Haltec collected. You can also see the yellow data points. They all fall outside the area that we have mapped. All I have to do is increase the scale to get most of them in.”

Jerry watched with amazement. He was familiar with word processing and several spreadsheet programs for data manipulation, but he had never seen anything like this. He heard Laura continuing.

“Once we have all of the data points on the map and have the scale adjusted, we can add some points to make the locations more understandable.”

Her fingers continued to stroke the keys.

LOGIN: CITY BNDRS

LOGIN: LAKES >100 ACRES

"Watch this, Jerry. I just told the program to go get the city boundaries for this area and superimpose them and to add the outline of any lakes in the area that exceed 100 acres."

Jerry stood dumbstruck as the screen flipped to reveal blue boundary lines and the outline of Lake Michigan. He could immediately recognize Evanston, Winnetka, Zion and all the Northern suburbs. This gave a real frame of reference to data.

Laura turned toward Jerry to finish her instruction. "Of course the data mapping will be a lot more complete when we get the rest of the information from Dr. Donnolly."

Obviously, Laura had given the computer a PRINT command, because paper began spewing out of a different printer that sat in the corner. Jerry walked over to it and bent forward slightly, straining to watch it print.

"Nifty huh?" Laura nearly whispered. "If you really perk up those ears, you think you can hear the jet spraying the ink on the paper—in 4 colors yet."

"I don't remember seeing anything like that," Jerry said.

Laura rose, brushing Jerry who was still bent forward. They caught each other and locked eyes for a micro second. Laura moved to the printer making a task of watching the print out.

The large 11-inch by 17 inch paper allowed the production of a multi-colored map that was remarkable in detail and precision.

As Jon was stuffing all of the information into a battered tan briefcase with its layer of dust, Laura and Jerry simultaneously called for him to see the printout just being completed.

Jon walked to the still spraying printer, unable to hear the sound it emitted. The brilliant white paper stopped moving out of the unit just as Jon was focusing on the multi-colored image.

It was immediately obvious to the four ragged scientists that there was no distinct or strong pattern. There did appear to be four primary areas of victim concentration. North of Chicago was the Waukegan Ditch area. Right in the City was Belmont harbor; followed by the new Park District area renovated from the old South Shore Country Club and the far South side's Calumet harbor.

The computer printed map showed some additional dots not located in those areas with no apparent pattern at all. Cindy, Jon, Jerry and Laura shifted from foot to foot and assumed various thinking positions while they silently allowed their trained minds to assimilate the data.

Breaking the silence, Jon almost whispered, "I can't figure it out, folks. If the disease is contracted by eating the fish, there would be no pattern. People come from all over to catch and eat fish from the lake. They even fish up at the Ditch, where the health department had years ago posted warning signs about the hazards of eating the fish that are contaminated with PCB's. Why would the sickness be in concentrations?

We need to convince everyone at the meeting about how serious this thing is. We must figure out if it spreads only by consumption or can it be transmitted by another mechanism. We know it's not a bacteria or virus."

"Laura, did you enter the data based on home address or hospital at which each person was treated?"

"I see what you're getting at, Doctor. Where they live or where they were treated doesn't matter. We really need to find out where they caught the fish or what kind it was."

Laura continued. "Another thing, Dr. Kepler. Does everyone get the disease that eats the fish or are there some who ward off the attack by the biotoxic chelator?"

They all stood like scarecrows, letting their minds boggle with that question. Jon was the first to move. He grabbed the printout and folded it haphazardly. Stuffing it into his already bulging briefcase, he began to move toward the door. He stopped.

"Laura! Something you said. It just dawned on me that we may be seeing isomers of the same compound in the human samples versus the fish tissues. Maybe they aren't exactly the same compound. There is even a chance that the chemical in the fish is like an intermediary. Then when it gets in the body, it goes through an additional metamorphosis to become this killer compound."

"That sure is a lot of maybes, Dr. Kepler," replied Laura.

Cindy interjected. "There is also a possibility that the same compound exists in both the human and fish tissues, but that it effects the bone structure of humans in a different fashion than it affects fish. Remember that humans are warm blooded and fish are cold blooded. They regulate their body temperature by finding an environment with the right temperature."

"That sure adds a whole new dimension to the problem," Jon summarized.

"Dr. Kepler, if you don't leave soon, they will finish the meeting before you get there," Laura warned.

With all of this information and new questions whirling around in his head, Jon began to get a feeling of insecurity. He had to convince some pretty heavy hitters that the problem existed and that there must be an immediate reaction to the problem. There was little doubt that the deaths were occurring faster and faster. However, did their data prove the connection between the deaths and the strange compound?

"Cindy, why don't you come with me to the meeting? I think that two of us presenting this rather mind-ripping concept we just developed, might carry more weight to convince everyone of its probability."

Jon continued with a renewed authority, "Jerry, if you don't mind, I would like you to go to County Hospital. Get the Medical Examiner's office to re-orient the data to type of fish consumed and where the fish was caught versus the onset of symptoms. Also find out if any people in the fishing parties have eaten fish but not gotten sick. Then massage the data with the plotting program to see if there are any patterns that might make sense. We'll go make the presentation and then head back here to continue with the testing and data studies."

Cindy wasn't certain that she could bring anything to the conference that Jon didn't already have, but she wanted to help wherever and with whatever Jon needed.

Getting an affirmative nod from Jerry and Laura on their assignments, Jon continued, “Well, let’s have at it team. We’re about to shock the shit out of the world.”

As Jon and Cindy walked rather solemnly out the door, Jerry looked to Laura who turned to her keyboard and tried to ignore the growing fear. Within moments she was also trying not to notice the warm, salty tears slowly streaking her face.

SECTION FIVE

THE DITCH

After demonstrating that the salmon would spawn the following year, it was decided that the Waukegan harbor was a good site to release 100,000 of the recently hatched fresh water Coho. The fry were poured into what was colloquially known as the Waukegan Ditch. In actuality, the ditch was a primary feeder stream to Lake Michigan and had proven popular with spawning Lake Trout. The Fish & Wildlife scientists waited for the following spring and rushed backed to the Waukegan Ditch in late April hoping for the return of just 5% of their yearlings. A Coho salmon is a survivor, but the aquatic biologists were well aware that it could take years for the salmon to adapt completely to this non-saline world. A yearling Coho will average about 1 pound. To the amazement of the small band of researchers watching from the shore, their sampling nets began to bulge with salmon returning to what they believed was their spawning ground. The biologists rowed out to their nets hoping to find healthy, golden-red Coho. The first net full had them gaping in total surprise. Not only were the fish healthy, but ranged in size up to three pounds. The females were ripe with roe and fighting to release themselves from the nets to continue up the ditch. For three days the biologists continued taking samples and estimating the fish count. By the time the stragglers arrived, the research team estimated a return of 23%. Exultation abounded. The Great Lakes was saved!

WEDNESDAY 2:45 p.m.

CHAPTER 24

Riding in the elevators of the Daley Center always made Jon think of some futuristic prison. The brushed stainless steel panels with the subdued hidden lighting were the City's answer to permanent graffiti. But they emitted a coldness that defied any real definition. Actually, he had only been here twice before and both times were for traffic tickets on Lake Street.

Escaping momentarily, Jon flashed back to his first weekend after starting at the EPA. He was half lost, only knowing that the Lake was on his right and that he was going north on the Outer Drive. While rounding the graceful bend in the Drive, Jon came full view onto Oak Street Beach. Not believing his luck he made the first right turn off the Drive and immediately saw a small street heading for the beach. While the lack of traffic didn't really register, Jon did appreciate being able to gawk at the summer's entire crop of decreasingly chaste bikinis.

One particularly ample young lady in a bright yellow, chamois bikini turned to smile at Jon. As he grinned impishly in her direction, he saw her smile turn to concern and then to an eye squinting grimace. It was then that Jon's Pontiac destroyed the much smaller aluminum grill of the relatively new Chicago Police car with a heart ripping sound.

As the officer ranted at Jon about the sign saying POLICE CARS ONLY, the yellow bikini strolled by and slipped Jon a mustard stained napkin with her name and phone number. The cop got madder the more Jon smiled.

As Jon awoke in Suzanne's apartment on the morning of his court date some 23 days later, he thought the hassle and probable fine would prove to be well worth the resulting frenzied relationship. He and "Suzanne" literally burned each other out in a few short months. Everything they did was with great intensity. Even her nickname was reminiscent of the Kingston Trio song about a torrid love affair.

"Jon," came the soft word dribbling into the crack in the door of his consciousness.

He shook his head mentally, in time to hear, "C'mon Jon. this is the nineteenth floor. This is where you said the meeting was.

He quickly returned to the present stepping out of the elevator to grab Cindy's waiting hand, while ignoring the quizzical look on her face.

Hustling down the corridor in the direction provided by the signage on the soft brown marble walls of the fifth floor, the two scientists were not sure what to expect from the politicians and bureaucrats who were going to be involved in this "highest level" meeting. Jon knew that Fred would be there along with the Department of Public Health Administrator. He also was certain that Mayor Thayer would be there. A guess added the Corps of Engineer's representative along with someone from the Governor's office, State Department of Natural Resources, State and Federal EPA's and who knows how many other local, state and federal department heads.

When they arrived at the end of the hall, another sign directed them to the left. Approaching the door simply labeled "Mayor"; Jon was gratified at the absence of reporters and news people. No TV lights destroyed the subtle nuances of the veined brown marble as they usually did whenever one saw the Mayor on a news program being interviewed as he left his office.

Pushing open the door into the office what was obviously the Mayor's Administrative Assistant, Jon couldn't help but notice that the door opened inward in direct violation of City fire codes.

Approaching the desk, Jon began, "Excuse me, but I'm to see the Mayor; my name is…

Jon was cut off in mid-sentence with a curt, "First door on the left. Go in, Dr. Kepler, but your friend must wait out here".

Jon was about to protest, but shrugged his shoulders to Cindy as he watched his name being dutifully checked off from a very fancy roster with both his name and photo.

As Jon moved to his left, he wondered about his credibility with the man that sat on the other side of the soft pecan colored door. Jon stopped with his hand on the knob. Turning to Cindy, he ordered, “In here, with me, Cindy. I need you.”

The aide was stunned by Jon’s authoritarian rebuttal of her order. While she recovered, Cindy nearly pushed Jon into the room. They were then silenced by the room’s hushed appearance and the frailty of the man standing behind the opulent mahogany desk.

“Dr. Kepler, I presume. I’m Robert Thayer. Please come in. Both of you,” he said with furrowed brows toward Cindy.

“With all due respect, Mr. Mayor, Cindy is one of the people that helped me get a handle on this situation, and I believe she is necessary not only to demonstrate credibility, but to stress the seriousness of the situation.”

“That’s just fine, Dr. Kepler. My aide is overly zealous about protecting my privacy, especially in my little hideaway here.”

Jon wondered how the mayor could hide out in his own office. He answered his own question with a recalled subconscious observation of just a moment ago. Jon had noticed that the “first office to his left,” when standing at the outer office desk, didn’t even have a nameplate. At the same time, he remembered the beautifully lettered, round topped door marked MAYOR THAYER in the center of the wall behind the aide’s desk.

Looking around, with Robert Thayer’s smile following them, they all realized that they were in a very small room that really looked like a library reference area. Bookshelves from the floor to the eighteen foot ceiling gave the room a curiously out of proportion look. The desk had absolutely nothing on it except a large scratch pad and a Chicago Bear’s mug filled with pencils. The soft light came from six wall sconces.

Cindy elbowed Jon and muttered, “There’s no telephone.”

“And no guest chairs either,” the Mayor beamed. “This used to be the administrative aide’s office, but I took it over and made it off limits to everyone. I like books and I like to research my own law references. I have rarely received anyone in this room, but felt that we needed to have a few words before the formal meeting begins in the conference room."

Awkwardly, shifting from foot to foot, Jon and Cindy stood in front of the desk and watched the Mayor of the City of Chicago go through a transformation.

Robert Thayer literally sagged into the chair behind the desk, losing the composed smile and the flamboyant air. Chicago's third black mayor had set strong goals for himself. He was supported by a majority of the people—white and black. He was simply an honest man trying to do a tough job.

"All right, Dr. Kepler, let's have it—pure and simple. Don't try to make your case here. Just tell me what you believe to be the truth about this whole situation."

Jon collected his thoughts and began, "Mr. Mayor, I believe that we have a public health crisis of potentially epidemic proportions with the gravest consequences. A toxin has been found in samples of human tissue and blood taken from some of the 41 people who have died from this lethal toxin. We have…"

The Mayor interrupted "You should know, Doctor, that the number now appears to be over 200."

Jon did not restart his explanation, but stood looking slack jawed at the man overwhelmingly selected by the people of Chicago to lead the city back to greatness.

The Mayor looked back at Jon with his soft bloodhound eyes that began to show fear. "Please continue, Dr. Kepler."

We have, uh, that's Cindy Farrell here, plus Jerry Wittner and Laura Thomas, my lab assistant and myself have isolated what we believe is the culprit. We were running analyses on fish samples for the Waukegan Ditch cleanup project and one of them showed a very strange chemical unlike any I had ever seen before. We got additional samples, but that was when Cindy's assistant was electrocuted. That is how Fred Donnolly and I got involved. We went to Purdue together. Dr. Donnolly needed GC/MS runs on tissue and blood samples. While running samples for him, we found the same chemical compound.

“Excuse my second interruption here, Dr. Kepler,” the mayor said quickly while looking from Cindy to Jon. “I was told that your friend Rubin was murdered.”

Cindy stepped right up to the Mayor’s desk as the mayor backpedaled in the chair responding to the threatening glare in her eyes.

“Mr. Mayor,” Cindy started with the conviction of a Mike Wallace. Rubin Anderson saved Jerry’s life. I am going to make certain that whoever did it pays.”

The Mayor relaxed, seeing Cindy’s rationality and then answered, “Apparently, the detectives were looking over the boat in their standard accidental death investigation and found a concealed wire leading from the special generator directly to some kind of railing.”

Jon explained, “The boat is equipped with a special generator and long metal cables in the water to shock the fish in the immediate area. A railing around the prow gives the people netting the fish, something to lean against.”

Looking to Jon with an unnerving earnestness in his eyes, the Mayor asked, “Has anyone considered that the murderer was trying to kill you, Dr. Kepler? My guess is that more than enough people now know you are the key person in this investigation.”

Jon was about to speak to that statement and quash the idea, when the Mayor abruptly stood up and beckoned that they all follow him.

Moving through the reception area outside the Mayor’s office past the chilly stare of the aide, the small somber group proceeded to the formal conference room.

Jon had not known what to expect. He assumed there would ten or twelve people in this meeting. He had felt that it was important that the group be sufficiently small that the various department heads would not be performing their usual jockeying for the Mayor’s attention.

Jon followed the Mayor into a room that was screaming with activity. It seemed that the people and even the words froze. All heads turned to the door, blinking at Jon and his followers. The Mayor proceeded to the head of the table, waving Jon and Cindy to the empty chairs on his left.

The Mayor had changed back to the penultimate politician. He seemed to be sequestering the attendees by acknowledging every single person with a nod of the head.

Jon got a vague head count during the movement. He became worried about what they might accomplish with somewhere around thirty-five people trying to arrive at a consensus. Then he turned to see a distraught Fred Donnolly slip into the room from another entrance.

WEDNESDAY 3:10 p.m.

CHAPTER 25

The Mayor's opening remarks were totally unexpected by Jon and his group. His words were those of a man concerned for his fellow man and not those of the politician always keeping the back door open or making certain someone else was to blame.

The three or four minutes were filled only with silence and the soft voice of the Mayor. He let everyone in room know that the purpose of this meeting was not to determine who did what, but he reminded every one to focus on what has happened and what could be done about it.

Robert Thayer made it clear that he would moderate this closed session and that no one should speak unless he asked them to do so. He also stated that this meeting would continue until a specific course of action could be determined and that action must have as its goal the resolution of this matter.

Jon noted that there were more than a few quizzical looks from the attendees. Obviously, there were a few people here who weren't sure why they were here. As Jon scanned the room from his vantage point, he caught the obvious glare from Dr. Engler who was not used to being upstaged by anyone, especially one of the people from the lab.

The Mayor finished with, "Now may I introduce to those who don't know him, the Medical Examiner of Cook County, who will update the situation for us.

Fred rose with a death-like somberness. To Jon he appeared to have just finished the Marathon. Then, as Fred's familiarity with the subject matter lifted the veil of exhaustion, he began to recap the situation for the still unsure audience. Jon was reviewing Fred's presentation in his own mind. He had his attention re-instilled when the room burst into a babble of voices all asking disconnected questions. The sound level rose quickly until the Mayor stood and glared the noise to a halt.

Jon had caught just the essence of what Medical Examiner had been saying, and it was undoubtedly his announcement of the current body count at two hundred that had stirred everyone.

Fred continued as Jon glanced at Cindy, who was riveted on Fred. "So, it is the conclusion of the Medical Examiner's Office that an immediate nationwide alert must be issued through every possible media method to warn everybody to not eat the fish from Lake Michigan. If they have any frozen fish they must call the announced health officials for testing and disposal. This disease deals only in death and it is excruciating. The announcement must make it very clear that we are not sure of the mode of transmission of the disease and that additional safeguards may be announced later."

All hell broke loose as Fred was trying to conclude his statement about the official position of the M.E,'s office and what steps should be taken. Everybody wanted a question answered. Everybody wanted to say something. The Mayor rose and while the group did gradually quiet, it was obvious that the Mayor would have to exert all of his authority to keep them under control.

"Dr. Donnolly," the Mayor continued, using another tactic to maintain control, "May I ask you to continue with your recommendations after we have heard the chemical side of things from Dr. Kepler?"

Fred turned toward the Mayor, acknowledging his request but pre-empted Jon's report with a statement of how Dr. Kepler and the ME's office have been working together on this since it surfaced on Monday night.

As Jon rose to organize his presentation, a call for recognition came from the rear center of the room. The chrome plated voice of the USEPA Regional Administrator demanded attention and was receiving it from everyone in the room.

Dr. Russell Engler continued his call for attention, "Mr. Mayor! Mr. Mayor! Please let me speak briefly to this matter. It is very important that I be heard at this time."

The diminutive, but impeccable Dr. Engler was pushing his way to the front, even as Jon was continuing his preparations. When Engler finally was visible to those in the front of the room, the Mayor stood and brought the room to attention.

"Dr. Engler, I thought I had made myself clear in the beginning of this meeting that we couldn't have individuals interrupting anytime they wanted. That would obviate any hope of an orderly session."

When Mayor Robert Thayer saw that the audience had quieted but were hanging on Engler's about to be spoken words, he used his flanking maneuver to take the wind out of Engler's sails and maintain control of the meeting. He simply said, "Dr. Engler, with all due respect to your position I must ask that you hold your questions until I open the floor. However, while Dr. Kepler completes the preparations for his presentation, you may make a comment as the spokesman for Dr. Kepler's efforts at the EPA laboratories."

Being a fair politician himself, Dr. Engler knew he had been put in his place by a professional. Without the aid of a microphone most would have assumed that Engler would never be heard. This was a mistake that many made based solely on Engler's stature. As the muted conversations in the rear of the room became rumblings, the voice of Russell Engler boomed throughout the room for all to clearly hear.

"Mr. Mayor. With all due respects to your office and to that of the Medical Examiner, it should be made perfectly clear that the United States Environmental Protection Agency has a very, very strict policy about the public announcement of information such as this when that announcement has not been cleared with the Office of Public Affairs in Washington. Dr. Kepler has violated the precepts of his employment by not even informing…"

"Sit down, Dr. Engler!" the Mayor nearly screamed.

Engler jumped noticeably, meeting the flaring blue eyes that didn't belong with the jet-black hair and blue-black skin. The words were choked off by the Mayor's order.

"Ladies and Gentlemen. It should remain clear that it is of the utmost importance that we do not take time at this point to begin making statements of position. Everybody has a position on this matter right now, but I guarantee that when you have all the facts, you will have a different position. Dr. Engler, I apologize if you took my interruption to be an admonishment. I thought perhaps that everyone might not hear me without a raised voice."

"Score a big one for the Mayor," Cindy whispered to Jon just loud enough for Fred to hear.

The Mayor continued to scan the room, defying anyone to speak without his recognition. He then turned slightly toward Jon and nodded.

Jon stood tall, completely aware of most people's thinking about scientists. He knew that they were already losing themselves in thought, assuming that he would be the typical boring speaker and try to bury everyone with technical information. Jon knew that several years in his favorite non-academic activity would come to the fore and change a few minds. Jon Kepler was a lauded member of the Purdue University debating team that had won national recognition.

He began, "Mr. Mayor, ladies and gentlemen. I stand before you a battered and tarnished Sir Galahad."

The heads began to lift and turn his way.

"I have fought the wars of science with my fellow knights." An extended arm swing indicated Jerry and Fred.

Cindy sat there, mouth agape. Fred smiled, remembering Jon's eloquent deliveries. Jon had everyone's attention.

"We have discovered a horrible enemy and now know that we have created him. Just six short days ago, a peak on a graph gave portent of the things to come. Since that time we have come to realize that we may have found an enemy more deadly than any evil black sorcerer or any nuclear weapon, for this enemy is unseen. It is a chemical. It doesn't have a name yet; we aren't even sure of its exact chemical structure. But let me assure you that there is no doubt in our minds that the deaths accounted by Dr. Donnolly were caused by this agent."

Jon paused momentarily to let the statements sink in and to shift from the "preacher mode" into the "technical mode". He flashed the first of several chromatograms onto the screen as a mayoral assistant dutifully dimmed the room lights in accordance with a mayoral nod.

Exactly seven minutes later, Jon Kepler hesitated while the lights came up and found a smattering of understanding nods from the assembled group. He prayed that most of them at least grasped the concept. Looking toward Cindy, he was greeted with a thumbs up and a supportive two-eyed wink from her.

Realizing that his conclusion was the single most important part of the presentation, Jon began slowly.

"In summary, let me say that while my scientific armor is dented with lack of collaborative data and dirty from the need of professional concurrence, the facts are indisputable. There does exist within our immediate ecosystem a KILLER. We have no way of knowing how fast the disease will spread throughout the Great Lakes and we do not yet even have the courage to ask the question about the world's oceans. I beseech you to support the Mayor, the Medical Examiner and the Department of Public Health in their quest for answers and for control over this killer. Let me also add, that we have recently theorized that the toxin can pass up through the food chain. What this means is that any foods that use fish byproducts or fish oil in their preparation, may now contain the toxin."

Glancing around at the stunned faces, Jon tried to judge the understanding of his last statement. He was troubled by the lack of comprehending nods.

"This toxic agent can spread throughout the food chain with electronic speed. There are hundreds of common food items that use fish products. We must warn everyone as quickly as possible."

Looking across the entire audience, Jon completed his statement with, "I will take questions when the Mayor deems it appropriate."

Even before the Mayor could rise, the room erupted in a cacophony of sound from screamed questions to just barely heard whispered statements of "scientific razzmatazz". Jon couldn't believe what he was hearing. He sat; unable to understand how they could doubt or, at least, not want to know more before they made a conclusion.

Cindy strained to hear the few favorable comments that included "We must get word to the people in the City before..."

The Mayor was struggling to regain control as the voices rose in question and spewed doubt.

When Robert Thayer's hand slammed onto the table, stunned order was restored. He showed his always present abilities and issued no admonition to the group. He simply called on Fred Donnolly to please describe the biotoxic chelation process as it occurred in the patients he had seen.

Fred scanned the listeners as he told of the soul-ripping pain that must be endured by the victims. He spoke of how the administration of nearly lethal doses of Demerol and even Heroin brought no relief from the inordinate pain that only ceased with the cessation of life.

Fred noticed that the same non-believers had their heads swiveling, trying to convince their neighbors of the lack of foundation, especially about the part where the so-called toxin continues through the food chain.

Fred then whispered to the Mayor, straightened and nodded to a technician. The same young man that assisted Jon, took a videocassette from the Medical Examiner, snapped it into the VCR, made two checks on speed and volume, and then, without introduction or warning, projected the picture onto the special screen that had again descended from the ceiling.

Within seconds, three people left the room, one turned pasty slumping onto a chair and one began to silently sob. When the technician decreased the volume of the ear piercing screams and thrashing, the mayor spun and exclaimed "NO!" to the startled young man, who fumbled to restore the volume to its recorded level.

Not needing to watch the screen, the sound replayed the picture of ignominious death for Fred. He had now personally witnessed eleven such deaths and it did not get easier. The initial writhing followed by screams for help. The sudden violence demanding leather restraints. By the time this victim was filmed, the doctors knew when to apply the leather cuffs to keep the victims from tearing at their own skin. Every part of their bodies moved. Heads flopped, mouths worked loudly and quite incessantly, chests heaved, hips rose and fell rhythmically, while legs and feet fought the restraints even more than the arms and hands.

Fred explained, "The process seems to take just about thirty hours. We have condensed that time period into about four minutes to show the degenerative process.

As the sequence proceeded, the powerful movements lost their rigidity without a reduction in their force. The voice of the victim did not reduce in volume, but its timbre was altered. The facial structure began to alter so much so that someone asked if this were the same victim, only to be pointed toward the unchanged nameplate in the lower left corner of the screen.

Three minutes into the sequence, the victim's widening face with its flattened forehead and sagging jaw, was truly unrecognizable. The strong arm and leg movements had become rubbery while the screams lost some of their vibrato.

Several people in the room gasped when the victim's left hand slipped out of the restraint with a blurred quickness. Some were afraid to look to see if the hand had torn off like some grizzly B horror movie. When they finally turned to the screen, it seemed somehow pathetic and sad instead of gory.

Nearly at the end of the videotape, the victim had now slipped two hands and one foot free of the bonds. It didn't matter. The arms and leg flopped about like gelatin filled tubes. It became obvious to all that the skeletal structure was gone. The pitiful flopping gradually subsided and both arms bent the wrong way to hang down off the gurney.

Finally, with his greatly enlarged "silly putty" face and grossly contorted body, the victim just ceased all movement, forever fixed in the audiences' mind like a full-sized Gumby.

Fred had meant to pay attention and alert the technician to turn off the video before the final few seconds played out to show the outrush of body fluids that had been muscularly retained in the slug-like body.

Everyone turned away too late. The technician hit the stop button with enough force to nearly tip over the small equipment table.

The Mayor slowly stood and asked the Director of the Department of Public Health to suggest an approach for the issuance of warnings to the people of Chicago and the cities surrounding the Lake.

The striking, tailored doctor stood, looking like a cast player from one of the soap operas. Sometimes called exotic, Dr. Tracey Ng had found her career blocked by her stunning good looks. She had accepted the post of Director following the fiasco with the Salmonella deaths caused by tainted milk from a grocery chains' dairy. She had been lauded as a brilliant leader in the field of public health and her credentials were impeccable. As she gathered her thoughts momentarily, she looked first to the Mayor and then to Dr. Donnolly and finally to Jon. Her silent acknowledgment of their efforts sufficed to applaud them but not to support them in any way.

Her voice crackled slightly, having forgotten to clear her throat before beginning. "Mr. Mayor, I believe that there exists a very strong case for a county-wide or even state-wide warning about eating the fish from the portion of the lake that borders on Cook County."

She held out her hand, palm forward, signaling Jon to retake his seat after Jon had risen to object to Dr. Ng's mistake.

Jon could not believe his ears and wondered how the Director of Public Health could not want or, even more, demand an immediate announcement at least around the entire Great Lakes about the dangers of eating the fish.

"How could Ng be that much of a chicken shit," Jon wondered aloud to Cindy, "Especially after her predecessor took gas for not issuing an emergency warning about the milk."

Cindy only shook her head in disbelief as Ng continued seemingly supported by the upraised arms of Mayor Thayer sternly calling for silence.

"Let me remind you that the unfortunate victim so dramatically depicted in Dr. Donnolly's tape is one of MAYBE two hundred victims. There were over three thousand hospitalized by the salmonella poisoning," Ng said, seeming to read Jon's thoughts.

"While I support the valiant efforts made so far by Dr. Kepler's analytical team and Dr. Donnolly's people at County, I fear that pandemonium would reign if we made a bolder announcement at this time. Please bear with me as I point to the missing information and call upon your good sense to resist the immediate call for declaring a war on an unknown enemy. This could be likened to the situation in Philadelphia during the first Legionnaire's outbreak when initial data from the area hospitals showed elevated numbers of deaths due to strange causes. This kind of thing takes some time to get the right data sorted from the wrong information. It appears that Dr. Donnolly has not even seen all of the death certificates from the other hospitals; he has only seen eleven victims. Dr. Kepler has only run two sets of samples and the first set showed the so-called toxin in one sample. In sum, let me again urge caution and recommend that you empower my office to direct the orderly compilation of information and data. With all of these people funneling their conclusions through me, I can promise you that I will personally be responsible for the protection of the health and well being of the people of this great city."

Continuing, Tracey Ng showed her own public speaking skills and sharpened body language that commanded attention. "We will quickly bring to bear the team, the equipment and the funds to make a sound scientific finding of the depth and extent of the problem. I am the first to warn against conservatism here. If what Dr. Kepler's initial findings show are borne out by just two or three more days of data, then we will enlarge the warning. Let me summarize by saying that the Department of Public Health knows its job. We praise both Dr. Kepler and Dr. Donnolly. However, all we know is that UP TO 200 people may have died from eating the fish from Waukegan Harbor and the Chicago area. There is absolutely no data that points to an epidemic spreading around the lake, nor is there a shred of data about the food chain theory. We will get the answers, Mr. Mayor. I will personally work with your public relations people following this meeting to draft the warning and the plan of attack.

The gray-suited new champion slowly sat to nearly thundering applause and calls of "Damn right" and "That's the answer."

The Mayor rose to quiet the group and then asked Ralph Holcum, the Public Affairs Liaison Officer for the Illinois Department of Water Resources to provide any additional information his group might have.

Ralph Holcum's statement was blunt. "I support Dr. Ng's position one hundred percent and will recommend that the Office of the Department of Water Resources do the same."

And so it went for another hour.

As a chagrined group exited the conference room with the vigor of Bataan death-marchers, they were thanked for their efforts by the Mayor and several others.

Jon only thoughts were of Dr. Ng's statement warning of the danger of a premature announcement and possible panic.

Cindy reached for Jon's arm, roughly spinning him around into the Mayor.

"Look here, Jon Kepler. Don't even think that crap about maybe he's right. You know that he's wrong. You know what is causing those deaths. You know what must be done to warn the people. Where the fuck is your nerve? If you won't stand up to the political meanderings and retreating that went on in there, I will. I'll talk to the Tribune and the Times myself."

Turning away from Jon, Cindy spun into the grip of the bewildered giant, Fred Donnolly. He nearly picked her up off the floor while softly lecturing her on what we believe to be true and what is true.

"Cindy, sometimes we are absolutely positive that we are right about something. We argue for hours about our information and our approach to the situation. When the dust clears, we find that our theory did have some holes. While I still believe that J.C. is right, there is a chance that we could cause a great deal of harm with a premature public warning that goes beyond DON'T EAT THE FISH."

The Mayor concurred with, "Ms. Farrell, Dr. Donnolly is giving sage advice there."

Cindy and Jon turned to see that Mayor Thayer had caught up with them again. His usual group was not in tow.

Thayer continued, "While there are some slippery politicians back in that room, there were a lot of knowledgeable people. The assistant Director of the Illinois Department of Public Safety supported Dr. Kepler but warned of an early advisement to the public. He handled the Tylenol poisonings and argued for quick warnings. Add to that, the fact that Chief of Police wanted at least 24 hours to gird his men for the foreseeable mass exodus from the city. Let's all take a few hours to search our minds and distill the information further. I will be contacting all of you as this thing develops. I want to offer my most heartfelt thanks, Dr. Kepler, for your astounding capabilities in the discovery of this threat to our people. Please call me as soon as you have more information."

With that, Cindy, Fred and Jon were summarily dismissed by a quick turn into his office. He had discharged them with a tight lipped nod.

As they moved sullenly down the corridor, Fred said, "Jon, do you have that strange mixed emotion that you hate feeling good about the job you did?"

Jon turned a morose face to Fred and only spoke with his eyes, saying, "I've got a very bad feeling."

WEDNESDAY 2:20 p.m.

CHAPTER 26

Laura was continuing her preparations for a third rerun of the fish and tissue samples using a different chromatography column. This technique was often applied to analytical methods when absolute confirmation of chemical composition was needed. This would also give them additional data by which to pinpoint the chemical structure of Dr. Kepler's biotoxic chelator.

For some unknown reason, Laura just realized that she had been humming the Battle Hymn of the Republic. That is weird, she said to herself. I don't even know the words. With a smile she continued her work just then noticing a sludge sample on the counter that wasn't there before lunch. Since it was in a standard EPA one liter bottle and had a regular EPA label, she assigned it a number and would add it to the run she was doing next. This would maybe save her some time. She ignored the usual notation FOR DR. JON KEPLER. Many of their samples were marked for Dr. Kepler to prevent delivery to the wrong lab.

Setting up the delicate glass extraction devices was always the part Laura detested. She knew that they were always being broken but there was just something spine shattering about the sound of an extractor bursting on the floor. It always took her several minutes to get over that happening.

As she concentrated very hard on tipping the 30 inch glass tube toward her for filling with the extraction solvent, she elbowed the new sludge sample off the counter. She knew what had happened and in the split second before the heavy walled glass jar hit the floor, her only thoughts were about all the time it would take to clean up the mess with the glass mixed in with the sludge.

She was certainly not thinking about the impact of the exploding glass as it ripped into her legs and traced a staccato pattern up her torso. She had not even begun to register pain as a large piece of the exploding jar struck the glass reactor like a bullet causing it to spew it contents into the air and Laura's eyes. The explosive force lifted her off the ground and tore at her clothes.

As the pain began to register, Laura could not grasp the concept of such a chain of events. She was lying on the floor, having been pushed up against the wall by the explosion. Her last thoughts before succumbing to the enveloping darkness were that the cleanup job would be terrible.

As Laura had struck the wall and collapsed onto the floor, Stewart Phillips was nervously spinning an elegantly fluted martini glass between his thumb and finger.

This was his third. He had felt the need overwhelm him right after he had prepared the miniature explosive device in the old EPA sample jar he retrieved from the Haltec storage area. Making the device was easy with the little prepackaged units that field seismologists used for underground wave soundings. He even figured out how to rig the flip switch upside down for it to explode as the lid was removed from the jar. He would get Kepler this time.

Phillips looked up to signal the bartender in the elegant "back room" of the Wrigley Building bar. This was his favorite place to hang out. He got to see a lot of famous people. He felt like he was part of the action. The bartender surreptitiously observed Stewart Phillips and decided that this one was the limit for this guy.

Stewart continued to mumble as the bartender moved to grab another flute from the overhead brass rack that contained a sparkling array of glassware.

"I'll show that bitch," Stewart mumbled. "She probably thinks I can't play in her league. But damn it, this will prove that I'm as good at it as any of her other division men. I'll bet when I call her to tell her about my latest scare tactic, she'll change her tone. That little tiny bomb will scare the shit out of them. I hope it blows that asshole Kepler's hand off. That'll sure make 'em wonder who's got their number."

Stewart called the bartender once more and as the white suited black man strolled along the wood slatted floor toward him, Stewart was trying to get his tongue to obey the command to say, "One more martini, please."

As the bartender was assisting Mr. Stewart Phillips into a taxi, with the help of the Wrigley doorman, he couldn't help but catch some of the delirium of the drunken executive.

"The bomb showed those fuckers, I bet," seemed to come out clearly to him as he stowed Phillips in the cab and directed the driver to the address shown on the driver's license from the eel skin wallet. The bartender stood on Michigan Avenue for a moment noting the bright afternoon sun and the warming air that signaled an early summer for Chicago. He looked around at the flowing traffic, caught the smell from the River, and noted the hurrying pedestrians. With a broad smile, he silently and proudly professed his love of Chicago—the city that works.

Hurrying back into the bar, he thought about calling the police to see if they were interested in the ramblings of a drunk. He debated whether the information could be of any use. He vacillated back and forth while he mixed a beer and tomato juice for the TV show host ambling through the door. Serving the strange colored fluid, the bartender had vacillated too long. As several more customers hurried in, the words of Stewart Phillips sounded less and less threatening.

WEDNESDAY 4:30 p.m.

CHAPTER 27

Fred had left the group saying only that he must get back to his office and see what the situation was. He promised to call Jon that evening.

Jon and Cindy were feeling the emotional and physical letdown that felt like they were on the losing team at the Super Bowl. They rode silently down in the cold elevator, which seemed to dump them onto street level at the Daley Center. The rushing crowds and the flapping pigeons on the plaza overloaded their senses.

Cindy suggested they consider a few hours of shut-eye before reconvening for a planning session.

Jon concurred with a nod of the head.

They stood on the edge of the plaza, not sure what to do next. Not sure of their defeat. Not sure of their conclusions.

Cindy was the first to speak. "Jon, take me home and hold me please. I feel like I've been beaten with a soft bat. I'm shot. I need you to hold me and hide me from what's out there."

Jon looked into Cindy's soft, drooping eyes and offered a weak smile.

"Cindy, I don't know where we stand or what we should do next. I'm convinced that all of these people are in danger from this biochemical menace and I am helpless to do anything. Honestly, my first reaction was to go the press and tell them everything I know. But I kinda go along with the thinking back there that maybe we don't have all the facts. Maybe we aren't drawing the right conclusions from the data we do have."

She just tugged at his hand, moving him toward a slowing taxi. Almost whimpering, she showed her loss of resolve.

"C'mon, Jon. We gave it everything we had and it wasn't enough, but I know you're right. We need to get the information and proof that everybody wants. It's really all there. It just needs to be put together. Please! Can't we rest and go back to it with some fresh brain cells."

Pushing him into the familiar green checker cab, she gave the nattily dressed Jamaican her address, assuring Jon that they would pick up his car at the lab later.

As the cab slid into the overly busy late afternoon traffic, Jon and Cindy could not help but notice the activity. They felt like part of a slow moving parade going north on Clark Street. Crossing Lake Street and then the rattling steel floor of the bridge over the Chicago River, neither of them had said a word.

The commercial buildings of the near north side did not invoke any reaction from the pair. As the cab finally jumped to a halt in front of Cindy's townhouse, the tug on Jon's arm only resulted in a perfunctory statement.

"Cindy, I've got to go back to the lab before I can get any rest. I have to review the data quickly and see if there could be a mistake. I'll be back here as soon as I can."

Waving the driver on with a flip of the wrist, Jon closed the door behind a somewhat stunned Cindy Farrell. Jon gave the address for the EPA lab to the driver without a glance back at a shuffling figure on her way up the steps, key in hand.

As the silent cab jockey threaded his way down Clark and whipped onto Wacker Drive, he finally acknowledged Jon's presence with eyes and nose in the mirror. He held up the green edition of today's Sun-Times and simply lowered his eyes and the paper in accordance with Jon's hand wave and shaking head.

Jon's mind was picking up speed as the taxi hung a hard left onto Washington to head east for the right turn onto Dearborn just two blocks north of the EPA offices.

Jon began to let the automatic drive slip into place and allow his trained reactions to assimilate the problems and devise the list of things to do that would solve them.

As the cab came to a jolting stop, Jon was almost back up to full speed. He threw a ten at the white-palmed, black hand and said a quick thanks to a politely lilted wish for a good day.

Jon failed to note the ambulance and police cars in the parking lot to his left as he entered the unattractive gray marble building through the stained brass double doors.

As he boarded the elevator to proceed to his lab, several policemen got in with him. They all followed the time honored tradition of not looking at anyone else, but carefully scrutinized the sequential display of floor numbers.

Jon had finally noticed the checkered hat bands on the three blue suited patrolmen when they stepped out of the elevator on Jon's floor. There had been an interesting array of people delivering samples over the years, and while that had included farmers and uniformed army personnel, it had never been a group of policemen. As Jon followed them toward the lab, he even noted that one of the men was a woman and her hat had the gold and blue-checkered band of a watch commander.

Jon's curiosity reached such a level that his mind had stopped listing the things to do and began to tune into his immediate surroundings.

He heard the commander say, "Get the officer that was first on the scene and bring the person that found the victim."

Jon wanted to ask what was going on as the police commander entered the door into the general lab section where Jon was headed.

She continued her commands with, "Get the evidence people up here right away and get these other lab people back to their jobs."

Jon was right behind the wave of blue serge, as they waded into the clot of lab people, all looking official in their typically spattered, white lab coats. He still had not gotten any clue as to what was going on, until he heard the voice that had been the first to interrupt that morning's conference.

"Get all of these people out of the waiting area," came the dulcet tones of Dr. Engler's command to Wayne Ely. "Let's turn this over to the police and let them figure out what happened."

Looking past the police who were gently prodding people to move along, Engler spied Jon and announced loudly "Well! If it isn't the missing crusader. Kepler, be in my office in 60 seconds."

Engler then pushed past the police and the white lab coats and nearly removed the door from its hinges while everyone fixed their eyes on the speeding back as it turned the corner toward the office section.

Jon was not at all pleased when all of the eyes that had recorded Engler's departure slowly rotated toward him. He was still standing there looking at the doorway, when a voice called for his attention.

"Dr. Kepler, I am Captain Lewis of the lst. Precinct. I have assumed command of the investigation of the apparent bombing of your laboratory. I will want your whereabouts and some other information when I begin interrogating…"

Jon pushed past the thin shouldered policewoman for some reason noting the silken blonde hair flowing from under the police cap. He cut her off in mid-sentence with the final awareness of the commander's statements.

The only thing Commander Terri Lewis heard as the scientist pushed past her was a softly whispered, "Oh, please God, not Laura."

She followed Jon Kepler into the lab waving back the patrolmen who were coming to her assistance.

Jon noted with fear the black ooze mixed with glass that seemed to be everywhere. The once gleaming stainless steel counters were leopard-looking with dark spots scattered about. As Jon approached the aisle that was flanked by opposing rows of benches he looked down at the spotted pattern that had been accented with red splotches. It appeared surrealistic to Jon as he spun to head back out of the building.

Again he tried to push past the policewoman who had been caught unprepared for Jon's retreat.

"Hold it right there, Dr. Kepler. I need to talk to you and we'll do it here and now."

Jon looked at the round face and demanded, "Where is Laura? What happened here? Where did they take her?"

Leading him into his own office, Terri Lewis had already categorized Jon Kepler. Twenty-two years with the Chicago Police had given her an education equivalent to degrees in Psychology and Political Science. She had learned how to handle people. She read Jon's face and found concern, worry, bewilderment and the look that a brother gets about a younger sister in trouble.

She began answering his questions, "Dr. Kepler, Miss Thomas is not dead. She is badly hurt. She has been taken to Presbyterian St. Luke's over on Harrison. They hope to be able to give me an assessment of her condition within the hour. Now what else do you want to know?"

Jon finally focused on the caring face and was still having difficulty with its adornment. The police trappings did not fit her soft features and voice.

Looking deeper into the nearly colorless eyes, Jon finally responded "Captain, was it?"

Her shake of the head prompted Jon's continued questions as he noted his once familiar, cramped office.

"What happened, Captain? That scene over by the prep station looks like a grenade went off.

"A rather astute comparison, Dr. Kepler. Laura Thomas was apparently working in that aisle when an explosive device was detonated. We can't quite figure why her legs were so badly riddled by glass, though. Her face was apparently showered with some kind of solvent that got into her eyes. There were also some glass fragments in her hair and mouth. She had lost a lot of blood within the few minutes that it took for someone in the lab to track down the muffled explosion. It must have been a very special device, Dr. Kepler, like a glass grenade. Any thoughts?"

Jon was shaking his head NO, while he whirled with the input from the Captain. His first reaction was numbness, until a connection arose from his subconscious and a suspicion flickered.

"Captain. Three days ago, I went with three other people to collect fish samples up at the Waukegan Ditch. Only two of those other people came back alive and detectives from that district said that Rubin Anderson had been murdered. It has been suggested that the "accident" had been meant for me. Now my technician is hit with a bomb that may have had my name on it. I don't want to sound paranoid, but this may all be part of my knowledge of the strange multiple deaths around the city."

The incoming evidence technician tapped on the glass to let Lewis know he had arrived. She acknowledged with a cursory wave and dragged Jon's lone side chair closer to the desk.

Removing her police cap and taking out a mangled note pad from her uniform, she said, "How about if we take it from the top, Dr. Kepler."

WEDNESDAY 5:40 p.m.

CHAPTER 28

As Jon completed his nearly forty-minute summation of the events of the last five days, Captain Lewis slowly closed her note pad and very methodically slipped it into her inside jacket pocket. Looking directly at Jon, she spent a few seconds digesting the story.

"Dr. Kepler, it seems to me that the public should be told of the total danger right away. My immediate assessment is that there is equal danger in telling the story prematurely and telling it too late. The only real problem that I see is a risk of panic. This panic will occur whether the story goes out now or later. However, and this is the thing that seems to stop everybody, what if you are wrong and these deaths are not related to your mystery compound?"

Jon was about to defend the work done and back it up with Fred's conclusions, when the police captain gave him one more thing to think about.

"Here's one fact you may want to throw into the calculations you've used, Doctor. Combining all the murders, suicides and natural deaths, nearly 270 people die every day in Cook County. How many of your 200 deaths might have mistakenly included some of those?"

Jon tried to assimilate those numbers into what appeared to be a rising number of deaths relating to the toxin, but failed when he admitted to himself that there were too many factors involved and he was too tired.

"Captain Lewis, I appreciate the fact that you have spent this time listening to the whole story. It seems that we do have some things to do before we can be certain that this compound is really some kind of biotoxic agent."

Locking his eyes on hers as he rose from the creaking office chair, he continued. "Captain, you have got to find out what happened here and at the Ditch. Are these two incidents related? Is someone really out to prevent further development of my concept or is there something else that someone is hiding? Please let me know if you find anything. I'll be here."

"I would suggest that you get some sleep, Doctor." This isn't the movies, you know. You are a real person and real people have to sleep." She smiled at him, arranged her cap on her head looking up at the underside of the bill.

"Always hated these things!" She turned to check on the other officers and any information they had gotten from the rest of the possible witnesses.

Jon walked out into the lab to see that the maintenance people had already begun to clean up the area following the thorough scanning by the evidence technician.

He stood there not sure what to do next. Slowly looking around the lab, he gradually remembered his list of things to do. The most important thing right now was obviously an in-depth review of the data to see if there were any analytical errors. Then he would have to make a list of the added technical data that was needed to both identify the mysterious compound and to better establish its origin. Somewhere on the list had to be a visit to Laura at the hospital.

Shrugging his shoulders at the exhaustion, Jon padded back into his office wondering how to ignite the computer's mind with probing commands for information. He knew that his GC/MS probably wasn't as tired as he was.

* *

As Jon slid his chair up to the terminal, Loretta Bonner was placing her ivory handset back onto the cradle.

Her expression was pensive. She wasn't sure what was happening with this whole Waukegan Ditch situation. She had talked to Blake Thompson at

Nautical Marine every day since the first call from that ninny Stewart Phillips. Blake had certainly been aware of the Army Corps of Engineers most recent study plans but was not aware of any difficulties or special attention to the study.

Loretta had kept Thompson updated. First she told him of the unfortunate death of Rubin Anderson, calling it an accident that would not have taken place if those other two hadn't been illegally out doing some additional sampling near the Nautical Marine plant site.

She also called Thompson the next day to tell him of Joan Blacker's seemingly unrelated accident. She had reiterated that the near-death of one of Haltec's upper management people had certainly had a negative impact on the morale and productivity at Haltec.

"It seems that her action had been brought on by the death of her only relative, a grandfather who, strangely enough, no one knew about," she had told Thompson.

Thompson had promised to do some checking through some contacts at the Kenilworth PD, knowing that there was probably little that the Chicago cops would tell any suburban police. That long forgotten knot had returned to Thompson's stomach. He had hoped that it was gone forever, but was beginning to realize that he had only suppressed it for these many years.

Blake Thompson's mind slipped back through the maze of daily decisions, trips, political dinners, show openings and the other crap he endured as a well known executive and found himself sitting in the same tile floored office on the third floor of the Nautical Marine offices in Waukegan, Illinois.

He did not want to relive those weeks and months but it was as if his mind was a projector and once the film had been loaded and started there was no retreating. The once familiar awards and plaques on the walls faded from his eyes. The leather couch and small conference table seemed to melt into the background as Blake remembered the news conference his first day on the job as President of Nautical Marine.

His having taken the job as head of Nautical shocked his fellow employees at the Ohio Feed Manufacturers Association. He had been Executive Director of the somewhat remote and little known association for almost three years and had successfully defended the feed distributor who had mistakenly contaminated 80 bags of special cow feed with PBB.

At the time little was known about the fire retardant chemical that was so highly praised by its users. Certainly the feed distributor should not have stored the feed in the same area as the retardant, but nobody knew the severity of its harmful effects. When the temporary worker assigned to the mixing room added the bags of polybrominatedbiphenyl, usually called PBB, to the cattle feed, he thought it was the vitamin supplement he had been told to use. As it turned out, all of the people who suffered the headaches, skin rashes and brain dysfunction summarily settled with the manufacturer of the PBB, the feed company and the association. In retrospect, the million and a half dollars to the farmers and consumers was but a fraction of the real cost. The State of Ohio spent tens of millions over the years since that time, tracking the effects of the contaminated beef, the milk contamination and continued deterioration of the health of the victims.

Blake Thompson had been contacted at his home directly by Loretta Bonner. She had only identified herself as the President of a holding company, ATI that controlled Nautical Marine Corporation in Waukegan.

"I've heard of your ideal handling of the PBB situation in Ohio, Mr. Blake," Mrs. Bonner had begun. "It appears that one of my companies may be going to face a similar problem and will need a very strong leader to see it through the pending crisis. I am convinced that you are that man."

Blake winced as he remembered the adrenaline flow when she told him of her plans for him.

"As President, I expect you to defend the company, see to it that the long range impact is negated and, finally, to make certain that your wife's mother is well cared for at her new home in the Kenilworth Sanitarium."

Blake had been stunned at her knowledge of him and his private affairs. The fact that she knew of his mother-in-law's debilitating brain cancer convinced him that Loretta Bonner was his kind of businessperson. Her offer of an annual salary of $350,000 was, at the time, an unheard of amount. That, plus the guaranteed care for his wife's mother and some other benefits, left Blake dumbfounded. He had simply shaken his head in affirmation to the phone following her command to be in her office the following Monday to devise the operating plans for Nautical Marine.

The weeks that followed had thrust him into the public eye with the impact of a new rock singer. His honest good looks and smooth demeanor had quickly quelled the outcry against NMC as he continued to succinctly and openly defend the company based on the fact that Nautical Marine stopped the use of PCB's in their manufacturing process the day that the EPA ordered it to be done. Their plea of "no solid technical information from the environmental community or the manufacturer until then" made it appear that NMC was totally innocent of any malice and forethought in its use of the suspected carcinogen.

For months he had appeared in front of the cameras, testified at EPA hearing and talked on every show and in front of every group that would have him.

Blake Thompson succeeded where all of Hooker Chemical had failed. Nautical Marine would not take the rap for the Waukegan Ditch like Hooker took the rap for Love's Canal. That was purely a marketing error by Hooker. They had utilized the very latest scientific methods to dispose of the chemicals from their plant in New York. They had sealed the waste canal with many feet of impenetrable clay and deeded the huge expanse of grassland to the City for use as a park. Hooker had made it clear to the city that the canal must remain untouched. They even itemized the materials that had been dumped. The EPA knew of the methods used and had approved. A few years later, the City violated the deed restriction on the park land and, against the written warnings of the legal department at Hooker, decided to trench through Love's Canal for some sewer lines to a new housing development. The city wanted the added tax revenue. They wanted the money to build a new grade school which they promptly located on top of the Canal.

"No, sirree!" Blake Thompson had said to his wife when they moved into their new home on the Lake in the richest suburb of Chicago. "There is no way, Hon, that I'll let the company get blamed for this. Nautical Marine may have caused a disaster, but there was no malicious intent. They didn't do it to save big disposal bucks. The company just didn't know any better. Before I'm done, I'll have the public supporting us in our quest to get the environmental ball rolling."

The entire activity surrounding the PCB's in Waukegan harbor never really ended. About two years after starting at NMC, the headlines stopped and some normalcy returned to the Thompsons' lives—for a little while. Within a year, Blake's mother-in-law had mercifully passed away having bravely fought the painful brain cancer that reduced her to a vegetable. It was only two months later that Gloria Thompson's internist diagnosed her with the initial stages of the same untreatable disease.

Sitting up to see his secretary's outstretched hand holding a pink message slip, Blake noticed her quizzical expression. It quickly brought Blake Thompson back to the present.

"Thank you, Rita. Please hold my calls when Dr. Lundberg is here. I'll need some time with him to review his research progress." Blake grimaced at the prospect of seeing the aging scientist again.

What had it been, he wondered. Let's see. We moved him to the Seattle laboratory and then to the research station in Alberta. I haven't talked to him in over six years. Let's hope that he's is still thrilled with his work and has forgotten about his earlier work here.

His continuing thoughts were almost prayers. His hope was to pull off one more coup, take the big raise promised by Mrs. Bonner and retire. His wife's cancer seemed to be progressing even more rapidly than her mother's had. He was feeling tired of it all.

SECTION SIX

THE CHEMISTRY

Over the next 8 years the research team continued its work, annually releasing some 4 million salmon fry and counting the returning adult Cohoes. The areas selected for deposition of the salmon fry ranged from Duluth Minnesota to Detroit and on to Cleveland. The rapidly rising population of Cohoes began to sharply reduce the count of Lamprey eels and the return of the perch was being heralded. The mixed stirrings within the ripening body of this thirty-four pound salmon, rarely confused her, but simply caused her to wonder about their origin. She had previously been able to shed these problems and this year was different. The strange sensations began to ebb and the Coho continued her trek toward the grounds. As she moved upstream, she again began to search for food. Her sack of roe created a demand on her body, that, coupled with the swim from deep water, caused her needs to nearly triple. Her rapidly changing body was nearly ready to release its 300,000 eggs in the safety of a nest she would create in the stream bed with her powerful tail. She began to notice more and more of her fellow species in the stream, knowing she would become one among the millions. She continued to devour any suitable food that was within reach in the stream. Mayflies, benthic larvae, worms wiggling up out of the gooey sediment. But mostly she ate the small crustaceans. These were her favorite and she knew that the high protein would give her fry the extra strength to survive the hatching process.

WEDNESDAY 7:30 p.m.

CHAPTER 29

Jon had completed extensive study of all of the raw data and the chromatograms from every analytical run they had made with the GC/MS. Reviewing each computer library search and compound identification had taken plenty of time and many ignored phone calls.

When he happened to glance at the wall for inspiration, he was shocked to find the time to be after 7:30. It took him more than just a moment to remember that it was still Wednesday and that just four hours ago, he was in the mayor's conference room giving his report.

Just then, Jon remembered Engler's stern notice to "Be in my office in 60 seconds." 'How long ago was that,' Jon wondered to himself.

Grabbing the files filled with his chromatograms and materials from the conference at the Mayor's office, Jon scurried to Engler's office. He hoped that Engler would be working late to avoid a confrontation tomorrow about ignoring Engler's orders.

Having practically run the entire length of the building, Jon arrived somewhat breathless and disheveled in front of Dr. Russell Engler's door with the gold highlighted, Ph.D. after the name.

Jon knocked and opened the door. He pulled up stunned to see Wayne Ely sitting in Engler's chair. Ely slowly raised his eyes to meet Jon's open mouthed stare. Jon could only think his description of Ely's expression as a "shit-eating grin".

"Well, well, well. If it isn't Dr. Jon Kepler back from the Holy Wars. Please! Sit down Dr. Kepler.

"Come on, Wayne. Knock it off. You know I'm here to see Engler. He told me to see him when I came in. Is he around?" Jon queried.

Indulging his position of power, Wayne Ely continued. "Dr. Engler was mighty pissed off, Jon. He was ready to can your ass on the spot for representing the Agency in an unapproved meeting. He has every right to do that, even with that bullshit Civil Service Act to contend with."

"Look, Wayne. I didn't come hear to listen to your crap. Is Engler here or not?" Jon asked vehemently, still on his feet.

"Well, Mr. Smartass, Dr. Engler is not here, but I was asked to fill in for him and deliver this message, er, command, to you about your conduct today. Engler said that you are to be reduced two pay grades. You will take 14 days off without pay. And, you will do so immediately. No questions, no rebuttals. He thinks you are lucky, and he hopes that you file a complaint so that he can bury you." Ely grinned.

"Jesus Christ. Help us," Jon said looking up to the heavens and noticing only the drab ceiling mounted fluorescent fixture.

Jon shifted the manila folder with its technical contents so that it was in front of him and held in both hands. "I always knew that Engler was a twit, but I thought that you had some good points, Wayne. I will take time off and I'll be glad to escape the absurdities."

Wayne Ely rose to hand something to Jon. He slid coming around Engler's desk, slipping on a pink Post-It Note left on the floor. From his near sitting position, he called after Jon as the scientist was already out of the room.

"You must sign this interview acknowledgment, Kepler. Engler wants this signed tonight, STOP!"

Jon turned to let Ely know that he had heard and was delighted to see him sitting on the floor, one hand raised to massage the knob on his head where it had struck the corner of the desk. Jon gave him the finger and smiled as he walked toward the elevators with his data and his pride intact.

Jon's smile began to wane as he rounded the corner to his office to pick up his jacket. "Where does this leave me," he wondered aloud. "I've really screwed myself now. What can I get done without a lab? How can I help without my tools?"

Continuing his internal quizzing, he boarded the elevator for the ride to the first floor and home. As he turned over the cold engine in the Pontiac, the beginnings of a campaign were just forming.

Twice on the ride home, he was startled into gunning the Pontiac to life when motorists had honked behind him. "I have to pay closer attention to my driving, he vowed.

Shaking his head, expecting the now too familiar horn blaring behind him, Jon saw that he again faced the wall that marked his stall in the apartment building. Groaning in disbelief and thanking St. Christopher, he remembered to change that to Mr. Christopher, mimicking the old joke popular since the Catholic Church had officially delisted him as a saint.

Jon nearly fell over Cindy as he bowled into her at the doorway to his apartment.

Cindy was trying to swallow her expletive when she recognized Jon.

"Well I see that you still walk like you're looking for quarters, Jon.

Continuing with one hand on her hip, she grinned with sparkling lust in her green eyes. "Jon, open the door or give me the keys.

Taking the keys from the outstretched hand and babbling on, Cindy said, "Hey Jon, you look like shit, if you don't mind some honest criticism."

Reaching around Jon to close the door, Cindy encircled his waist with her arms and leaned back to look up into eyes that were nearly void of the normal color. Cindy knew instantly that something else had been piled on top of the whole mess. She didn't ask. She only reached up to bend his head to her shoulder where it slowly began to dampen her blouse. She began to feel the exhaustion, hate, fear and other emotions that poured from Jon's soul.

"Let go of your coat, Jon."

She threw his coat to the wobbly wood chair near the door and led him down the hall to the bedroom. Slowly undressing him to his awful purple boxer shorts, Cindy pulled back the covers and laid his head on the pillow. She pulled the covers up to his chin and rolled over the top to squeeze next to him. She held him and stroked his hair. Eventually the soft sobbing was supplanted with the whisper of sleeping sounds.

Cindy held him and continued to soothe him while she began to cry. "Please Lord, let us really know each other when this is over. I want to love Jon Kepler for the rest of my life."

THURSDAY 8:45 a.m.

CHAPTER 30

Jon opened his eyes slowly and without moving his head, he looked around the dimly lit room. Not much was registering. He didn't recognize anything and drifted easily back to sleep just barely perceiving the soft luxuriant smell of Cindy nestled against him.

Not too far downtown, Stewart Phillips flew awake with his heart pounding. With each increasingly louder series of thunderous knocks on the apartment door, he became more and more irritated. He had no idea of the time or the date. His head and stomach told him that it must not be daylight.

"No one can feel as bad as this after sunrise," he mumbled to himself.

Delicately sliding his left leg out from under the expensive flannel sheets and blankets, Stewart was dismayed to discover that he was still dressed, except that his shoes were off. The banging on the door continued causing him great pain. He fumbled for his watch to check the time.

"Christ!" he said, a little too forcibly for his bulging head. "It's 8:45. What the hell day is it?" he asked aloud, with no answer.

A voice boomed through the apartment as if the person were inside. Stewart's eyes flew open at the prospect of an intruder.

But wait, this intruder called me by name, he thought. Robbers don't do that.

The call came again even louder. "Open up, Phillips. This is the Chicago police and we want to ask you some questions."

Stewart froze wide eyed on the edge of the bed. He waited for another demand while his head pounded and his stomach rolled in agony. They'll go away, he hoped.

Wait, he thought. They probably only want to talk to me about Rubin's work and that kind of thing. They can't possibly connect me with his death. He continued this debate with himself through several more door and head poundings.

Vacillating several times, Stewart finally decided that he was safe from suspicion. He slid from the bed to a barely upright stance. He held both sides of his head as if it were sure to burst from the pressure.

"I'm coming," he belatedly replied to the demanding inquiry.

Grabbing a robe and shuffling to the door, he opened it with bravado to a surprising emptiness.

"Goddamnit!" he swore into the elongated nothingness.

"Shit!" Phillips continued to swear as he slowly closed the door, angrier at his hesitancy to answer it than at the fact that the police were already gone.

"Goddamnit, Sybil, why didn't you get the door," he screamed. I didn't hear them until it was too late."

Opening his wife's bedroom door and dreading her morning mousiness, he continued, "Why couldn't you have just…"

Stewart's eyes fixed on the empty, unwrinkled bed. The pink envelope perfectly set in the center of the Country French spread accenting the light wood of the slender four-poster. He scanned the room searching for his wife and found nothing. Everything was in its place, but no Sybil.

"Son of a bitch," he ranted. "Where the hell did that woman take off for now. Just when I need her?"

Stewart stomped across the cornflower blue carpet and snatched the note off the pillows trying his best to mess the bed. Tearing it open, he threw the envelop into the air to demonstrate his defiance. He had to read the note a second time to be certain that he understood it. Having always treated his wife like a second-class citizen, he still wasn't certain that she could have written this note.

Phillips read aloud to confirm his impressions,

> "Stewart—I have found your behavior of late to be deprecating and licentious. You have eliminated all possible hope that I could continue to live with you. I have decided to visit my parents in Vermont and will let you know if I will ever return."
>
> "The fate of your Ms. Blacker was rather sad, but not as sad or disgusting as your arrival last night in a drunken state."
>
> "Please do not try to contact me."
>
> Sybil Phillips

Stewart Phillips couldn't believe that the dolt had signed her last name to the note. As if there were more than one Sybil living here.

As Stewart walked out of Sybil's bedroom, he was wrestling very hard with his emotions. Should I be glad she's gone so I can really hustle the young stuff at the office? What about daddy's money and position? That's why I married the little dullard in the first place.

Still staring at the note, he continued into his own room and began getting dressed. As he bent over to pull on his trousers, he was dramatically reminded of his hangover when he began to wobble and the pounding in his head returned.

Grabbing the suit valet for stability, he held his forehead with one hand, massaging the temples. "Christ. I think I need a little hair of the dog this morning," he said aloud to the inside of his eyelids.

Zipping his pants, Stewart went down the hall into the plush gray and mauve living room to the bar. He bent over much slower this time to retrieve the Bloody Mary mix from the undercounter bar refrigerator. He poured a healthy slug of vodka into a tumbler with no ice and filled it to the top with the black-speckled, spicy mixture. With a sizable draught of the Bloody

Mary working its way into his system, Stewart felt that he would regain control of this whole situation soon. He would call the police from his office and give them whatever facts they needed on the Anderson death and then he would deal with his wife.

"I don't need her anymore," he declared to the air. "I've gotten this far and I can go even farther. The old dame in Tennessee will come through for me and I'll probably move into ATI corporate headquarters soon. Sybil would never have liked Tennessee, not sophisticated enough for her."

Stewart continued talking to himself while dressing and all the way to the elevator. He had been doing it so long, he failed to realize that these conversations with no one were nothing more than the way a pathological liar convinces himself that it's all true. He was smiling as he left the front door of the posh apartment building at 1000 North Lake Shore Drive. He looked out onto the green rolling surface of Lake Michigan wondering how it could look that color with the gray skies hovering at ground level.

With the always-variable April weather, Stewart pulled up the collar of his Burberry coat and noted that the wind had a real bite to it.

* *

Meanwhile, Jon and Cindy continued to lay in each other's arms not willing to break the silence that allowed them to escape the real world outside. The small movements that occurred seemed to deepen their intertwining. The tiny guttural sounds were more than just unspoken forms of "I Love You."

Finally, Jon said softly, wondering if Cindy had drifted off to sleep, "We have got to go face the rest of the world with this, Cindy. We can't hide here. Let's have something to eat, while we clear our brains and then we'll contact Fred.

No answer.

Jon moved away just far enough to look into Cindy's eyes. He couldn't move any further, she was lying on his arm and had her leg completely over his thigh.

“Cindy. I know you’re awake. I see your eye moving under there. Open those lids and talk to me.

“Jon, please hold me a little longer,” she replied to his searching. “I’m not ready to look out into that shitty world we left a few hours ago.”

Squeezing her eyes tightly and holding onto Jon even harder, Cindy was genuinely afraid.

Maybe it was a dream and this is last Saturday, she thought to herself. With a start, she whipped open her eyes and held Jon’s gaze and face in both hands.

“Jon, what day is it?”

Returning her intense look, Jon replied, “It’s no use Cindy. It’s Thursday morning and this is no dream.”

Cindy flipped her leg off Jon and rolled over to face the huge battered dresser Jon had claimed to be a Shaker antique.

“C’mon, you. Let’s get up and see what we can do,” Jon demanded with a gentlemanly softness.

Cindy did not turn to him. She only slid from the covers and walked toward the bathroom. Without turning, she said, “OK, Jon. But today had better be a hell of a lot better that the last five days have been.”

Jon silently joined in Cindy’s wish, but without much hope. He too felt the depressing sourness of the gray skies and he had not yet raised the blinds.

THURSDAY 9:20 a.m.

CHAPTER 31

Blake Thompson sat in his office this dreary Thursday morning with a gnawing concern that his past and future would soon meet and destroy the present. The meeting with the research chemist from Alberta and a bad night in his wife's battle against her cancer had combined with the grayness outside to depress him to an unusual depth.

Blake had long ago learned that the best philosophy for life was to do a good job and to pray a little just in case. He rarely let the mood around him have a negative impact and tried very hard to keep a good attitude about what happened in his life.

Today was very different. He was in the process of admitting to himself that the meeting with Dr. Lundberg had caused a great deal of concern when he was interrupted by his secretary for a call from the scientist.

The hair on the back of his neck began to tingle. Blake Thompson wasn't sure why. He lifted the receiver to hear Dr. John Lundberg's raspy old voice begin with no salutation or thread of small talk.

"Mr. Thompson, I have been thinking about our conversation yesterday and am somewhat puzzled about its conclusion."

"Please tell me how I can clarify anything for you, Dr. Lundberg," Blake answered with a tightness in his throat.

"I want to know precisely why Nautical Marine Corporation is funding this research project of mine and why the work has to be conducted at a facility in remote Canada. And, while I've got you on the phone asking questions, what has become of my old project on the potential mutagenicity of PCB's?"

Just the mention of the concept made Blake wary. Always known for thinking quickly, Thompson asked, "First, Dr. Lundberg, I thought you said that you were returning to Alberta last night. I am surprised to hear from you today. Was there some delay or any other problem?"

"No. No problems at all. I was a little tired last evening after dinner and changed my return flight to later this afternoon. As long as I was still here, I wanted to ask you these things because I always forget once I'm in my lab."

"Well doctor, NMC has a very strong interest in your continuing efforts in the biotechnology field and especially in the approach you are taking to the cleanup of oil spills with oil-eating bacteria. As you know we and our parent corporation have long been supporters of scientists working on the edge of technology and feel that it is our national duty to see that this kind of work is done. We also hope that the technology that results from these efforts can be used in a beneficial product that will improve the company's sales and profits."

This was essentially a bunch of excerpts from Blake's standard speech about the basic goodness of American corporations. He felt that it was true in principle, but it had long been known that the potential profits had better be realistic or no company could afford long-term research projects. He also knew that this was all a lie when it came to Dr. Lundberg's work.

"Well, that sounds very nice, Mr. Thompson," replied the chemist while he sat on the edge of his bed at the quaint old Michigan Inn on the Lake in downtown Waukegan.

"However, I keep wondering about the status of that work I had started. I never get any progress reports or anything. You have always promised me that the work would continue and that when anything significant appeared, I would be called in as a consultant."

Thompson's forehead began to bead as he formulated an answer for the aging scientist. Up to now Lundberg had never pressed the issue but always seemed satisfied with the verbal run-around he got from the Research Director at Nautical Marine.

"Dr. Lundberg, I will personally see to it that you get a copy of the research status report that is due from that group in about six weeks. That should give you a complete run-down of what has happened and where they are headed. Now if you would..."

Lundberg interrupted with an uncharacteristic abruptness.

"Mr. Thompson, what I am saying is that as long as I'm here why not let me sit down with the Director and his team this morning. Then I won't have wasted the day. I'm certain that it wouldn't take more than an hour of their time."

The beads of perspiration began to dampen the armpits of Thompson's shirt as he retained control of himself and continued the conversation.

With an increasing note of authority, Blake tried to dissuade the chemist's inquiring track.

"Dr. Lundberg, the staff at the research center would not be prepared to give you a report at this time and would most certainly prefer your getting a copy of their regular report.

Please, let's just handle it that way. You could use your time today to visit the LabCon show at McCormick Place. That would be very beneficial to you."

"Well, I see that I can't fool you, Mr. Thompson. I really wanted to meet those people to find out if they are diverting their research funds into other projects. I was at a real turning point in my work just before you begged my help on this Recombinant Bacteria project. They should have been able to publish some real definitive data years ago. I was worried that the project had been shelved, or worse yet, was being funded with no work being devoted to it. If you understand my concern, you can see why I'd like to visit the Research Center in Evanston and check for myself."

Blake knew there was no way he could let Dr. Lundberg into the Research Center to begin nosing around like an old ferret. Blake Thompson already knew full well that there was no progress on the PCB project because there was no PCB project.

"Sir, I will personally see that a copy of the next research report is sent to you. You have my word," Blake finished.

The little-known scientist now researching the decontamination of oil spills with bacteria had been working at Nautical Marine Corporation for more than twenty-three years, when he received permission to publish a small article in the regionally distributed Chemical Bulletin.

No one could have guessed the rush of publicity that was to come to Nautical Marine when the U.S. Environmental Protection Agency released its information about the Polychlorinated biphenyl contamination of the Waukegan Ditch. The area of the Ditch by the NMC plant became the most photographed stretch of waterway in America. Its oily black waters with the rainbow swirls would be shown to the public until everyone was overwhelmed.

Blake remembered that it was several weeks after he had been brought in by Loretta Bonner to save the company that his secretary came in to announce that a Dr. Lundberg from Research kept insisting that he had something important to discuss with Mr. Thompson, but he wouldn't say what. His secretary had become so protective of Blake's time with the publicity onslaught that she hesitated to put the research staff man in direct touch with the new company president.

In his usual effort to placate everyone who could be remotely involved in the PCB mess, Blake had agreed to meet the scientist the next day right after lunch.

Blake could for some reason remember that day as if it had just taken place last week. He could picture walking back into his secretary's area from lunch more than twenty minutes before his 1:30 meeting with Lundberg. As he rounded the corner, he saw the scientist sitting on the chair facing his secretary. She glanced at Blake, rose quickly and tried to forestall Dr. Lundberg but she failed. The bright-eyed chemist had immediately introduced himself to Blake Thompson and turned to go into Blake's private office even before he received an invitation.

Dr. Lundberg slid a copy of an article across the desk. He announced that it was to be published in the next edition of Chemical Bulletin. The article was entitled, "Theoretical Mutagens of Complex Chlorine Compounds."

Even though Blake was able to maintain his calm exterior, he knew that the material the scientist had just shown and explained to him would more than likely wipe out the tremendous strides Blake had made in his reconstruction of Nautical Marine's image.

That technical report described the kind of chemistry that could take place if the right conditions were available to the PCB's that currently lay locked in the gooey, black sediments at the bottom of the Waukegan Ditch. The report was an unexploded bomb.

The press would have a heyday with this, Blake had thought at the time.

I must get this researcher off onto another project and gain some time to figure out what to do here, he had reflected then.

Standing, Blake vowed to get back to the scientist first thing in the morning with a plan. This gave Thompson at least until the next day to think the thing through and not have to act in haste.

Blake Thompson recalled that next day with a certain sadness and shame. He knew that it was the first time in his entire career that he had found it necessary to blatantly deceive another person. Sure he had told the usual childhood and teenage lies, but that was about the worst blow Blake had ever suffered to his ethics and personal perspective.

Sure, he had been able to justify the action to himself, remembering that his wife was being consumed with her mother's battle against cancer. He knew that he could not face losing this job that provided the money that gave his mother-in-law those few remaining comforts. Those justifications all seemed rather hollow now.

Blake knew that there were other ways to handle his wife's mother and the cancer, but the way it had been done was easiest at the time. He also had full comprehension that he had sacrificed his principles for her sake, but no matter how much he pushed it under the rug, he also was aware that he could've done it differently.

He feared the possible retribution of the government and the public if they found out about the report written by Dr. Lundberg. No one in the entire company or the scientific community suspected that the research paper had been buried. The few inquiring calls that had come to Dr. Lundberg's office regarding his work, had been easily diverted with a letter ostensibly signed by Dr. Lundberg announcing that his work had contained several unbeknownst errors and the concept was being withdrawn.

Blake Thompson remembered the entire story like it was yesterday. It was his cancer. It gnawed at him with no outwardly effect. Thompson knew that he had sold his soul for an easier way in life. He could not take any comfort from the usual potpourri of excuses that many business people used for their own transgressions. He also knew it could not be rectified now.

Blake was talking out loud as if presenting a defense to an unseen jury. "If it was ever discovered that I withheld that report, they would crucify me. I hoped that Lundberg was wrong. It seemed remote that PCB could react to form a biotoxic compound. It seemed even more remote that it might somehow cause hundreds of deaths."

Blake Thompson was still presenting his case to the nonexistent court as his secretary was glancing at the paper she had bought during lunch. An article caught her eye even though it was on the bottom right hand corner of the second page. The small 12 point headline read:

DEATHS DUE TO POLLUTANTS

The first paragraph was even more interesting with its acknowledgment of the "reliable source within the mayor's office having stated that the recent mystery deaths around the city could possibly be linked to a chemical contaminant in Lake Michigan.

The secretary shrugged with the usual news appraisal adopted by people in these times. This position was confirmed with her turn of the page and statement, "Tomorrow they'll tell me that pantyhose cause breast cancer."

THURSDAY 09:55 a.m.

CHAPTER 32

As Jon and Cindy puttered around his tiny kitchen, both were somewhat absorbed in their own thoughts.

Jon had been reviewing the entire project up to date and he was mindlessly chewing toast and drinking coffee. Cindy was concentrating on the subject that had continued to plague her thoughts.

Jon found himself staring at Cindy. He was thinking about how this whole thing had begun at the same time they had met. He was not sure how he would have gotten through it without her help and affection.

Both continued their reflections. Jon looked at Cindy's tousled hair, sparkling eyes, the sensuous curve to her lips and Oh, God, those long legs.

Finally, Cindy spoke, "Jon, you have the strangest look on your face. I think it's a new one."

"Cindy, I love you." If you hadn't been here last night I am not sure what I would have done. I was so burned out I couldn't even remember to go to your house. However, I am sorry to say that we are still involved in this thing. I reviewed every bit of data and every chromatogram and found no mistakes. Everything is within all guidelines. Laura has done a hell of a job."

Cindy's smile disappeared with the mention of Laura's name. She thought of Laura and instantly became incensed at the stupidity of the situation.

Jon noted the strong mood change and he too thought of Laura. He was thankful that Captain Lewis would be diligently pursuing any information that might locate the bastard that planned that fiasco.

Jon reminded Cindy, "I really think that this police captain will do a good job of finding whoever did that to Laura. She took a great deal of time to listen to me and the whole story of the PCB's and the testing."

"Why don't we get dressed and go see Laura," Jon said.

"Maybe we should call first, Jon, to make sure that we can see her. I wonder if anyone has called her parents yet."

"Cindy, I've got another problem. I have been ordered to take two weeks off. Dr. Ng is in charge of the whole thing at this point. It sure is interesting that her team is being organized and they haven't even tried to contact me as far as I know."

"I suggest that the second call you make, Jon, is to Dr. Donnolly and fill him in on where we stand. Then we should swallow our pride and go to Ng's office to see what we can do to help them get up to speed on this thing. I really hate to think what will happen if the number of deaths continues on the progression that has started."

After his shower, Jon was toweling his hair and strolled into the living room to find Cindy glued to the TV. He didn't tune in to the voice right away because he was immediately distracted by Cindy sitting in the large overstuffed chair clad only in one of his old shirts. He smiled at her but she was looking intently at the screen and appeared to be straining to hear what was being said.

Jon reached down and adjusted the volume hearing, "It seems that the Mayor's office is not yielding to pressure from the media and steadfastly refuses to issue a statement until late this afternoon. This reporter has spoken with the Health Department and the Medical Examiner's office. The same story comes from all sides. There will be no statement until this afternoon. We will interrupt the regular programming to keep you updated on any new developments. I repeat, forty-three people were found dead this morning at the Lake Lodge at Illinois Beach State Park. More details as they become available."

Cindy turned to Jon and said, "Jon, I just realized what has been bothering me for the last few days. I have kept wondering about the data and the mapping that Laura was doing with Jerry. It has been nagging at me and it just hit me."

"The fish have your biotoxic chelator in them, but the fish couldn't all have been in the Waukegan Ditch, could they?"

Jon looked at her with a quizzical expression while lines of water were running down his neck. "Go over it for me again, Cindy. I'm not sure where your thought started."

"Remember, the four of us were looking at the plotted map trying to figure out the pattern and on what kind of data to base the next map?"

Jon nodded, struggling to get the days straight in his mind. Well," she continued "None of us were sure about the best way to look at the data. You wanted Laura to re-plot based on what the people had eaten and where they were when they got sick. Well it was bothering me about the data points being in three pretty distinct locations and not being limited to the area of the Waukegan Ditch."

The towel almost fell to the floor as Jon's hands relaxed at his sides. His face contorted with the burst of thoughts that rushed through his mind.

"Cindy!" he exclaimed. "This is incredible. You've hit on the real heart of the situation. The fish aren't becoming contaminated at the Ditch; they're being infected by each other. That's why the original three areas of concentration at South Shore, Waukegan and Belmont Harbor. Those are just convenient fishing spots. The salmon are being caught and some were being grilled by people right where they were fishing."

"My God, we've got to call Fred right away and make certain that we can convince the Health Department to issue an immediate warning about the fish throughout the Lake Michigan and, maybe, the entire Great Lakes. It's definitely too dangerous to wait any longer."

"Jon, there is something else. You really didn't finish the thought out to its final point. It would be unlikely, no impossible that everyone who has gotten sick has eaten Coho salmon."

Cindy sagged with the weight of her statement.

"I think the original contamination may have taken place in the Ditch and it may well have been caused by some reaction between the PCB's and the salmon. It may have been the result of the fish ingesting crustaceans that were contaminated by living in the bottom sediments. But, the overwhelming thought is that the disease, or whatever we should call it, is now being transmitted from fish to fish. It may take some time but there is the possibility that every fish in Lake Michigan may be a carrier soon."

Jon was trying to grasp the impact of the Cindy's prediction when the first ring of the phone made both of them jump.

Before Jon could even say hello, Jerry Wittner was speaking too fast and too loud. Jon quickly moved the phone away from his ear with a grimace.

Cindy hearing the familiar voice just hollered, "WHOA! Wittner!"

Jerry paused and restarted, "Sorry. Is that you, Cindy? Have you and Jon had the news on at all? What's going on? Has anybody talked to Laura? You didn't call me last night. Why not?"

"Whoa Wittner," Jon repeated.

"Sorry, Jon. I thought Cindy was on the line. Tell me. Where do we stand?"

"Well, Jerry, a lot has happened. It would take quite a while to try to explain it all over the phone especially Cindy's latest thoughts on the transmission of the disease. Why don't you come here? I will be making some phone calls before you get here and hope to be up to date with Fred and the Ng' group."

No coaxing was needed. Jerry just replied, "On the way, chief," and hung up.

"Jerry's on his way over now, Cindy. Let's start making notes about who is involved and what we have to do before we try to convince Dr. Ng about the warning."

Jon picked up the phone and began dialing Fred's direct line number at County Hospital.

"Dr. Donnolly's office," answered the obviously feminine voice.

"This is Jon Kepler. Is Dr. Donnolly available?"

"Oh, Dr. Kepler. He has meant to call you several times, but with everything happening, he hasn't had a chance. He told me that if you call, you should leave word where you can be reached. I'd get Dr. Donnolly for you, but very honestly, I would hate to interrupt his first sleep in several days."

"OK. Just tell Dr. Donnolly to call me at home. I will not be in my office."

Not even hanging up, Jon punched the number for the Department of Public Health.

"Is that what you used to do with your time before you met me, Jon? Sit around and memorize phone numbers," Cindy asked playfully.

Jon smiled and stuck out his tongue at her. He almost bit it when a harried male answered, "Health Department. Please hold."

Alternately clenching and relaxing his jaw muscles, Jon was apparently on hold and Cindy interrupted with a statement. "I am going over to Haltec to see what's happening. I'll be right back. Don't you and Wittner decide to desert me either."

Flinging on her brown leather bomber jacket, Cindy was out the door in a flash, leaving Jon thinking, 'Good thing I didn't want to say anything before she left.' He just smiled at her usual flit-about persona.

"Can I help you," interrupted Jon's toe-tapping, impatient wait.

"This is Dr. Jon Kepler from EPA. Is Dr. Ng available please?"

"I'm sorry, Dr. Kepler, but Dr. Ng is not taking any calls right now. She is in conference with a number of people and left orders not to be disturbed. If you can tell me the nature of your call, I'll be glad to give Dr. Ng a message."

“Just tell her that I called and it is very important that I speak with her as soon as possible. There are additional developments on the Waukegan Ditch matter.”

“No insult intended Doctor, but everybody that calls has something new about that matter. Can you give me any details?”

Jon was quickly infuriated. “Look. I’m not some reporter or stooge. I’m calling to give Dr. Ng the results of our latest study,” Jon lied.

“I’ll give her your message,” said the irritated male voice with no goodbye.

“Up yours, too!” was Jon’s answer to the treatment he had received at the hands of some harried switchboard person.

Pushing down the button to stop the shrilling of the open line signal, Jon immediately dialed the general police information number to find Captain Lewis’s phone number. He wanted to see if there was anything new in her investigation and to ask if she had been able to tie the case to Rubin Anderson’s murder.

“Chicago Police Information. If you are calling with an emergency, please dial 911. If you have an administrative question, please hold the line and an officer will be with you. Do not hang up, please. Your call will be taken in the order in which it was received.”

“Well, this is very productive so far,” Jon said to the Muzak coming from the police phone.

“This is Officer Delaney, how may I help you,” came the soft almost motherly voice.

“Officer Delaney,” Jon always found that using a person name back to them was a good start when you wanted help. “I would like to talk to Captain Lewis but I don’t remember her precinct. Could you give me her number?”

I’ll connect you to Captain Lewis’s office. Please hold.”

Again tapping to the strains of Montovani, Jon worked at being calm.

“This is Lewis,” came the loud brusque answer.

“Captain, this is Jon Kepler. Are there any new developments in the two cases?”

“Interesting that you should call at this time, Dr. Kepler. There was a development a few hours ago that we checked out. By the time an investigator went to Haltec to talk with some of the people about information and came back here to report, we had wasted some time. You should know that I have sent two detectives back to Haltec to arrest our prime suspect and bring him here for questioning.”

“You did say HIM, Captain Lewis?” Jon queried.

“Why do you ask that, Doctor? Did you have some suspicions about who was behind this?”

“Well, it just occurred to me as we spoke that the only person who might have known about the late night fish sampling and the analytical work being done at my lab was Joan Blacker. I’m sure that you know she had a serious accident a few days ago.

“Dr. Kepler…”

“Please call me Jon, Captain.”

“Ditto, Jon. My name is Terri. As I was going to say, we are satisfied that Joan Blacker did not try to commit suicide. By the way, Doctor, umm, Jon, did you know that her real name was Blackman. It seems that a few people that we talked to about her said how she was concerned that her Jewish background might hinder her career. Apparently, she tried to hide it with the name change.”

Ignoring the usual Chicago reference to heritage, Jon said, “I only thought she might be involved because Joan Blacker was Cindy’s boss and probably found out about everything that was going on. I didn’t want to infer that Rubin’s death or the explosion at the lab had anything to do with Blacker’s accident.”

“Don’t worry, Jon,” Lewis continued. “We’ll keep everybody straight here. Also, do you know where I can find Jerry Wittner? He hasn’t been back to work for a few days and wasn’t home a few minutes ago.”

Jerry is on his way to my place for a get together with Cindy Farrell and me."

"We want to check on his relationship with all of the parties involved in this matter. We would like to especially talk to him about Cindy Farrell and what he knew about your lab assistant's work on this project. We were told by several people at your lab that he had been with you and this Cindy working in the lab."

"You can't seriously suspect Jerry Wittner in this matter. Why he was…"

"Don't jump to conclusions, Dr. Kepler," Lewis said returning to her official voice. "I didn't say anything about Mr. Wittner being a suspect. We want to talk to him about Stewart Phillips. We have some fingerprints from…"

"Captain, wait a minute. I just remembered that Cindy is on her way to Haltec now and I'm sure that everybody there knows about her part in this by now. Could this guy be on the lookout? Would he hurt Cindy?"

"Easy Jon! The suspect is Stewart Phillips. He is the Vice-President of the Chicago division of Haltec. He called a little while ago to offer information and I doubt he would know we suspect him. However, to be on the safe side, I will radio the detectives and tell them to be aware of Cindy Farrell."

"I apologize, Terri, but two people associated with this project have been hurt already. I didn't want anybody else on my mind. What did you say about fingerprints?"

"We were able to lift three prints off the black plastic lid of the glass sample bottle. The lid remained intact. One of our bomb experts thinks the bottle fell to the floor and exploded instead of going off when the lid was removed. That would explain the strange pattern to your technician's injuries. How is she doing by the way?"

Jon was embarrassed that he still hadn't checked on Laura's current status.

"I'm sorry to say that I don't know. Cindy Farrell and I have turned up some additional chemical information that is really horrifying and I've been trying to get a hold of the people involved with the Health Department. But all I'm getting is the run-around. I'm leaving messages but haven't talked to anyone yet."

“I don’t know how to help you there, Jon, but the press is starting to get people scared. It’s like we were saying yesterday. Should they release a warning risking that it is premature or be very cautious and let people know right away. Even with the new deaths, this isn’t a Salmonella crisis yet with 18,000 cases, but it is starting to give me bad feelings. I’ve got to contact those detectives. Let me know if I can help.”

As soon as Jon thanked her, and hung up, the phone rang.

“J.C., its Fred. I told the girl to wake me if you called. Where the hell are you?”

“Well, Fred. Engler told me to take two weeks off without pay because I really pissed them off by going over their heads.”

“No shit, Jon,” he exclaimed.

“By the way, did you know that I called Engler yesterday and left a message for him that you had simply acted on my orders and weren’t trying to circumvent the system. He must have really been pissed at you to ignore it. If you’re worried about what to do, come over here and give my people a hand setting up this Mass Spectrometer that Hewlett Packard just delivered. They are letting us use it during the crisis. Its bad out there, buddy. We have logged another 94 deaths and our latest phone survey indicates that we are looking at another 300 or more who have the disease. I don’t know what that asshole Ng wants, but I have calls into the Mayor’s office, the Governor’s office, the Feds at HEW and everybody else I can think of. It’s time to move on this thing. Fuck the precautions. People are dying and some of their deaths might have been prevented.”

“Fred, we’ve got some additional thoughts that make this whole thing even a bigger potential disaster. Cindy and I believe that all of the fish in the Lake can become carriers and not just fish that have been in the Waukegan Ditch.”

Fred interrupted with, “God no, Jon. I had hoped that this message from the Milwaukee Medical Examiner did not mean what I thought. I’ll get back to you in a few minutes, Jon. Let me call this guy and see what’s up.”

He was gone before Jon could say anything else.

“Milwaukee,” Jon said out loud. “That’s 71 miles north of here. That’s makin’ good time for a fish.

THURSDAY 11:15 a.m.

CHAPTER 33

Jon was rustling through his papers and making notes when Jerry's pounding resounded through the small apartment.

Opening the still vibrating door, Jon looked at Jerry's Labrador face and smiled.

"C'mon in Wittner. It's about time you came to help. How about following up on some of my phone calls where I left messages. We got some other possible problems to discuss too."

"Christ, Jon," Jerry interrupted, "I do want an update, but let me at least take a whiz first. It's just cold enough out there to make me want to pee every time I go outside."

Jon couldn't help but smile at Jerry's usual down-to-earth expressions.

"Jer," Jon spoke loudly through the bathroom door. "Cindy just left for Haltec to see what's happening over there. Before she left, she laid a new theory on me about the spread of the biotoxic chelator. Cindy thinks that the only logical explanation for the appearance of the disease outside of the Waukegan Ditch is that the fish are now infecting each other. That is based on her supposition, which I support, that not all of the fish could have been in the Ditch and that the fish can't all be Cohoes anyway".

Jerry opened the bathroom door slowly. The growling of the commode was the only sound Jon heard. Jon looked to Jerry for some confirming movements of the head but found only a slack jawed expression on his face.

"Oh shit! Jon," Jerry finally replied. "The thought of this thing being able to spread like that is too frightening to grasp. My work in fisheries management and the ecosystems of large lakes tells me that intermingling of species and the ranging of the various fish throughout the Lake means that the entire fish population could be carriers within a few weeks."

That thought must have stunned him even more, because Jon noticed that Jerry had forgotten his zipper, at least for the moment.

"Jon, did you say that Cindy had gone to Haltec?"

"Yeah, Jer. She went to see what was going on."

"Well, I'll see if I can get a hold of her there and have her grab my papers. I'm sure that I have some reference materials on the migration and range of the various species that populate Lake Michigan in and around the Chicago area."

"Umm, Jerry. You had better expand that reference to include Milwaukee and who knows what else. Fred returned my call just before you came in and then interrupted it to say that he had a call from the Medical Examiner up in Milwaukee. I just hope it wasn't what I'm thinking."

Jerry slowly removed his jacket and sat in the squeaky chair by the phone. He quietly removed the handset from the cradle and punched in the number for Haltec. His whole character seemed altered. The spirit was gone. It had been replaced by fear.

Meanwhile, Cindy was almost running down Pearson Street to get to Michigan Avenue and grab a bus to the Haltec building. Normally she would have strolled down this quaint narrow avenue admiring the brick three flats and townhouses that were stacked in the four blocks that was Pearson Street. Tree lined and clean, for the near-North side, Cindy's thoughts were not on the surroundings but on her espoused theory about the transmission of the biotoxic chelator. At the same time her brain was whirling with thoughts of Jon and Laura and everything that had brought the lot of them together. She filed most of those thoughts by heading them all FOR A BETTER TIME. She concentrated on her theory as she hopped aboard one of the nearly empty, serpentine, buses put into service by the RTA.

Still struggling with the enormity of the concept, Cindy stepped off the bus and rounded the back as it sped South on Michigan toward the Chicago River. A blaring horn brought her attention to the traffic as she deftly side stepped a yellow streak emblazoned City Cab. She strolled into the Haltec building to what was normally an accepted auditory stimulus. The paging system was quietly but forcefully directing her to call the switch board.

She focused her attention to the repeating message. "Cindy Farrell, please call the operator. Cindy Farrell, call the operator please."

Cindy was always impressed with the beauty of the two story lobby of the Haltec building. It was genuinely pleasant. It had not been designed to convey the stately bank image but was broken up into small independently designed areas that almost gave a homey feel with all the plants, soft brown onyx and the wood.

She walked to the information desk and reached across to grab a phone and dial the operator. The receptionist spun around to put a glare on Cindy for touching the phone, but recognized Cindy right away and smiled.

Cindy listened to the message to call Jerry at the number she recognized as Jon's. As she dialed for an outside line and waited for Wittner to pick up, she was beginning to feel the merry-go-round effect of keeping everyone informed.

Jon's perfunctory hello sounded down, but Cindy ignored it with her best sultry voice.

"Hi! You big sexy Pollack. How would you like…"

"Cindy! I'm glad we caught you. That theory of yours knocked Jerry right off his feet. He wants to talk with you. Fred also called and is checking out something in Milwaukee. I hope it's not our biotoxin, but that would support your theory. No Coho salmon could make it to Milwaukee that quickly, could it? Hold on. Here's Jerry."

Cindy didn't get in a word after Jon's interruption and the way Jerry blurted out the instructions to get to his files and bring back everything having to do with fish life in the Great Lakes, made it clear that this would be a short conversation.

Trying to reflect on everything Jon had mentioned while remembering all the stuff that Jerry wanted, Cindy jogged over to the elevators reserved for staff people.

As she punched her floor, she turned to look into the black, black eyes of a gray suited giant. She thought the guy was King Kong.

He's got to be close to six ten, she thought. Unable to resist she turned and smiled at those unsmiling eyes, half expecting a returned grin. Nothing.

Quickly facing forward, Cindy's subconscious had registered the bulge under the left armpit of the nicely tailored beige suit.

"Christ, this is like being on an episode of Dallas," she whispered to no one.

As she stepped off on her floor, she was relieved to turn and not find the giant with the bottomless eyes behind her.

Turning quickly into her shared office, she immediately noticed that the room had been rifled. It wasn't that it was like the movies with stuff tipped over and papers strewn all over. This was a poorly done quick search for something. Nearly all of the tan desk drawers were partly open. The papers on her desk and especially Jerry's were all in one even pile.

While Cindy had no idea what somebody was looking for, her thoughts of wandering around and talking to some friends were instantly gone. She quickly went through Jerry's technical files and grabbed what she remembered he wanted. She snatched up a bag from the latest trade show and stuffed the files in the gaudy orange and green plastic that heralded some new hazardous waste treating equipment.

Cindy casually looked left and right as she left the office, having become a little paranoid. The whiteness of the general office area glared at her. She thought there was a pervading sense of emptiness in the place and quickly noted that there seemed to be only a few people in the office. Although that wasn't too unusual, it spooked her.

Nonchalantly, she walked back to the elevator and pressed the DOWN button while praying it would come quickly. She could not understand the feeling that had come over her. She felt like a thief. She looked at the back of her hands to check for dirt.

As the doors opened she squeezed through the slender opening and shouldered into the giant who had greeted her on the way up. The jostling caused the small-looking man next to the giant to look up. Cindy looked unbelieving into the panic stricken eyes of Stewart Phillips.

He practically spat out the words. “She’s the one. She took Rubin Anderson out on the boat. It’s her fault that he’s dead. That bitch killed the poor kid.”

Even in her shock at the outburst, Cindy realized that Phillips’ eyes weren’t red from crying. They were obviously irritated by booze or drugs or both. Cindy noticed the slight flinch of the giant’s forearm as he tightened his grip on Stewart Phillips. The sloppily dressed man holding Phillips’ other arm looked like a TV detective. Ashes on the tie, wrinkled tweed sport coat and stained shirt seemed part of a costume for the detective look-alike contest.

Phillips had said nothing since the squeeze of the upper arm had brought sweat beads to his forehead. The giant had not moved.

He returned Cindy’s look and simply said, “Excuse us Ma’am, but this gentleman does not know how to act in the presence of a lady. However, would you please identify yourself and tell me why Mr. Phillips would say those things?”

All of this was said with a fluidity that surprised Cindy. She said nothing, while following the man’s hand to his inside suit pocket where he deftly recovered a badge case, flipped it open, and held it steady for Cindy to read.

Looking up into those black bottomless pools, Cindy answered with a frog in her throat, “I am Cindy Farrell and I work for Haltec as an environmental biologist. Mr. Phillips was my supervisor’s boss. Her name is Joan Blacker.

What are you going to do with him?” she interjected.

“Well, Ma’am,” replied the soft spoken leviathan, “That is police business. I’m sure that you understand my refusal to answer that question and possibly violate this man’s rights. Also I must ask you to accompany us down to police district headquarters for a visit with the Captain who would probably like you to refute Mr. Phillips’ claims in person.

He turned a little and placed his huge hand around Cindy's upper arm and lightly but firmly gripped it, much like Stewart Phillips'. Cindy did not say anything but only wondered how the situation could get any worse.

Just a block away, Cindy couldn't see the print proof that had just been handed to Managing Editor of the Chicago Tribune. The gum chewing stopped as the man looked carefully across the banner headline losing out to an old habit of first checking its spelling carefully. He read aloud to the print man as if the breathless runner from the main plant four floors below had not looked at the Special Edition on his rush up here.

"EPIDEMIC POSSIBLE—FISH ARE UNSAFE TO EAT"

SECTION SEVEN

THE MATING

Suddenly she knew. She was there. The surroundings were immediately familiar. She had traveled a distance of nearly 27 miles in less than one day; knowing only the direction and the primal urge to get there baring all obstacles. The rocky area just below a shoreline was perfect. Within moments she sensed the presence of another. As she whirled to face the intruder, she knew there was no danger. The gigantic golden-red body of the male Coho salmon moved toward her nesting area. They began a ritual of darting, tail lashing and nipping that controlled their movements with no conscious effort on their parts. Together they began to swing back and forth in their mating dance finally ending in a tail-to-tail position. Combined, their lengths filled the five foot circumference of the rocky nest. They began to move their tails in long, low sweeps to clear the recently deposited silt from the rocks. As this continued, the female's body began to spasm with the peaking of her eggs. Uncontrollable muscle contractions began to eject nearly a steady stream of roe. The male immediately proceeded with the fertilization process, depositing his fertilizing stream onto the eggs as they fell into the nest. This miracle of gene-directed reaction was always the strongest urge she felt.

THURSDAY 12:15 a.m.

CHAPTER 34

Jon turned to Jerry and asked, "How long has it been since we talked to Cindy?"

Jerry tried to look at his watch while holding the receiver to his ear. He immediately felt like Lou Costello doing the old routine with the coffee. Jon smiled at Jerry's embarrassment.

"Jon, I've been having so much fun on the phone I hadn't noticed the time. Cindy should have been here thirty minutes ago even if she crawled. As long as I'm on hold for the Health Department, I'll hang up and call Haltec."

Rapping the cradle button with the handset, Jerry rapidly punched in the direct dial number for Mickey in his office. After four dutiful rings, the call was transferred to the message center.

Before the operator could even finish her little spiel, Jerry interrupted, "Helen, this is Jerry Wittner. Have you seen Cindy Farrell?"

"Hey Jerry, this place is hopping. You should be here. They just arrested Mr. Phillips and Hey! Cindy Farrell was with them."

"What in the hell are you talking about, Helen? Cindy is with what company?" he screamed into the receiver, while delivering a wilting look at its hole-ridden mouth piece.

“Back off there a bit, Jerry. I was getting to that. Two cops hauled Phillips out of here and one of then had Cindy by the arm. You couldn’t miss this guy. He looked like that wrestler Andre’ the Giant. He was…”

“Do you have any idea what precinct they were from or where they were going? Helen,” Jerry interrupted again.

“None whatsoever, but it must be local. It wouldn’t make sense to send guys from some…”

Jerry hung up and looked up to see the questions forming on Jon’s mouth.

“Hold it, Jon. I’ll tell you everything. The cops have arrested Phillips at Haltec. The main receptionist said that two of them were hauling Phillips out the door a few minutes ago and one of them, a giant of a guy, had Cindy by the arm. That’s all I know.”

Jerry flinched as Jon grabbed the phone from in front of him. He just wasn’t sure what Jon’s reaction was going to be with this latest development.

“This is starting to become a nightmare, Jerry. I’m not sure what to do next, but we’ve got to get some control and find out the status of this thing. I’m going to call Captain Lewis and get the scoop on Phillips and Cindy. Don’t worry, I’ll straighten it out. It looks like we’ll have to go into manual override on this program.”

Jerry noticed that Jon must have formulated a plan. That big spark was in his eyes. He had come alive.

“We’ve got some big problems in the Windy, Jer. Let’s see if we can’t find some answers. Why don’t you hop in the Pontiac and shoot down to Fred’s and get the latest stats. If he is around, fill him in on Cindy’s new theory. I’ll track her down and get her back here. If I can’t get Lewis, I’ll check the Clark Street precinct. If Cindy’s not there, I’ll bus it down to police headquarters and see Lewis in person.”

Jerry’s hand was on the door to the hall, as he motioned for Jon to flip him the keys for the Pontiac. A quick two fingered salute and he was gone.

Jon pondered the situation as the phone rang in Captain Lewis’s office. As he was about to hang up, he immediately recognized the strong voice of Police Captain Terri Lewis.

"Captain Lewis, I was just told that Cindy Farrell has been arrested at the Haltec building along with Stewart Phillips. What the hell is going on?"

"Hey, Jon! Easy! In the first place, I ordered Phillips' arrest based on some witness's testimony. It's a little thin right now, but he will break like a winter twig. Second, when Detective Samuelson was escorting Phillips to the car, Phillips fingered your Miss Farrell as the person who planned the whole thing. I cleared it up as soon as I saw that foursome come in the door. Samuelson did the right thing by bringing her in. He is driving her back to your place right now."

"When I asked her how goes the technical war, she gave me a quick synopsis of her theory and I don't like it at all. It is starting to sound like nothing is being done and everybody is running to nowhere. Jon, let me ask you something. Do you really think that this thing could go the way Cindy says? Could all of the fish in Lake Michigan become infected? We've got to do something."

It seemed to Jon that there was hidden crack in the Lewis rock.

"Captain. Terri. We have got a problem so massive and frightening that I am afraid to talk about it. I keep hoping it will just go away. The Mayor's team, headed by Ng from the Health Department, is going nowhere. They just keep delaying the inevitable announcement. I just sent Jerry Wittner down to Dr. Donnolly's office for the latest statistics and I kinda hope he doesn't come back."

"Jon, you must turn this thing around. You seem to be the emerging center of a team. Now use it! Do Something! I'm coming to your place to see if I can help."

She hung up before Jon could explain further. He softly replaced the phone on its cradle. He starred at it for some time.

He jumped when it rang, fumbling with the receiver and dropping it to the floor. As he bobbled it, Fred's voice coming weakly from the instrument.

Finally he got control of it in time to hear Fred, "J.C. we've got a big fuckin' problem."

THURSDAY 2:30 p.m.

CHAPTER 35

Fred had just finished telling Jon of all the new victims of the biotoxic phenomena and had given him the bad news about the outbreak in Milwaukee, when the kick to the door came simultaneously with the yell from Cindy.

"Open the damn door, Jon. This frigging bag of Wittner's crap has been all over town with me and it is getting heavy."

Jon reached over his shoulder to twist open the doorknob. He didn't remember sitting down.

Cindy burst into the room and successfully threw the bag of reprints, maps and books onto the floor in front of Jon's feet. He was obviously just finishing a phone call with someone.

As Cindy stripped off her jacket, she heard, "All right, Fred. I'll fill everybody in here. I'm sorry about all of this. Maybe I could have been more persuasive. I should have been more forceful with my presentation at the Mayor's office. I could…"

"OK, Fred. You're right. Let's see what we can do from here on out. How long before you can get out of there and meet us. That Police Captain who is handling Laura's case is on her way over too. I'm beginning to think that she and I might be on the same channel. Later, buddy. Hang in there."

Cindy was just returning from the refrigerator. A plink and a spurt preceded a man-like swig from a Diet RC. She almost sputtered trying to speak with the swallow about half way down. Jon motioned her to silence.

He stood, pinned her arms to her sides while surrounding her with himself. She molded into him with a purr.

"Cindy. It has started."

Cindy did not like that statement and pretended for a warm happy moment that it hadn't been said. She felt safe in Jon's arms. Too many things were happening and too many of them were bad.

"Hey! You two should close the door, if you're going to do that," Jerry blurted with a smile. "C'mon kids. I've got the answer to our problems right here."

Jerry moved toward the kitchen with a large white sack with a blue logo and printing that Jon couldn't make out over Cindy's turning head.

Moving out of Jon's embrace, Cindy said with a grin, "Jerry, I'd know that smell anywhere."

The warmth of Cindy's hug held Jon to the spot for a moment. Jerry and Cindy were rustling about in the kitchen emptying the sack of its little blue and white boxes. The kitchen counter began to fill with them. Jon grinned too.

He knew what Wittner was doing and he respected Jerry's ability to pull it off. He ambled into the area designated as kitchen by the change in the floor covering. Jerry Wittner and Cindy both turned to face him. Each had cheeks bulging with rivulets of grease running down onto their chins. They grinned at Jon and then at each other as they sat the plates on the tiny table chewing and "ummming" the whole time.

Jerry declared with a wave of the hand, "Eats for the king from the Castle—the White Castle that is." Stuffing what must have been his third into an already full mouth.

Jon looked down at the little hamburgers picturing the soft, clear onions on top of the square patty of meat with the holes in it. He couldn't believe he was so hungry. Jon picked up two White Castles as Cindy was passing around the fries and asking what Jon and Jerry wanted to drink. For a moment Jon retreated from the catastrophe. He knew the reprieve wouldn't last.

"Hey! Doesn't anybody want to hear about my adventure?" Cindy blurted. "I have decided to tell you guys that the detective that took me in with that toad, Phillips, had to be an NFL guard or tackle. Easily two ninety or three hundred and six nine or six ten. He was lucky that I didn't give him a shot in the family jewels for arresting me on Phillips' say-so," Cindy continued unabated.

"That weasel, Phillips, just whined and whimpered all the way to the station. First, a story about how I planned Rubin's death. Then, he changed it to Jon Kepler being the cause of all the trouble. Finally, he began blubbering about Joan Blacker and how she was undoubtedly behind all of this."

Jon broke in. "Cindy, did you hear anything about how the police came to arrest Phillips?"

Well, after sufficient apologies, when they were releasing me, the linebacker explained..."

Jerry interrupted with, "He was a guard or a tackle before." A feigned jump-back by Jerry brought a snicker from Jon.

"As I was saying before that inconsiderate interruption, the fullback (tongue out at Jerry) tells me that Joan Blacker managed to tell the police about Phillips' suspicious activities during a short recovery from her coma. Also, our Mr. Stewart Phillips got shit-faced after delivering the bomb to your lab, Jon. He was ID'd by the bartender from the Wrigley Building when the guy called in about a mumbling drunk who mentioned "getting someone with a bomb."

Little more was said as the threesome finished devouring the tiny slabs of meat and square buns. Finally, with a last swig of nearly warm Coors Light, Jerry belched so loudly that it insulted Jon's sense of manners while forcing him into uncontrolled laughter.

"That is the finest meal a guy could ask for," Jerry stated with authority. As he leaned back in the chair, reaching for his Swiss Army knife and its secreted tooth pick, he ignored the squeaking protests from the chair.

"Well, Jon, Cindy, the shit has hit the fan," Jerry said with no trace of the jolly belcher on his face.

Jon wiped his face with a paper napkin, simultaneously pushing away the last White Castle burger. His head drooped momentarily as he appeared to be gathering his thoughts. He looked up to find Cindy's inquisitive eyes and concerned face.

"Yeah, I know, Jerry. Fred called and gave me the bad news."

"Cindy, that was Fred on the phone when you came in. He has just finished his review of all of the demographic data on patients, number of deaths, total reported cases, locations, etc. Just as he was finishing that, he got a call confirming that there has been an outbreak of the biotoxin in Milwaukee. He says that it looks like we have a full blown epidemic on our hands and he is not sure how to stop it, short of an announcement to the entire Great Lakes Region."

Cindy just continued to look at Jon and Jerry alternately while absently turning the RC can around on its circle of condensation. She didn't even speak when her eyes dropped and a single tear fell onto her lap, almost unnoticed.

"Cindy, do you understand what the possible ramifications are? What does all of this portend for the Lakes?" Jon asked.

"Fuck you, Jon. I don't want to hear it. I've had enough."

Rising quickly, Cindy nearly upended the table spilling some little blue and white cardboard boxes across the floor.

Spinning toward Jon's living room, Cindy spewed, "Kepler! I have known you for six days. Those have been the six worst and six best days of my life. I cannot continue to handle this kind of emotional stress. It's tearing me apart."

Jon broke from his stunned silence, hopped up to bring Cindy into his arms where she finally broke into racking sobs.

Jerry watched as Jon soothed Cindy and seemed to soak up her vitriolic outburst. He contemplated what all of it meant. In six days, his life had also totally changed. He had been transformed from a respectable, career-minded biologist to an out-of- work environmentalist bearing the kind of load usually set aside for world crusaders. Jerry Wittner, the Clownfish, had become Jerry Wittner, the Haggard. The lack of sleep, Joan Blacker's accident, Laura's tenderness, the attempt on her life…

"Oh Christ! Jon, where do they have Laura? What is her condition? Have you talked to her?" Jerry rattled out the questions.

Jon turned, while not releasing his pressure around Cindy who had finally quieted.

"Jer, she is at the McCauley Pavilion of Michael Reese. I am a total bastard for my neglect, but I have not seen or talked to her. If you're thinking of going, hurry back. It is important that you are here for the confab with Fred and Captain Lewis."

Jerry nodded his determination and respect to Jon. He softly touched Cindy's shoulder as he stepped past her and Jon toward the door.

"Just remember that poster in your office, Cindy."

He was out the door by the time Cindy had lifted her face to respond. It was like someone had pasted the poster to the inside of her eyelids. She saw the soft green background, the bare branch, the helpless kitten with its front paws slimly holding on, back legs dangling, stripes running 70% around its middle meeting on the edge of the white furry belly—with a smile on its face. The words at the bottom in bold black letters exclaimed HANG IN THERE BABY!

Cindy looked up at Jon with reddened, puffing eyes and said, "Jon, do kittens smile?"

Jon replied simply, "I sure hope so."

As Cindy lowered her face to Jon's chest, she was startled by the too loud knock at the door. As she raised her head to turn toward the sound, Cindy gave Jon a quick kiss on the chin and said, "Thanks! Jon, I do love you very much."

Twisting the knob, Cindy was taken aback when it revealed a short blonde in jeans and a sweat shirt that was emblazoned:

P —Pride
I —Integrity
G —Guts

Pushing the door aside, the figure took several strides into the room, eyes quickly assessing the spaces and fixtures. She stuck out her hand and said, "Hi! I'm Terri Lewis. You must be Cindy. I came as soon as I could, Jon. What's the lowdown? Give me the whole story."

Cindy released the potent handshake and watched the woman complete her cataloging. Turning toward Jon in near unison with the much shorter, white headed dynamo, Cindy was somewhat dumb-struck by the black handle of a pistol protruding from the top of a holster stuck down in the lady's pants. As they both came to face Jon, he formalized the introduction.

"Cindy, this is Captain Terrianne Lewis of the Chicago Police Department. Terri, this is Cindy Farrell, the biologist at Haltec who has been involved with me on this thing."

Cindy reddened wanting to correct Jon's disregard for use of an ambiguous term like "involved".

She again stuck out her hand in that automatic reaction that follows an introduction. Cindy tried to withdraw her hand before anyone noticed and failed. The reddening deepened.

Terri Lewis smiled at Cindy, "Well, you've done a hell of a job so far as a team. I hope that I can help."

They all moved toward the sofa with Terri in the lead saying at too fast a pace, "Jon, I just heard from the Doctors at Reese and they told me that Laura will lose the sight of one eye, but that she will be otherwise unimpaired. She will be one sore, stitched up mess for a while, but she will come out all right. You probably know that we arrested Stewart Phillips for endangerment and attempted murder. That's when your gal, Cindy, got corralled by my best detective who was avoiding the loss of a possible contributor."

They slowly seated themselves as if the whole thing had been choreographed.

The vibrant policewoman continued, "Jon, there is more involved in this whole thing than Phillips running around trying to blow someone up for no reason. I think he knows more than he is letting on and will probably be willing to tell-it-all as soon as we lock him up in the holding tank. We'll put him in with the meanest looking bunch of butt-fuckers we can round up Oops. Sorry, Cindy. When he spills his guts to get out of there, we'll know a lot more. Until then, we haven't been able to tie anything else together. Rubin's murder still sits out there by itself, but I have a hunch that Mr. Stewart Phillips won't be too far out of focus in that picture."

"We also got a call from a Dr. Anna Froehlich about Joan Blackman. This Doctor reported that Blackman had said something about Phillips and a messenger and a Loretta Bonner. We aren't quite sure what it means or who this Bonner might be, but we…"

Cindy jumped in. "Captain, I assume you mean Joan Blacker from Haltec."

"Well, Cindy, we were told that Blacker or Blackman went to see her grandfather, Isaac Blackman at the urging of this Dr. Froehlich. The Doc then told Blacker about her grandfather's critical condition and when the Doc was paged, Blacker left the building. The grandfather died shortly thereafter and Dr. Froehlich has been attending the granddaughter ever since."

Jon asked, "Do we know why there is this name discrepancy, Terri?"

"No, Jon, but the interesting part is that Joan Blacker seems to be struggling to tell us more about Phillips and whoever Bonner might be."

Cindy nearly spurted the newly remembered knowledge. "A Mrs. Loretta Bonner is Chairman of the Board of the company that owns Haltec!"

Lewis said, "I'll track that down, Cindy, thanks. Could Blacker/Blackman be trying to help us pin all of this on that shithead Phillips?"

Jon leaned forward, his elbows on his knees and realized that he had just mimicked Terri Lewis's last move. Sitting up quickly he began his recital of known information to date, saving Fred's determination to last.

"…and it now stands that there are a total of 485 known dead from the biotoxic chelator and an estimated 750 cases with every one of those expected to die. There has not as yet been a single survivor."

The WAC training came out in Captain Terri Lewis with her first question.

"Has anyone studied the concept of a contaminant added to the Lake by some terrorists?" She asked in all sincerity.

Jon flinched at the obviousness of Terri's military training and her hammered-in distrust of society.

"Really, Terri, I think that the discovery of this compound in the fish tissue makes it difficult to conceive of the Russian biotechnology project that could have spawned this. It looks to be a bastardized relative of the compounds called by a group name—PCB's."

"Oh sure!" Terri replied without need. "I remember when the big scare hit town about all of the PCB's up in the Waukegan Ditch. That must be at least 10 years ago. That keeps coming up for discussion in the media whenever the Feds want to do something about it. The latest was a proposal to dredge the Ditch, wasn't it, Doc?"

Jon began to reply and then realized that the question was rhetorical. He simply nodded as the police captain continued her thought.

"That's where you came into the picture, isn't it Cindy?"

Cindy nodded, following Jon's lead.

"Then we have the analytical wizard here finding a strange new compound. He elicits the aid of two biodetectives who collectively watch their compatriot fry."

Hearing the sudden intake of air by Cindy, Terri Lewis quickly touched Cindy's wrist and apologized for reviewing the case aloud in typical police jargon.

"Go on, Terri. I would like to hear a summation of this whole thing from a police perspective. You might spare us the graphic terminology, though."

"OK, Doc. Now, as I see it, as soon as you guys start to deepen the investigation into this strange compound, people start turning up seriously hurt or dead. Not only the ones who ate the fish, but Joan Blacker, Rubin Anderson and your assistant, Laura. We nail Phillips, for blasting Laura—

OOPS! Sorry. He babbles on about how it's not his idea. Then he tries to finger Cindy as the culprit. I just don't see a common thread."

"Well, let's see," Cindy took up the case summary.

"We know that the fish contain some weird new chemical, related to PCB's. Jon calls it a biotoxic chelator because of its effect on humans."

"Jon! Shit!" Cindy Jumped up so quick again that she almost tipped over the low coffee table in front of the sofa.

"Remember the rat in my refrigerator?"

"Oh God, how could I forget those beady eyes glaring at me out of its Baggie prison." Jon chided.

"Jon, I'm talking about the fact that it may have died of the same thing. That rat was stone cold when I picked it up at Monroe harbor. I made a mental note to check the rat the next day, but everything began to happen too fast. I remember the main reason I even picked up the damn thing—it didn't look dead. The rat was still soft and pliable. It was cold but not stiff. Don't you see? Its bones were chelated. Shit! That's our proof about the food chain contamination."

Jon interrupted her with, "And do you realize that any animal that is fed with the fish or fish by-products can become infected. I'm not just talking about somebody's pet cat. I'm talking about calves that are fed fish along with the grain to increase flavor and reduce fat. I'm talking about fish waste that is ground and used in meal with cheese whey for pigs and sheep. I'm talking about a major portion of our food supply."

Spinning to look up at Cindy in particular, Jon spat the question, "Cindy, do you think that this chelator could be transferred to vegetable products if fishmeal is used in powdered form as part of a natural fertilizer program?"

"Goddamnit, Dr. Kepler." Terri injected. "Are you serious? You mean this thing could be transferred to any product that is even remotely connected with the fish from Lake Michigan?"

"That's exactly what I mean, Captain."

The shift to formal address was signaling a rise in the tension which was shattered with a loud knock to their left. Heads turning in unison, Jon called, "Yah! It's open.

Fred pushed the door wide open and brought a look of shock from his scientific comrade. The look from Jon kept Fred at the doorway.

Looking at the strange group, Fred mentally tallied Cindy sitting near Jon, who was looking at a head full of blonde hair seated opposite him.

"Can I come in, please?" Fred murmured shuffling into the room.

Dr. Fred Donnolly looked strained in his effort to reach the lone, unused chair in Jon's small living area. Six eyes tracked his movements and waited for him to plop himself into the hideous orange and brown wingback.

"Fred, this is Captain Terri Lewis, Chicago Police. She is handling the investigation of Laura's accident. Now fill us in on the status of things."

"Well, folks. Here it is. We've gotten ourselves in the center of a crisis of unbelievable magnitude. I see the early inaction of the Ng group as one of gutless perversion that is being fed on the fear that they will make a mistake by issuing a warning without the documentation called for in the regulations. The Mayor is counting on Ng to handle the whole thing on an intelligent basis. He doesn't seem to understand the geometric progression of this kind of problem. I have heard that a news bulletin is on its way to the public by tonight. I'll bet you a dime to a dollar that the warning is restricted to this area and to Coho salmon only. All these careful steps are so goddamned political," Fred adjudicated.

"Fred, before you go on, you should know that we have two additional theories that will not make you any happier. We figured that the fish were beginning to infect each other somehow and that explains the flare up in Milwaukee."

Cindy interrupted by jumping up just seconds after having sat down when Fred began his summation.

"What are you talking about Jon? What flare up in Milwaukee are you referring to?" She asked.

“Well, it’s been non-stop talking since I hung up with Fred and I haven’t had a chance to tell you. I was getting to it in my review. The Medical Examiner up there contacted Fred to discuss the concept of a possible link between several unexplainable deaths and our rash of victims here in Chicago. Fred has talked at length with him and they agree that action must be taken, NOW. We can’t wait until we are sure of every detail.”

Jon continued, “So it appears that the only way for there to be cases in Milwaukee within a few days of the first case here is if the fish are becoming infected with biotoxic chelator in a chain contact situation. It is inconceivable that a fish would have made the seventy miles to Milwaukee in that time.”

Fred broke in with, “Why have we not gotten word of cases from the South in Indiana or to the East in Michigan?”

“That could be something to do with lake currents or the travel patterns of the Coho in Lake Michigan. When Jerry gets here we’ll see if he can address that issue.”

“Jerry’s here and he can most certainly cover that point. The goddamn fish have broken their usual pattern and appear to be wandering.”

Standing in the doorway with both hands holding the jamb at shoulder height, Jerry continued to the turned heads, “All of the data seems to be pointing to the fact that the fish are not acting according to normal patterns. At this time of the year, all of the Coho and Steelhead should be up in the streams spawning, not out swimming in the Lake.”

Stepping into the now crowded room, Jerry surveyed the party and announced, “You should all know that Laura is doing OK. She is out of surgery and is hungry. However, Captain, guard Mr. Phillips carefully or I may sneak in and save the City a lot of money by gutting the bastard.”

Terri Lewis did not take that statement as a joke and simply inclined her head with a nod and said, “I’m really glad that your Laura is OK, Jerry. Now sit down and finish your thought.”

“From the death patterns we see so far, the fish aren’t just wandering aimlessly though. They seem to be making in a straight line north. I suggest that we all get ready for inquiries from the other cities around the Lake within a few hours. The known currents, fish concentration and a few other factors only vary the time that it will take for the biotoxin to show up in South Chicago, Gary, Green Bay, Duluth, Detroit, and Cleveland…"

Fred interrupted weakly, "Let me add to that, folks. I have had a call from St Ignace. If you all remember your American geography, that is the little city on the Upper Peninsula of Michigan across the Mackinaw Straits from Mackinaw City. That means only one thing. The chelator has made it to the mouth of Lake Michigan. I don't know how we can stop it now."

While the others sat in totally stunned silence, Jon rose and went to his desk. He returned to his seat and opened an atlas retrieved from the pile of vacation memorabilia still standing on the battered roll top.

Jon exclaimed when he found it, "Here it is. St. Ignace. Holy Shit, Fred. That's got to be close to two hundred miles."

"More like two hundred fifty, Jon. On the drive over here I had hoped that you guys would be brimming with some ideas for containment. I'm really sorry that all I did was add to the burden," Fred lamented.

Cindy added to the lamentation with, "Fred, we have also theorized that the biotoxin might be carried over into any and all fish products. There is also the chance that whatever consumes the fish products, will then transmit the chelator right on up the food chain."

"Cindy, are you saying that there is food in the stores right now or on its way there tomorrow, that could be contaminated?" Fred asked.

"A number of things point to that possibility, Fred," Jon explained. "Cindy has a rat in her refrigerator that may be contaminated. She found it last Friday night when she, Jerry and Rubin came in from sampling the Ditch."

Jon looked at all of the others. He guessed that this was the team that had to do something. No one else was yet willing to grasp the dire consequences of this twist of nature's plan. He remembered all the familiar chants from the 70's. Recollection flooded back with thoughts of Earth Day and Silent Spring.

He silently prayed for the strength to see it through. He looked again at the faces of the haggard group and wondered about his own vulnerability. 'What am I supposed to do,' he wondered silently. 'Am I supposed to be the leader of this pathetic band of crusaders?'

"I hope to God that we can think of something soon", Jon said, shivering.

Then suddenly Jon blurted, "It just dawned on me that this plague could infect the entire world. Fish are the primary protein supply for over half of the world's population. All that needs to happen is for the fish to transmit the disease along a chain of their fellow non-mammals, right into Lake Huron, Lake Erie, Lake Ontario and out through the St. Lawrence Seaway into the Atlantic."

"Using the distance it has been transmitted thus far, and the fact that the number of fish infected is geometric, my quick estimate is that the biotoxic chelator will reach the Atlantic Ocean in 40 hours."

FRIDAY 4:00 a.m.

CHAPTER 36

Looking for all the world like a band of hippies that time had forgotten, Jon and Cindy sat together with Fred, Jerry, and Terri Lewis on the few pieces of furniture that were usable in the living room. They had been talking for several hours now, noticing the time slipping by with no ideas or resolution about attacking the heart of the problem.

The obvious ideas of closing the St. Lawrence Seaway Locks had been discussed and discarded hours before, because of the fish ladders that had been constructed years ago to allow free access throughout the Great Lakes system and into the estuaries along the Seaway. Additionally, unknown numbers of fish "tunnels" had been added by various local and state agencies for their own reasons. The group was convinced that there really was no way to insure the complete closure of the Seaway.

Around 2:00 in the morning, Fred suggested that they all catch a few hours of sleep in preparation for what was likely to be their last rest in the coming days.

Jon was about to rustle around getting sleeping bags or whatever he could find, when he noticed that Jerry simply took a roll onto the floor and was asleep before Cindy could get a throw pillow under his head. Fred Donnolly, long a practitioner of sleeping on his feet, felt very comfortable in the wingback in front of the silent TV.

The police captain looked around, smiled and said, "What gentlemen, leaving the couch for the lady. Jon tossed her a pillow and a comforter from the closet. Cindy covered both Jerry and Fred with blankets. Jon and Cindy then shuffled silently toward the single bedroom.

Without a word being spoken, the two sought comfort in each others arms as they slowly removed their clothes in that strange ritual of trying to always touch while undressing. Their arms and lips became entwined, their clothes fell away and they sank into the bed in each other's embrace.

With a nearly breathless "I love you," Jon and Cindy fell into a death-like sleep. The entire apartment rumbled with the sleeping sounds of exhausted warriors.

Less than one and a half hours later, Jon sat bolt upright and shook Cindy far too hard.

Cindy awoke with a fright and a tiny scream that indicated her unwanted dream had not yet ended. She stared wide eyed at Jon and said with fear-shortened breath, "You bastard, Jon. You could have given me a heart attack. What in the hell did…"

"Cindy! I'm sorry, but I would have shaken you awake anyway. I know who can help us. I know who can figure out what to do about the spread of the chelator."

Jon was out of bed in a flash pulling on his shorts and pants throwing a shirt around his shoulders. He was still talking and too loud at that, as he walked into the next room for the telephone. He flipped on the light to the immediate curses of one Police Captain, who just happened to be sleeping with her head on the arm of the couch directly under the bright reading light on Jon's end table.

Cindy was trying to reorganize her clothes from the piles scattered around the room. She was skipping along behind Jon when a voice dampened with sleep, pierced the brightness.

"Jesus Christ in Heaven Above! Turn off the friggin' light before I shoot it out!

Jon announced to the chagrin of all the volunteers that he had an idea about who would solve the problem containing the biotoxic chelator. He continued his march through the group each of whom was slowly coming upright.

All except Jerry, who had not moved. The deep throated gurgling from the floor near the couch was a strong indication of his attentiveness to Jon's words.

Cindy walked over to Jerry, knelt on the floor and lightly touched his cheek with her fingertips. She noted the two day old, blue-wire mask Jerry had. She just kept stroking his face until his eyes slid open forming narrow slits that sparkled.

"Wake up, Wittner," Cindy said purring.

"Lord, if you are there, will you make this a dream like I've never had before? Make this the dirtiest dream you've ever conjured up for man. Make the voice be attached to a naked Cindy Farrell poised to take me to Nirvana."

Jerry was trying to continue his lurid dream description when Cindy punched him with her usual assertiveness.

Jerry yelped for someone to rescue him, when Jon turned from the kitchen and asked how many cups of coffee he should brew.

He should not have asked because he got almost as many answers as there were people there. He was sure that at least two answered more than once, including, "Forty cups for me." Another said, "I'll need six cups directly injected into my left ventricle." The final answer came, "How many cups were consumed in all of World War Two?"

Finishing up the minor task of coffee making, Jon turned to nearly knock Jerry down as the biologist was rooting in the refrigerator for anything edible.

Jon said, "Listen folks. I know that we would all like about fifteen more hours of sleep, but I think I know who can help us with the Seaway problem."

Turning to face the living room contingent, Jon continued, "If you will all recall, we at EPA were actually working for the Corps of Engineers on the

Waukegan Ditch Project. Haltec was just a contractor for the sampling. All of the analytical work was being done by EPA directly for the Corps."

"The Project Manager is an old timer at the Corps. He has probably got 20 years of service, but he's not some stodgy old fart. This is the guy who did a lot of the design work on the lock system for the St. Lawrence Seaway when it was rehabbed a few years ago. I first met Kurt Jackson in Kuwait."

"Hold it right there, buster," Cindy interjected. "This is the first time you mentioned Kuwait."

"Well, Cindy. I don't talk much about that experience, because it wasn't exactly a delightful trip."

Jon had flipped open his personal phone book, quickly locating Kurt Jackson's home number.

Jon's eyes darted from person to person around the room. It was almost as if all of them were holding their breath waiting for Jon to pull a rabbit out of his hat.

They all heard, "Kurt! Kurt Jackson. This is Jon Kepler from the EPA. Yes! I know what fucking time it is, Kurt, but we've got a group assembled at my place that is the total spectrum of information on the recent deaths around Chicago."

Jon allowed Kurt Jackson a minute to chew on Jon's ear and then continued.

"Kurt, I know that it is hard to imagine why this group should include a dirty old engineer, but you are the man of the hour. Sincerely, Kurt, we need you. I can't explain over the phone; it's too unbelievable"

Jon scanned the others for support and got unknowing stares.

"Kurt, I'll drive over and pick you up myself. Give me your address and be out front. Yes! No more than ten minutes.

"Oh! And Kurt! Please dig out any good map you have of the St. Lawrence Seaway. No! No! Not now. Trust me. We will all explain when you get here. Thanks, Kurt." Jon hung up the phone with near reverence.

"Well, folks, I guess that we will all get to see if I'm a little wacky or if this could be the guy that saves us all."

Fred hardly waited for Jon to finish, when he said, taking charge momentarily, "All right everybody. Let's divide up the assignments and get busy."

They all looked at him as if Fred had just announced Bill Clinton to be the next Pope.

"Jerry, you take breakfast orders and run to the Golden Cup around the corner. We might be able to work without much sleep, but I don't know anyone who can work without food."

Turning toward the still reclining Terri Rosa, Fred asked, not ordered, "Terri, can you get someone in the department to go to my office at County and gather the most recent printouts from the system manager. I'll call there and set it up. If they could be brought here by the time Jon's savior is here, we could make some real time."

"What else do we need, Jon?" Fred asked bowing to Jon's obvious leadership position.

"Fred! Good idea on the chow. Jerry, I hope you don't mind. Cindy, could we get someone over to your place to pick up the rat from your fridge for analysis down at County. We need to know the extent of the danger of food chain contamination."

Terri Lewis was already speaking into the phone in a soft yet authoritarian voice that conveyed the importance of the order to dispatch one blue-and-white to County to deliver printouts to Jon's. Another would wake the superintendent of Cindy's building to let them in to pick up the rat for delivery down to the County Lab.

She cupped the phone and asked, "Fred, who should the officer see at your the Lab?"

Fred gave Terri the name of the Chief Technician at the County's toxicology lab where all of the analyses were being run since Jon was put out of business.

Fred then asked for everybody's attention and posed a very poignant question. "If this Kurt Jackson can really help us solve the problem of the Seaway cutoff from the Atlantic, who is the person to solve the problem of notifying the public of the horrifying disease that threatens us all."

Obviously that was the easiest question of the recent past because everybody pointed back at the asker.

"Fred, I think you can see that all of us agree that any announcement must come from you. You are the only one with the title that would warrant the public's belief. Anyone else could be shot down by the media or Hasting's team as a purveyor of rumor and unproven theories. Captain Lewis might want to consider notifying the Department as soon as we decide what the announcement will be. Also we need the names of some press and TV people that we each might know well enough to get a sympathetic ear."

Just then Jerry was standing with his hand on the doorknob waiting for a chance to get final food orders when he said, "Hey, Shit! Jon. If there really is a chance that the food chain will be or even is toxic with the Chelator, what the hell do I get for everybody to eat?"

They looked rather stunned until, the police came to the rescue again. "Get tuna fish sandwiches and potato chips or French Fries. The tuna would have had to been canned several weeks ago and the fish haven't been contaminated that long. Anything else you can think of that was canned or processed at least a week ago should be all right."

Everybody was impressed with the sprightly blonde's intuitive assessment and logical thinking. Jerry was gone in a flash and back just as quickly.

"I only have two bucks," he said sheepishly with his head through the small space he had reopened.

Fred walked over and handed Jerry two twenties and pushed the door closed, sending him on his way.

Fred leaned against the door for a moment. Then he looked at Jon saying, "Well! Get going you lazy turd. You had this depth-of-the-night flash of brilliance. Go get your Mr. Jackson."

Jon was walking to the closet to grab his jacket. He turned as he opened the door. "I just pray the Kurt can help. If he can't bring his know-how to bear on the problem, we'll have to go public without a rational solution. That will panic the whole city or even the entire population around the Great Lakes."

He walked toward the door, head down. He wasn't sure himself. He hoped that the inspiration to call Jackson had been enough and that they could rely on the wiles and years of experience to bring forth the saving commands.

Jon swiveled his head as he was closing the door behind him and said slowly and succinctly. "I'm sure that Kurt will grasp the situation immediately and offer the best solution."

However, as the elevator descended to the garage level, Jon's mood seemed to sink with the downward movement.

Getting into the Pontiac, Jon was searching for words to contact God and pledge everything Jon ever hoped to possess in return for some inspiration. Jon didn't think he could offer enough.

FRIDAY 5:30 a.m.

CHAPTER 37

Jon and Kurt Jackson walked onto the elevator in the basement garage of Jon's building. It was as if the elevator had not moved since Jon went to pick up Kurt. The snail's pace of the lift was even more annoying than usual to Jon. As an additional irritant, the elevator shuddered to a halt at the main floor, the doors sliding open with a slight whoosh.

Jerry practically burst into the tiny space, cursing his armful of food bags, while trying to push the button for Jon's floor. After balancing everything on one arm and a lifted leg, Jerry saw that the button was already lit and was not wary of insulting his fellow passengers with "Oh sure, fuck you, button!"

Jon tapped Jerry on the shoulder and asked if he would like some help.

Jerry whirled in surprise at Jon's voice nearly dropping the precious bag of French Fries and condiments.

"Shit, Jon. You scared me half to death. Hell yes, I want help. Take this bag of smelly stuff and I'll take this one with the fries. I love to eat them out of the bag before I even get home. Anyway, I just buy an extra bag of fries to eat on the way home so I have the regular order with my food when I get there."

Jerry looked at Jon as if he expected verbal agreement to his complex explanation of ordinary phenomena.

Jon shook his head slightly and made the formal introduction, "Jerry, this is Kurt Jackson, the Chief Liaison Officer for the Chicago District Corps of Engineers."

"Hi Jerry. I think I am pleased to meet you, although the circumstances of my being here make me a little wary of believing this guy." He indicated Jon with a toss of his head.

"Hello, Engineer Jackson. I'm Jerry Wittner, biologist and fast food connoisseur. And, oh yes, formerly of Haltec, the sampling contractor to the Corps for the Waukegan site."

As Kurt was about to ask his first question, the doors parted and they hustled into Jon's apartment, which sounded very busy for 5:30 am.

Opening the door and allowing Jerry to pass, Jon paused for the cheers to subside.

Over the rustling of white butcher paper and the crinkling of little French fry bags, Jon introduced Kurt Jackson to everyone and couldn't resist grabbing one of the tuna sandwiches for which the Golden Cup was famous. Kurt dug in too, wondering why he was so hungry at this time of the morning.

As they were filling up, it became obvious that the serious nature of their conclave was resurfacing. The chatter had diminished, the rustling of paper quieted. Fred quickly gathered the remains and cleaned up the table.

From the kitchen he asked if Kurt had looked at the newspapers or TV this morning.

Kurt responded with his head tilting toward Jon "God! No! This crazy chemist got me out of bed to come and eat tuna fish at 5:30 in the morning."

Jerry leaned his chair forward and interjected, "I bought one at the corner machine and I don't want to read it. Just seeing the headlines, I can tell that the city is about ready to panic. The word is obviously out about the deaths. Every story probably has a different theory about how and why. Each of them is based on different rumors, I bet."

Fred came back into the living room to pluck the paper from Jerry's outstretched hand. He quickly unfolded it and scanned the headers of the front page. Flipping open the first and second pages, everybody had their eyes on the now open front page with the headline screaming in bold print:

500 DEAD—THOUSANDS STRICKEN

A couple of people sucked air while the others stared with stunned expressions—the best of all appeared on the face of Kurt Jackson.

Kurt's eyes never left the paper, when he said, "I had heard that there were some health problems and even a minor epidemic, but all I heard about was a possible new strain of influenza and that the mayor and health department had things under control. Is this why you brought me here, Jon? Do you know more about this?"

Kurt had a stern, sour expression clamped to his face. His still conditioned body was not extraordinary, but it was obvious to anyone who met him that he had not gone soft. He had a slightly thinning head of dark brown hair atop an angular, aquiline face whose edges softened when he smiled. Not many would see him with soft edges for a while.

Jon started at the beginning by asking Cindy to relate the fish sampling to Kurt, followed by their meeting and on through Rubin's death to Laura's close call, and finishing with their conclusion that the fish could infect each other. He commanded a postscript about possible contamination of the food chain right out into the Atlantic within an estimated 40 hours. Each person filled in the areas where they had first hand knowledge.

While Jon listened to the others, he felt a seeping dread. It seemed to him as if this was some kind of surrealistic play, carefully rehearsed with everybody saying their lines at the right time. Jon knew it couldn't be a script when he listened to Fred fill in the details of the horrible 30 hour death rite to which every victim succumbed.

Terri Lewis noticed the unwavering eyes when Fred told of the screaming sufferers, but caught the clinching jaw that almost completely hid a gut-tightening fear.

Jon resumed the tale of horror with a more detailed recap of why they felt that the St. Lawrence Seaway had to be closed off somehow.

Fred interjected with, "Remember too, Jon, that we must deal with Dr. Ng's group soon. It is obvious that they will have to make a public announcement today. They have to stop hiding.

Jon came back to the subject of the Seaway and asked, "Well, Kurt is there anything that we can do to contain this thing in the Great Lakes."

Kurt Jackson reached into his inner sport coat pocket and slid out two of those really expensive onion skin maps that nobody can ever seem to buy. He opened the first to reveal a beautiful, full color overview of the Great Lakes region.

"Let's put this into perspective, first. The Great Lakes are the second largest body of fresh water in the world. The largest is in the Soviet Union. From Duluth, Minnesota to Watertown, New York is nearly 700 miles as the crow flies. To get from Chicago to Watertown, you must pass up through the entire length of Lake Michigan, through Lake Huron, Lake Erie and Lake Ontario. That is almost 900 miles. Even though I've known Jon a long time, it is difficult for me to believe that this thing could spread that fast, threatening the Atlantic in less than 40 hours."

Jon nodded to Kurt's rhetorical question, adding, "We think that fish to fish transmission is the only explanation for the rapid rise in the number of cases and for the distance covered already. The outbreak in Green Bay, Wisconsin shows that."

Kurt continued, questioning, "Am I also supposed to believe that your so called biotoxic chelator is being carried into the whole food chain, and anything or anyone that eats an infected fish, has the Calcium leached from his system or becomes a carrier?

His swing past all of the faces in the room did not require a verbal confirmation.

Kurt rose, thumb and forefinger pinching his chin in thought "Well, folks. You aren't making my digestive system handle greasy French fries too well. If, and that is still a big word, what you theorize is true, then the only way to prevent the spread of the disease is to seal off the St. Lawrence Seaway, just as you said. You were right to reject the idea of simply closing the locks. There is no way to be certain that the locks would not leak nor is it certain that all tunnels or fish ladders would be sealed. Furthermore, it would seem best to seal the St. Lawrence close to the Atlantic to be certain no fish can escape before we complete the closure."

Walking back and forth while he thought his way through this thing, Kurt Jackson looked the role of the construction engineer. Inward thinking and outward doing, he held everyone's eyes as he paced. It looked like a championship tennis match with all the heads following his movements back and forth.

"OK, everybody! I've got an idea, but it will take a considerable effort from each of us to pull it off. We have got the basic team, but we would certainly need some inside help especially with supplies and the like."

Jerry, Jon and Cindy were seated close together right below the pivot point of Kurt Jackson's turnaround. They kept glancing at one another while occasionally looking to Fred and Captain Lewis to read their faces.

Whatever Kurt has in mind, it must be big for him to talk about all of this like a military maneuver, Jon thought.

'Does he have a strong concept of the criticality of the time frame involved?' Fred wondered to himself.

Going around and around in Terri Lewis's head were thoughts of the panic in the city and certainty that no amount of preparation would get the Department ready for the turmoil that would surely follow any announcement.

"It is obvious to me that we cannot spend much of the time remaining in getting permission or a blessing for our plan," Kurt continued.

It was apparent that Kurt Jackson was taking charge. Jon was pleased with the thought that he might not be spearheading the resolution of this crisis. Just then his mind turned from its inner thoughts to the sound of his name.

"…And Jon can help me when we try to convince the President that the only safe action is an immediate implementation of our plan," Kurt stated emphatically.

Jerry chimed in with, "Hell, Kurt. What is the plan? Tell us how this motley crew, no offense to anyone, is going to pull off the closure of the Seaway in a short enough time frame."

Fred was speaking as Jerry finished, "And how is it that you find us to be the group that can do the job. Don't we need to get the involvement and blessing of the necessary local and state agencies that control the Seaway?"

"Without them," Cindy interrupted, "We cannot get the assistance and things we need."

Jon interrupted with, "Wait a minute, Kurt. What president?"

Kurt watched each of them voice a concern for the ability and welfare of the team members. It was obvious that none was concerned about his personal safety or professional status, but wondered how the job could get done.

"Each of you is confusing the real job with the obvious one. You each think that we must convince the local or state authorities to undertake a plan that they cannot be convinced about. It is also obvious that those agencies would have done something already if they were convinced that there was a genuine long term problem. Those same people also don't want to take the responsibility for the final decision," Kurt lamented.

They all agreed with that while Cindy, Jon and Fred remembered the discouraging meeting with the Mayor.

Kurt continued, "Right now what we need is a kickoff to this campaign and I see only one person in the room who can pull it off."

Every bleary eye in the place searched around looking for Kurt Jackson's kickoff man. The suspense was ended immediately when Kurt's eyes locked in on Fred Donnolly.

Fred quickly glanced around to make sure that everybody had come to the same scary conclusion.

He quickly began, "Well Kurt, I never was a kicker but I used to run pretty mean interference at Purdue. What exactly do you have in mind?"

"We need you to announce the full truth about the crisis as this group understands it. You must do it because that rather brazen act will take the level of credibility that only you can muster. You have an official bureaucratic title that provides certain of its own authority and can be the anchor to which the public can secure their concerns," Kurt pronounced from his plan.

"What is the thrust of my announcement, Kurt?" Fred asked.

"Shouldn't we at least warn the Hasting's team about our intentions, Kurt?" Jon wondered aloud. "Aren't they likely to try to discredit Fred and regain control?"

Kurt was obviously prepared for some backtracking by the team due principally to lack of experience in these matters. He addressed Jon's question expertly.

"We will simply ask the President to invite them to Fred's news conference. We need two people to call the media and set up the presentation at Cook County Hospital from Fred's official bastion of power.

Looking around for more volunteers, Kurt settled on Cindy and Terri.

Smiling he began, "We really have an excellent group here. Cindy, you and Captain Lewis will start by calling the three network TV stations, the two radio news outlets, along with the Tribune and Sun-Times. Oh and don't forget AP and UPI. That should do it. If we insult somebody by not inviting them that's just tough shit. We have more to worry about than anyone's ego."

Stammering slightly, Cindy asked, "What the hell do we tell all those people, Kurt? We aren't in a position to state unequivocally that our theories are true. Sure all of the obvious evidence says we are right, but what are we going to tell them in response to the questions about our plan?"

Kurt was quick to allay Cindy's fears. "You and Terri will tell the media that the Medical Examiner's office has an important announcement concerning the mystery ailment and the subsequent deaths related to it. You do not explain anything at that time nor do you answer any questions."

Looking to Fred, Kurt continued that thought, "Fred, what is the name of the PR person at County who usually handles the media when the hospital has someone famous in for a workup?"

Picking up on his idea, Fred turned to Cindy. "Just tell them that you are from Frank Carlton's office at Cook County Hospital and you were instructed to inform the media of the pending news conference. Nobody will ask any questions at that time."

Fred continued, "Hey, I've got an idea. Let me make our last announcement call to Ng. I think that I can convince her, one on one that this requires action NOW! My guess is that she will be there or will send someone. With the right approach, I can probably save them some embarrassment which just might result in their supporting our plan."

Kurt was happy to note that it had gone from 'his' plan to 'our' plan.

"OK, ladies," Kurt announced with a firm look, "Let's figure that it will take the networks about an hour to shoot a crew over to County and another hour to set up. You can begin making the calls right now," glancing at his watch, "and tell them that the press conference will begin at 11:00 am sharp."

Quiet, up until now, Terri Lewis asked softly, "What in the hell do you need me making calls for? There must be something that can best be served by my badge?"

"You didn't really think that you were getting off that easily did you, Captain?" Kurt grinned. "Oh, no. We need your ability to move about the city in a quick, guaranteed fashion. Timing will be of the essence as the day wears on."

Looking to Fred, Kurt said, "I think you should go to the hospital, prepare your statement and wait for our call confirming that things are all set up. I know that you think its bullshit, Fred, but make certain that you wear your white labcoat and the whole getup. It's all part of the credibility factor."

Terri, could you arrange safe transport for Dr. Donnolly to County affording him sufficient time to prepare his announcement?"

"Absolutely," Terri replied reaching for the phone and ordering a squad car to Jon's address.

"As long as you are on a roll, Captain, please see if you can have a squad available to us for our trip to O'Hare Airport," Kurt announced with a dip of his head to Jon.

"Alright, Goddamnit! Jon yelled. "Why in the hell am I going to O'Hare? And, what president do you keep referring to? Jon demanded.

Kurt went on. “I’ll fill you in on your assignment, Jon, as soon as we get the others started. I’ll answer your second question with two words—THE President.”

Returning his gaze to the group, his eyes settled on Cindy, who still had an impressed, questioning look on her face.

“Do you think that you can compile all of the data and information on the Waukegan Ditch project, Cindy? That should include everything. Not just the current work, but all of the historical data and reports that you might have. Get all of that and prepare it as a backup to my report for the President. Since this is command center, find some organizational supplies. Standard stuff. You know—files, labels, binders, etc.”

“Jerry,” Kurt went on with hardly a breath, “I want you to go to Jon’s EPA office and make off with all of Jon’s chromatograms, computer runs, printouts, sample logs and everything else related to this project. Then get it back here.”

Some were beginning to doubt their new leader as he glanced about for concurrence on the latest round of assignments.

Jerry was first with, “What in the hell do we need all of that stuff for, Kurt? I thought this was the action team and not the paperwork team.”

Kurt looked first at Jerry and then slowly scanned the group with a firm commanding look.

“All of this gathering of data and paperwork is the basis for our defense when they come to take Jon and me to jail.”

SECTION EIGHT

THE SHIMMERING

The male and female Coho salmon took up positions above the nest aware of a growing need for nutrition. They would not leave their nest for 8 days, their only food being the flotsam and jetsam that drifted by in the turbid waters of the stream. The female's body was now beginning to relax after its ordeal, when suddenly a slight tremor passes through overworked muscles. Another tremor quivered through her. Then she was jolted by a shocking, nerve jangling pulsation along her spine. The male salmon turned, watching her undulations and the increasingly apparent shimmerings of her flanks so frightened him that he leaped from the nest into the main current of the stream to escape her presence. After nearly thirty minutes, the shattering pains and strange body reactions began to quiet. Her fluttering gills gradually returned to a normal breathing pace. She knew she now carried something more within her body. She felt the presence far more strongly than she had felt the ripening roe at the start of her journey. When the physical reactions were totally gone, she took stock to find no particular impairments had appeared and her sides were still. The presence was there. She was different but she would not know why for some time to come. For the first time in her thirteen years of returning to the Ditch, the female Coho left her nest without a single twinge. The eggs were forgotten—only the presence within her was on her mind. She gradually moved out into the main part of the flow and let the current push her downstream.

FRIDAY 8:20 a.m.

CHAPTER 38

Blake Thompson was once again in his office before any of the staff people arrived. He had noted at breakfast, that his continuing problems sleeping were bound to manifest themselves in his job performance before long. Blake's troubled sleep was not the usual insomnia, but a strange compulsion that awakened him every twenty or thirty minutes throughout the night. It didn't matter if he was dog tired from an evening of racquetball or if he was half loaded from a boring cocktail party.

Sitting with the twenty ounce foam coffee cup in his hand, Blake knew that he was suffering from some strange form of guilt that required him to formulate "what-ifs" and to solve them as the night passed. He had dealt with 'What if someone digs up Lundberg's research article?' He had also studied 'What if the USEPA learns that I hid vital information from them during their investigation of the PCB contamination?'

Slouched at the desk with his head cradled on his right hand while slurping the stinging black brew, Blake reflected on what his options really were at this point.

Softly debating the air around him, Blake Thompson said, "If the media discovers the Lundberg statement, they will hang me without a trial. If the Feds get wind of that, it will be all over for the company and me personally. However, if the company makes the right kind of statement now, it could save face and save itself from ruin. Maybe I'm losing my grasp on reality, but I've got to decide what to do or I will lose my mind."

Making at least one decision, Blake slid the black, sleek phone closer and lifted the receiver to punch up the private number for Loretta Bonner. Maybe the strange old matriarch will have a suggestion for me, Blake thought without much hope of assistance.

Maybe she will be able to see that I must call…"Hello! Derrick, this is Blake Thompson at Nautical Marine in Waukegan. Could I please speak with Mrs. Bonner?" Blake's hopes rose a single notch with this activity toward lessening the quiet.

"Mr. Thompson, I'm sorry to tell you that Mrs. Bonner has taken ill today and might not be available. However, I'll check the house and see if she could talk to you," came the lilted reply followed by Blake's Thompson's involuntary shiver.

"Thank you, Derrick," Blake replied. "See what you can do."

Slowly lowering the handset onto its cradle, Blake resented the fact that Loretta Bonner picked today to be sick. He felt even more repressed and depressed than before. That little lift he had gotten from the movement to action, had been replaced with a downward thrust in his mood.

For maybe the third time, Blake Thompson tilted the empty cup to his lips and cursed the addiction of coffee. Pitching the white foam cup toward his walnut wastebasket, he saw the cup bounce off the credenza, bounce against the wall, hit the rim of the basket, teeter momentarily and fall in on top of yesterday's memos. A cheer began to rise in his throat. He stifled it with remorse knowing that he didn't deserve to have his spirit lifted.

Blake was literally disgusted with himself. He no longer had a justifiable logic for hiding the possible truth from the public. He had also been subconsciously recording incoming information about the mysterious deaths in the Chicago area. He was beginning to put two time-divergent sets of data together concerning the horrible sounding deaths and Lundberg's work. When the phone rang, Blake jumped to grab it and answered almost breathlessly.

"Mr. Thompson, this is Dr. Lundberg in Alberta. I know we just spoke yesterday and you assured me that I would be getting some reports about my research on PCB. However, just this morning, I was reading the Chicago Tribune I picked up at the airport last night. Have you read that paper, Mr.

Thompson? It talks about some very strange deaths that have occurred in the area around Chicago and I wondered if…"

Blake interrupted with a strong voice that sounded more in control that he had been for several days, "Dr. Lundberg. It is imperative that you return to my office on the very next plane. I believe that there could possibly be a connection between the deaths you speak of and the work you did on PCB mutagens. Will you please arrange to call my private number immediately upon your arrival? I will personally pick you up at the airport. Don't bother to confirm your reservations with me. Just call as soon as you are at O'Hare."

Before Lundberg could respond, Thompson continued "Oh, and Doctor, don't tell anyone that you are coming back to see me again. It might make waves before we can talk."

Once again, before the white haired scientist could answer, Blake cut him off, "Bring a copy of your original Research Paper with you, Doctor. I don't know if we have one here."
Blake Thompson hung up with an abruptness that startled John Lundberg.

Blake smiled and felt good. A feeling that he was searching for the last couple of days. His sudden desire to make it all right was precipitated by Lundberg's call. It was time to clean the slate. Beginning to feel free, Blake decided to move more quickly to check any connection with the deaths and the PCB's laying in the bottom sediments of the Waukegan Ditch. Blake walked the few paces and looked down through the dusty glass at the oily black surface of Waukegan Harbor. With resoluteness, he went back to the desk to begin a list of things to do which would bring the public's awareness back to Nautical Marine Corporation. However, the first name he listed to call was that of Loretta Bonner. Her underlying evil greed must be exposed, he thought.

The smile on his lips stayed in place even though the growing headache seemed to be much worse since he had finished the coffee. He turned his chair to bend toward the lower drawer of his desk for his stash of Extra Strength Bayer when a bolt of lightning seared his brain from within.

Blake Thompson slowly slid from his chair onto the floor. He noted that there were dust balls under his desk as his cheek slapped the cold tile. I'll have to complain to the janitors about that, was his last thought as the aneurysm burst and completely deprived his brain of its oxygen-giving blood flow.

Blake Thompson's body was not even found until 9:15 that morning when his secretary came into his office to check Blake's appointment book for some scheduled event she had not recorded.

Martha Rigby had been ringing Blake's com-line all morning, with no response. She assumed that he had gone to some meeting and had forgotten to tell her the day before. When the call came from Mrs. Bonner's office, Martha put the boy or girl, she could not tell which, on hold while she went to check Blake's office calendar. As she opened the door, Martha noticed that his chair was up against the wall. When Martha walked around the desk, she saw Blake Thompson looking like he was asleep partly under his desk.

Bending down, Martha saw his glaring eyes and ran from the room screaming for help.

About sixty seconds later, Derrick hung up the phone making a note to call Mr. Thompson back to tell him that Mrs. Bonner was unable to call him, but would do so on Monday. Derrick also made a note to tell Thompson that his secretary was very rude and more than a little inefficient.

FRIDAY 1:00 p.m.

CHAPTER 39

Loretta Bonner had not gotten to her position of wealth and power by being slow witted. She had observed her husband for many years. She had come to know the people at his companies and all along the chain of command at the many social functions and company gatherings.

Loretta had taken the reins of ATI when her husband died. Her action was much to the chagrin of the stodgy Board of Directors. She fixed that quickly and efficiently. With her quiet control and skill, Loretta had an entirely new Board within 11 months. ATI was becoming one of the largest privately held corporations in the U. S. Its far-flung empire included silver mines, computer manufacturing, lumber mills, environmental engineering companies and Nautical Marine Corp.

With the waning of the 1973 gasoline crisis, Loretta and ATI grabbed Nautical Marine because its stock price had hit rock bottom. The company had one of the lowest price-to-earnings ratios of any basic manufacturer. Within one year, the outdoor recreation business boomed and Nautical Marine was booming with it. The plant was expanded and the staff beefed up. The production lines hummed with the increased output of outboard engines.

Sitting on the swing of her cabin porch, Loretta reflected on the days she shared with her husband and on those exciting first days after taking over ATI. She thought of the invigorating proxy fights, the acquisitions and especially the dramatic growth of the company. Loretta also knew that many people thought of her as being a cold, heartless woman whose only goal was to make more money. This reputation rarely bothered her. While she admitted being a tough businesswoman, didn't think she deserved the negative comments.

She worked relentlessly toward her growth goal of ATI being a billion dollar company. Something her late husband, Lawrence, would have never conceived.

Loretta knew that there had been occasional uses of dubious tactics and that her ethics had been questioned a time or two. She just put that out of her mind. 'It was probably the jealous ones anyway,' she thought.

Her reflections continued right up to her receiving the word on Thursday. Was that only yesterday? Loretta asked herself.

When she had not heard from Stewart Phillips by late Wednesday afternoon, she became concerned that something had gone awry. Her phone call to his private line had not elicited any response. Finally in desperation, Loretta contacted Derrick, her administrative assistant, and instructed him to find Phillips.

It was not until Thursday morning that Derrick finally talked to Stewart Phillips' secretary. Finally some of the story made its way to Bonner's huge suite of offices. Derrick had chatted at length with the busybody to find that Stewart Phillips had just arrived at his office. Before the secretary could get him on the phone, she told Derrick that two Chicago police detectives had come to arrest Mr. Phillips. The secretary claimed that she didn't know the reason for the arrest, but might have overheard the police saying something about a girl named Laura.

Shortly thereafter, Loretta Bonner absent-mindedly sat in her dove-beige executive chair tapping some musical number on the desktop with her letter opener. Derrick came on the tone controlled intercom buried in the enameled surface of her desk. She remembered their conversation very clearly, because she felt that first twinge of fear when she learned of Phillips' arrest.

Then, on Friday morning, Derrick regretted interrupting her, but felt it important enough to do so. "Excuse me, Mrs. Bonner, but I have just received a call from Nautical Marine Corp. His secretary has just found Blake Thompson dead on the floor of his office."

"Thank you, Derrick," she replied in a monotone. "You were right to disturb me with the news. Please arrange all the standard wishes and condolences to his family. Then find out from his secretary exactly who had appointments with Mr. Thompson every day for the last week. Also find out what social events he attended and what appointments he has scheduled through the end of the month."

"Oh, Derrick," Loretta caught herself. "Please see to it that the nursing home payments we make for Mr. Thompson's wife are stopped immediately."

Loretta Bonner continued to move slowly back and forth on the old chain hung swing at the cabin's front door. She had built this palatial "log cabin" nearly ten years ago. Everything one could need was here. Loretta had always used it as a retreat, a place to hide from it all. Many times when she had difficult problems to work out she would come here. While it was only twenty-two helicopter minutes from her office in downtown Knoxville, it felt like a million miles as soon as the copter was out of audio range.

Loretta looked south over the top of the pine trees that swept down toward the lake. In every direction, it appeared that civilization had vanished. Mile after mile of trees of every size. This reforested area was part of the ATI empire and would one day yield millions of board feet of sturdy Southern pine for houses up north. Loretta smiled with a feeling of accomplishment and achievement.

The cabin itself was an eleven room building with an expansive living area and master bedroom. The fireplace in front of the main seating arrangement was a work of art. Hand-laid flagstone rose from a huge hearth nearly eighteen feet to a paneled ceiling. Every piece of building material had been flown in to construct the cabin, thus avoiding any roads to the place that only invited unwanted guests. The workers had been housed in tents for the ten and a half months of construction.

Even now, with some difficult problems to work out, Loretta felt the inner peace returning. She was weighing her exposure in light of Stewart Phillips' arrest. She knew that Phillips would tell the police every thing. Loretta was prepared for that with Stewart's conveniently prepared memo regarding Rubin Anderson's death.

The death of Blake Thompson had hit hard. She was counting on him to tie up all the loose ends at Nautical Marine. He had proven his loyalty throughout the PCB incident. He had brought Nautical Marine up out of the business doldrums and had even buried the report and work done by that crackpot chemist.

"I wonder if that scientist will cause any trouble at this stage of the game," Loretta said out loud, coming forward to the edge of the swing.

Settling back, she assured herself that the chemist was so old by now that he must be senile.

"Nope, you're OK, Loretta. You're clean on this one," she said, continuing her conversation with the blue sky and softly blowing breeze.

A couple of more days on retreat here should give it time for the whole issue to settle down, she confirmed to herself. Then I'll sell Nautical Marine to one of the clamoring buyers.

She was looking forward to her favorite dinner, prepared as always by here Cantonese chef at the cabin. He had personally ordered the salmon and would slowly poach it in its own juices. He had wanted a large female, rich with roe to be used in the special sauce he made for Mrs. Bonner. He had called his usual supplier in Chicago.

* *

Meanwhile, in an overly warm Boeing 757, Dr. John Lundberg was fidgeting with a little plastic cup, occasionally sucking the one ice cube left in the bottom. Looking down into the blackness outside the plane, he said to no one, "We must be somewhere over Minnesota about now. I'll be glad when we get there."

Squirming in the seat, trying to get comfortable, John Lundberg thought to himself, 'I wonder why Mr. Thompson wants me back so soon. He will be pleased that I found a copy of my original report on the possible mutagenic effects of PCB's that the company dumped in Waukegan Ditch. I wonder if Mr. Thompson is having me come back because there has been a discovery by the team working on my project back at the Waukegan lab.'

The aging blonde stewardess interrupted his thoughts with the question, "Care for a copy of USA Today, Sir? It is compliments of Canadian Airways."

Shooing her away with a look and a shake of the head, Dr. John Lundberg missed the blaring headline for Friday.

THOUSANDS ILL - HUNDREDS DEAD AND MORE DYING

FRIDAY 8:50 a.m.

CHAPTER 40

They all began to clamor for more information. Of course, Jon wanted to know the full extent of the plan and his involvement, especially the part about going to jail.

Kurt quieted the group with palms forward. He said, "I really think it best that the plan I'm hatching not leave my mind as yet. I need to talk to some people and run it up the flag pole to see who salutes. Then, I will give every one of you the whole story. Until then, how about if we all get our jobs started."

While Cindy began looking up the phone numbers in the white pages, Terri Lewis was busy trying the various radio, TV and print media.

Jerry announced his departure for Jon's office following a little discussion with Jon regarding the information.

Cindy glanced up from the phone book, smiled toward Jerry who had turned back to face the room. "Good Luck, cowboy!" Cindy said with a look of feigned confidence.

Fred stopped vacillating and decided that Kurt Jackson was right. He asked, "Jon is it all right to use the term BIOTOXIC CHELATOR at this point? It sure seems to describe our enemy the best."

Jon looked into those tired eyes and replied, "Sure, Fred. Whatever you think will help people understand that the only present danger is from eating the fish and other products that may be in their food chain."

As Fred was readying himself to leave, Jon added, "Fred, how about the idea of telling the media that Dr. Hasting's office will be preparing a list of foods that should not be eaten. Not only is that something that needs doing, but it might force the Hasting's group to respond with positive assistance."

Kurt interjected with, "Great idea, Jon. Use it, Fred. Now get going. You will need the time to get ready before the news conference starts at 11:00. Let me know if I need to get the President to make a call to Ng. It would cause some unnecessary delay, but can be handled."

As Fred was leaving, everyone wished him a heartfelt 'Good Luck.' He signaled his appreciation with a hand wave from the hallway.

Jon surveyed the remaining team members.

"Jon! Don't stand there like some dork, get busy with your task," Cindy chided.

Before Jon could respond, Kurt answered for him, "He doesn't know what his job is yet, Cindy."

This time Jon flipped Cindy the finger. The continued teasing eased the tension that had begun to mount towards normal breaking point.

Trying to give Jon a disgusted look, Cindy got up, walked over and sat on his favorite, and only, chair in the living room.

Terri Lewis continued her job by calling the last one on her list—WGN television. She knew that the so called "local" station could have the greatest impact because of its status as a TBS Superstation on the cable network.

Cindy watched Terri and was impressed by her authoritative approach to the operators and newspeople. She is really one hell of a woman, Cindy remarked to herself. Continuing her thoughts, Cindy surmised that having risen to Captain in the male dominated Chicago Police Department must have taken some real ability and the backing of a strong Alderman.

Cindy rose suddenly and said, “I’m going to head over to Haltec now.” Turning toward Jon, she warned, “It may take me several hours, so don’t worry. If I not back here by 2:00 at the latest, then you can assume that something has gotten screwed up.”

Jon looked deeply into her eyes, stood and lightly kissed her on the mouth. “Be careful! I love you. Now get going and take a cab. Here’s extra money. Get a cab back, especially with all the crap you’ll be hauling.”

Cindy wanted to stay and simply ignore the mess outside. Jon gave her a tender shove. She smiled and reminded him that she would need cab fare, now that she was unemployed.

As the door closed behind her, with Jon’s eyes fixed on a last view of her, Kurt Jackson abruptly stopped pacing and almost dove at the TV pulling the knob to bring it to life. Turning immediately to WGN Channel 9, Kurt Jackson devoted his entire attention to the screen just as if he knew something was about to happen.

On cue, it seemed, the rerun of “My Three Sons” was replaced with a grim faced reporter doing his best to look serious without looking depressed.

“Ladies and Gentlemen! We have a special bulletin from our News Room. WGN has just learned that the Medical Examiner’s Office of Cook County has called a news conference for 11:00 o’clock this morning. Our sources tell us that we are to get some serious information about the strange disease that has struck our city like a plague. Dr. Fred Donnolly has stated that he has recently correlated information from the area hospitals and other health officials that should carefully and concisely be brought to the attention of the people of this City. More on that meeting when we take you live to Cook County Hospital with VIEWCAM 9. Now this message.”

Terri Lewis wondered how the newscaster had inferred all of that from her simple call made to WGN, but smirked knowingly about the media’s hopeless tendency to embellish and make every story just a little more dramatic.

Kurt turned to Terri and softly asked her to contact Fred at County for him. He asked in such a way as to not insult a Chicago Police Captain.

This did not go unnoticed by Terri Lewis. Kurt Jackson had immediately impressed her.

The commercial for some detergent was just ending when Jon's attention was drawn by the TV's quiet statement, "We have additional information for you on the outbreak of disease that seems to be making its way throughout the City."

As they all looked to the flickering screen, the same newsman had reappeared, only this time he was standing in front of a map of western Lake Michigan ranging from Green Bay in the north down around the tip of Lake Michigan to its tiny border with Indiana.

Nervously twirling his pointer, he began, "Ladies and Gentlemen, it appears that this strange illness that is plaguing the area has grown beyond Cook County. Cases have started showing up in Milwaukee, Wisconsin and Gary, Indiana." He hesitated while the pointer found those two cities.

"Our news department has determined that there are nearly 600 reported deaths and over 3,000 people hospitalized…"

Jon, Terri and Kurt stood mummified. They could not believe what they had just heard. The early morning paper had reported just the 400 dead. They re-tuned their minds to hear the continuation of the news.

"…while the special health commission appointed by the Mayor says that a statement will be released very soon. However, Channel 9 will bring you the recently announced news conference from the Medical Examiner's office, when it is broadcast at 11:00 a.m."

The newscaster continued his non-descript recitation of the information, almost as if he didn't believe what he was saying. It seemed to Jon that the aging carefully crafted newsman was struggling with the overall concept. The voice from the narrow range speakers continued, "There have been rumors that this is some kind of food poisoning. All of the early victims who contracted the disease had eaten some kind of freshly-caught Lake Michigan fish. However, the last several hours have brought reports of victims who had eaten at a local Japanese restaurant. They all succumbed to the same strange disease, but each had something different to eat."

Jon was amazed at the relative accuracy of the report considering that they had little hard scientific facts to go by. The team members looked at one another and unspoken fear began to pervade their faces.

Gaining familiarity with the subject, but seeming reticent about his next announcement, the newscaster went on, "We would like to advise our viewers that the next sequence of film was shot at a health clinic just several blocks from our studios. Apparently, one of our camera crews was getting shots of a truck and school bus accident in front of the Museum of Modern Art, when terrible screams were heard from inside the clinic. Investigating, our reporters found a young man being held down by two nurses and a doctor. They were trying so hard to control the patient that they were unable to treat him. What you are about to see is footage shot not more than 15 minutes ago. It is absolutely unfit for viewing by youngsters due to its violent nature."

With an emphatic nod, the newscaster called for the tape to be played. Jon jumped to turn down the volume. The screeching and screaming were akin to the wail of bloodthirsty wolves. The writhing form on the examining table would alternately appear and disappear as the nurses and doctor fought to gain control.

Jon and Kurt were cringing while Terri just glared at another death scene played out with a higher degree of pain than she had ever seen before.

The three could not bear to watch and couldn't turn away. Jon saw that the physician was finally able to get the top off a syringe filled with some depressant to quiet the man.

Just then the reporter commented, "We have learned that the doctor administered an incredibly heavy dose of an intravenous barbiturate with little lasting effect. The pain returned within minutes. The patient has since died."

Each of the three realized they had been holding their breath. One by one they released the building pressure in their lungs with an audible rush of air. Then the camera refocused on the newscaster who was obviously shaken. He stared, mesmerized by the off-camera monitor.

Leaning forward, Jon switched the set off, while they got their breathing back to normal.

"Well, Jon," Kurt began, "It looks like we are in for a hell of a night."

Breaking her hypnotic-like trance, Terri Lewis stood and announced to no one in particular, "I know you guys need help, but the entire police department will be going crazy. I think that it's time for me to get back to what I know best."

She took two strides up to Kurt Jackson, shook his hand firmly and said, "Just get the fucking job done soon, Kurt."

Two more steps to Jon. "Be careful, Jon. You have a big job to do, but a solid group to help you with it. Tell Cindy she is great and also tell that homely hunk from Ohio State that he can eat burgers at my house when this is all over."

Captain Terri Lewis stepped quickly to the closet, grabbed her jacket, checked the position of her belt holster and saluted the two men as she opened the door.

Stopping with the door open just a few inches, Terri called in to Jon, "I'll check on Laura for you and let you know if she is OK."

Jon and Kurt watched her go, feeling a sudden loss.

Kurt said to Jon, "What that young man went through on TV might be preferable to what we will be undertaking over the next 38 hours," glancing at his watch.

Kurt walked to the tiny kitchen set and motioned Jon to a seat. Kurt then unfolded a larger detail map of the Quebec City area and began explaining his plan to Jon.

FRIDAY 10:50 a.m.

CHAPTER 41

As 11:00 a.m. neared, Jon and Kurt reluctantly turned on the TV for Fred's news conference. They watched as the organized turmoil of the news people quieted when Fred walked to the temporary podium.

Kurt noted that Fred was in full uniform—the white lab coat with his nametag.

Fred began with no preamble, "Ladies and Gentlemen, my name is Dr. Fred Donnolly. I am the Chief Medical Examiner for Cook County. We have been working for three straight days to try to determine the cause of death in the many lives lost to this plague-like disease that has begun to run rampant in our City and elsewhere."

Jon noticed that the pens and pencils all began to write more furiously when Fred emphasized "and elsewhere." Kurt just stared intently at the screen as the camera stopped panning around and focused fully on Fred.

"This office, in conjunction with other scientists, has determined that an unidentifiable chemical mutation has created a BIOTOXIC CHELATOR in the fish from the estuary to Lake Michigan known as the Waukegan Ditch. A chelator is a chemical that surrounds and dissolves other compounds. Some of these chelators are routinely used to treat lead poisoning. By surrounding the lead that has accumulated in the body, a chelator can safely carry the toxic metal out of the blood stream via the kidneys and urinary tract."

Fred was proceeding with deliberation during this part of the presentation to give everyone time to absorb the concepts and to get it right. He wanted to make certain that the public was not misinformed after this.

Continuing, he said, “It is believed that this BIOTOXIC CHELATOR is causing the deaths around the City. We believe that this compound has never existed before. Obviously, you know from the statistics available that the chemical is extremely toxic.”

Hands flew up and reporters asked for recognition. Fred raised his hands and forcefully said, “Please! Please! Let me finish and then we will answer every question.”

“To the best of our ability we have analyzed this new chemical and have found it to be a derivative of the PCB chemical family of compounds. The Polychlorinated biphenyls, or PCB’s, are known carcinogens. They have been present in great quantities in the bottom sediments of the Waukegan Ditch for over 20 years.”

Hesitating for just a moment to look for their nods, Fred continued, “It has become apparent that the fish ingested the PCB’s, either directly or indirectly through the food chain. Once in the fish’s system, the PCB began to mutate or alter its chemical formula. Fish samples analyzed showed the chelator, just the same as did the blood samples taken from the initial victims. It appears that this chemical enters the body when any of the contaminated fish are consumed.”

Jon watched as Fred scanned the audience, never really looking at anyone in particular. Great technique, Fred, Jon said to himself.

Waiting momentarily for the murmuring to subside, Fred could see that the newspeople wanted to bolt to the phones. He was ready to drop the big one.

“Continuing, we also believe that this chelator has made its way into other levels of the food chain.”

Fred noticed the audience’s quizzical looks. He also felt the heat of the lights building and motioned for some cooler air.

“As I was saying, we now have found the chelator in a number of other food items that have been prepared within the last few days. It is difficult to conceive of the number of products in which fish, fish oil and fish by-products are used today. While I am asking the Department of Public Health to prepare a list of foods that should not be eaten, I believe that the safest thing to do is eat only canned goods that you have had in your possession for more than a week."

The background noise level in the room was rising as the whole idea sunk in. Voices started to call out again.

Once more Jon watched Fred quiet them with raised palms.

"I demand that all of you news people present this crisis as it is. I want no embellishments, no panic headlines and no sensationalism. It is your job, right now, to inform the people of the hazardous situation in which we find ourselves. Before you write any story, think of your own families and how you would like them to get this story."

That got their attention, Kurt thought while elbowing Jon to make sure he was paying attention.

"Finally, it has become apparent that the BIOTOXIC CHELATOR is spreading much faster that we would have thought possible. Cases have been reported in Milwaukee, Green Bay, Traverse City and even in St. Ignace near Mackinaw City. Uh, excuse me."

Fred stepped from the podium for a moment to turn an ear to one of his assistants. The room broke into bedlam with everyone talking at the same time.

Looking somehow grimmer, Fred moved back to the microphones and declared that he was very sorry to announce that cases had now been reported in Duluth and Detroit.

Jon and Kurt were stunned. Kurt jumped to his maps and began calculating the movement of the disease. Jon didn't know whether to watch him or Fred. Settling on the TV, Jon listened intently.

"Ladies and Gentlemen, let me make it perfectly clear. The Chelator is not directly contagious. However, be acutely aware that it is far more dangerous than influenza, ptomaine poisoning and even the Salmonella that killed 18 people just a few years ago. This is more akin to a burst appendix. The pain is excruciating. The dissolution process that causes your bones to decalcify goes on for nearly 30 hours. And, I'm sorry to report, we have absolutely no idea how to stop the chelation process, once it starts."

Looking into upturned faces with mouths agape, Fred dropped the big one, "There is no cure. Hell, there is no way to even alleviate the horrible pain. Anyone who has eaten fish from Lake Michigan within the past few days is in jeopardy. Any food product that was made with fish or fish by-products, within the last 72 hours, will likely transmit the disease. Warn the public. Tell them to contact any Poison Control Center or Cook County Hospital if they have consumed any product that is suspect."

Taking a folded computer printout from an offering hand, Fred referred to it and looked up to announce, "There are now 1,100 reported deaths and several thousand people diagnosed from this man-made terror. I just hope it can be stopped somehow."

Obviously finished, Fred wanted to leave the podium, but the questions came like thunder. Trying to sort them out in the melee, Fred pointed to a rather attractive girl he recognized from the PBS station in Chicago. He thought he had heard her question and just wanted to get it over with.

Andi Barrett asked in a full voice, "Dr. Donnolly, what is to prevent this disease, this Biotoxic Chelator, from spreading to the ocean fish population, especially in light of the fact that one and a half billion people on this planet subsist on a principal diet of fish?"

The audience had moved to the front of their seats. It appeared that no one else had thought of that terrifying global consequence. Fred looked at them directly. Then he turned to Andi Barrett and said, "I wish I knew."

FRIDAY 2:00 p.m.

CHAPTER 42

At precisely 2:00 p.m. Jerry knocked once and opened the door looking for the entire world like a misplaced Santa Claus. Hung over his back was a huge green plastic garbage bag nearly filled with rectangular protrusions, all a couple of inches thick.

Apparently proud of his accomplishment, Jerry announced, “Maybe I should be a cat burglar. When I got to your lab, Jon, the place was still pretty busy with investigators, EPA people and even your old boss sitting in your office. I was really at a loss until I spotted the Janitorial service cart nearby. Now this is the good part,” he continued excitedly.

“While all of these dudes wandered around and your boss sat at your desk on the phone, I picked up a garbage bag and began emptying wastebaskets.”

Even with the news they had witnessed before and the rather risky plan just laid out by Kurt Jackson, Jon and the Corps Engineer had to grin with Jerry’s portrayal of his stealth.

“Then I just slid a stack of printouts into the garbage bag. You should see your office, Jon. It hasn’t been this clean in years. I even asked your boss to hand me your wastebasket making like he was in my way. He wouldn’t demean himself by handing the basket to me, so he just scooted the chair way in under the desk. So, get this, I ‘accidentally’ gave him a good push into the desk while I squeezed by to get the waste can. I heard a good WHOOSH from him.”

Jerry was opening the garbage bag to remove its contents, when Jon noticed that the bag also bulged with other paper and smelled faintly of food and cigarettes.

Jerry looked down into the bag, removed a second green garbage bag from his back pocket and turned to smile at Jon and Kurt.

"Outside of a few coffee stains and gray powder from the ashtrays I emptied, I'll have all of your materials out of here in a jiffy," Jerry informed them.

Kurt and Jon spoke together in congratulating Jerry on his successful raid on the EPA office.

While he continued his sorting of good stuff onto the couch and garbage into the second bag, Jon returned to his study of the map laid out by Kurt Jackson. This very special map was apparently prepared for some purpose other than the standard geological survey of U. S. territory. Covering an area only about two miles in each direction, the City of Quebec, centered along the bank of the St. Lawrence River, has long been the capitol city. However, it has always been overshadowed by its showy neighbor to the west, the crown city of Canada—Montreal.

Jon continued to scan the map, noticing that there were no denotations for typical tourist attractions, but yet the parks were all plainly labeled. He saw that the major roads were well marked but did not bear the standard miniature mileage numbers from city to city. Instead, each road was labeled with two numbers separated by a dash.

Tapping Kurt's arm, Jon softly asked the meaning of those numbers.

Kurt replied somberly, "That is the width of the road followed by its carrying capacity in tons."

Pointing to a road just northwest of Quebec, Kurt explained further. "This road is 32 feet wide and will carry 24 tons. Obviously it is not a good military road, because of the weight limit."

Jon really didn't want to hear an answer with those undertones. He continued his study.

A racket fell on their ears along with a string of curses that made even Jerry scrunch his head down into his shoulders.

"Cindy's back," Jerry announced matter-of-factly. "Don't you think you should help her, Jon?" Jerry gestured toward the thundering hall.

Jon spun quickly to visually scold the grinning Wittner for placing him in jeopardy. He took a number of small reticent steps toward the door, only to be barely missed by its edge as the door burst inward followed by Miss Cindy Farrell livid with anger.

"That fucking cabby ditched me. I gave him this big tip to help me unload the boxes and carry them onto the elevator. He said, 'Sure Lady! No problem. Just show me where.' Then when I led the way with this first big box, I turned to see if he had made it, only to find that he hadn't even started into the building. "Fuck me! That kind of thing really pisses me off," she almost screamed to the others.

Jon, Jerry and Kurt reluctantly filed onto the elevator for the ride down to grab the boxes for transport up to Jon's apartment.

With that mission complete, Cindy began asking for an update only to be shushed by Jerry who had turned to the TV after glancing at his watch.

Jerry was about to chastise Jon and Kurt for not filling him in about Fred's news conference, when the announcer began hyping another SPECIAL BULLETIN.

The picture flickered momentarily then focused on a face of the well known female Chicago newscaster. Kelly Larson appeared vibrant as always, but she had a true depression about her. This was not the so called somber look used by TV people when they report a death or tragedy. This was real.

"Following the initial presentation of the information from the Chief Medical Examiner's press conference, there has been a mass exodus from the city. In less than two hours, a panic appears to have gripped the people. They are simply trying to get away from the Lake for fear of the plague it holds. The expressways are all jammed with people heading west and southwest. The hospitals are reporting people lined up outside emergency rooms wanting to be checked for fish poisoning."

The picture moved without a flip to show Madison Street just west of the loop where some looting had begun. The police were moving in to control the situation and arrest looters.

“The entire police department is on alert and patrols have been beefed up. The Governor has ordered the National Guard to stand by for possible assignment to the City and along the North Shore,” Kelly reported.

The camera refocused on her face close-up. She said, “Please everyone, the Mayor pleads with all of you not to panic. There is nothing to fear except the contaminated fish and food. There is no need to leave the City. All of the supermarkets and stores are hastily removing all foods from their shelves that cannot be declared absolutely safe. For your information, all canned vegetables and canned meats are known to be safe. If you find it necessary to go to the market at this time, expect to wait in a line that is police controlled. This is simply to avoid panic buying and hoarding.”

Kelly Larson turned quickly to take a typewritten page from an off camera assistant. She glanced at it and Jon swore that she visibly wavered before regaining her composure.

“Ladies and Gentlemen, I am sorry to report that cases of the BIOTOXIC CHELATOR poisoning have been increasing around the borders of Lake Michigan and Lake Superior. A limited number of cases have been reported around Lake Huron into Detroit.”

Again, the hesitation. Again, the update sheet flutters to rest in Andi Barrett’s hand. She struggled to maintain control.

“An update from Detroit. The State of Michigan has called up its National Guard. They suspect that it will become necessary to use the Guard to control traffic and prevent looting. There is reported to be an area within the City of Detroit that is vacant of police. They lost control of a 12 square block area about an hour ago and will not risk the manpower and lives to go back in. There are other reports of mob violence, panic buying at stores and always the mass movement, which is away from the Lakes.”

Andi Barrett’s face was replaced by a picture from a mobile camera panning along Oak Street beach which is normally crowded with midday walkers. The day in Chicago had warmed considerably and the sun was shining beautifully. The beach was barren, except for one dead seagull slowly rocking back and forth in the light waves that broke with a white froth on the beige sand.

Jon noticed that there were no other gulls flying around or on the beach scavenging. For some reason, Jon sadly wondered how many of the gulls had died.

The TV reports only seemed to tighten Kurt Jackson's jaw. He was apparently resolved to prepare the plan and execute it in a well timed fashion within the timeframe available.

With those announcements, it seemed to Jon that time was growing short. He turned to Kurt to get a better grip on the timing of their plan.

Kurt had picked up the phone and was punching in a lot of numbers, Jon noticed. He looked up to see Jon watching. He covered the phone with his hand, saying, "That was my long distance access number, Jon. I am calling Washington to get permission to proceed with the plan on an emergency basis. It looks like this chelator is beating us to the punch with the rapidity of its movement through the Lakes."

Kurt dropped his hand and turned away from Jon while speaking softly. Jon was curious about his actions. It seemed like Kurt was playing at being a spy or something. Jon slid over to where Cindy was still standing near the doorway. He continued to help her stack the reams of material from Haltec. All together she had five boxes of paper.

"Cindy," he said quietly, "How in the world did you get all of this stuff out of Haltec?"

"Oh, Jon, the place is up for grabs. People are coming and going, talking about nothing but the chelator and the fish, etc."

"Still, I can't imagine your carrying all of this to the elevator and out to your car," Jon queried.

Cindy responded with, "It was simple. I just went down to the storage level where we keep all of the sampling equipment and supplies. I grabbed one of the little hand carts there, went up to my and Wittner's office and just loaded the stuff into boxes. Nobody seemed to even notice, let alone care," she shrugged trying to sort out the reams of paper.

Kurt replaced the phone in its cradle very softly. He turned to the other three and announced that the plan was underway. "General Walters, the Commandant of the Corps of Engineers will be meeting with the President within the hour. The Chiefs of Staff would be at the meeting and the Commandant suggested we proceed as if the plan is approved, but that we are to remain in direct contact with his office and only proceed to the eastern base. We will wait there for the final go ahead."

Jerry and Cindy just stared at Kurt. Cindy slowly turned to Jon and asked bluntly, "What in the hell is going on here, Jon?" What is Kurt talking about?"

Jon moved to put his hand on Cindy's arm to make contact and reassure her that everything would be all right.

She pulled away from Jon, steely eyes glaring.

Jerry jumped in with, "How are we supposed to help when we obviously don't know what's going on."

Kurt looked up from his maps at Jon and said, "Well, Jon, tell them."

Just then there was a knock on the door. Jon called, "Who is it?"

"Sergeant Rios. Captain Lewis said to be here at 4:00 sharp to transport you to the airport."

"Come in, Sergeant," Jon replied, opening the door at the same time.

Cindy looked at him with a mixture of fear and distrust. Jon shrugged his shoulders as if to say, 'It's not my fault.' I was going to tell you 'til the cop showed up.

Kurt said, "OK. Let's saddle up. You should each grab a warm jacket, a heavy pair of jeans and warm shoes. We have to be at the military section of O'Hare in time for our 4:00 flight to Bangor."

Jerry stopped them with a question. "Kurt, I'm not trying to get out of helping, but if I'm not really needed, I'd rather go make sure that Laura is OK. She hasn't had much attention from us."

Kurt said very honestly, "I wasn't really sure how you could help now, Jerry. It would even be better if we kept the number of people directly involved to a bare minimum. We will need to organize all of the data for a full presentation to the Corps Commander and the President within 24 hours. If you could get that started, we will be that far ahead.

"Kurt, you don't have to convince me. I have felt bad for two days that we haven't had the time to go see Laura."

Picking up his jacket, he said a cursory goodbye to Kurt. Then Jerry walked to Cindy and Jon saying, "You two be damn careful. I want to see you back here soon, so we can all go to the Sippery again."

He smiled. Cindy kissed him. He was past the policeman in a flash.

"Let's get going, people!" Kurt declared.

Cindy ran into the bedroom to change shoes while Jon grabbed both their jackets and waited at the door.

Kurt, for some reason, turned and surveyed the apartment before they went out the door with Sergeant Rios. The introspective engineer thought rapidly through a series of mixed scenes, ranging from Cindy never questioning that she would accompany them on the mission to Jon's unwavering belief in his theories.

Kurt assured himself that if Jon Kepler once expressed any doubt about the plan, Kurt would bring everything to an instant halt.

Friday 8:00 p.m.

CHAPTER 43

It all seemed so improbable to Cindy. She was rocketing along an old narrow two lane highway, reviewing the last few days in her mind, but was having difficulty with the last couple of hours.

First she is swept into a police car in the basement of Jon's apartment building. Then she has a rather hair-raising ride to the Air National Guard building at the Northeast corner of O'Hare airport. The police car is directed out onto the tarmac where a camouflage painted 707 was sitting on the runway, engines running. Kurt later corrected Cindy when she was told that the military version of the 707 was officially called the KC-135.

Cindy climbed the metal stairs to find, not the typical row after row of six seats across jammed into the plane's fuselage, but a large elongated cylinder that was barren. The entire cargo area of the KC-135 was empty except for four seats anchored in slots about half way up the plane. Straps and cargo slings and ropes hung everywhere, making the cigar shape even more like a haunted house. Cindy had to be pushed by Jon, to continue onto the plane.

Now, she was bumping along over the tar-stripped, crack repair lines, which could be felt through the cushy ride of the huge Lincoln Town Car. She reflected on the strange flight to the Air Force base at Bangor, Maine. The young airman on board served them a piping hot dinner in aluminum trays that was far better any she had ever eaten on a commercial airliner. All three of them fell into a dead sleep for the remainder of the two and a half hour flight.

Cindy remembered a dreamless sleep that had apparently eluded Jon and Kurt, for they looked even more haggard than before. When the airman had awakened them to announce that they were 15 minutes from touchdown, Jon had finally told Cindy the remainder of the plan.

She had been thinking about nothing else since. The temperature had gotten into the mid 60's in Chicago the day of their departure. It was only in the 50's in Bangor. The wind was none too kind either. Blowing at nearly 20 miles per hour, it seemed to carry graveyard dampness.

All three of them were cramped into the front seat of the black Lincoln as it rolled from Johnson Airfield at about 9 p.m. Cindy sat in the middle with controls for the special radio telephone digging into her knees. The back seat and trunk were filled with equipment. Cindy had watched the Air Force personnel load all of it. She only guessed at what some of it was. The heavy wooden cases marked explosive were the easiest to guess.

Cindy was surprised but not shocked to see that Kurt Jackson picked up the radio phone and asked for a secure line to the Corps Commandant.

Each time the conversation was the same, "We are progressing. When do you think you will have permission to proceed? Yes, we will contact you again in 30 minutes."

She had heard three of those radio checks only to be informed that she would hear more. Cindy was told by Kurt Jackson that they would have to travel a total of 155 miles. They would be crossing the Canadian border just north of Moose River, Maine.

Kurt guaranteed them that they wouldn't have to worry about seeing any people after that.

When they got close to the Canadian border, they turned off onto a horribly rutted dirt road that wound up Boundary Mountain part way and then back down, reappearing on the same highway now marked Canada 173.

As Kurt turned the car onto a dirt road, the pace slowed. After just a few miles, he brought the Lincoln to a halt.

Cindy said, “Kurt, you’ve really got to level with me. You seem to be a pretty powerful guy for a civilian liaison officer in the dowdy, old Corps of Engineers. I thought all you guys ever did was build bridges and dams.”

Turning to face her better, Kurt opened his door a little to relieve the cramped interior. The chilled dampness hit them instantly.

“Cindy, I have served two government agencies nearly my entire career. My duty with the Corps has been to oversee the relationship between civilian contractors and the Corps. I have worked on many of the large Corps projects, like the Ten Tom dam in Tennessee. At the same time, I report to the National Security Council as to the performance and integrity of the Corps. In that regard, I might add, I have never had anything but the highest regard for the job the Corps has done throughout the world.”

“OK, that explains the power you have. Now explain what we are actually doing here and how all of this appears to have been preplanned,” she demanded.

Kurt proceeded as if he had been asked to describe the workings of a garden tractor.

“As you have probably heard, the Joint Chiefs hire these Think Tank consulting companies like RAND Corporation in Palo Alto to play mock war games. From these theoretical clashes come ideas for maneuvers and tactics. The military has plans for every possible contingency…”

“You don’t mean a theoretical plan for war with Canada!” Cindy blurted.

Without wincing, Kurt nodded in the affirmative. “It was my review of those plans, as an advisor to the Joint Chiefs, that gave me the basis for this idea.”

“Sometimes, I think that the military has too much money and isn’t sure what to do with it,” Cindy retorted.

“Sometimes I agree with you,” Kurt replied.

Still not satisfied with her emotional venting, she continued with, “I suppose we have invasion plans for Mexico, too!”

Seeing Kurt wince, Cindy knew the answer.

He reached for the radio telephone once more. The conversation was nearly the same. Jon opened the door and stepped out because his legs were cramping. They had done the 155 miles in a little less than three hours over some pretty hairy roads.

Stretching to wring the weariness from his body, Jon felt Cindy come up behind him and slid her arms up inside his jacket to rub his lower back.

Jon moaned, saying how good that felt. Cindy rubbed harder. "Before Kurt finishes his call, let me say again that I love you deeply, Cindy Farrell," Jon said turning to hold her in his arms.

"Oh, Jon, I hope this passes. I pray that we can get the job done and stop the spread of this man-made curse."

Kurt interrupted with, "That's it you two. The President has spoken with the Prime Minister trying to convince him of the necessity to close off the Seaway. The Prime Minister says that the entire Canadian population would lynch him for committing an atrocity against nature of the magnitude the President wanted."

"Couldn't the President convince him of the need to stop the fish from getting to the ocean?" Jon interjected.

"It seems that the relatively small number of deaths in Canada, around 500 has not been sufficient to convince the Canadian military to assist the U.S. Army in the undertaking. The Canadians went so far as to warn the President that should the plan be attempted without Canadian sanction, the Prime Minister would consider it an invasion of their sovereign territory, and any such invasion would be repelled with force."

"So that's why we're out here all alone," Jon said. "A large military force would be easily noticed. Well, Kurt, we best proceed with sealing off the Seaway. If we don't, I am convinced that we will release this terrible plague on the rest of the world. At least if it is contained in the Great Lakes, we can stop its spread. Out in the ocean, I doubt if there would be any stopping it," Jon explained.

Kurt quickly added that the fish in the Great Lakes could all be killed with one of the environmentally safe chemicals. The lakes could then be restocked and back to normal in eight to ten years.

"If it will help, Kurt, I believe that there is no other way," Cindy said adding her support.

"Well, for your information, the Commandant told me that there are officially 11,500 deaths so far and it's mounting fast. Let's get the car closer to the bank and begin setting up the equipment.

Hopping back in the car, the three drove about another 500 yards until the edge of the earth seemed to disappear from in front of them.

Getting out and zipping his jacket, Kurt looked straight ahead and said, "Well, there they are. The cliffs of Quebec."

Jon and Cindy followed him to the very edge. They looked up and down the St. Lawrence River and across at the other bank. Kurt was obviously studying the terrain for access down to the river.

Walking to his left, Kurt said, "Here is the path over here. Right where they said it would be. Let's bring the equipment over here and get ready."

The three began unloading the crates and one large soft bundle. As Kurt began to untie the bundle, Cindy and Jon stopped to watch, wondering what it was.

Kurt turned and said, "Now stand back, I'm not quite sure how big this thing is."

With a healthy tug on a bright yellow rope the dark gray bundle popped loudly and the brilliant hiss of carbon dioxide could be heard. Within a few seconds, Jon could already make out the unmistakable outline of the boat made so famous by Jacques Cousteau. The Zodiac was nearing full inflation, when Kurt pried open the top of the only rectangular crate to reveal a compact battery and strange looking electric boat motor.

"Kurt, that thing doesn't look like it can do the job on this trip. While the current probably isn't too strong here, we have a lot of work to do in just a short time."

"Jon, I think that the marines know what they are doing with these. This battery is no standard lead-acid job. It's a silver-zinc type that they use to start jet planes. It'll do the job as will the motor with the extra thrust from the counter rotating propellers."

Jon was walking around the boat trying to agree with Kurt. Cindy stood waiting for the men to quit showing their macho crap and get on with it.

"Jon. Cindy. Would you begin unloading the charges from those crates? Be careful to keep them in their air cushions for safety, while we get the boat down the hill."

Jon and Cindy began prying open the boxes with the little pry bar from Kurt. Extracting the first one, Jon held it up as if that would help in the near moonless light.

The ball encased in the blow up cushion appeared to be slightly smaller than a volleyball, with one flat side. It was silvery, while the cushion itself was red, clear plastic.

Jon had assumed that every crate would be full of these, because it was going to take a lot of explosive to do the job they had planned. Much to his surprise, there were two balls in each of the fourteen small crates. That made twenty-eight explosive charges total.

"Hold it, Kurt. There is no way that this much explosive will accomplish what you say. I don't care if it is C-9, C-21 or whatever the hell they call it now."

"Jon, nobody ever told you that we would use a standard type of explosive."

Kurt grabbed each of their arms and steered them to the edge of the gorge. They automatically looked down at the peaceful, yet chilling waters of the St. Lawrence.

Kurt explained. "Look at the cliffs across the Seaway," he said pointing into the blackness. "It is six hundred feet from this bank to the cliffs. Actually these are fascinating geological formations because this side of the River is so much lower than the other side. One theory is that this was once the ocean shoreline where we are standing."

Cindy and Jon both looked at their feet. Then they raised their eyes to the towering cliffs across the way.

"Those cliffs rise 720 feet above the surface of the water. The eroded bank below them means that the cliffs are about 60 feet back from the water. That all means that we must lift a 700 foot high wall of dirt out 60 feet and dump it into the Seaway. In order to assure a leak proof blockage of the River, the Engineers all agree with my calculation that we should move at least a 200-foot width of that cliff. If we use the depth of the river plus 10 feet as a safety factor, then we have to remove about 45 feet from the front of the cliffs."

Turning toward them now, "That comes to somewhat over six million cubic feet of dirt and rock, which in turn translates to 220 million pounds or a hundred thousand tons."

Smiling slightly, Kurt said, "Even a chemist and a biologist can figure that there is no way to get that amount of explosives here short of an armada of trucks working day and night for a week."

Jon bent down and picked up one of the flat-sided volleyballs. "Well when did we come up with this little beauty?"

"OK, Jon, what is it?" Cindy demanded.

Kurt answered, taking the unit from Jon he set it lightly in the Zodiac. "That, my dear, is a miniature atomic device."

Jumping back as if it had suddenly grown white hot, Cindy exclaimed, "You mean a fucking thermonuclear warhead!"

"No! No! Not as powerful as that Cindy," Kurt explained. "We tried to make the Canadians understand that these atomic bombs were the only way to get the job done fast enough. They absolutely refused, saying that as soon as their scientists evaluated the situation, they would be glad to work with the U.S. and find a solution. They were talking weeks—we were talking hours."

Cindy wanted to scream that all of this had gotten out of hand. She wanted more time to think—but there was no time. The radio telephone had reported to Kurt that so many people were already dead and Nobody knew how many more would die. It appeared that the word was getting out to everyone around the Great Lakes but it was too late for many of them.

With that, Kurt finished his explanation by saying, "These were originally designed to be used as excavation devices."

Looking up, Kurt asked, "Do either of you remember the flap about five years ago when the Corps of Engineers proposed digging a new canal across Panama. It was to have been a sea level canal with no locks. The only problem was that the canal would have been 130 miles long and to dig it by conventional methods would have cost untold billions of dollars. Well one of the scientists at Jet Propulsion Labs in California, came up with the idea of using miniature atomic bombs to dig the canal. Along with the Corps designers, he estimated the cost of the canal at less than one billion dollars with a total construction time of 10 months. This process was fairly well researched, even to the point of formulating these so-called clean bombs."

"Was it ever tested?" Cindy asked quickly.

"No!" Kurt replied glumly, while loading the 28 bombs into the Zodiac.

"Kurt," Cindy called, stopping her movements. "Are these bombs really clean, or are we just trading one huge problem for a large one.

Kurt walked over to Cindy, while Jon looked at the two of them with naked fear in his heart. Kurt took Cindy's face in his hands and looked into her eyes as deeply as he could.

"Cindy, I have no desire to die, either today or in a few weeks from radiation poisoning. I have reviewed the design of the bombs and all of the theories. It is my opinion that all of the bombs will release less than one-tenth of radiation that was given off in the first tests in New Mexico. Some of the equipment in the car is a measuring unit for radioactivity and special air sampling devices. They want us to stay after we detonate the bombs and see how bad things are."

He released her and searched Jon's face to see if there were any more doubts.

Then Kurt said, "Let's uncoil the rope and slide the boat down that path toward the river," pointing at an area with flattened grass.

"Then we'll carry the motor and battery down. We'll rig up all of the equipment and cross the river to the base of the cliffs. Once we have everything in place, we'll come back to this side, take cover away from the river and use a radio detonation device."

The team tied the lightweight polypropylene line to the now weighted Zodiac. They let it slide the 70 feet down the steeply slopped bank. When the line went limp, they knew it was down. They picked up the motor and battery and began carefully picking their way down toward the water.

Cindy noticed a certain peace around her. She heard a few gulls crying in the night as they dove about. She reached for Jon's hand and held it tighter than ever before.

Once down to the boat, Kurt had to talk much louder to be heard over the sound of the river. It had seemed so quiet to them up on the bank, but the black, swirling water looked foreboding. Each of them shook their heads in turn, to rid each of their minds of the undeniable fear and dread that had seeped in.

Moving very quickly, Kurt fastened the little motor to the support between the two pontoon sides. He popped the battery clips in place, told Cindy to get in and told Jon to shove off.

It seemed to take forever to cross the River. Cindy felt a chill pushing deeper and deeper into her. All of a sudden, the cliffs loomed above them through the blackness. More sensing the shore than seeing it, Jon hopped from the boat, didn't quite make dry land and pulled the Zodiac up onto the bank cursing his wet shoes.

Glancing at his watch again, Kurt instructed, "We only have an hour and a half until dawn. Jon, you count forty paces along that bank and set the first charge with the flat side right up against the cliff. Then walk three paces back this direction and set another. That will give us a charge every eight to nine feet. With a total of twenty eight bombs, we will easily give us the two hundred feet of cliff we need. I know it means quite a few trips back and forth, but it is really only safe to carry two of these at a time."

Watching Kurt remove the protective balloon from the first bomb, Jon began to wonder about the contributions that man had made to the planet and what man's future might be. Picking up his first two bombs, he started up river counting his paces out loud.

Kurt told Cindy to make certain nothing happened to the boat and to carefully unwrap each bomb for them to save time.

Cindy stopped Kurt with a touch on the arm. “Kurt, I love that man who just walked away carrying some kilo-tonnage of atomic bombs. I want to have his children. Please tell me with your heart that this will work.”

Kurt looked directly into the depths of those fearful eyes and said, “Remember. Keep your eye on the boat. Without it, we won’t get back.” He turned and began his fifty pace march down river.

SATURDAY 6:16 a.m.

CHAPTER 44

As Jon and Cindy each pulled themselves out of the light rubber Zodiac, they turned to face the nearly smooth clay colored cliffs as they loomed over the water on the other side of the river. Kurt was trying to disconnect the tangled wires from the electric motor.

Just then the ear splitting thunder of whining jets could be heard. As all of them spun toward the east just noticing the dim, gray first hint of daylight. Two Canadian Harrier jets were already passing over. The three people turned to follow the roar, mocking the viewers of a tennis match. The planes veered off, one going west, the other east in a well practiced, flawless turnaround maneuver.

Jon moved closer to Cindy and pulled her down into the long grass while he stroked her hair with his cheek. "It will be done soon and we can sit around explaining it all to each other", he murmured.

Jon really didn't know what the planes were or to whom they belonged. He could only sense that they were harbingers of failure.

Cindy pulled him closer as her arm went around his waist. They were both wet from the drizzle that had begun, making the sky even darker gray and their mission even more sinister.

Kurt Jackson was still sitting in the Zodiac, working on the motor. He had followed the Harriers' pattern and knew what was to follow. His face seemed to reflect the gray light from the water's surface. Suddenly, Kurt called to Jon and simply pointed toward the cliffs some 700 feet away.

"Jon, I think we'd better finish our job. We've got company coming," Jackson said.

Jon and Cindy looked up to see a Canadian K-400 troop carrying helicopter hovering over the cliffs. Just then the words boomed into their minds from the loud speaker suspended below the red striped white helo. The thrumming of the blades seemed to intensify to compensate for the message from the loud speaker. Jon was trying to concentrate on the words.

"Stop where you are. This is the Canadian Coast Guard. You are under arrest. Your activities violate Canadian sovereignty. If you have not yet started your mission, please signify by raising your arms."

Jon continued the commitment to his convictions and slowly raised his arms while lowering his head. Cindy squeezed Jon's hand even harder, as he lifted hers along toward the sky.

"Kurt, how can we get them away from the area? We can't consider blowing them up. The specter of death has blackened us enough. I don't want it to be any deeper in my soul," Jon said. As Jon turned slowly away from the helicopter toward the Army engineer, all he saw was Kurt pushing the Zodiac back out into the current.

Jon and Cindy both came alive to begin screaming at Kurt. He was obviously bent on diverting the Canadians to allow Jon the time and space to detonate the charges.

Cindy grabbed Jon as he was about to lunge into the water. They nearly fell when each slid on the weedy clay that was damp with the drizzle of the night.

Cindy pointed toward the copter and hollered at Jon to make him understand. "Don't you see, Jon? The helicopter is following Kurt. They think he's up to something. They'll go after him and we can finish."

Jon looked from the water to the Canadian chopper and back to Kurt in the Zodiac. Kurt had managed to get the clumsy boat out into the current far enough that it was rapidly pulling away from the Cindy and Jon.

Apparently, the Canadians felt he was up to something, because the chopper had banked steeply and was closing on Kurt and the bounding Zodiac.

Jon and Cindy scrambled up the bank and ran for the big Lincoln. They jumped in and Jon fumbled with the keys. With a roar the engine came to life. Jon spun the wheel right, and then left in a Hollywood reversal to get back from the edge of the cliffs. He was whirling his head constantly to locate the chopper and to gauge its distance from the point where the bombs were set.

As the Lincoln scrunched to a halt some five hundred feet from the edge of the St. Lawrence, Jon turned just in time to see the side mounted Gattling gun on the Canadian helicopter spit fire down into the river. He cringed and swore silently with a hatred for the waste of another life.

Cindy was reaching for the transmitter when the car engine died. Jon jerked it away from her with a violence she had never seen before. They looked at each other. One with anger, the other with compassion.

"Jon," Cindy said pleadingly, "you know why Kurt did that. Now, finish the job or I will".

Jon slammed his left hand on the oversized steering wheel trying to expel the emotions that were tearing him apart. Cindy slipped the transmitter from his hand.

The thing looks like a garage door opener, she thought. The large green button at the top edge was nearly the color of her eyes. With no further thoughts she pushed the button.

The shattering roar of the miniature atomic bombs was muted by the directional design that drove the main blast into the cliffs. Cindy turned in her seat to see a solid wall of gray limestone and clay towering into the sky. Then, as if a giant hand was cupped toward the Seaway, the dirt and rocks moved over the water.

Jon felt the earth shudder as the 28 blasts moved the hundreds of thousands of tons of earth into the air. He grimaced while gripping the wheel in the dead car. It never dawned on him that they might die. He could not get the picture out of his mind that had burned its way onto the back of his eye lids—the helicopter with its nose dipped between the opposing cliffs, a short burst of red spitting from its high caliber machine gun.

As Cindy watched the earth stop moving and the sky stop shaking, she reached for the door handle. Jon stopped her just as the wind tore at the heavy Lincoln rocking it from side-to- side with a force over several hurricanes. Cindy screamed as Jon held her, pulling the back of her head into his chest in case the windshield didn't hold against the force of the blast.

The shock wave dissipated as quickly as it came. Stepping out onto the trembling ground, Cindy realized that the wall of dirt was gone. It had been replaced with a mighty cloud of dust. Even that was settling fast back into the river.

Jon joined Cindy in getting out of the car. Meeting in front, they automatically sought each others hand. As the air cleared and the sky brightened, they could just make out the cliffs on the other side of the river. Reaching majestically up out of the gray waters, the cliffs looked untouched.

Jon screamed, "Oh my God, Cindy, we failed.

Cindy looked and then pointed. "Jon, it worked! It worked! Look!"

Jon looked toward the St. Lawrence Seaway not understanding Cindy's shouts. Then he saw the land bridge across the entire width of the river. He looked harder at the Quebec cliffs to see how it had happened. Then he noticed that the other side was considerably further away.

"It worked!" he said repeating Cindy's words as if she had never said them.

They stood together not touching. The adrenaline had left them weak. Their hyper states of a few minutes ago had completely disappeared.

Jon smiled, He picked up Cindy's hand, turned to her and said, "Want to walk to Quebec City for some breakfast".

Just then, the Canadian helicopter appeared to their left, moving fast toward them. It seemed like it came from a different time. Jon barely recorded its reappearance, with a feeling of gratitude for the safety of the Canadians. Suddenly a mighty wind ripped at their clothes and eyes. Dirt blew into their faces and the only thought in Jon's head was—did we do it in time?'

Then he realized that the chopper had landed very close to them. He tightened his grip on Cindy's hand until her reflex was to pull away. Six camouflaged figures jumped from the helo even before it had settled to the ground.

Jon's still foggy mind was querying itself on the men's actions when it dawned on him. "Rifles", he said aloud.

As Jon began to move in front of Cindy, the men fanned out in a semi-circle as they approached the pair.

The fully arrayed Canadian marines moved quickly toward Jon and Cindy with menacing looks and poise to kill.

"Hands on your heads," the apparent leader shouted above the decreasing roar of the chopper blades.

The wind still beat at Cindy's hair and Jon had closed his eyes to the invasion of dust and dirt. The soldiers grabbed each of them by the arms almost dragged them into the menacing wind machine.

Just then Jon heard first one and then another explosion that rocked the helicopter. He tried to find a window as he was pushed to the floor by one of the Canadians, only to be jerked from his seat back outside.

He and Cindy, still hand in hand, stood facing some smiling Green Berets bedecked in full battle gear. Jon looked around to see the hands of his captors in the air and the pilots of the copter sliding out of their seats with upraised arms. To the right and left knelt more of the U.S. Army Special Forces facing the Canadians with the menacing launching tube of a wire guided missile pointed straight at the chopper.

The Colonel leading the Green Berets grabbed a bullhorn and sternly declared that the Canadians were on United States territory. However, it they would leave peacefully, no harm would come to them.

One of the Green Berets moved to pull Cindy and Jon away from the doorway of the helicopter. The Colonel motioned the Canadians back into the helo. As the blades revved up, the faces of the Americans turned somewhat softer. The Colonel then called his men to attention and saluted the Canadians as the helicopter began to rise into the air.

As the copter banked toward the chalky, new face of the Quebec cliffs, the Colonel turned to Jon and said, “Excuse me, sir. Would you and the lady care for an escort. The President is waiting to speak with you.

Just a couple of minutes please, Colonel. He pushed Cindy into the car and raced it toward the Seaway. He jumped out and walked with Cindy onto the rubble land bridge they had just created. As he faced east, he squinted into the morning sun. The emotions of the past hours began to rip into him. Just as he was about to break down, a voice hollered, “Hey, Jon, Cindy, it looks like a nice day.

They both wheeled to see a blackened and tattered Kurt Jackson standing on the bank with the help of one of the Green Berets. They rushed to embrace him as he explained that the Canadians had sure managed to put a lot of holes in that Zodiac, but none in him.

The three turned to look once again at the dam of rock and mud, each hoping that the job was done in time.

EPILOGUE

The salmon had been swimming for some time now. She continued to feel the surge of evil within herself. The glowering menace inside the salmon had been driving her for 30 hours now. She had not eaten in some time.

Just as she had noted a faint taste of saltiness in the water, a back shattering vibration rocked her very being. She was tossed about and totally disoriented by the blast that had blown the facing cliffs into the St. Lawrence Seaway.

As the boulders and rocks and clay tumbled into the water, it became a fight to dodge the projectiles falling about her. The water seemed filled with them. She dodged right and left. The water became darker and darker with the soil and rocks. The explosion impaired her sense of direction. She was not even sure if she was going in the right direction.

As she swam rapidly to and fro, responding to inner stimuli helping her to avoid a head-crushing blow, she noticed that none of the other salmon were to be seen. How could she have lost them, she wondered.

Looking to her left, the now nearly crazed fish drove toward what seemed a lighter area. Had she only risen closer toward the surface or was this really safer water, she wondered.

As the huge rocks, amid the great muted clatter piled up behind her, the salmon could sense the lessening of the fallout. The roiling clouds of silt and sediment began to choke her gills, but she noted her decreasing effort to avoid descending objects.

She slowed her beating fins somewhat to find that the water was settling. The vibrations were decreasing and the water was clearing somewhat.

Standing on the rock and clay strip that now connected the two sides of the river, Jon looked down from his eastern watch toward some motion just below the surface of the water. Cindy tried to follow his eyes when he jerked his hand upward to point.

Just then, Cindy and Jon felt the low rumble near where they were looking. A mammoth boulder settled into a more stable position in the bomb-made rock dam. One-half turn was all that was needed to seat the huge piece of dolomite that crushed the life from a single silvery shadow that had been heading toward the sea.

Cindy screamed with near panic in her voice, "Jon, what the hell did you see?"

Jon said, "Never mind. It's nothing. I thought I just saw something there, but it's gone now. I'm sure it was nothing."

ABOUT THE AUTHOR

William Gartner is a graduate scientist with 18 issued patents and more than 30 years experience in the environmental field with many appearances on television and in the press. This father of 5 children has long been a prolific technical writer and wanted to combine that scientific knowledge with a vivid imagination and motion picture mind to create the ultimate novel of environmental terror.

Mr. Gartner has traveled extensively throughout Asia and Europe visiting industrial sites that have been heavily polluted. The author lived in the Chicago area for more than 25 years and based the novel in the area. Many of the locations, buildings, lakes, tributaries and other geographical places are real. The circumstances on which the concept of a biotoxin is based is not outside the realm of possibility.

His education includes a degree in Chemistry from Lewis University and graduate studies at Northwestern University.

Mr. Gartner is working on two additional novels. The first, titled *Canals*, is about the first manned mission to Mars and what they fined in the Canals. The second is titled *2022* and is about a judicial computer program that loses its goals and direction.